FINDING THEIR FOREVER FAMILY

CAROLINE ANDERSON

REDEEMING HER HOT-SHOT VET

JULIETTE HYLAND

KT-377-252

MILLS & BOON

First published in Great Britain 2023
by Mills & Boon, an imprint of HarperCollins*Publishers* Ltd,
1 London Bridge Street, London, SE1 9GF

www.harpercollins.co.uk

HarperCollins*Publishers* Macken House, 39/40 Mayor Street Upper, Dublin 1, D01 C9W8, Ireland

Finding Their Forever Family © 2023 Caroline Anderson

Redeeming Her Hot-Shot Vet © 2023 Juliette Hyland

ISBN: 978-0-263-30599-9

03/23

FINDING THEIR FOREVER FAMILY

CAROLINE ANDERSON

MILLS & BOON

Thanks to my daughters Sarah and Hannah and their families for the extensive opportunities to savour the agonies and ecstasies of parenting/step-parenting. So much material! Love you all. xxx

CHAPTER ONE

SHE WAS LATE. AGAIN.

She hurried in, racked with guilt and frustration as usual, and bumped straight into James Slater—clinical lead, department cheerleader and stickler for punctuality...

He quirked a brow and smiled wryly. 'Morning, Emily. What is it today?'

She rolled her eyes. 'Billy. I'm so sorry. He wouldn't put his shoes on.'

James chuckled. 'Take him to school without them. They only do it once. Anyway, I'm glad you're here. I'm putting you in Resus. I'm a bit tied up with meetings, and I need you to look after our new consultant.'

She felt her eyes widen. 'He needs babysitting?'

James laughed again. 'Hardly. He just needs to get to know the department. We were really lucky to get him. He's ex-LMTS.'

That surprised her. The London Major Trauma System was world-class, and for a moment she wondered why on earth he'd chosen to come to Yoxburgh. Not that it wasn't a great hospital, but even so... Still, at least he'd be competent, unlike their last locum.

'OK. Give me a second to change. What's his name?'

'Oliver. Oliver Cavendish.'

She felt the shock all the way down to her toes, but there

wasn't time to stop and think. Not that she knew *what* to think...

She nodded and walked away to the locker room, heart racing, her mind in turmoil.

Why's he here?

It might not be him. There had to be more than one doctor called Oliver Cavendish. She changed into scrubs, scraped back her hair into a messy bun and headed to Resus. The red phone was ringing as she opened the door, and she picked it up and tried to focus.

'Yoxburgh Park Resus.'

'Code Red, eighteen-year-old male, motorbike versus car, open book pelvis and lower limb fractures, right-sided chest, possible clavicle, query head injury...'

The list went on, and as she wrote it down, her heart started to race. If they got the young man in alive, it would be a miracle. Code Red was as bad as it got, and Oliver went clean out of her mind.

'ETA?'

'Five minutes. He's in the air.'

'OK.'

She hung up, put the message out on the Tannoy and fast bleeped the anaesthetist, orthopaedics, radiography, interventional radiology, and then booked a CT slot and checked the fridge for blood. Four units. Hopefully it'd be enough until they could cross-match.

She could hear the sound of the helicopter overhead as it came in to land, just as the door swished open behind her.

'OK, what've we got?'

She turned at the familiar voice, her heart racing, and over her mask she met striking blue eyes she hadn't seen for nearly twenty years. Eyes that widened in shock.

'Emily?' His voice was incredulous, and for a second

they stared at each other, and then the door swung open again as more people came in, and she gave herself a mental shake and snapped back into doctor mode.

'Right, we have a Code Red, eighteen-year-old male, motorbike versus car...' She reeled off the list of injuries as the other members of the team poured into the room, and Oliver stood there, his focus absolute.

His eyes met hers. 'OK, this is a complicated polytrauma by the sound of it. Do you mind if I lead? I've done a lot of these.'

'No, not at all. Do you want me to go and meet them and you can brief?'

'Sure.'

She ran out to meet the casualty, and as they wheeled him into the now crowded Resus, she was wondering how on earth he was still alive. Not only alive, but conscious enough to moan and mumble something she couldn't understand.

'It's OK, Jack. We've got you,' she told him gently, and grabbed a corner of the sheet. 'On three. One, two, slide—'

'Right, what do we know?' Oliver asked, taking over.

The air ambulance doctor rattled off the list of injuries from top to toe, detailed the treatment he'd received so far, including a pelvic binder, and then told them the family were on the way. As she finished, he nodded and moved straight to the patient's head and bent over him.

'Hi, Jack. I'm Oliver. I'm one of the doctors here. Can you tell me where you hurt?'

The boy's eyes rolled a little, and he mumbled something incoherent.

'Jack, can you squeeze my hand?' he asked, then shook his head. 'He's not obeying commands. We need to send him off to sleep so we can get a proper look at him. Do we have an anaesthetist here?'

'Yup, I'm on it,' Peter said, and while he put Jack under and intubated him, the rest of the team were assembling the equipment they'd need, putting up drips, warming blood, cutting off the rest of his clothes to reveal his injuries to Oliver.

'OK, he's got reduced air entry on the right, so let's get a chest drain in. Emily, can you do that, please? And there's something very wrong with that pelvis. We need to scan him as soon as we can, but we need to get him stable and I don't think we're quite there yet. Let's get the chest drain in and a catheter to check his bladder and see where we are then. Can you start rapid transfusion, please, and take bloods for group and save? And that left foot's very pale.'

The orthopaedic consultant was already looking at it. 'Yeah, it's the ankle. I'll reduce the fracture now,' Dan said, and while he and a nurse did that, Emily prepped for the chest drain, aware of Oliver's every move, every breath, every word, not sure if the surge in her heart rate was because of him or because of their patient or both. Either would have been enough, but Oliver Cavendish could wait. Had to wait. It had been almost twenty years. Another hour or two wouldn't matter.

Jack was their priority, and until he was stable, scanned and shipped off to whoever was going to tackle his complicated injuries first, her feelings were on the back burner. As for Oliver's feelings—well, she had no idea what they were. Her own were enough to deal with and she wasn't sure what they were, either.

She shut her eyes for a moment, took a steadying breath and inserted the chest drain...

* * *

It took nearly an hour, but finally Oliver felt confident that Jack was reasonably stable, or at least for now. 'Right, I think we need to get him to CT. Are they ready for us?'

'Yes. I've asked them to hold it.'

'Good.' He looked up, catching Emily's eyes briefly before he dragged his own away and scanned the team. 'Do we all think he's stable enough to go? Anyone got any concerns?'

'Well, he's not great, but I think he's as good as we can get him without more information,' Peter said quietly, echoing all their thoughts.

'OK, I'll go with him. Peter, can you come, too, please? And, Emily, could you talk to the family?'

'Sure.'

And heaven help them if Jack died.

He's only a year older than Charlie...

They wheeled him down to CT, then stood side by side, watching the images appear. They weren't pretty, and not for the first time he wondered if his first case was going to survive.

He had multiple fractures—his pelvis, the right side of his ribcage, his left ankle and right wrist were all fractured, but there were no spinal or skull fractures, and at least his aorta was intact. That had been a worry from the start.

As had the quality of the team. Because the last thing he'd needed was an unskilled crew on a case like this, but to his immense relief they seemed to work well together and know what they were doing. And Emily—so calm and competent, she'd quietly got on with it, and he was pretty sure if he hadn't been there, she would have coped fine alone. Impressive. And disturbing.

Why's she here?

He refocused on the screen and frowned. 'Wait—can we have another look at his heart, please?'

And there it was.

'Pericardial effusion. Damn. Right, can you get Dan Wheeler to look at the images immediately, please, and let's get him back. He might need that drained. Thank you.'

They got back to Resus and found the orthopaedic surgeon studying the images with Joe Baker, the interventional radiologist, while Emily was on the phone trying to book a theatre.

'He's a mess,' Dan told him, and he dragged his eyes off Emily and concentrated on Dan's words. 'We need to sort this before he bleeds out. I'm going to need IR to deal with that, so Joe's coming in if the crossover surgical suite's available.'

'It's on standby for you,' Emily said, hanging up the phone. 'What are we doing about the pericardial effusion?'

'I'm not sure,' Oliver told them, glad to see that Emily had spotted it. 'How's he doing, Peter? Is he stable?'

'No,' Peter said, shaking his head. 'BP's dropped to eighty over fifty, heart rate's up to one thirty, and his jugulars are distended.'

'Tamponade,' he said, and looked around. 'Right, let's get some imaging of this. I'm going to do a pericardial tap.'

'The trolley's ready,' Emily said, moving it into position with everything laid out for him, and he picked up the long needle and took a steadying breath, grateful that she was on the ball.

Under image guidance he advanced the long needle up through Jack's diaphragm and into the blood-filled space between his heart and the pericardial membrane, slid a fine tube up through the needle and withdrew it, then took off thirty-five mils of blood.

And waited.

'Come on, Jack, you can do this,' Oliver muttered, and then after a few heart-stopping seconds, he started to respond.

'BP's up to one ten over sixty, heart rate's down to eighty-six,' Peter said, and he felt the tension in the room ease a fraction.

Not his. Not yet.

'So far so good,' he murmured, and checked the images again. Better. He withdrew the fine tube, watched the monitor for a few more moments, then turned to Peter.

'How's he looking now?'

'Good. Better. The jugulars are back to normal.'

He nodded, relieved, and turned to Dan.

'Happy to take over?' he said, and Dan nodded.

'Absolutely. I want to get him sorted asap.'

Oliver thanked them as they wheeled him out, Peter going with them, then looked around at the rest of the team, feeling the tension drain out of them all as the responsibility for young Jack was passed on up the line.

'Thank you. That was great teamwork. He's not out of the woods yet, but we've given him a fighting chance, so thank you all for that. It's good to know I've got a strong team with me.'

And then he turned his head and met the soft, beautiful but very guarded grey eyes that he knew so well. 'We need to talk to the parents. What have you told them?'

'Only what we knew before the CT. They're in the family room.'

'Come with me?'

'Sure.'

* * *

They were distraught, but sobbed with relief when they were told he was still alive, stable and on his way to Theatre.

'We'll keep you in the loop,' he promised. 'When he comes out of Theatre, they'll give you a call and update you on his condition, but he'll be going to ICU while they monitor his progress, probably for a few days, and then it'll be a long, slow job, I'm afraid. He's still not out of the woods by any means, but he's very lucky to be alive and at least now he stands a chance.'

'How long will the operation take?' his father asked.

'I don't know. It could be several hours. It's tricky surgery.'

'And will it work? Will he walk again? And what about his heart?' his mother asked, her eyes wide with fear and worry. He could understand that. If this had happened to Charlie...

'I would very much hope so, but his pelvis is quite badly broken and it'll take a lot of skill to sort it out. In the meantime his heart seems to have recovered from the bleed, so that's one hurdle crossed.'

'Is the surgeon any good?' his father asked, and before Oliver could open his mouth, Emily jumped in.

'He's excellent. If that was my son, I'd want Mr Wheeler working on him. He really is in very good hands.'

He saw the tension drain out of them, and after answering a few more questions, they showed them the way out to the main café where they could wait for news.

Oliver watched them go, her words echoing in his head. *If that was my son...* Did she have a son, too?

'Emily, have you got time for a debrief?'

* * *

Had she? She didn't know. Maybe, maybe not, but now the clinical pressure was off, the emotional pressure was well and truly on, and her heart kicked behind her ribs.

'Sure.' Damn, why did her voice sound breathy and ridiculous? 'Of course,' she said, injecting a bit more oomph into it. Better...

'Right. First stop, coffee.'

She stared at him, stunned. 'Seriously?'

'Absolutely dead seriously. I've been here since six and I haven't had breakfast, and if I'm not going to fall over, I need something fast and filling right now. So where do we go?'

She was about to say the staff-room, but the coffee was vile, the biscuit tin would be empty, and anyway, it wouldn't tick the 'fast and filling' box.

'Park Café. We can go round the side.'

She turned on her heel and headed out through a staff door, and he followed her, before reaching past her to push the door open, bringing his body so close to her that the remembered scent of him filled her nostrils and made her ache with longing.

He fell into step beside her. 'Thanks for your help this morning. You're good,' he said, and she shot him a look, desperately trying to ignore the leap in her pulse at his nearness.

'You don't have to sound surprised.'

The low chuckle rippled all the way down her spine. 'I'm not. I'm just being honest. I was glad to have you in there. They're a sound team. I was very relieved about that.'

She found a smile from somewhere. 'Yes, it wasn't exactly finding your feet gently, was it?'

That chuckle again. 'Not exactly. And there I thought I might get bored doing a nice quiet little job, in a pretty seaside town where nothing much happens…'

Emily laughed at that. 'Quiet? I wish. You do realize this is a major hospital?'

'It's beginning to dawn on me,' he said, his grin wry and achingly familiar.

'So how come you're here?' she asked, partly because she was desperately curious and partly to fill the silence. 'Why on earth would you leave an LMTS hospital to come to Yoxburgh? Because it doesn't sound like you were looking for a quiet life.'

'Family reasons,' he said, without elaborating, and then added, 'and I could ask why you're here.'

'You probably could,' she said, and deliberately didn't answer it, just walked into the café and joined the queue. Better the silence than getting into that one…

He ordered a large cappuccino, picked up an egg and cress sandwich and a banana, and watched while she dithered over the pastries, then chose a chicken salad sandwich, a yogurt and a fruit tea.

'That's not like you.'

'Actually it is—well, it is now. I have a bit more respect for my body than I did twenty years ago, and it looks like you have, too.'

'Touché,' he murmured, then his mouth kicked up in a smile, and her world tilted sideways. This was such a bad idea…

'In or out?' she asked, looking hastily away.

'Out. It's a gorgeous day.'

He picked up the tray and headed through the doors, and she followed him to an empty table for two. It was set against the wall in the sun, and there was no alternative but to sit opposite each other.

He ripped open his sandwich and took a huge bite, and for a moment neither of them said anything. He, she guessed, because he couldn't talk with his mouth full, and she because she was too busy searching for all the changes the last however long had etched on his face.

That and wondering what the 'family reasons' were…

He glanced up, and she peeled open her yogurt, stuck the spoon in it and looked up again, finally meeting his eyes. Thoughtful, questioning eyes.

'I can't believe you're here,' he said softly after a pause that stopped the breath in her throat, and she looked down again and fiddled with the yogurt, stirring it mindlessly.

'Ditto.' She looked up again, studying him as he took another huge bite. The new lines around the eyes, the creases at each side of his mouth, the touch of grey threaded through his dark hair at the temples.

And then her curiosity got the better of her. 'So what have you been up to for the last—what is it? Eighteen years?'

'Something like that.' He gave a rueful huff of laughter and turned his attention to his coffee, avoiding her eyes, as she'd just avoided his, then when she'd given up expecting him to answer, he gave a shrug and smiled, but it didn't reach his eyes.

'Working too hard, trying to decide what I wanted to do—you know how it goes, but the move back to a major London hospital was the decider.'

'I'm surprised it took you so long to work out. You always were an adrenaline junkie.'

'And you weren't, so why are you here doing this?'

She looked away from those suddenly searching eyes.

'I've changed. I guess we both have. We've been doctors almost half our lives, seen all manner of things that most people never get exposed to. It would be weird if it hadn't changed us.'

He nodded slowly. 'Yes, I guess it would. Are you going to eat that yogurt or just play with it, because we really need to get back.'

And just like that, he shut it down.

He swallowed the last bite of his sandwich as she scraped out the pot, then finished his coffee and looked at her. 'Ready?'

'Sure.'

She drained her cup and stood up, stuffing her sandwich into her scrubs pocket. 'Lunch,' she said, and he rolled his eyes.

'If we get that lucky.'

They didn't. So much for his nice quiet little job...

The rest of the day was chaos, with ambulances queueing up outside, waiting to offload as they dealt with a deluge of patients with chest or abdominal pain, head injuries, nasty fractures and all the rest, not to mention the never-ending supply of walking wounded, most of whom could have been seen by their family doctors.

As for lunch, that was never going to happen. Still, at least he wasn't bored, and it was a good introduction to the efficiency of the department, the skill sets of the various team members and the lack of ego amongst the doctors in particular.

He'd met some egos in his time, especially in the early days, and it was a relief to see that everyone here was treated with respect regardless of their grade or position. He was all for that. He knew just how hard it was to forge a career in medicine, knew the toll that working in trauma and emergency medicine took on you, the drain on your reserves, the destruction of your personal life brick by brick until there was nothing left.

He knew all about that one from bitter experience. And if you felt unsupported at work, that was the last straw, and it was the reason so many good doctors and nurses walked away.

But not Emily.

Emily was still there, working alongside him on the more complex cases, independently the rest of the time but always in the background—and it was getting to him.

He'd never in a million years imagined he'd end up working with her, not least because eighteen years ago she was aiming for surgery, and now she was working in the ED. Why had she changed her mind? And where had she been? What had she done with her life? Was she married? Did she have children? Was she happy?

That most of all. He hoped so. He was, but it was a qualified happiness, underpinned by a lot of regret and remorse. Not to mention failure.

He looked across the central desk and saw her, her face lit up with laughter as she shared a joke with a colleague, and it hit him like a punch to the gut.

No. He wasn't going there. Not again. His heart had been broken enough times without him throwing it under the bus for the hell of it, and that particular bus had run him over before.

'You OK? Has Emily been looking after you?'

He turned his head and conjured up a smile for James.

'Yes, thanks. She's been great.'

His new boss smiled wryly. 'She is great. It's a pity she can't work full time, but her children come first and it's a bit of a juggling act. She's a very good doctor, though, and we're glad to have her. She's an asset to the department.'

So she *was* a mother, working part-time, presumably with a husband and family around her. He told himself he was happy for her, and he was, but it just underlined how much he'd lost over the years.

Starting with her...

He walked round to the other side of the desk just as she reached it.

'I've had some news about Jack,' he told her. 'His pelvis came together better than expected, and they've taken him up to ICU. They'll keep him under for a day or so, sort out some of his other issues, and then slowly ease off on the drugs and see where we are, but it's looking good and his heart seems OK now, so that's a relief. I thought you'd like to know.'

Her smile was genuine and heartfelt. 'Absolutely. I've been really worried about him. His parents will be so relieved.'

'They are, apparently. They sent their thanks to the team and said everyone's been brilliant.'

'Oh, that's nice. It's good to feel appreciated. Right, I'm off. See you tomorrow,' she murmured, and he dug out a smile.

'Yeah. Thanks for holding my hand today.'

'You're welcome. Sorry, I have to go.'

Presumably to pick up her children from school. Interesting—and none of his business. She hurried away, and he turned back to James. 'So, what's next?'

She couldn't believe he was back in her life.

And why, oh, why did he still have to be so ridiculously gorgeous? Why couldn't he have got saggy and paunchy and lost his hair or something? Instead he was slimmer, more toned, and age had done his insanely good looks no harm at all. If anything it had honed them—that and his charismatic manner, the way he made a point of thanking his team, the quirk of his lips when he smiled…

He was just too darned perfect.

And she needed to stop torturing herself. She wasn't in the market for a relationship, particularly not one which had already failed nearly two decades ago.

No, not failed. Just been put on hold when he'd gone to Chicago, and then crashed and burned, taking her heart and her trust with it. Should she have gone? She'd kicked herself for not going at the time, and maybe she'd been wrong to let him go without a fight. How different would their lives have been?

Too late to worry about that now…

She parked the car, walked to the school gate and waited for the children to come out. There were a couple of older women there, standing chatting, and one looked vaguely familiar, but she couldn't place her. An ex-patient? Maybe, although she didn't think so. She hadn't seen her here before, certainly, but then she was often a bit late.

The children ran out, Phoebe straight for her, Billy detouring to chase another boy, then eventually ambling over to her before being sent back for his jumper.

'So what did you do today?' she asked Phoebe, scooping her up for a cuddle. It was an unnecessary question, as she was splattered with paint from her hair to her shoes, but Phoebe told her, moment by moment, and she nodded and smiled and felt relieved that her little daughter was so happy in school.

By the time Billy re-emerged, his jumper trailing on the ground behind him, almost everyone had gone, and she took them home, sent them out to the garden with a drink and opened the fridge.

'Can we have pasta?' Billy asked, sticking his head back into the kitchen, and she rolled her eyes.

'Again?'

'I like pasta.'

'I'll see.'

He went, not looking convinced, and she stared at the fridge again. There was a chicken, which wouldn't keep, so she pressure-cooked it, stripped some of the meat off and threw it in with a bowl of pasta and pesto, added some peas and sweet corn, and called the children in.

'Yay, pasta!' Billy said, and Phoebe pulled a face.

'We *always* have pasta,' she grumbled, but frankly putting anything on the table that was edible was a miracle, the way she felt today.

Confused didn't even scrape the surface.

'We'll have something else tomorrow,' she promised, and gave the ever-hungry Billy another dollop.

'So how was your first day?'

He straightened up from fussing the dog and gave his mother a wry smile.

'Interesting. Pretty full-on, really, but good. We had a boy just a year older than Charlie—his motorbike hit a car head-on. It was pretty messy, and I had no idea how everyone there would cope. Back in London I wouldn't have worried, everyone knew what to do, but actually it was brilliant. They're a good team, and he's doing OK, so that's good.'

She eyed him thoughtfully. 'And?'

'Well, it was touch and go and just a bit close to home.'

'I'm sure, but it's not what I'm talking about.'

He laughed. He'd never been able to hide anything from

his mother, and he gave up trying. 'Emily's there. She was one of the team.'

Her brows creased in a thoughtful frown. 'Emily Harrison?'

'She's Emily West now. She's a senior specialty registrar—what? Why are you looking at me like that?'

'Does she have children?'

'I think so, maybe.'

'A boy and a girl?'

He raised his hands, confused. 'I don't know. I have no idea. Why?'

'Because I saw someone today after school who looked rather like her, but I thought I must be imagining it. She had a little girl with blonde hair—about four, I suppose, and a boy of about five or six called Billy, with grubby knees and the cheekiest smile you've ever seen.'

That made him laugh, but his breath caught and deep inside there was a tiny pang of regret for what might have been. If they'd stayed together, those could have been their children, his and hers. He stamped on that before it had time to take root, and made his voice deliberately light. 'I have no idea. I don't know how old they are or what they're called. More to the point, how was Amelie's first day? She seems to have enjoyed it, from what she said just now when I went up.'

'I think she's fine. She certainly didn't seem unhappy, but it's early days. But you know her, Oliver. She makes friends really easily.'

'She loses them again pretty quickly, as well,' he reminded her with a wry smile, and she nodded.

'She'll learn,' his mother said soothingly, and slid a cup of tea across the island to him. 'Are you hungry?'

He gave a slightly hollow laugh. 'You could say that. I

had a sandwich about eleven thirty, and a banana at some point, and probably way too much coffee. What are you offering? Because I could eat a horse.'

'Sorry, no horses, but I made a fish pie.'

His stomach growled, and he smiled wearily. 'That sounds amazing. Bring it on...'

She didn't let it rest, of course.

She wanted every last detail of his day, every last detail of how Emily looked, how she'd sounded, how he felt about her being there.

That was the tough one to answer, because he really didn't know. It had certainly made it harder to settle in and focus, because she'd been all he could think about, all he could hear, all he could see. Everywhere he turned, she was there, or there was the echo of her laugh, the soft murmur of her voice soothing a patient, talking to a relative, comforting a frightened child.

And then, as if the day itself hadn't been enough to contend with, that night he dreamt about her and woke up with a racing heart and a body that was more than ready to welcome her back into his bed.

This was going to be impossible to ignore. *She* was going to be impossible to ignore. And seeing her again had brought a whole lot of memories flooding back. Memories of her in his arms. Memories of them laughing together at something ridiculous, laughing at each other and themselves. Fighting about silly things, and then making up...

Damn. He rolled onto his back, stared up at the ceiling and wondered if moving here had been the biggest mistake of his life.

No. That prize had to go to his decision to go to America, and then to try and forget her in the arms of another woman, and look how well that had turned out.

Except it had given him Charlie, and for that he'd always be grateful. He looked at his watch. Two fifteen. It would be nine fifteen in Boston. He'd still be up.

He sat up, dragged a hand through his hair, reached for his phone and called his son.

CHAPTER TWO

THE ED WAS busy as usual.

For once that was a good thing, because if she wasn't busy, she'd have time to think about him, and she really, really didn't want to do that. The last thing she needed was to get sucked into that again. It had taken her years to get over him, and yesterday had made her realize she wasn't really over him at all. She'd just learned to live with it in the background.

Seeing him again had brought all those old feelings rushing back, the good ones as well as the bad, and it wasn't conducive to sleep, apparently. She'd had three, maybe four hours, in fits and starts, and in the end she'd got up and busied herself in the kitchen, making tonight's meal out of the leftover chicken and freezing the rest for some point in the future.

Then she'd curled up in the sitting room for a few quiet minutes, staring out over the garden as the sun came up and sparkled on the dewy grass, before she'd showered and dressed. And dithered over make-up.

To wear, or not to wear?

She'd scowled crossly at herself in the bathroom mirror, put on her usual flick of mascara, a touch of lippy and a streak of concealer to hide the shadows under her eyes, and got the children ready for school.

They were surprisingly cooperative for once, which meant she was early, and James opened his mouth to comment and was firmly shut down with a challenging look.

His lips twitched. 'I never said a word,' he murmured, but her relief was short-lived because he followed it up with, 'Can I ask you to work with Oliver again? Just until he's found his feet?'

He'd looked pretty sure on his feet yesterday, but she agreed, wishing she could say no but knowing it would demand a whole bunch of explanations she wasn't inclined to give right then. Mostly because she had no idea what to say.

It didn't matter. James just nodded and strode off to speak to Tom Stryker, leaving her to deal with her tangled emotions as she worked side by side with Oliver on one case after another.

And then at half past one it went weirdly quiet.

For the first time she could remember, they had no urgent cases that weren't already under control, leaving her to twiddle her thumbs.

She stuck her head into Minors and found everything there running smoothly and under control, so she was redundant. It wouldn't last, she knew that, but as she walked back into Majors, she all but fell over Oliver.

'Where is everyone?' he asked, looking puzzled.

'Who knows? It's like everyone's left town.'

He chuckled. 'It was a busy morning. Maybe they've got it out of their system.' He glanced at his phone. 'Quick coffee in the park?'

No! Not again. Too dangerous...

'That's asking for chaos.'

'I'll take the risk. You can fill me in on everything I need to know about everybody.'

Really? She shrugged and gave in. 'OK, but you're buying, and I'm hungry today—I need lunch. Just so you know.'

They found a bench under a tree, and sat down with their coffees and sandwiches, pagers at the ready because it really couldn't last.

'So, what do you want to know about us?' she asked, just to break the silence that was echoing with memories she'd really rather have forgotten.

He shot her an odd look, as if he knew what she was thinking, then followed up with a crooked smile.

'I don't know. You tell me. I'm sure I'll work it all out, unless there's anything really out there that you think I should know in advance?'

She shook her head, partly to clear it, and stuck to the script. 'Not much. Andy Gallagher's part-time. He had a benign meningioma removed a few years back and wanted a better work–life balance, and Tom Stryker's got retinitis pigmentosa and his peripheral vision's a bit dodgy, so if you end up working with him, you need to bear that in mind. Otherwise, no. Sam's an ex-army medic like Ryan, and he's pretty gung ho, but he's very good, so is Ryan, and James is just great. The junior doctors are by and large OK, there's the odd one that needs watching, but all the nurses are lovely.'

He nodded slowly. 'OK. That's good to know.'

He searched her eyes, and she had to look away because there was something in his steady gaze that made her heart race and her breath catch.

'And you?' he asked, his voice low and slightly husky. 'What do I need to know about you?'

Nothing…

'There's not much you don't know. I'm still just me,' she said lightly. 'I've been here for a year and a half, initially covering Tom's wife, Laura, on her maternity leave, and when she decided not to come back, I stayed on in the post and took on a bit more. Anyway, enough of us all,' she said, changing tack. 'What do we need to know about *you*?'

He gave a soft laugh, but his eyes changed, as if he was shielding himself somehow. Why? Although she could talk…

'I'm still just me,' he echoed with a slight smile. 'I've been working in London, as you know, and it was time for a move.'

She wondered why. He'd said family reasons yesterday but didn't add any more, so she probed a little deeper.

'So when did you come back from America? The last thing I knew you were in Chicago and you were getting married and having a baby.'

And breaking my heart in the process…

He looked away. 'Yeah. That didn't last too long. Just long enough to move back to the UK, have Charlie, and for Sue to meet someone else. They're living back in the States now—been there for four years, since he was thirteen, and I hardly see him.'

Wow. That shocked her. 'You couldn't have gone back there so you could be near him?'

He shook his head. 'No. I was married again by the time they moved back, we had a child, and Kath was working a lot in Europe, so it wasn't practical.'

'You've got another child?' she said, feeling a curious pang of something she didn't want to analyse, and he nodded.

'Yes. Amelie. She's five and a half now, and she's just a bundle of mischief.'

His eyes softened, and she could see the love in them.

She'd bet her life he was a wonderful father, and he must miss Charlie so much. How would she feel if that was Billy?

Gutted.

'So tell me about you,' he went on, switching the subject back to her. 'James said you only work part-time, and Mum said she thought she saw you outside the school yesterday, so I gather you've got children, too.'

'It was *her*!' she said, the penny dropping at last. 'I was sure it was someone I knew, but I couldn't place her. So how come she was there?'

'She helps with the school run,' he said, but there was something else he didn't say. She had no idea what it was, but now wasn't the time because he was moving on, or rather back, to the subject of her children.

'She told me you had a little girl with blonde hair and a boy called Billy with the cheekiest smile?' he added, which made her laugh.

'That sounds about right.'

'Well, come on, then, tell me more.'

She wasn't sure she wanted to—it seemed too personal, but what could it hurt? It wasn't like she was ashamed of them or anything, and she could hardly hide them if his child was at the same school, but he didn't need the whole sorry saga.

She gave a little shrug. 'There's not much more to tell. Phoebe's four and a half, and Billy's just six.'

'And their father? What does he do?'

Trust him to get to that.

'He's an accountant, but we're divorced,' she said reluctantly, looking away. 'He has our two every other weekend, which is good because I then work two long days, which gives me a chance to make up some hours. Otherwise, I wouldn't be able to afford the house.'

'Doesn't he pay maintenance?'

'Yes, of course he does, but I wanted a house in a good school catchment area, so I have to pay the premium for that. It's only a modest little house, but it's big enough for us and it's going to be mine one day, but it does mean I have to work more than I want to while they're so young.'

'You couldn't have stayed in the family home?'

'No, because it was in Nottingham, and he moved down here, so when this job came up I followed for the sake of the kids. It's just a bit tough at the moment, but I'll get there, one day.'

He stared at her for a long moment, then shook his head. 'I'm sorry.'

'What for? It's not your fault. You haven't done anything wrong—well, apart from dumping me nineteen years ago to follow your dream.'

His mouth twisted into a bitter little smile. 'I didn't exactly dump you. I asked you to come.'

'And I couldn't, you knew that, and you were going for a year and coming back. That was the plan. You going off with someone else wasn't *exactly* on the cards.'

He frowned and looked away. 'No. No, it wasn't. And I am sorry about that.'

'Is that it? "I'm sorry" is supposed to make it all OK? Is that what your letter was all about?'

'Of course not. I'm not that stupid. I didn't know what else to do, how to tell you, and you didn't reply.'

She gave a tiny humourless laugh. 'What did you expect? Congratulations? A wedding present? There was nothing to say, Oliver. Sue was pregnant, you were getting married. End of.'

He was looking down, peeling a crust off his sandwich and throwing it to the robin who was eyeing them patiently, his face sombre. 'I've often wondered what happened to you.'

'You could have asked me. I wouldn't have been difficult to find if you'd tried.'

'No, you wouldn't, but I didn't try.'

'Why?'

He shrugged. 'I didn't think it was fair. I thought I'd done enough damage, and I had nothing to offer you, and it wouldn't have changed anything, except to make it harder. Then when I did eventually look, I couldn't find you. I thought you were probably married, but I'm surprised you changed your name.'

'I did it for the children,' she said simply. 'I didn't want them having the confusion of a different last name to me, so it made sense.'

'Yes, I can understand that—oh, here we go...'

He picked up his pager and sighed, just as hers went off, and as they scooped up the remains of their sandwiches and their coffees, they could hear the sound of the helicopter overhead.

'So much for my quiet life,' he said drily, and they headed back to Resus in a slightly awkward silence.

She left barely in time to collect the children from after-school club, and found Phoebe in tears because she'd lost her teddy and Billy with a plaster on his knee after a fall in the playground. He started to limp as soon as he saw her, but she wasn't fooled, just rumpled his hair and gave him a hug, scooped Phoebe up and headed for the car.

'I can't go home without him,' Phoebe sobbed. 'What if Mrs Ellis can't find him?'

'Don't worry about Mister Ted,' she soothed. 'He'll turn up. I'll bet when you get to school tomorrow, he'll be waiting for you.' And heaven help us if he's not...

'What if he's lost for ever?' she asked, and started to sob again as Emily strapped her in.

'I'm sure he's not,' she said, crossing her fingers and sliding behind the wheel. 'He'll turn up, you'll see. So what did you both do today?'

'We've got a new girl in our class this week,' Billy told her. 'She's called Emily. Or I think she is, but she said it funny.'

That caught her attention. 'Amelie?' she suggested, with a little hitch in her heart.

'Yes. Why doesn't she just say Emily?'

'Perhaps because she's actually called Amelie. It's a French name, and someone at work has a daughter called Amelie who's just started at school near here, so maybe it's her.'

'Oh.'

She watched him in the rearview mirror, working that one out while she did the same thing. Was it purely coincidence that their names were so alike? Must be. And she really shouldn't start reading things into that...

'Can we have pasta?' he asked, moving on to his favourite subject, and she rolled her eyes.

'No. Not again.'

'I want chicken pie,' Phoebe said.

'I hate chicken pie!'

'Well, I *like* chicken pie,' Phoebe said, 'and I lost my teddy and it's my turn to choose. I want pie.'

'Well, isn't that lucky, because it's what we're having,'

Emily told them, turning onto her drive with an inward sigh of relief. 'Come on, let's get that knee cleaned up and then we'll go in the garden. I need to cut the grass before we can eat.'

She was single.

So was he.

And he had no idea how he felt about that. Wary? Nervous? Excited?

No! He wasn't going there, not ever again, and certainly not with Emily! Not that she'd have him, judging by what she'd said today.

Smart woman. He wasn't a good husband. Couldn't be, could he, or two women wouldn't have left him for someone else. Although Sue's justification was a bit different, but Kath's wasn't. She'd found someone who'd be there when she was able to be at home, not someone who might well be on duty for the two days she was back in the country before her own better-paid high-flying job took her away again.

She'd wanted a house husband, but he hadn't realized that until it was too late, and there was no way he'd been going to give up his career to sit at home and wait for her, any more than she'd have done it for him. And that was the kiss of death for their marriage. Not that it had been great to start with...

No. Never again, not with Emily, not with anyone. He had his mother on tap if he wanted adult company, Amelie any time he needed a cuddle, and Charlie was on the end of the phone. Failing that, there was the dog who was always up for a hug and a bit of affection, and absolutely never judged him.

What more could any man want?

A friend?

He had friends. Good friends. Although he'd lost contact with most of them over the years, like he'd lost contact with Em. Work pressure, lifestyle differences, geography—there weren't many people left who he could call a real friend, but a part of him yearned to be friends with Emily again.

Not lovers. That was messy and would open all sorts of wounds, but…friends? She'd said her ex had the children every other weekend and she worked then, but not for forty-eight hours straight. Maybe he should take her out for dinner?

Except he'd have to ask his mother to babysit, and she did enough already—and besides, her matchmaking antennae would be having a field day.

Best not. Even if it would be nice…

Mrs Ellis and Mister Ted were waiting for Phoebe when they arrived, and Phoebe grabbed him and hugged him tight.

'I told you he'd be all right,' Emily said, and Phoebe ran off smiling. Billy was long gone, playing with his friends in the playground, and as she walked towards the gate, she spotted Oliver's mother, with a small shaggy dog and a little girl.

Amelie. Had to be. She was the spitting image of Oliver, and her heart thumped. Long dark hair scraped back into a bouncy ponytail, pink dungarees and a unicorn on her T-shirt peeping over the top of the bib, she was the picture of health and happiness, and Emily stood rooted to the spot.

The woman kissed her goodbye and then turned and greeted Emily with a wide smile and open arms.

'Emily, it *is* you! How lovely to see you again!'

'Hello, Elizabeth!' she said, and found herself engulfed

in a warm motherly hug that brought tears to her eyes. She'd loved his mother, and it seemed it was mutual.

Elizabeth let go of her after a long moment, stood back and smiled. 'Oh, it's so good to see you again. Are you off to work?'

She nodded. 'Yup, afraid so.'

'Oh, that's a shame. It would be lovely to catch up with you. How would you feel about a play date after school one day? You can come round to ours.'

Ours? Her heart skipped a beat. They'd been living in Hampshire when she'd known them, so they must have moved up here. Or did she mean Oliver's home? And what about his wife? It was a minefield, and she tiptoed her way out of it.

'Why don't you come to mine?' she suggested, opting for safety, and Elizabeth pounced on it.

'Oh, that would be lovely! How nice. We can take it in turns. How about after school today?'

She hesitated, mentally ran an eye over her house and decided it would do, then nodded. 'OK. Actually, that would be great. I'll meet you here?'

'Perfect. Have a good day. I'll see you later.' Elizabeth kissed her cheek, and Emily walked away with a whole bunch of mixed feelings and tumbling emotions.

Was it wise to get reeled in? To forge a relationship with his mother at the same time as trying to keep him at arm's length to preserve her heart and her sanity?

Too late now; she'd agreed, but if the children didn't get on, she could always use that as an excuse to avoid it happening again, and it would give her a chance to find out a little more about him and his life now.

'My mother says you're going on a play date.'

Emily laughed at him and shook her head. 'That sounds

so weird. She's coming round to mine with Amelie after school. It's not very exciting.'

'She's looking forward to it,' he said, searching her face and wondering whether she was. Possibly not, judging by the guarded look in her eyes, and he certainly wasn't thrilled.

'You could always put her off if you don't want to do it,' he added hopefully after a moment, but she shook her head.

'No, it's lovely to see her again. I was very fond of her.'

'Yes, it's mutual,' he said wryly. 'I'm not sure she's ever really forgiven me for breaking up with you.'

Which made at least two of them, if not three. He certainly hadn't forgiven himself, and from what she'd said yesterday, Emily might not have, either.

Too late now. The damage was done, and he wasn't going there again, but he wondered how much his mother would tell Emily about him. Nothing, hopefully, but it was probably a vain hope.

'So how come she's doing the school run?' Emily asked, ignoring his last comment, and he looked away from those all-too-seeing eyes.

'We needed help with childcare,' he said, being distinctly frugal with the truth. 'We lost the live-in nanny, and Mum stepped up. That's why I took this job—to be closer to her.'

The red phone rang just as Emily opened her mouth, rescuing him from a conversation that was about to get into very tricky waters, and he sighed with relief as she scooped up the phone. The last thing he needed while he was at work was an in-depth discussion of his second failed marriage...

'Right, we've got a thirty-four-year-old woman, fall from a horse, query spinal injuries, short loss of consciousness, ETA ten minutes.'

* * *

She got away just about on time, and Elizabeth was there with the dog. There was no sign of Billy, of course, but Phoebe ran up to her, and she bent and hugged her as Billy and Amelie appeared.

Billy was chasing Oscar again around the playground, but Amelie ran over to her grandmother, her pink dunga-rees reassuringly grubby, with grass stains on the knees and bottom, and a blob of something that could have been tomato sauce on her unicorn T-shirt. She was beaming, and her smile reminded Emily so much of Oliver that her heart squeezed.

'Amelie, this is Emily,' Elizabeth said, and Emily smiled at the child that could so easily have been hers.

'Hello, Amelie,' she said gently. 'It's nice to meet you. Billy told me you'd started in his class. This is Phoebe, by the way. Have you met?'

'I saw her at lunch,' Amelie said. 'Grandma, Lucy asked me on a play date. Can I go?'

'Not today, darling. We're going to Emily's house with Billy and Phoebe, but another day, I'm sure.'

Her face fell. 'Oh. OK. Can I go tomorrow?'

'Let me talk to Lucy's mummy tomorrow,' Elizabeth said, just as Billy ran up.

'Mummy, can we have pasta?'

Emily laughed and ruffled his hair. 'Again? We'll see. Amelie and her grandma are coming to ours now for a play date.'

'Cool,' he said, and then, 'can we have pizza instead?'

Elizabeth didn't really mention Oliver, but Emily did glean that Amelie's mother was based in Germany and made fleeting visits at the weekends.

'Gosh, doesn't Amelie miss her?' she asked, unable to imagine what it would be like to see Phoebe or Billy so little.

'Oh, yes, of course,' Elizabeth said, 'but I do what I can to fill in the gaps and we get by.'

She tilted her head and smiled at Emily. 'Enough of us. Tell me about yourself,' she said, switching the conversation back to Emily. 'I'm longing to hear all about you. I've often wondered what you were doing with your life, and Oliver tells me you're divorced. I'm sorry to hear that, but you seem to have made a lovely home for your children.'

'Thank you. I've done my best—'

And that was as far as any revelations went, because the children came running over, demanding pizza, and she ended up cooking for all three of them, and while they piled in, seeing who could eat the most pizza, the conversation moved to what she thought of the hospital.

'Oliver seems quite impressed,' she said, and Emily smiled wryly.

'Yes, I think he imagined it would be a bit quiet, but so far it's been pretty hectic. He's good, though. He's going to be an asset.'

'I'm glad. He was worried it would be the end of his career, I think, but Kath didn't really leave him any choice. The job in Germany was too good to turn down, and I couldn't really live in London with them long-term. My life's here now.'

'Yes, I was going to ask you about that,' she said, her curiosity getting the better of her. 'The last thing I knew you were living in Hampshire.'

'We were, but I moved up here when Martin died.'

That shocked her, and she reached out and laid a hand on Elizabeth's arm. 'Oh, no, I'm so sorry. When did he die?'

'Five and a half years ago. It was very sudden.'

'Oh, Elizabeth, I'm so sorry. You must have been absolutely devastated.'

'I was. I am.' She glanced away, staring at something in the distance. 'He had a heart attack out of the blue. I found him in the garden, on the bench under the trees. It must have been very, very quick. He looked so peaceful.'

'But what a shock for you.'

'It was. There was nothing wrong with him. He was fit and well and hadn't had so much as a twinge that I knew of. I keep telling myself it was better than a slow, lingering death or a horrible stroke that left him unable to move or communicate, but it doesn't stop me missing him every single day, and it'll always hurt that I never got to say goodbye. Anyway, I was rattling around in the house on my own, so I sold it and moved up here to be closer to my sister, and then Oliver needed my help with Amelie so—Amelie, no, don't fight over the last slice. That's rude, darling.'

'But he's had more than me!' she protested, and Billy denied it, but couldn't look her in the eye, so Emily solved the problem by giving it to Phoebe because she'd been left trailing by their competition.

'Sorry, he's a bit feral,' she said to Elizabeth, but she was laughing.

'Don't apologize. It's nice to see children with healthy appetites,' she said with a smile, then glanced at her watch. 'We ought to be going soon, but it's been lovely, Emily. It's so good to see you again. You must come to us next time. We only live round the corner.'

'That would be really nice,' she said, slightly torn because she wasn't sure if Oliver would be open to that. He'd looked a bit cagey earlier today, as if he hadn't wanted them together.

Why? She had no idea, and Elizabeth had been disappointingly discreet. She could always ask him about himself, but she wasn't sure she wanted to know about his complicated domestic arrangements, and she certainly didn't want to talk about her own messy life.

Which didn't stop her being curious...

Thankfully, James decided that Oliver's hand didn't need holding any more—not that it ever had, she was sure—so she was freed from the constant contact, the weird tug of tension in her chest every time he was in the room, which meant she could truly concentrate on her work.

And there was plenty of it. They were as busy as ever, so the days flew by, and before she knew it, it was the weekend.

She picked the children up from school on Friday, took them home and packed their things, and at five on the dot Steve appeared to take them to his.

'Be good,' she said automatically, but they'd gone, telling their father all about what they'd done this week, and she waved them off as they drove away, then closed the front door.

Silence.

Silence and emptiness, and she spared a thought for Elizabeth. How had she coped when Martin died? When she'd walked back in from the garden and knew the house was empty for ever?

Not that this was the same thing at all. Divorce was hardly in the same league as bereavement, but it still left its wounds.

She gave herself a mental shake, tackled the laundry, changed the sheets, put on another load and ran a bath.

She was going to read a book, but she was already in the water by the time she realized she'd forgotten to bring it.

Which left her mind time to wander, which of course it did, without asking her permission, straight into Oliver territory.

What kind of a marriage did he have? It couldn't be much of one if Kath was in Germany all the time, but maybe that suited him? Suited both of them, perhaps, but Kath must be made of sterner stuff than her.

When Steve had moved back here to be with his first wife, Amanda, and their two children, it had left Emily, Billy and Phoebe bereft. He'd given up his whole new life and gone back to his old home, and she'd been left with no choice but to follow him here for the sake of her children, so they could maintain their relationship with him.

She knew why he'd done it, because like her he'd never got over his first love, so she could understand, even sympathize, but he'd destroyed her trust and left her sad and lonely.

Just as she'd been when Oliver had left her.

How different would their lives have been if she'd gone with him to Chicago? He'd wanted her to, he'd begged her to go, but her father was waiting for bypass surgery, and the prospect of being so far away if anything had happened to him had held her back. She'd told herself if she'd really meant that much to Oliver, he would have stayed, but in her heart she knew he couldn't. He'd signed up to a course, he'd paid for it, he was committed, and so he'd gone, and she'd kissed him goodbye and waited for him to come back.

Only he didn't, or not to her, because he'd met Sue and that had changed everything.

If only she'd gone, or he'd stayed, their lives would have been completely different. They might have had children of their own, but instead between them they'd had two failed marriages and four children, none of which would probably have existed if they'd stayed together.

But they hadn't, and painful though her break-up first with Oliver and then with Steve had been, she couldn't unwish her children, never in a million years, and she didn't imagine Oliver could unwish his, either.

But that didn't stop her wondering where they would have ended up if she'd gone, and what kind of a family they might have had—

Oh, for goodness' sake! She had to stop obsessing about him. Their relationship was over, done with long, long ago. Her fault? His? Whatever—it was over.

Except now he was here all the time, getting inside her head, haunting her sleep and driving her crazy. Still, it was the weekend and James was on tomorrow, so she'd get a bit of respite…

CHAPTER THREE

SO MUCH FOR RESPITE. She walked into the department at seven the next morning and practically fell over him.

'What are you doing here? I thought James was on today. You've been here all week!' she said, and he shrugged and gave her a wry smile.

'I swapped. Connie's out and their childcare fell through, so I told James I'd cover the morning. Do you have a problem with that?'

She felt herself colour slightly. 'No—no, of course not. Sorry. I was just surprised.'

'Yeah, I got that. So how come you're here? You've been here all week, too.'

'It's Steve's weekend for the children, so I work both days.'

He cocked his head on one side and studied her thoughtfully. 'Do you do twelve days straight, or do you have time off next week?'

'No, I work twelve days, but ten of them aren't full days. It's not ideal, but it's not as bad as it sounds and at least I pull my weight.'

'It still makes getting life stuff done tricky.'

She laughed at that. 'Isn't it always?' she said. Then she added, 'It's weirdly quiet without the kids, though, so I'd rather be at work. It feels odd and empty. They drive me mad, but when they aren't there, it feels all wrong. I mean, there's quiet, and there's too quiet.' Quiet enough to start thinking about him...

He nodded again, his mouth kicking up in a smile full of irony. 'Yeah. I know how that goes.' And then out of the blue he added, 'So what will you do this evening?'

'Oh, I have no idea. Put away the washing, I expect. It's the highlight of my weekend.'

He laughed, then pulled a thoughtful face. 'How do you fancy going to a pub? Nothing flashy, just a drink and something to eat?'

She stared at him, slightly stunned. 'Are you asking me on a date?'

'No!' he said hastily, and then softened it with a smile. 'No, not at all. I was asking if you want to come and hang out with an old friend so I can pretend to have a life that doesn't involve Amelie or work. I don't know anyone here, and it's a bit...'

'Lonely?' she offered, torn between contemplating the 'old friend' thing and wondering if things were all right with his rather odd marriage, and he nodded.

'Yeah, pretty much.' He gave a soft huff of laughter. 'Although it's hard to be lonely when I'm always surrounded by people, but...'

'Yes.'

'Yes?'

'Yes, it's hard, but it happens, and yes, that would be nice. Saturday night is always a bit dull somehow. Seven thirty?'

His mouth kicked up at one side. 'Sure. Amelie should be in bed by then. I'll check with my mother that she's OK to babysit, but I'm sure she will be and we won't be out late. Any idea where we could go?'

'Not really. I don't go out a lot, but James is a fan of the Harbour Inn down by the river mouth. We could try that?'

'OK. I'll check it out. In fact give me your phone. I'll put my number in and you can send me your address and I'll pick you up.'

She handed it over, wondering at the wisdom of agreeing to all this, and he tapped in his number and handed it back.

'Right, I suppose we ought to go and tackle the backlog from last night,' he said. 'I think they're still wading through the revellers. I don't know where the young get their stamina.'

'You mean you can't remember the nights we stayed out till five and fell into bed for two hours before lectures?' she teased, and just like that she'd scrolled them back almost twenty years, the memories so vivid it could have been yesterday.

Her breath caught as he held her eyes, and then he turned away before she had a chance to read them properly.

'That was a very long time ago,' he said quietly, and headed off towards the desk, leaving her wondering why on earth she'd said that. So awkward. And they were going out tonight? So much for 'old friends'.

'Idiot,' she muttered, and followed him.

Why did she have to talk about bed?

And specifically their bed. He closed his eyes, breathed in and counted to ten, then picked up a file and headed towards the cubicles. Frustration was burning a hole in him, and he was annoyed with himself for reacting to her. Especially as they were now going on a 'not-a-date' date!

So much for taking her out for a nice platonic little chat...

* * *

What to wear?

It's not a date!

She rifled through her wardrobe, discounting everything on the grounds of being too boring, too provocative, too bright, too tight, too loose—all her clothes were too something, and she sat down on the bed and sighed.

Jeans and a pretty top? Less controversial than a dress, and it wasn't really warm enough for sandals yet, not in the evening.

Jeans, then. Definitely jeans. And a totally uncontroversial top. She pulled them on, looked at herself and sighed. She looked as if she was going to the supermarket!

'Why did I say yes?' she wailed, and ripped the top off, going back to the wardrobe for an alternative. Better. Prettier, but still not overly dressy.

She checked the time, studied her face and decided it would do. Enough make-up to have made an effort, not so much that she looked as if she was going 'out' out.

A car pulled up outside, and she grabbed a cardi, slid her feet into simple ballet pumps and ran downstairs. She could see him through the obscured glass, a fuzzy shape heading to the front door, and she pulled it open as he reached for the bell.

How could he look so hot in jeans and a shirt?

He gave her a guarded smile. 'Hi. All ready?'

'Yup.' She scooped up her bag, locked the front door and followed him back to the car, relieved that he was wearing the same sort of thing as her, less relieved at her reaction to it, which was doing nothing for her plan to keep it strictly neutral. She got in as he slid behind the wheel and glanced across at her.

'I've booked a table at the Harbour Inn—it seems to have good reviews, so I hope it's OK.'

'So do I, as I suggested it, but really I have no idea. My work–life balance means I'm either at work being a doctor, or at home being a mother, which is my life. I can't even remember the last time I was just me.'

He gave a soft laugh. 'You and me both, but we're doing it now, so let's go. You never know—we might even have fun.'

They pulled up in the car park, and over the top of the sea-wall she could see the masts of the dinghies on the fore-shore silhouetted against the sky.

They went in and were ushered to a table by the window, and she looked around as they sat down. 'Oh, this is lovely.'

'Your choice,' he said with a smile, and she smiled back.

'Not really. I was going from what James said, but he clearly doesn't lie.'

They ordered drinks, pored over the menu for a while and ended up with traditional fish and chips.

'Not the healthiest, but hey,' he said wryly. 'We can't be good all the time.'

'I try, but if I listened to Billy, we'd have pasta every night.'

That made him laugh. 'I don't have that problem. I hand over the money and all the responsibility for that to my mother and let her deal with it.'

'You're lucky to have her.'

His smile faded. 'Yes, I am, and I'm glad I'm there for her now Dad's not around, but I use her more than enough as it is, which is another reason why I hardly ever go out. I don't want to take advantage. It simply isn't fair.'

'Life isn't,' she said softly, then added, 'I was so sorry to hear about your father. He was such a lovely man. It must have been a terrible shock for all of you.'

He dropped his eyes. 'Yeah, it was awful. Very sudden. And it was right before Amelie was born as well, and I was gutted that he never got to meet her. And then Kath only took three months' maternity leave and went back to work as soon as we could get a live-in nanny, so I barely saw Mum in that time.'

'That must have been hard.'

'It was, juggling trying to keep an eye on her and help her, find any time to bond with Amelie, not let my work colleagues down—it was a nightmare, but she was brilliant. They'd already talked about downsizing, so she sold the family home, bought herself a lovely flat in Woodbridge so she was closer to her sister, and then when the nanny left eighteen months ago, she dropped everything and stepped up without hesitating, and she's been amazing ever since. Then this job came up and I sold my house, she let the flat, and we've bought a house together.'

They all lived together? 'Gosh. And I thought my life was complicated! So how does Kath fit into all this?' she asked tentatively, and his mouth twisted into a rueful little smile.

'Ah. Yeah. Kath and I aren't together any more,' he told her, and her heart gave a little jolt. 'She's always travelled a lot with her job, but about a year ago she was offered a stunning promotion and she's now based in Germany, and there's a new man in her life, and we've both moved on.'

'And Amelie?'

'Lives with me full time. That was the deal in our divorce settlement. I wasn't losing another child to a broken marriage, and to be honest she wasn't the most involved of parents. I mean, don't get me wrong, she loves Amelie, and Amelie loves her, and she comes over from Germany whenever she can, but she simply doesn't have the time to devote to Amelie, and my mother does.'

'And are you happy?' she asked.

'In a way,' he said after a lengthy pause, and his eyes searched hers. 'What about you? You've been through a lot. Are *you* happy?'

She rolled her eyes. 'Gosh, that's a hard one. I would rather it had been different, but it is what it is, and yes, I'm happy, I suppose. I love my job, I love our little house and I adore my children, so I have a lot to be thankful for, but I'm never going there again. Divorce leaves its scars.'

'Yes, it does. It certainly does, but Kath and I—well, it was a disaster once Amelie was born, and to be fair it wasn't great before that. She basically wanted a house husband, someone happy to hold the fort and be there as and when she had time to come home to change the contents of her suitcase, and that was never going to be me. She understood my commitment to my job, because she had the same commitment to hers, but she had no commitment to our marriage, and that—'

He broke off, then said, 'I was going to say it hurt, but actually it just annoyed me more than anything, but I guess it was my fault.'

'How was it your fault?'

He shrugged. 'I should have realized what she was like, but I was grateful initially that she understood my work schedule. Or I thought she did, till the crunch came and she said I should give up my job. That was never going to happen, not at that stage in my training.'

'Could you both have cut back?'

His laugh was humourless and a little surprised. 'No way. It would have been career suicide for me, and she wouldn't even consider it, so we got a nanny and we managed, but it was never really satisfactory, not till Mum stepped up. Then all I felt was relief. As I said, it wasn't much of a marriage and it was definitely a mistake.'

'So how did you feel about Sue when you split up?'

His mouth tilted into a wry smile. 'Ah, well, that was a whole different ball game. We'd been back in the UK awhile, and she'd had Charlie, and I was working ridiculous hours—you know how that goes—and then she found a babysitter and enrolled on a cookery course one evening a week, and met a woman there called Donna. They had a lot in common—they were both from the States, they loved crafts, they loved cooking—and it dawned on them that they loved each other. Game over.'

'Wow,' she said softly. 'I wasn't expecting that.'

He laughed. 'No, nor was I, but let's just say it explained a lot of what was wrong with our marriage. I'd blamed it on my work schedule, but it wasn't that—or not all that, but it was what it was. There was no way I was in competition with Donna and at least it left my ego intact. Charlie was more of a worry, and I was gutted for him at first that we weren't going to be bringing him up together, but you know, Donna's lovely, Sue's happy with her, they're married, I'm still in regular contact with Charlie and he's happy, well-adjusted...'

His little shrug spoke volumes.

'But you're really not,' she said, realizing she could still read his eyes.

This time he didn't look away, and she could see the sadness in them as clear as day. 'No. No, I'm really not. Not with that. Not because of our marriage, that wasn't working anyway, and we really only got married because she was pregnant and it made it easier for residency and stuff, but Charlie… Now they're back in the States, I hardly see him in the flesh, and there's only so much you can gain from a video call, and I miss his hugs.'

She was sure he did. It must be heart-breaking. 'Did they *have* to go back?'

'Yes, they did. Donna's parents were ill, and she needed to be near them so there really wasn't an option, but—yeah, it hurts.'

'And you couldn't go back because of Amelie. Oh, Oliver, that must have been so hard. I can't imagine how I'd feel if that was Billy.'

He shook his head. 'No. You can't, not till it happens. You think you understand, but—I had no idea. He was so much a part of my life. I saw him whenever I could, and losing him like that was really tough. And there was no way we could move there, so I stayed here with Amelie while Kath invested all her energy into her career and I tried to hold mine together and maintain my relationship with Charlie, and this is how it's all ended up.' He laughed again, but his eyes were still sad. 'Great, isn't it? I'm forty-two, divorced twice, and I'm back living with my mother. Happy days.'

'It's not quite like that,' she said gently, but he just gave a little huff of what could have been laughter but sounded more like self-mockery.

'No. No, it's not quite like that, but it feels like it. So anyway, that's me. I want to know about you.' He cocked his head on one side. 'Mum said the children had fun the other day.'

'They had a fight over the last slice of pizza,' she pointed out, and he laughed.

'Yes, she said. She also said they were lovely together.'

She chuckled. 'They were, in between times.'

His smile faded. 'So what went wrong with you and Steve?' he asked softly. 'How did you end up here?'

She wasn't sure she wanted to talk about it, but he'd spilled his guts, so it was only fair. But...

'Well?' he said, just as their meals arrived, and she picked up her knife and fork.

She hesitated, wondering where to start with the sorry saga of her failed marriage. 'I don't know where to start.'

'The beginning?' he said, his smile gentle.

She smiled, picked up a chip as a stalling tactic, put it down in defeat and did as he suggested.

'OK. I was working in Nottingham, I met Steve, and I knew all about his ex and his two boys—he was quite up-front about the fact he saw them every other weekend, and I was pleased he felt the need to keep in touch, so I was fine with it and we seemed happy enough. Anyway, we got married and had the children, and Steve was back there every other weekend and for a week at a time in school holidays, staying in his old house with his ex and the kids, and then it slowly dawned on them that they still loved each other, always had done, and they wanted to be together.'

He frowned. 'Ouch.'

'Absolutely. It came totally out of the blue, but they were quite certain, they'd thought about it for a long time, so we split up and he moved back to them, and every other weekend he was coming up to me.'

'And?' he prompted as she hesitated.

'And it felt wrong. I didn't like him being in my space, the children were confused about Daddy not being there all the time, they didn't understand why we were in different bedrooms, and in the holidays he took them to his other house and they'd come back after a week really confused and unhappy. It just wasn't working, not for any of us. He was really unhappy about leaving the little ones, but it was right for him and his other family.'

'They couldn't have moved to Nottingham?'

She shook her head. 'No, his kids are in secondary school and one of them has a learning disability, so it really wasn't an option to unsettle them.'

'Ah. That's tough.'

'It was tough, tough on all of us, but it was the right thing for them. I was still in my old job for a little while, but then Laura's maternity leave post came up and it had my name written all over it, because Steve's only ten miles away. There were actually two posts going, so I said I'd do eight tenths, but short days and working every other weekend, with more time off in the holidays, and that gives me time with the children, but it's not really ideal and James would love me to do more. That's why I do the weekends when I can to make up for it, but it seems to be working a lot better for all of us.'

He studied her thoughtfully. 'You're very understanding.'

'What, like you with Sue and Donna? Sometimes you just have to deal with what life throws at you and move on, so I did. And anyway, when I look back on it, our marriage was far from perfect, and I wouldn't have stood in his way even if I could. This way we're all better off.'

He chuckled and shook his head. 'What a pair we are. Four kids, three marriages, two compromised careers—'

'Stop,' she said firmly. 'Stop right there. You have your mother, you have two children who you love and who love you, you have a good job in an excellent hospital, even if it's not the cushy little number you thought it was going to be—'

'I never said anything about wanting a cushy little number!'

'Well, that's good, because you aren't going to get it in

Yoxburgh. And I've got two beautiful, healthy children who I adore, a job I love, a house I can just about afford—what more could either of us want? We have so much to be thankful for.'

He studied her face, a slow smile tilting his lips, and he stifled a grin at the last second. 'I'd forgotten how gorgeous you are when you get feisty,' he murmured, 'and you need to eat that if you're going to or it'll be stone-cold,' he added softly, and went back to his own food, that smile still playing around the corners of his mouth.

She picked up her cutlery again and picked at the remains of her fish, but his words were echoing in her head.

'I'd forgotten how gorgeous you are when you get feisty...'

There was a touch of colour in her cheeks, and he was busy kicking himself for saying what he had, but hell, she was glorious when she got on her high horse. He'd forgotten that—forgotten all sorts of things, like how easy she was to talk to, how honest she was about her feelings, how responsive she'd been...

He cut his thoughts off sharp, and leaned back in the chair.

'I'm stuffed.'

She put her knife and fork down and met his eyes, then looked away. 'Yes, me, too. I don't think I can finish this. It's a killer.'

'Probably in more ways than one, but it was delicious.'

'It was. Pity, the dessert menu looked really wicked.'

'We could share?'

Their eyes met and held, and she looked away first. 'Depends. What did you fancy?'

You...

'The chocolate fondant?' he suggested, knowing it was her favourite. 'I love a melting middle chocolate pudding.'

'Cream or ice cream?'

'Ooh. I'll let you choose,' he said, knowing she'd say cream. And...

'Cream.'

Right on cue. He smiled. 'Done.'

Except sharing was tricky. Too intimate, too cosy, too reminiscent...

He found himself watching her every spoonful, and he was relieved when it was over and she stopped sighing with delight over every bite.

'Oh, that was good,' she said, and he wiped his mouth and nodded.

'It was. Good choice. Coffee?'

'No, thanks. I think I'm done, but don't let me stop you.'

He met her eyes, and for once he couldn't read them.

'OK. I'll get the bill.'

He drove her home, pulled up outside and looked across at her.

'Thank you for coming out. It was really good to do something normal.'

'Yes, it was. Thank you for taking me.' And then before her brain could take over from her tongue, she added, 'I could make you a coffee? I know you wanted one.'

He hesitated and she could see him looking at her, but it was too dark to read his eyes. And then he spoke, his voice a little odd somehow. 'Yeah, why not? That would be nice.'

They went in, and she flicked on the lights and led him through to the kitchen, thankful that she'd had a blitz the night before, and he looked around.

'This is lovely. I like what you've done with it.'

'I haven't really done very much, and to be honest it wasn't difficult because it's so small, but it does the job and I couldn't afford anything more.'

'Do you need anything more?'

She smiled. 'Not really. A playroom would be nice, or another room downstairs, but that would mean moving or extending and I can't afford to do either. We're warm, we're dry, we're fed and we're happy. What more could we need?'

He shook his head slowly, and his smile was gentle. 'You always were good at putting a positive spin on things,' he murmured, and she laughed.

'Was I? Or was it just a case of learning it out of necessity? Anyway, tea or coffee?'

He hesitated, mostly because, standing in the small kitchen with her, he could smell the enticing fragrance that had teased his senses all evening and stirred up a hornet's nest of want and need and frustration. Not to mention longing.

Get a grip, man. You aren't going there again.

She turned round, two mugs in her hand, and raised an eyebrow. 'Hello?'

'Sorry, I was miles away. What did you say?'

She sighed and smiled. 'Tea or coffee? I have decaf, if you want?'

No, it's you I want...

'Decaf coffee would be lovely. Thanks.'

'You go and sit down, then. I'll bring it through,' she said, and turned back to the mugs, so he retreated to the living room, wondering why he'd agreed to come in, but he was here now, so he took the few moments he had to look around.

She was right, it was small, but it worked, with a dining

table at the garden end beside the kitchen, and a big comfy looking sofa under the window at the other end.

One end of the sofa had a table with an open book lying face down on it, so he headed for the other end and sat down, hopefully far enough away that he wouldn't be able to smell her.

Except she brought the coffee over and put it down next to him, and left a subtle drift of scent behind that did nothing at all to settle down his raging libido. Nor did the way she curled up on the sofa, tucking her now bare feet under her bottom and wrapping her hands around her mug.

'It's been really nice spending time with you again,' he said softly, and she turned her head and met his eyes.

'Yes. It's been a very long time.'

'It has. A lot of water under all sorts of bridges.'

'Most of them leading to divorce,' she added wryly. 'And the odd lucky escape.'

'Really?' That shocked him a little, although why he wasn't sure.

Her smile was wry and a little bitter. 'Yeah, really. I nearly married another doctor, but we were like ships in the night. We shared the same bed, but hardly ever together, and it was like having a flat-mate. And then he got a different job, so did I, so we just split up and went our separate ways.'

'Like me and Kath.'

'Yes, except we didn't have any children, so there was no guilt, just disillusionment, really, and disappointment. So I picked myself up and vowed never again, and then a few years later I met Steve, and he worked from home and was flexible so we could actually have a life together. I thought it would be fine, only I was wrong and it all fell apart. And of course, this time there were children involved—two sets.'

'I'm sorry. Life stinks sometimes.'

'Yes, it does.' And then she added, totally out of the blue, 'I often wonder if it would have been any better if I'd gone with you to Chicago.'

Her voice was a little wistful, and for some reason it made his heart beat faster. 'Why didn't you?' he asked quietly, and she gave him a sad little smile.

'You know why. My father was ill. I couldn't. And anyway, we hadn't been together that long, I'd already accepted a placement starting that summer and I had debts. I needed to get on with my career, start to earn some money, and there was no guarantee I could find a job over there, you were going to be busy on your postgrad course—'

'You could have enrolled for the course.'

'But I didn't want to. I couldn't afford it, and anyway, my father was waiting for a heart bypass and I was worried I'd be hours away if anything happened. But I did regret it, for a long time.'

He let that sink in, then searched her eyes and asked the question that had nagged at him for years.

'Did you love me?'

Her mouth opened, and she closed it and looked away, then looked back, her eyes sad.

'Yes. Yes, I loved you—but I wasn't enough for you, was I? You found Sue and that was that. I thought you'd be back after a year—I was waiting for you—but you weren't, or at least not on your own, so I moved on with my life, but I missed you.'

He swallowed. 'I missed you, too.'

'So why did you sleep with Sue?'

He couldn't hold her eyes, couldn't bear the rawness in her steady gaze, so he looked away.

'I have no idea. I'd seen her around at the college, and I went to a party and she was there, and we ended up together. She was warm and sweet and funny, and I guess we'd both had a bit too much to drink, and we just ended up in bed. And then a few weeks later she told me she was pregnant and I was devastated, but she was young and innocent, and I didn't feel I had a choice except to stand by her, even if it meant the end for you and me. And yes, it was a mistake, no, I shouldn't have done it, but it gave me Charlie, and I love him more than I knew it was possible to love anyone. He's such a huge part of my life I couldn't imagine what it would be like without him, so I couldn't turn the clock back. No Charlie, no Amelie...'

She nodded slowly, her face sad. 'No. I couldn't turn it back, either. Billy and Phoebe are everything to me, and they have to come first, before anything, but if it helps, I did love you, and not going with you broke my heart.'

'I'm sorry,' he said, his voice gruff, and he looked away, blinking back sudden uninvited tears.

'Don't be,' she said softly. 'We both did what we had to do. The decisions had already been made, and we were both committed.'

He met her eyes again. 'I didn't need to sleep with Sue,' he pointed out bluntly, and her smile tore his heart.

'No, you didn't, but you didn't abandon her, either. I couldn't have forgiven you for that. And as you said before, there's a lot of water gone under a lot of bridges. We've both made mistakes. We're human. We have to learn from them and move on.'

Learn from them? So what the hell was he doing here now?

He put his mug down and stood up. 'I need to go,' he

said, his voice a little gruff to his ears, and she uncoiled her legs and stood up and walked with him to the door.

He stopped in front of it, stared down into her eyes, and with a resigned sigh he pulled her gently into his arms and hugged her, burying his face in her hair and breathing her in for an age before he dropped his arms.

She eased away and looked up at him, her lips just a breath away from his, damp and slightly parted.

Don't do it...

With a ragged sigh he took a step back, and with a quiet, 'Goodnight, Emily,' he turned and opened the door and walked out of her house.

She watched him stride away, get into the car and drive off, lifting a hand in farewell, and she closed the door, leant on it and touched a hand to her lips.

Had she imagined it, or had he nearly kissed her? She could still feel the touch of his breath on her skin, the shiver of anticipation, the yearning need—or had she just imagined it?

Of course she had. And even if he hadn't nearly kissed her, it was too late for them now. It had been too late for close on twenty years.

She scooped up the mugs, put them in the dishwasher and went upstairs to bed.

At least she'd get some respite tomorrow. A whole day without him.

Suddenly it didn't seem all that appealing...

CHAPTER FOUR

'HELLO, DARLING. I didn't expect you back so early. Did you have a lovely time?'

'Yes, thanks. It was very nice.' Right up until the time he hugged her...

He bent and kissed his mother's cheek, and dropped onto the sofa beside her. 'How about you? Was Amelie good for you, or has she been up?'

'She was up for a little while, but not long. She just wanted some time with her Grandma.'

'I bet you spoiled her.'

'We might have read a book or two.'

'Or three,' he said, smiling indulgently at her. 'Honestly, you're a star, Mum, but you are such a pushover.'

'And you never spoil her, of course.' She chuckled and got stiffly to her feet. 'I'm off to bed. I'll see you tomorrow.'

'Anything I can do?'

'No, no, everything's done. Just relax. You don't do that nearly often enough. Sleep well.'

'You, too. And thanks again.'

'You're welcome. I'm glad you enjoyed it.'

She kissed his cheek, gave it a little pat and walked through into her part of the house, her book tucked under her arm, and he watched her go, torn between gratitude and guilt.

Well, it made a change from frustration, he thought as he went upstairs to check on Amelie. She was fine, sleeping peacefully, and he bent and kissed her tousled hair, then came down and sat on the sofa, scrolling through messages on his phone.

One from Charlie, saying there was something he wanted to tell him. He glanced at the time. It would be mid-afternoon in Boston.

The phone rang once, and Charlie picked up, the sound of his voice instantly grounding, and his whole life fell back into place. This was who he was, the father of two wonderful children, not some crazy hormonal undergraduate.

He settled back and listened to his son.

Work the next day was as busy as ever, with loads of sporting injuries as a result of the lovely weather.

Luckily most of it was routine stuff, because she was struggling to concentrate.

Had he been going to kiss her? She had no idea, but for a breathless second she'd wondered, and she'd dreamt about him last night…

She made herself concentrate, and by the end of her shift she was exhausted, her brain was reeling and her feet were numb, but the second she walked in through her front door, she was straight back to that not-quite kiss.

Madness. It would be folly to start something like that with him.

Wouldn't it?

What if—no. Bad idea.

She heard the scrunch of tires as Steve's car pulled up on the drive, putting a stop to her endless circular thoughts.

'See you in two weeks,' their father said, kissing the

children goodbye, and they shut the door and ran in and hugged her, fizzing with excitement.

'They've got a puppy, Mummy,' Phoebe said, eyes sparkling, and her heart sank.

'That's nice,' she said, waiting for the inevitable. She didn't have to wait long.

'Mummy, please, *pleeeeease* can we have a puppy, too?' Phoebe said, her eyes wide with longing.

She gave a tiny sigh. 'You know we can't, darling. My work schedule won't allow it.'

'But Amelie's got a dog and her daddy's a doctor, too, so you could,' Billy reasoned.

'But her grandma lives with them, and it's her dog,' she said, crossing her fingers behind her back and hoping she wasn't lying.

'So why can't *our* grandma live with us?' he asked, and she sighed again.

'Because she and Grandad live near Nottingham, Billy. You know that.'

'But they could move,' he said with all the logic of childhood. 'We moved to be near Daddy.'

And left her parents behind... She swallowed a little ache. 'I know. I'd like them closer, too, but they live where they live, and they've got lots of friends there, so they aren't going to move, and besides, we haven't got room for them here. Anyway, tell me all about this puppy. What's it called?'

He was back in the ED by seven Monday morning, leaving his mother to deal with a fractious Amelie who'd apparently decided she hated school.

He didn't have time to dwell on it, though, because he was straight into Resus, taking over from the team that had been working for the last hour on Dylan Reed, a teenager who'd fallen from a height.

'So what's the story?' he asked Sam, and was told he'd sneaked out of his bedroom window and was coming home drunk and/or drugged and had slipped and fallen backwards off the drainpipe onto the patio below.

'Pupils are equal and reactive, but a bit sluggish, and he's been semi-conscious throughout but he's not really making any sense. Reflexes are weak in the lower limbs and his right arm, so we're looking at head and spine. There's no obvious disruption on palpation but something's going on. He's booked for a CT shortly, and in the meantime we've done a tox screen and we're waiting on the results. Parents are in the family room and I'll go and talk to them now and update them. Over to you.'

'Great. Thanks. Anything else going on in the department I should know about?'

'Not as far as I'm aware. Have a good day.'

Oliver grunted and turned his attention to the boy. 'Right, is he good to go down to CT?' he asked, checking his stats on the monitor, and they nodded.

'Yes, he's stable.'

'OK. I'll go down with him and have a look,' he said, not liking the sound of the sluggish pupils or the weak reflexes. Drugs, or head and neck injuries—either way he was still far from ideal.

He was right to be worried, as it turned out. There was a small brain contusion, and what looked like bruising on the spinal cord, but there was nothing more to do in the ED, so he was shipped up to Paediatric HDU, pending the result of the drugs screen, and his parents went with him after an update, torn between worry over his condition and anger that he'd been so stupid.

He could empathize with that. It was how he felt about Charlie from time to time, but he had minimal control from so far away, which made it easier in that he didn't know when to worry about him, harder because it just meant there was a low-grade stress going on all the time.

Still, at least he was coming over for three weeks in June, so that was something to look forward to.

And then Emily walked in and gave him a slightly forced smile that didn't quite reach her eyes, and his stress levels ramped up again.

'Hi there. Good weekend?' she asked lightly.

He grimaced and looked away, cross with himself for whatever it was that had made their relationship strained. They'd been OK last week. Now? Not so much, apparently, probably after that almost-kiss moment. Or him spilling his guts. He ignored that and answered her question.

'Up and down. Charlie's decided to come over in June, for three weeks, which is the up. The down, Amelie's decided she hates school.'

'Really? She looked happy enough in the playground this morning. She ran off with Billy and Phoebe, and they were all giggling.'

He felt one layer of tension ease, replaced by another, the never-ending tug of war between his brain and his body. Or was it his heart?

'That's good to know.'

The silence yawned, and he was almost begging for the red phone to ring when she spoke.

'Are you OK?'

'Of course I am.'

'Are you? Are you really?'

Her voice was soft, teasing his senses, and he met her eyes and read concern behind the wariness.

He gave up the pretence. 'No. Not really,' he told her, going for honesty. 'Can we grab a coffee later?'

She hesitated a moment, then nodded.

'Sure. Of course. Assuming we get time.'

Big assumption. It was a quarter to two by the time they paused for breath, and they went straight to the Park Café, grabbed drinks and something to eat, and sat on a bench in the shade of a tree.

'So, what's wrong?' she asked, because something obviously was. 'Is it Charlie? Amelie?'

He shook his head slowly. 'No.'

No? Then…

'Is this about Saturday?' she asked, probing deeper.

He met her eyes, his still wary but steady on hers as he nodded. 'Maybe. We got into a lot of stuff, and…'

'And?' she coaxed as he trailed off, and he shrugged.

'I keep thinking we should have left it alone.'

'Why? It was good to know what you've been doing. We were together briefly half a lifetime ago, and I still care about you, but we're different people now, things have changed us, and it was really great to catch up and find out more about you now, about where you've been and what you've come through.'

He looked away. 'I just don't want it to change things, to make them awkward. I don't want you thinking—we can't go back, Emily. Even if we want to. There's too much at stake—the kids—all of it.'

She reached out and laid her hand over his. 'I don't want to go back. Believe me, I'm not looking to find another relationship to screw up. It would just be really nice to be friends.'

He looked back at her, his eyes doubtful, and then he gave a quiet sigh and his mouth tilted into a sad little smile.

'Yes. Yes, it would.' He looked away again. 'We are screwed up, aren't we? Both of us, in our own way.'

'I suppose we are. How does that song go? "Pick yourself up, dust yourself off and start all over again"? Except I can't even think about the last bit. I have bigger fish to fry now, and so do you, so that's OK. We understand each other. Friends?'

He reached out and cupped her cheek in a firm but gentle hand. 'Friends,' he said softly, and raised his coffee cup to her.

She clinked hers against it, as far as you could clink a paper cup, and smiled sadly.

'Good. And don't worry about Amelie. She'll be fine. They all go through this, and you've got Charlie's visit to look forward to.'

He nodded, bit into his sandwich and was about to take another bite when the pagers leaped into life.

'And here we go again.' He sighed, and they walked quickly back, eating as they went, binning the last bites as they went through the door, but her heart was lighter.

A friend was exactly what she needed in her life, especially one who was on the same page. No misunderstandings, no false expectations, no hidden agenda. Just friends…

He felt hugely relieved after their little chat, and working together was infinitely easier.

Amelie seemed to be settling in school, despite her protests, and his mother was making a few friends at the school gate, other grandmothers on childcare duty doing the school run.

She'd invited Emily and the children back to theirs for a play date, and he crossed his fingers it would go well and Amelie wouldn't have a strop about something trivial, but he didn't hold out much hope. She seemed to have a reluctance to let people close, having reeled them in in the first place.

Because of Kath's absence? Maybe. She was supposed to be coming over this weekend, but that always left Amelie tearful and fractious, and he wasn't sure he wanted her to come at all.

Except she didn't come. She deferred it, sending him a text on Thursday, while he was working with Emily.

'Oh, for heaven's sake! She can't keep doing this,' he growled, and Emily raised an eyebrow.

'Who can't do what?' she asked, and he dropped his phone back in his pocket and met her eyes.

'Kath. She was coming this weekend to see Amelie, but now she can't. Something more important has come up.'

His words were loaded with sarcasm, and Emily frowned.

'What's more important than not letting her daughter down?' she asked, and he swore.

'Exactly. It's ridiculous. Apparently someone's flying over from Japan, an important client, and she has "no choice".'

Emily hmphed and went back to writing up her notes, and he did a bit of hmphing himself, went and got a cold drink from the staff kitchen, and was tempted to throw it over his head to cool himself down.

And then the following weekend she couldn't manage Friday, and said she'd come on Saturday afternoon instead, and he was so angry he nearly told her not to bother.

He really, really didn't want to see her. Hard to avoid it, considering she was going to be in the house—unless she took Amelie somewhere else for the weekend? She might. Or he could take himself off somewhere and leave her to it. His mother was away for the weekend, staying with her sister, so maybe he could hide out in her part of the house.

Although Amelie would know he was there and would keep coming in, defeating the object.

He was slumped over the desk with his head in his hands when Emily walked into Resus.

He straightened up and swivelled round, and she eyed him thoughtfully. 'What's up?' she asked, and he shrugged.

'Kath. Again.'

'What again? Not the weekend?'

'Not the whole weekend, no, but she can't come tomorrow, she can't come till Saturday afternoon, so Amelie will be gutted, all over again, and to make it worse, because she was coming, Mum's going away, so it'll just be the three of us in the house and I'm so cross I could kill her.'

'You don't mean that.'

'No, of course I don't mean it literally, but it's just going to be difficult, and if I'm there they won't get the one-to-one.'

'You could always hide out at mine,' she said, and he searched her eyes, so wanting to say yes, but she was only being kind. Wasn't she?

'Really?'

'Really. The kids are with Steve, I'm at work, and you can have Billy's room. It's got a decent bed in it, so you can even stay over if you want and leave them to it.'

She was actually serious. His heart thumped a little, and he ignored it, but it was so tempting…

'No, I can't do that,' he said after too long a hesitation, and she smiled.

'Well, you can, and you're very welcome to,' she said matter-of-factly, 'but you can cook for me if you like so I don't have to when I get home, if it makes you feel better.'

He was so, so tempted, but he shook his head slowly.

'No. It's not fair.'

'Why not?'

Because I still want you...

'Because it's the only downtime you get, the only time you can do stuff.'

'And it gets very dull. There's only a certain amount of fun you can have cleaning the house and doing the washing. If it makes you feel better, you can cut the grass and weed the garden while I'm at work.'

That made him chuckle, but he still shook his head.

'No. It's very kind of you, but no. I don't want to take advantage of you.'

'I don't think I asked you to,' she retorted with a grin, 'but suit yourself. The offer's there. Take it or leave it.'

And with that she walked out and left him staring after her.

It's too dangerous.

He growled softly, closed the file, and got up and followed her out.

Would he come?

She wasn't sure, but to be on the safe side she changed the sheets and cleaned the house on Friday night after the children had gone, and she sent him a text when she got to work on Saturday morning.

Key under blue plant pot on right, mower in the garden shed, key in kitchen by door. Feel free. X

She pressed send, then instantly regretted the kiss. Too late. He'd make of it what he would and she had bigger things to think about because the revellers had been out in force. Three stabbings overnight, one still in Resus with his chest open when she hurried in there to help.

Tom was there, up to his wrists in the young man's lungs, trying to stem the bleed without any success.

'We're waiting on a surgeon,' he said, 'but I didn't think we had time to do that and it turns out I was right. Emily, could you do me a favour and get through to cardiothoracics and NAG. I need advice on this if we aren't going to lose him. Oh, hang on, I've got the bleeder. Clamp, please.'

The door swished open, and a CT consultant came in, took one look at him and shrugged. 'Well, you seem to be doing my job OK,' he said, and she heard Tom chuckle in relief.

'Pure luck. He's all yours,' he said, and stood back and let the CT consultant take over.

'What on earth was going on last night?' Emily asked as they wheeled the man away to Theatre. 'It sounds like carnage.'

'It was. It all kicked off at two this morning, apparently. They were all drunk, there were drugs involved, two gangs of youths—just utter carnage. We lost one, stabilized one and shipped him out, and this lad didn't seem too bad, and then he just suddenly went downhill. They're just kids. It's sickening what they're doing to each other. Anyway, I'm done, I think the worst is over and I'm going home now. Enjoy.'

Not a chance.

As the last of the overnight admissions were being dealt with, the usual 'we've got the weekend off so let's tackle the DIY/garden/guttering' brigade turned up, together with a succession of sporting injuries—a dislocated shoulder, a squash ball in the eye, a dislocated kneecap—which kept her busy for the rest of her shift.

By the time she clocked off, she was tired, hungry, mildly irritated and more than ready to crawl into a hot bath and do nothing.

And then she turned onto her drive and found Oliver's car there, and her heart skipped a beat.

'Hello?' she said, walking in and kicking off her shoes, and he came out of the kitchen, bringing a waft of something delicious with him.

'You're here,' she said, unnecessarily, and he smiled.

'Yeah, sorry, I took you up on your offer, but I've mowed the lawn, weeded the beds, swept the patio and cooked you supper.'

She laughed. 'I can tell. You don't need to apologize—it smells amazing.'

'It's just chilli, but I wasn't sure what time you finished, so I did something that would keep hot for hours. How was your day?'

'Crazy. It started with stabbings, and ended up with the usual sporting injuries and people who have no idea of how to keep themselves safe when they do stuff they're clearly not qualified to do.'

'Oops. I'm guessing DIY?'

'And walking backwards with a rotary lawn-mower and falling down a slope with it on top of you. Luckily it had stalled before it did too much damage, but he had multiple severe cuts, he was soaked in petrol, and he'd landed on his hip on the path below and driven the head of his femur into his acetabulum, causing a lovely starburst fracture.'

'Ouch. I thought those mowers had an automatic cutout?'

'Not if they're ancient. And then there was the elderly woman who fell off a ladder and down the stairs trying to put stuff in the loft without help, and the guy who slashed his hand in half trying to lay a carpet—need I go on?'

He was laughing by then, and he shook his head. 'I get the drift. Do you want to change and shower, or just eat?'

'Do you know what I really want?'

'A hot bath and a nice cold glass of wine?' he asked, and she stifled a laugh.

'How did you guess?' she said, and he opened the fridge and poured her a glass of perfectly chilled Chardonnay.

'Enjoy,' he said, and she took it from him and went upstairs, her heart suddenly lighter.

He poured himself a glass, went into the living room and tried not to think about her lying naked in the bath somewhere above him.

He hadn't had to guess what she'd want. His mind scrolled back to the times he'd sat on the floor in the bathroom, chatting to her while she lay in the bath after a long day. Sometimes he'd share it with her, but always, always, when she was done, he'd wrap her in a towel and carry her to bed.

Don't go there. You'll just make it worse.

Hard to imagine how. Oh, this was such a mistake—although looking at her as she'd walked through the door, she hadn't looked like someone who was relishing cooking a meal before she could relax. He could understand that. The weekends were often killers, peppered with tragedy and liberally sprinkled with accidents that should never have happened.

He tipped his head back and rested it against the sofa, eyes closed, yet again trying not to think of her body lying naked just a few feet above him. It wasn't fair, and it wasn't why he was here. She'd offered him a way out of a difficult situation, and he'd taken her up on it and done some things to help her in return.

Because they were friends. Friends. Not lovers, not even contemplating it.

He heard the gurgle of water, and went back to the kitchen to reheat the chilli. She wouldn't be long, he guessed, and he sliced thick chunks off the fresh, squishy tiger bread and put them in a bowl, carried it through to the table, and stirred the chilli, just as she came running down the stairs.

'Oh, that smells so good—tiger bread? Oh, you are amazing!' she said, and before he knew what was happening, she slid her arms around him from behind and hugged him briefly, then let go and stood back.

'Anything I can do?'

'Ah—yeah, you could find the soured cream and the grated cheese in the fridge and take them through,' he said, his mind and body totally scrambled by the hug. 'I won't be a moment. You could use a mat on the table—this is hot.'

She left, and he sucked in a low, slow breath and blew it out even slower, then picked up the pot of chilli and followed her.

'That was so good,' she said, putting down her fork and leaning back against the chair, too tired to sit up straight any more. 'Thank you. I was starving.'

'You're welcome,' he said, and topped up her glass. 'Go and sit down and put your feet up, and I'll clear the table.'

'That's not fair,' she protested, but he just quirked an eyebrow at her and jerked his head towards the sofa, and she stifled a smile and went. If it made him feel better to wait on her, then she was fine with that.

She sat down, rested her head back and closed her eyes, and a short while later she heard his quiet tread, and felt the sofa dip as he sat down at the other end.

'Give me your feet,' he said, and she turned her head and looked at him. 'Come on. You know you want to.'

She gave up the inward battle she really didn't want to win, turned round on the sofa, put them up and closed her eyes as he set his thumbs to work, massaging the sole of her right foot.

'Oh, that's amazing,' she groaned as he finished. 'You always did give the best foot massage.'

'We aim to please. Other foot?'

How could feet be so sexy?

Except hers were, and always had been. Perfectly shaped, with neat, straight toes and a perfect arch. She'd always painted the nails way back when, but not now. Now they were bare, translucent, neatly clipped.

She'd rested her head back and closed her eyes, but she made the odd tiny sound as he worked, and when he stopped, she opened her eyes and smiled lazily.

'That was lovely. Thank you.'

'My pleasure. You look tired.'

She laughed, a soft little huff of sound filled with irony. 'I'm always tired. It's a constant juggling act, trying to balance my job with caring for the children and giving them the love and the opportunities they deserve.'

He nodded slowly. 'Yeah. I completely get that. If it

wasn't for my mother, I'd be sunk. At least you have Steve reasonably close and he's doing his bit.'

'Oh, absolutely. I couldn't possibly work the hours I do if it wasn't for his input, and they all get on well now, so I don't need to worry about them when they're with him.'

He gave a soft huff of laughter. 'You're so lucky having him close. If only Kath could do more, but it is what it is.' He dredged up a smile. 'Can I get you another drink? Tea, coffee, fruit tea?'

She studied him thoughtfully, a little smile playing around her mouth. 'You're being very solicitous. Are you trying to earn brownie points?'

That made him laugh. 'No, I'm just being a decent human being. You've been at work all day. I haven't.'

'But you work longer hours and this is your time off.'

He lifted her feet off his lap and stood up. 'I really don't think making you a drink counts as work. I'm having decaf tea. You're having...?'

'Blackcurrant, please.'

He nodded and went into the kitchen, put the kettle on, found a container for the rest of the chilli and put it in the fridge, added the pan to the dishwasher and switched it on, then turned to find her propped in the door, watching him.

'You are super domesticated. What happened?'

'What happened? Um—I grew up?'

That made her chuckle, and the sound rippled through him like a tiny electric shock along his nerve endings.

He turned back to the kettle, and she came over to him, reaching past him to put the teabags back in the cupboard, and the scent from her skin was so enticing, so evocative that he groaned out loud.

'What?' she said, turning to look at him, and he put the kettle down with a sigh.

'I can't do this,' he said, his voice low and hushed. 'Deal with this—whatever it is, this tug, this undercurrent between us. It was always there, but that was fine then, and it's not fine now. It was half a lifetime ago, and we aren't those people any more. We've changed, and yes, I want you, but I don't know if the you I want is the old you, or who you are now, and it's getting in the way of everything,' he said, the confession dragged out of him. 'I'm not sure I even know who you are now, but I know I'm not who I was then, not by a mile.'

She held his eyes for a moment, hers soft and luminous, filled with sadness. 'Nor am I. I want you, too, but I can't trust myself, my own judgement, because maybe I just want to turn the clock back, and we can't do that. I never want another relationship where my children are exposed to hurt, and I'm sure you don't, either, so we can't let ourselves get sucked into anything that might affect them. And if it means our lives are a loveless desert, so be it, but I can't risk my kids' happiness, and nor can you. I just know we can't go back to what we had, because it's gone for ever. It died when you slept with Sue, and I don't know if I'll ever be able to trust you again.'

He turned away, his eyes prickling with sudden tears for all they'd lost, all he'd thrown away.

'I'm so sorry I hurt you,' he said, his voice broken, and he sucked in a breath and let it out again. 'I never meant…'

She slid her arms around him and rested her head against his back, and her warmth seeped into him.

'I know,' she said softly. 'We were too young, too foolish, too far apart, and if I'd been able to come with you, who knows how different it might have been, but it is what it is, and we're where we are now, and if we can somehow find a middle ground where we can be friends and still keep our hearts safe, then I'd love that. I need a friend right now far

more than I need a lover, and I think you do, too. Someone we can talk to, someone who understands where we're
coming from, someone we can understand. And that's so
rare, so precious.'

He nodded slowly, and turned towards her, pulling her
gently into his arms and holding her for the longest time.
Her head was on his shoulder, his cheek against her hair,
and he could feel the beat of her heart against his, the rise
and fall of her chest as she breathed, the warmth of her body
thawing the ache of loneliness deep inside him.

'I've missed you,' he said gruffly, and she sighed.

'I've missed you, too. It's good to have you back.'

She took a step back and looked up into his eyes, resting a hand against his cheek in a tender gesture that nearly
broke him.

'I'm going to bed. I'll see you in the morning.'

He nodded and watched her go, his resolve in tatters,
his heart aching.

I don't know if I'll ever be able to trust you again.

He closed his eyes, squeezing back the tears of grief
and regret for all he'd thrown away by one careless act so
long ago.

Where would they have been now if he hadn't gone to
that party and ended up with Sue? Would they still have
been together? He had no idea, but his track record wasn't
great. Maybe he was so fundamentally flawed that he could
never make a relationship work.

Well, he was going to make this one work, this friendship, if it killed him. He owed her that, at least. And maybe,
in time, she'd learn that she could trust him again...

CHAPTER FIVE

SHE LAY AWAKE, listening for the sound of him coming up to bed, going over and over their conversation in her head. Could they do this? Really do it, put aside the huge sensual tug they both felt in favour of a straightforward friendship?

No. It was never going to be straightforward. Not with their history.

She heard his quiet tread on the stairs, the click of the light switch, the sound of running water and then silence. So near and yet so far...

It was hours before she went to sleep, and all too soon she was woken by a quiet tap on the door and Oliver's voice interrupting her dreams.

'Emily, it's six forty-five. What time does your shift start?'

Shift? She sat bolt upright and stared in horror at her alarm clock, then catapulted out of bed, heart pounding, and ran for the bathroom. She left the house five minutes later, arriving just after seven to find the department already busy.

If Oliver hadn't woken her... Then again, if he hadn't stayed, she wouldn't have had such a terrible night, and she certainly wouldn't have had those disturbing and unsettling dreams.

Would he still be there when she got home? No, of

course not. She gave herself a mental shake, took a deep breath and joined the fray.

Kath went at three to catch her flight, and left Amelie in floods of tears. To her credit Kath had looked upset, too, but as long as she put her career first, this was always going to be the way of it.

He scooped his daughter up in his arms and hugged her as they went back inside and closed the door, and eventually she stopped sobbing and snuggled into his side on the sofa.

'So what would you like to do for the rest of the day?' he asked, and she shrugged, all forlorn.

'I don't know.'

'How about going to the beach?' he suggested to cheer her up. 'It's a nice day, and maybe we can get an ice cream?'

'Can I have a curly one with a chocolate stick in it?'

He ruffled her hair and smiled, happy to have his sunny little girl back. 'Sure, if we can find one. Let's go and see.'

He changed into shorts and trainers, found the bucket and spades, and they headed for the beach, and to his relief the stall was open and had the right sort of ice cream cone. Crisis averted. They sat down to eat them on the edge of the prom with their legs dangling, while the gulls swooped overhead, and when they were done, they took off their shoes, put them with the buckets and spades in a space on the beach and went down to the sea to wash their hands.

'It's freezing!' she shrieked, running and giggling back up the beach, and he followed her slowly, his heart aching for his little girl with her fractured life.

It wasn't all Kath's fault, either, however easy it was to blame her. He was busy, too, and it would have been career suicide to drop to part-time before he became a consultant. Maybe he could consider it now, so he had more time to share her precious childhood years? Or maybe both he and Kath could cut back a little? After all, compromise was a two-way street.

Like Emily, who was all about compromise, making things work, putting her children front and centre of her life in a constant juggling act, and yet still trying to find a way to fit him into her hectic life. But only as a friend, which was more, really, than he had any right to ask...

He felt a sandy little hand grasp his and tug. 'Come on, Daddy, you have to help me. We're going to build the biggest sandcastle in the world!' Amelie said, and he put his emotional and physical needs on the back burner and knelt down next to his little daughter in the damp sand and reminded himself that this was what mattered, and all that could ever matter.

Monday was a bank holiday, so she'd taken the day off and spent it taming the garden, but Tuesday morning came all too soon.

She'd had to listen to the antics of Steve and Amanda's puppy all yesterday evening, and the begging and pleading was relentless.

'Phoebe, we can't have a dog, darling. You know we can't,' she'd said for the hundredth time as she tucked her up for the night, and then of course in the morning at school drop-off Elizabeth was there with Amelie and her little black dog, Berry, and Phoebe rushed over and cuddled it.

'Careful. You don't know her very well,' she warned, but Elizabeth smiled reassuringly.

'Don't worry, she's always fine with children. She loves them. How was your weekend?'

'Busy. I was working, apart from yesterday.' And apart

from the time she was trying to seduce Elizabeth's son...
'How was yours?'

'Oh, lovely. Quiet. I went to my sister's, and we had a walk through Woodbridge and a coffee near the Tide Mill, then did some shopping. I actually found a new top that I like, which was the most exciting moment,' she added with a wry grin that reminded Emily so much of Oliver that her heart twisted in her chest.

She found a smile. 'Well, it sounds better than mine. I spent my weekend patching up DIYers and sports enthusiasts for the most part.' And having my feet massaged, and getting silly ideas about Oliver... 'Go on, in you go, Phoebe. Time to say goodbye,' she coaxed, and Phoebe kissed the dog on the nose and ran off to join the others.

'We should have another play date,' Elizabeth said. 'Come to ours. I'll bake us all a cake. How about tomorrow?'

She agreed on autopilot, and just hoped Oliver would be OK with it. He should be, it didn't affect him, but Amelie was his daughter, after all. He deserved a say in how much Emily was involved with her.

She told him in the first quiet moment, which wasn't until almost eleven. She found him in the staff kitchen washing down a sandwich with a glass of water, and he gave her a slightly wary smile.

'Hi. Everything OK?'

'Yes, fine,' she said, digging out an answering smile and wishing things could be different. 'Your mother's asked us round for another play date tomorrow. I just wanted to OK it with you.'

He gave her a puzzled frown. 'Of course it's OK. Why wouldn't it be?'

She shrugged. 'I don't know. It's your house, your daughter...'

'Emily, it's fine. I'm more than happy for Amelie to make friends with your children, and it's lovely that you and Mum are getting on so well. Really, I have no problem with it at all. You go for it.'

Except it didn't happen.

She turned up at school on Wednesday, and Elizabeth wasn't there. Amelie came out with the others, and she waited there with the three of them, but there was no sign of her. She tried Elizabeth's phone and it rang and rang and then went to voicemail, so she left a message and went to the office, but they hadn't heard from her, either.

'I'll call her,' the school secretary said, but Emily shook her head.

'Done that. She didn't answer. I'll try Amelie's father.'

She went back outside, scanning the road outside the playground, but still nothing, and then Oliver answered.

'Hi. What's up?'

'Do you know where your mother is?'

'My mother?' he said, sounding puzzled. 'She's with you, isn't she?'

'No. I'm at school with all the children, and there's no sign of her, and her phone went to voicemail. Do you want me to go to the house?'

'Uh—yeah, if you could? Take Amelie with you, and let me know as soon as you get there. Do you want me to come?'

'No. Don't worry, Oliver, she's probably just broken down somewhere without signal. She'll be fine. I'll call you when I know a bit more.'

'OK. I'll have my phone on me.'

He gave her the address, cleared it with the school, then they left and went straight to his house and found Elizabeth's car on the drive.

So where was she?

She turned and looked at the children. 'OK, stay here, all of you. I'll go and see where she is. I won't be long. She's probably just lost track of the time.' Or had an accident?

Elizabeth didn't answer the door, but she could hear the dog barking, and the door opened when she tried it, so she stepped inside.

'Elizabeth?'

Berry was running round her, then away again, and she heard a voice calling, so she followed the dog and found Elizabeth sitting on the blood-spattered kitchen floor in a sea of broken glass, clutching her right hand with her left.

'Oh, Emily, I'm so glad you've come,' she said, tearful with relief. 'Where are the children?'

'In the car. What have you done?' she asked gently, picking her way through the shards and then crouching down, her hand on Elizabeth's trembling shoulder.

'I've cut my palm. I slipped on some water and fell with a glass in my hand. So stupid. And I can't let go of it or it just bleeds and bleeds, and I could hear my phone ringing and there was nothing I could do. I couldn't get up without my hands, and I'm so worried Berry'll cut herself on the glass.'

'Right. Let's deal with that first, as you seem to have the bleeding under control,' she said calmly, 'and then we'll get you sorted out.' She straightened up and called Berry over to the bifold doors to the garden, checked her paws, then let her out before calling Oliver.

'I'm with your mother. She's cut her hand in the kitchen, so I'm going to bring her in, but I'll have all the children and I'll have to bring the dog because there's glass everywhere. Meet me at the door in ten minutes?'

'Sure. Is she OK?'

'She'll be fine,' she said reassuringly, not wanting to alarm either of them, then she swept the glass out of the way and smiled at Elizabeth.

'Right, we'd better take you to hospital and get that looked at,' she said, comforted that at least it wasn't still bleeding heavily, although from the look of her index finger she had some tendon damage.

She got Elizabeth up, shook the glass off her clothes and then wrapped her hand in a clean tea-towel, 'so we don't scare the children too much!', and led her out to the car and left Elizabeth explaining to the children while she ran back to pick up her bag, keys and the dog, and lock the door. She put Berry in the back, then jumped in the car and looked over her shoulder at the children.

'OK, everyone?'

Her two nodded, but Amelie looked worried. 'Are we taking Grandma to see Daddy?' she asked.

'Yes, he's expecting us.' And hopefully he'd be there.

To her relief he was, armed with a wheelchair, and Elizabeth shook her head.

'I don't need a wheelchair,' she protested, but he just raised an eyebrow and helped her into it, then turned to Emily, his eyes fraught with worry.

'Could you be a star and take Amelie and Berry back to yours?' he asked.

'I have a better idea. They were all expecting cake, so why don't I take them to the café, and then we can take her home when she's done? Berry can come with us.'

'That would be brilliant,' he agreed, and stuck his head into the back of the car.

'Hi, Amelie. Hi, guys. I'm Amelie's dad, and I'm just going to take my mum and get her fixed, OK? You're going to stay with Emily and I think there might be cake, if you're good.'

'Will Grandma be all right, Daddy?'

Emily didn't hear his reply, just the gently reassuring tone of his voice, and then he straightened up, gave her a fleeting smile and wheeled his mother away.

Emily parked the car and led them round the outside to the Park Café. 'Right. Let's have a look. What do you fancy, guys? Chocolate brownie, blueberry muffin, apple turnover, rocky road—'

She was drowned out by the chorus, so she started again, one by one, and loaded up the tray, picked up three cartons of juice and a coffee, and headed to a picnic bench.

'Right, here you are,' she said, and they settled down to munch their way through the cakes.

They were just finishing when her phone rang.

'Is that Daddy?' Amelie asked, looking a bit worried still, and Emily nodded and answered the call.

'Hi. How's it going?'

'OK, but she's going to need to stay in. She's done a proper job on it,' he told her, his voice stressed. 'It needs microsurgery and we can't do it down here. She's cut the tendon in her right index finger and severed a world of blood vessels, so we've put a compression dressing on it and she's going up to Theatre in a minute. I don't suppose there's any way you can take Amelie home with you until I finish work?'

'Of course I can,' she promised, and then handed the phone to Amelie who was desperate to talk to him.

'Is Grandma going to be all right?' she asked, and Emily could hear his voice cheerfully reassuring her, then telling her to give the phone back.

'All OK?' Emily asked.

'Yeah, I guess. I told her Grandma was very excited because she was going to have a sleepover here, and she'd be back home tomorrow. Not sure they need to know more than that for now.'

'OK. Well, come round when you're done and I'll feed them—not that they'll need a lot. They've eaten their body weight in cake.'

'No, I'm sure they won't. I've seen those cakes. Right, got to go. Take care. I'll come as soon as I can.'

'OK. No rush. We'll be fine.'

She hung up and turned back to the children.

'Well, that's exciting, Amelie, your grandma having a sleepover! I bet she wasn't expecting that! So Daddy wants you to come back to ours and he'll come when he's finished work, OK?'

'OK,' she said, but she still looked a bit worried.

'What's wrong?' she asked, and Amelie's eyes filled.

'She's not going to die, is she?'

Oh, bless her worried little heart. 'No, sweetheart, she's not going to die. She's just cut her hand!' she said reassuringly. 'They're going to mend her, and then she'll have a lovely rest and she can probably come home tomorrow.'

'Oh. That's OK, then. Can I have a sleepover, too?'

'I think we'll have to talk to Daddy about that,' she said, but it sounded like a good idea, because juggling the logistics was going to be tricky otherwise. 'Right, home, or shall we go to the playground first?'

It was well after seven before he arrived, and the children and Berry were lined up on the sitting room floor in front of the television, watching a film.

She saw the car pull up and went to the door, letting him in quietly.

'How is she? Did they fix the tendon?'

He shook his head. 'No, and it's not great. It was even

worse than I thought. They've done the blood vessels, but the tendon damage is extensive and there's more than one involved, so they're operating tomorrow when the specialist hand surgeon's in. I just need to go home and grab her some things and take them back, and then I'll come and get Amelie.'

'And do what with her in the morning?' she asked gently.

He stared at her, gave a short sigh and dragged a hand over his face. 'Yeah. I don't know. I haven't thought that far ahead.'

'No, I'm sure you haven't. I have. Leave her here—she's already asked anyway. Go and get her things and your mum's, and some dog food, then come back and say goodnight to her. She'll be fine here and so will Berry.'

'Are you sure?'

'Of course I'm sure. She's totally up for it. They're watching a film right now, but it's nearly ended, so if you go quickly and come back with her things, you can spend a few minutes with her before you go back to the hospital.'

'And what do we do with Berry tomorrow? She can't spend your whole shift shut inside.'

'Leave it with me. James and Connie have dogs, so do Ryan and Beth, and so do Tom and Laura, and they're all in easy reach. One of them will have her, I'm sure.'

He hugged her briefly, mumbled, 'You're a star,' and went back out. Fifteen minutes later he was back, by which time she'd heated up his leftover chilli that she'd put in the freezer because she was sure he hadn't yet found time to eat.

'Sorry, you're eating,' he said, but she shook her head.

'I've eaten with the children. This is for you because I bet you haven't. Feed the dog while I dish it up.'

He sighed, a frustrated, unhappy sigh. 'Em, you didn't need to do this.'

'I know, but I work there, too, and I know how busy it gets. Plus I knew if you'd had a spare second, you would have been with your mother... It's not rocket science, and it's not exactly haute cuisine, either,' she added with a smile, and his mouth kicked up at one side, but it was a stressed, weary effort.

'Just eat,' she said gently. 'Tea, coffee, cold drink?'

He grunted. 'A glass of water would be great, but be careful with it,' he said with a wry grin. 'I've just cleared up the mess at home. She did a proper job, didn't she?'

'Yes, sorry, I had to leave it.'

'It's fine. I'm just grateful for all—'

'Yes, you've said that a thousand times,' she pointed out with a smile, and went to get his drink, putting water down for Berry while she was at it, and by the time she was back, he'd polished off the chilli. He wiped the plate with his bread and sat back with a weary smile.

'That was amazing. Thank you. Thank you for all of it—for finding her, for bringing her in, for looking after Amelie and Berry, for feeding me—I owe you big time.'

'Yes, you do,' she said, trying to keep a straight face. 'Don't worry, I'm keeping tabs on my brownie points. But you did make the chilli, so sadly it's not as big a tally as it could be.'

He chuckled and shook his head. 'You always were sassy,' he said softly, and then it was there again, that connection, the link between them that time had frayed but not severed.

'I haven't changed *that* much, Oliver,' she murmured, just as the film ended and Amelie got to her feet and ran over and hugged him, saving them from any further awkward conversations.

'How's Grandma?' Amelie asked, holding his face and staring into his eyes.

'She's OK. How are you? Are you still full of cake?'

'Up to here,' she said, holding her hand at nose level, and his eyes widened.

'*That* full? Wow. So how do you fancy a sleepover to-night with Billy and Phoebe?'

'Can I?' she asked, excitedly bouncing up and down, and he laughed and hugged her.

'I think that's a yes,' he said, and met Emily's eyes over her head. 'If Emily's OK with that?'

'Emily's very OK with that,' Emily said, and they all trooped upstairs. 'How about I put you in with Phoebe?' she suggested. 'She's got a pull-out bed you can have.'

'Cool. Can you read us a story, Daddy?'

He shook his head. 'No, darling, I'm sorry. I've got to take Grandma's stuff to her, but I'm sure Emily'll read to you.'

'Of course I will. Why don't you all get changed into your PJs and clean your teeth, and then we can find a book?'

He rang at nine thirty to see how she was coping, and they talked for a few minutes about his mother.

'I'm not sure how this is going to go. They're talking about her maybe needing to have it in a cast for several weeks while the tendons heal, if they have to graft them, so I have no idea how she's going to manage. She does so much for me. All the house stuff, the cooking, lots of the gardening, and she won't be able to drive. It's a nightmare.'

'I'm sure between us we can sort that out,' she said, trying to reassure him, but she heard his sigh and knew what he was going to say.

'You can't—'

'I can. Stop arguing and worrying, keep me posted if

there's any news, and I'll see you in the morning after I've dropped Berry off with Laura and done the school run. And try and get some sleep, please?'

She heard a humourless huff of laughter, then another sigh. 'Fat chance,' he murmured, 'but thank you. I'll call you tomorrow.'

She put her phone down, put the dog out for a minute, then headed up to bed. The news hadn't been good, unlike the children who had been positively angelic for a change. Berry, though, was understandably unsettled, and she spent the night on Emily's bed for the sake of peace.

She dropped her off with Laura, then took the children to school. By the time she arrived at work, he'd spoken to the hand surgeon, and they were going to have to graft the tendons of Elizabeth's index and middle fingers.

'He's doing it this afternoon after his elective list, and he thinks it could be quite a long op, so she's going to be in for another night, and when she comes out, she won't be able to do anything. And as if it wasn't enough worrying about her and her recovery, I just don't know where to start with how I cope without her.' He raked his hands through his hair, stress written in capitals all over his face, and she laid a reassuring hand on his shoulder.

'You don't need to worry about that yet. I'll look after Amelie. One more is no harder, and I'm doing the school run anyway. We can do this, Oliver. We can manage. It's not a problem. You worry about your mother and leave the rest to me.'

'How? How can I do that? Amelie's hardly ever been away from me, and I tuck her up every night and wake her every morning, and that's if she doesn't wake in the night and come and get into bed with me. And it's not just her. What about the dog? I can't expect everyone to pick up the pieces for me.'

'So we'll find a dog walker for the days, and we'll live at yours for now,' she said calmly, although she wasn't at all sure how it would work. 'Assuming you've got enough space?'

'We've got tons of space, it's got four bedrooms and Mum's annexe, but that's not the point.'

'Yes, it is, and I'm sure we'll cope,' she said, as much to herself as to him, and then looked around. 'So, where do I need to be first?'

'With me in Resus? And this conversation isn't finished, just so you know. We can talk later when I get home.'

'I'll need keys.'

'There's a key safe by the door. I'll send you the code.'

By the end of her shift Elizabeth's operation was under way, she'd spoken to a dog walker who sounded as if she might be able to help, and she went home with all the children and Berry, and sat them down and asked them how they felt about going to stay at Amelie's house for a few days.

Billy and Phoebe were ridiculously excited, but Amelie looked worried.

'Isn't Grandma coming back?' she asked, and Emily re-assured her hastily.

'Of course she's coming back, sweetheart, but her hand is a bit poorly, so she won't be able to do very much, so we're all going to have to help her. That's all it is, and we can do that, can't we? Make her life a little bit easier?'

They all nodded, and she smiled at them and mentally crossed her fingers that it would really be that easy. 'Great. Right, we need to pack some things!'

By the time he finished his shift at seven, his mother was in Recovery, and he ran up to see her, then left her in the care of the surgical team and drove home. Not for long, he'd have to go back, but he had to be there for Amelie, and he had no idea how Emily was coping.

Brilliantly, as it turned out. He opened the front door and was greeted by Berry and the wonderful smell of something delicious. He followed the sound of the children's voices and found them in the kitchen sitting at the table in their pyjamas, heads bent over their drawings.

Emily was standing at the stove, her hair scraped back into a messy ponytail with the odd escaping wisp, and she turned and smiled at him, her eyes searching as she mouthed, 'OK?'

He nodded and went over to the table, laying a hand on Amelie's shoulder, and she looked up at him and reached up her arms.

'Daddy! How's Grandma?'

'She's fine,' he said, stretching the truth as he bent and hugged her. 'She's very, very sleepy, but she's going to be fine. Her hand's all mended now and it just has to finish getting better, but that's going to take a long, long time, so we'll have to look after her, OK?'

She nodded. 'Emily said we were going to help her,' she told him, and then wriggled out of his arms and picked up a sheet of paper with a drawing of...

'Is that Grandma?' he asked, looking at the picture of a person with a humungous bandage on one very over-sized arm.

'Yes. And that's blood,' she said, all matter-of-fact, pointing to a red splodge on her bandage. 'Emily's cooking you a surprise,' she said, her eyes theatrically wide. 'You'll never guess what it is.'

He knew exactly what it was, because paella had been

her signature dish all those years ago, just as chilli had been his, and anyway even if he couldn't smell it, the pan was a dead giveaway.

'Um—fish pie?'

She shook her head.

'I know! Frog's legs on toast.'

That made her giggle, and he saw Emily's shoulders shake as she tried not to laugh.

'OK, one last guess. Um…cauliflower cheese?'

'No. See, I told you you'd never guess,' she said triumphantly, and picked up the crayons again.

He met Emily's eyes again over their heads and smiled.

'Is there anything you need me to do?'

'Yes. I need you to sit down and chill for a minute. Drink?'

'Don't worry, I'll get something. I've got to go back and see Mum later, after I've put Amelie to bed and eaten whatever it is you're cooking up over there.'

He winked at her, and she smiled an enigmatic smile and went back to her pan, and he got a glass of water from the fridge dispenser and perched on a stool at the island, watching her cook as he had so many times before. She lifted the lid, testing the grains of rice, adding a spoonful of stock, before covering it again.

'Is it done?'

'Not quite. Right, children, I reckon it's time to clear up the table and head upstairs to bed, don't you? Oliver, maybe you need to come and make sure everyone's in the right rooms.'

'Whatever you've done will be fabulous,' he said, 'just so long as we've all got a bed to lie on. Come on, guys, you can show me where you're sleeping.'

* * *

It was after eight before the children were all settled and
they were able to eat, and almost half past ten by the time
Oliver got back from the hospital.

She knew the second his car pulled up on the drive, because Berry was up off the sofa and straight to the front
door, tail wagging furiously.

He gave her a quick stroke, then walked into the sitting
room with a weary smile.

'Hi. Everything all right?'

'It's fine, all quiet. I want to hear about your mother,' she
said, and he let out a long, slow sigh and shook his head.

'She's OK. She's a tiny bit sore, so they upped her pain
meds and she's sleepy now, which is a good thing, but she's
worried, which isn't.'

'About her hand?'

'No. Not at all. She hardly mentioned it and I'm not sure
she's understood the significance of it long-term. No, she's
worried about us—about me having to cope without her,
about you taking on so much, about Billy and Phoebe being
uprooted—all of it, really.'

'Did you reassure her?'

He laughed, a soft, hollow huff, his eyes closing and his
head tipping back.

'I tried, but I agree with everything she said. She's in-
dispensable, and while she loves to be needed, she's really
angry with herself for daring to have an accident.'

'That sounds pretty typical. She's always put everyone
else first.' She studied him, lying there with his eyes shut,
looking shattered. 'Do you want me to get you a drink?'

He sat up. 'No, you're fine. I'll get one. How about you?
Fancy a glass of wine? I reckon we've both earned it.'

She smiled slowly. 'Yes, I think I do, actually. Only one. I can't stay up too late, but I'll have one with you.'

He disappeared for a moment, then came back and sat down at the other end of the sofa, but it wasn't a big one and Berry was between them, so it was…cosy, to say the least.

Cosy, and intimate, and just a teeny bit dangerous for her peace of mind.

He shifted slightly and turned so he was facing her a little, his arm along the back of the sofa, fingers just inches from her shoulder, and smiled a little sadly.

'I can't get over what you've done for us, yesterday and today. I don't know where to start to thank you. I'm just so ridiculously beholden to you.'

'Well, what can I say? Just look at all those brownie points I'm clocking up.'

'I am. Right now it's looking like I owe you two months on a tropical island, lying under a banana-leaf shelter, sipping a hideous blue cocktail rammed with ice with a ludicrous umbrella stuck in the top of it, while your personal beautician finishes your foot massage and pedicure.'

She closed her eyes and leaned her head back with a happy sigh.

'Keep talking. I can hear the waves breaking on the shore, and smell the sea. I might even go diving tomorrow from a boat, if I can be bothered. Or I might just have another foot massage.'

He chuckled, and she felt him shift and the warm weight against her side lifted as Berry was hoisted off the sofa.

'Feet,' he said, putting his wine down and beckoning, and she swung them round and rested them on his lap, closing her eyes again with a groan of ecstasy as his fingers got to work.

'See, I don't need to go to a tropical island,' she said lazily. 'I can just lie here like this and pretend.'

She'd fallen asleep.

He sat sipping his wine and watched her—not for long, not really, because he needed to go to sleep soon himself, but long enough that the urge to scoop her into his arms and carry her up to bed was almost overwhelming.

No. Not appropriate. He didn't need to mess with the fragile status quo before the metaphorical ink on her generous offer of help was even dry. And anyway, there were three kids in the house who'd be a mess of questions if they got caught.

He shifted her feet, lifting them gently and sliding out from under them, threw her wine, virtually untouched, down the sink and put both glasses in the dishwasher, then went back and sat beside her and laid a hand on her shoulder.

'Hey, sleepy-head. It's time for bed,' he said softly, and she stirred and opened her eyes.

'Oh. Sorry. Long day.'

'Tell me about it,' he said, dredging up what might pass for a smile. 'You go on up. I'll sort the dog out. I'll be up in a minute.'

She nodded and got to her feet, and he watched her go, an ache in his chest. How long could he expect her to help him out? She'd stepped up without a thought for herself, taken over where his mother had left off and done it all with a smile.

He really, really didn't deserve that. Not after the way it had all ended, which had been pretty much all his fault. He'd let her down, lost her trust for ever, and yet here she was, playing the good Samaritan and bailing him out.

He couldn't let her do it indefinitely, but for now he had little choice. He'd just make sure she realized how grateful he was, and maybe somehow return the favour.

He got to his feet with a heavy sigh. 'Come on, Berry, time for bed. You need to go out,' he said, and headed for the door.

CHAPTER SIX

ELIZABETH WAS DISCHARGED the following day, and Oliver took the afternoon off and drove her home.

She was exhausted, and even though she denied it, he could see she was in a certain amount of pain, but she seemed glad to be home.

'You need a rest,' he said, and she nodded. She even allowed him to take off her dress, the only button-through thing he'd been able to find in her wardrobe, but she drew the line at her underwear.

He lifted back the duvet so she could get into bed, and as she turned, he could see bruises coming out all over the place from her fall. He sorted her pillows, covered her up and fetched her a glass of water to put by the bed, and she eyed it ruefully.

'That's what got me into this mess,' she said, and he smiled.

'Just don't get out of bed with it,' he said, and kissed her cheek. 'You have a sleep. I'll see you in a bit. Call if you need me—your phone's right here. Berry, come on, Grandma doesn't need you on her bed.'

'She's fine,' she said, reaching out her good hand and stroking her loyal little friend. 'Leave her here. She's good company.'

'OK. You know where I am.'

He left her to it and walked back into the main house, leaving the door ajar so he could hear her.

He had about half an hour before Emily would be here with the children. And they'd be here all weekend, which wasn't really necessary and would add to the noise, which might tire his mother. Unless she wasn't planning to stay for the weekend? As neither of them were working again until Monday, there was no need to, and she was doing more than enough anyway.

Still, as she'd said, it was only temporary, and there would be no need for her to be here at all once he could find a temporary replacement for his mother. He really needed to get on that. He picked up his phone, but he'd hardly started to look for au pairs when he heard a car on the drive. He closed his mother's door softly, and went to let them in.

Time for a conversation…

The front door opened before they reached it, and Oliver let them in with a finger pressed to his lips.

'Grandma's having a rest,' he murmured, 'so if you could all be really quiet, that would be very helpful.'

'Is she OK?' Amelie whispered, and he nodded.

'She is, but she's tired.'

'Can I see her?'

'Not till she wakes up, but I'm sure she'll be delighted to see you then.'

Emily met his eyes over their heads, and she raised an eyebrow questioningly.

'Everything OK?'

He nodded. 'Yeah. Fine. She's just getting over the anaesthetic.'

She wasn't convinced. 'Why don't we settle the children down with a drink and a biscuit in front of the TV,' she suggested. That way she could find out what was wrong, because something clearly was.

They left them in the sitting room watching cartoons and migrated back to the kitchen, and she turned to face him.

'So what's up?' she asked softly.

'Nothing—well, not with her, but as neither of us are working now till Monday morning, I think there's no real need for you to be here over the weekend. Mum's quite tired and bruised and a little shaken up, so some peace and quiet wouldn't go amiss, but if you think that's too disruptive for the kids—'

She shook her head. 'No, that's fine. I was thinking the same thing myself, so long as you're sure you can cope?'

'Of course I can cope.'

'Good. So what else is bothering you? Because it's not just that.'

He scrubbed a hand through his hair and sighed. 'You. Well, no, not you, just—I'm putting on you, so I've been doing some research, and I'm going to get an au pair.'

She frowned. 'I thought we'd had this conversation?'

'We have, but realistically I can't expect you to do this indefinitely. When you offered, we were talking short-term, but her injury is worse than we'd thought and it's going to be weeks—months—before she's properly up and running again, and if I don't get someone in to cover for her, she'll be overdoing it, and I know perfectly well she will, whatever I say. She's stubborn.'

'Well, that runs in the family,' she said bluntly. 'So what did you find out?'

He shrugged. 'Not much, I've only just started looking, but I'm so conscious of the massive disruption to your lives. And I know you're going to argue, but it's not fair on you and it's not fair on the children, so I need to sort this.'

There was more to it than that, but she let it go. For now. 'OK. By all means look, but really, we're fine. This makes sense for everybody, especially for Amelie, and yes, it's disruptive, yes, it's not ideal, but does she really need to be looked after by a total stranger?'

'But my mother would be here.'

'And she would feel she had to help, which could be awkward. For goodness' sake, Oliver, just accept my help. It's not for ever. Unless you really don't want us here?'

He held her eyes, something unreadable in his, then looked away. 'It's not that. Not that at all. I just feel guilty.'

'Well, don't. It's fine. We'll go home this weekend, which I'd planned to do anyway. It'll give your mother more peace and quiet to get over the anaesthetic, and there are lots of things I need to do, like pack a few more things, do the washing, sort out the fridge, cut the grass—life stuff,' she said with a smile, and he gave a soft huff of laughter and returned her smile.

'Thank you. And it's not that you aren't welcome, it's not that I don't want you here—'

She took a step forward and put a finger over his lips, stopping him in mid-sentence.

'Oliver, it's OK,' she murmured. 'I understand, and it's fine. I'll take them home, sort out my house, and we'll see you on Sunday evening, shall we, after supper?'

'Come earlier,' he said. 'I'll cook for us all.'

'If you're sure?'

He nodded slowly. 'I'm sure. Of course I'm sure. It's the least I can do under the circumstances, and I'll get another solution as soon as I can.'

'Don't be silly,' she said. 'You look after your mum, and we'll come back on Sunday and we'll see how it goes from there.'

* * *

Emily and the children went, and the house felt weirdly empty. He reminded himself that that was a good thing, because his mother needed quiet, but it still felt somehow wrong.

His mother woke a little later and called him, and he tapped on the door and went in, to find her sitting on the edge of the bed looking helpless.

'I can't get dressed,' she said crossly, and he could tell she was on the verge of tears. That shocked him, because his mother never, ever cried. Well, that wasn't quite true. There'd been a lot of crying when his father died, but since then she'd just soldiered on. Maybe for too long…

He sat down on the bed beside her and put his arm round her shoulders. 'It's OK. I can help you.'

'You can't. Not really, not enough. I must have hurt my left wrist as well when I fell, and I've been lying here thinking about it, and there are all sorts of things I'm not going to be able to do for myself. I can't even make a cup of tea, because I can't lift a kettle with either hand, and anyway there's all the personal stuff, like getting washed and dressed.'

'I can help—'

'No! Oliver, you can't,' she said, her voice firming up. 'I know you're a doctor, I know you've seen it all, but you haven't seen *mine*, and you're not going to. You're my son, not my doctor, not my carer. Can you ask Emily to come and help me, please?'

He sighed quietly. He hadn't anticipated this at all. Perhaps he should have done. 'She's not here.'

'Not here?'

'No. She's gone home with the children for the weekend. I told her we could manage.'

'Well, I can't, apparently, and you aren't going to do those things for me and that's an end to it.'

'So what do you suggest?' he asked, feeling totally blindsided by this, because he really, really hadn't thought it through.

'I'm going to ring Catherine.'

'Catherine?'

'Yes, Catherine. My sister. Your aunt.'

'I know perfectly well who you're talking about, Mum, but what are you suggesting? That she comes and stays here?'

'No. I'm going to ask if I can go and stay with her for a few weeks. I'm sure she'll say yes, and it'll give me some company in the day.'

'*Weeks?* Really?'

'Well, why not? She's alone, I'm alone, she's got a garden suitable for Berry, she can walk her—I don't see what's wrong with it. Emily will have enough to do without worrying about me and the dog, and anyway, she won't be here in the day so what happens then?'

He frowned. 'It might not be Emily.'

'What do you mean? You said she was going to stay here and take over from me for a little while.'

'She is—she was, but it's a heck of an imposition, and I assumed you'd be here, so I was thinking of getting an au pair. She could help you, just until your other wrist is better.'

She frowned. 'Never mind about me, I don't matter, but are you saying you're going to get a total stranger to look after Amelie while you're at work?' She laid her hand on his knee. 'Poor little thing. Don't you think she's had enough change and disruption in her little life without that? She's got to know Emily, she knows the children, it's all familiar—how is a stranger possibly better?'

Because I won't have Emily getting under my skin at home as well as at work. It's already impossible to think straight.

'I don't want to take advantage of her—and I can help you.'

She gave him a level look and got to her feet with difficulty. 'We're not going over that again, Oliver. Could you please help me put my dress on? And then I'd love a cup of tea. You can make it while I phone Catherine. And don't argue.'

He didn't. It was pointless, so he did as he was asked, and the tea was waiting for her in the kitchen when she emerged. He could hear her in the sitting room talking to Amelie, so he picked up the tea and went through, and found them snuggled up together on the sofa.

He removed Berry who was lying sprawled across them both, and put the tea down beside her.

'Thank you, darling. I've spoken to Catherine. She's coming over in the morning to collect me,' she said, and picked up the tea with a little wince.

He opened his mouth, met her eyes across the top of the mug and shut it. He'd seen that look enough times in his life to know what it meant. It didn't solve all his problems, though, because he really, really didn't want to have to rely on Emily, but he still hadn't got the slightest idea what else he could do.

He picked up his phone, and while Amelie spent the next half hour decorating her grandmother's cast with felt-tip pens and a running commentary, he scrolled through all manner of websites about au pairs. There were lots of comments, too, some singing their praises, and others outlining the perils and pitfalls.

OK, they were few and far between, but what if the person he chose was a disaster? What if Amelie wasn't safe? How could he know if he could trust a stranger with his precious child?

He couldn't. And his mother was right—she'd had enough change in her short life and at least he knew he could trust Emily implicitly. He'd just have to keep his mind and his body under control.

His heart, well, that was another matter. It was already a lost cause.

Emily spent the weekend blitzing the house and the garden, doing the washing and packing up the things they'd need for the next week.

Clothes were a bit of an issue. The children got through them at such a rate, and Phoebe had shot up and outgrown most of her summer clothes. All last year's dresses were too short, her favourite dungarees weren't long enough in the body, and Billy wasn't much better off.

She could always wash them at Oliver's, she supposed—or run back here and do them after Oliver was home and the children were in bed?

Or she could go and buy more, so she had enough to last a week at a time. That made sense.

She took them to the supermarket, found a few things which fitted and which they didn't hate, then loaded up the car and went back to Oliver's at five.

She rang the bell, and he let them in with a puzzled frown.

'What's wrong with your key?'

'I didn't want to presume—'

'Don't be ridiculous, Em. You're living here! Treat it as your home, please?'

'But it isn't— OK, OK! Sorry. How's your mother?'

The children ran in, looking for Amelie and Berry, and he rolled his eyes and stifled a laugh. 'Stubborn and awkward. She's gone to her sister's with the dog.'

Emily felt her eyes widen, and her heart gave a sudden thump. 'Really? For how long?'

'Really. And—weeks, she said, until she can manage her personal care. She wouldn't let me do anything even remotely personal for her. I didn't realize it, but she'd hurt her left wrist as well, so doing anything was difficult, and apparently I'm her son and some things are out of bounds.'

Her mouth twitched and she bit her lips. 'OK.'

'Don't laugh at me. It just hadn't occurred to me that she'd be so…'

'Protective of her privacy?'

He laughed at that. 'I was going to say coy, but—yeah. She asked for you. I had to explain you'd gone home. And I told her I was going to find an au pair.'

'And how's that going?' she asked, sensing it wasn't good.

He shook his head and turned away. 'Come into the kitchen while I cook. The kids are OK. They're in the garden and we can see them from there. They can't come to much harm.'

She climbed onto a stool at the island and watched him thoughtfully, her mind assimilating the fact that without Elizabeth here the evenings were going to be…interesting, to say the least. 'So—the au pair thing.'

'Yeah. It's a minefield. I've been trawling the advice threads. Some au pairs are amazing, some not—oh, and some are man-eaters.'

That made her really laugh. 'You are rather making the assumption that they'd *want* to seduce you,' she said, trying not to think too much about him being seduced, but he just rolled his eyes.

'Whatever. I can cope with a hormonal teenager—that's the least of my worries. What I'm worried about is my daughter, her safety, her emotional security. How will she feel being looked after by a total stranger? She's been through enough and right now everything's new—the school, the house—she doesn't need this.'

She stifled a smile. 'Well, you know what I think,' she said, and resisted the urge to say, 'I told you so'.

'Yes, I do know, and for now at least I have very little choice but to accept your help with Amelie, but I'm not happy about it.'

She got up, walked round the island and put a hand over his mouth. 'Oliver, shut up and cook the supper, and stop beating yourself to death over it. It's temporary. Cope with it.'

'OK, OK,' he mumbled, and she felt his lips pucker as he kissed her hand, his lips soft and warm and slightly moist against her skin.

Their eyes locked, and she dropped her hand as if his mouth was red-hot and turned away. This had suddenly got a whole lot more complicated...

'So what are you cooking?' she asked, hoping her voice didn't really sound quite so strangled as it felt.

'A one-pot chicken recipe of Mum's. It's easy, Amelie eats it and it's reasonably healthy.'

'Sounds like a win. Are you serving it with pasta?'

His lips quirked. 'No. I'm not. I'm serving it with peas and new potatoes. Will they eat that?'

'My kids? They'll eat anything, Billy especially.' And then, just because it was getting really hard to sit in there and watch him, she added, 'How long before we eat? Have I got time to bring the stuff in from the car?'

He glanced at the clock. 'Ten minutes? The chicken's ready. I've just got to do the veg.'

'Great. I'll do it now,' she said, and escaped from the kitchen with a tingling hand, a silent sigh of relief and a vow never, ever to touch him again.

The week started well, considering.

Work was busy but not horrendously so, and the children seemed to be getting on OK, which was a massive relief to him as Amelie could be tricky sometimes with her friendships. But on a personal level, it was an exercise in frustration and denial.

It was fine until the children were all in bed, but then they were left alone together. They didn't have to be. He could have taken himself off to his study, she could have gone in his mother's rooms and made herself at home, or he could, but without fail they ended up on the sofa listening to music, watching the TV, reading—and all the time his senses were filled by her.

Every move, every breath, every drift of the scent of her body, every page she turned registered. And if they talked the conversation was either artificial or straying into dangerous territory, and the last thing he wanted was to rehash all the might-have-beens, so he held it together and kept telling himself it wasn't for ever.

And then on Thursday his run of luck at work ran out, with the day from hell, and it all fell apart.

It was late by the time Oliver got home.

He stuck his head into the kitchen, and she took one look at his face and knew it wasn't good.

'Are the children in bed?' he asked, and she nodded.

'Long ago. I told Amelie you'd come in and say good-night, but I haven't heard a sound.'

'OK. I need a shower anyway.'

She was standing in the kitchen with her back to him when he came down a few minutes later, and she heard his quiet tread as he walked over to her.

'I'm sorry I was so late. Do you need a hand?' he asked, but there was something in his voice that troubled her, and she turned her head and smiled at him, but his face was expressionless.

'No, you're fine.'

Except he wasn't fine.

She switched off the hob and turned back to him, and for a fleeting second his eyes were unguarded, raw and touched with pain.

'Tough day?' she asked gently.

He closed his eyes and nodded, and she reached out for him. 'Come here,' she murmured, and he walked into her arms and stood there, his head resting against hers, and she sensed his body was held up by sheer willpower.

'Want to talk about it?'

He shook his head, just the tiniest movement, and then opened his eyes and stared into hers.

For a moment they just stood there, and then his lips were on hers, his kiss wild and a little desperate. She understood, because this wasn't about them, it was about him, and as his hands cupped her face, his mouth urgent, his body taut, she held him and kissed him back as the storm raged through him.

And then finally she felt the tension go out of him, and the kiss slowed and gentled, his hands cradling her head tenderly as he stroked his lips against hers, the damp skin clinging before he pulled away.

'Sorry, I don't know what that was all about,' he said gruffly, his voice echoing with sadness, but she did, and she touched his cheek in comfort.

'Tell me,' she coaxed.

He shook his head and moved away a fraction, but she pulled him back, and he rested his head against hers with a slow, heavy sigh.

'Her name was Helena. She was just a kid. Twelve. She was knocked off her bike on the way home from school, and she didn't make it. Telling her parents was the hardest thing I've ever done.' His eyes squeezed shut. 'How does that feel? To be her parents? To know she's never coming home again? How will they do that, Em? How will they go on?'

A tear slid down his cheek, and she kissed it away.

'I have no idea. I'm so sorry, Oliver.'

'Don't. You should be sorry for them, not me.'

'Why not you, too? I know what it's like. They all say, don't get involved, and when you're working you don't, but when it's done and you walk away, then it all comes crashing back and of course it hurts, because we're human, and we care, or we wouldn't be doing the job, and every one we lose stays with us for ever.'

'I can't get her out of my head. I want to forget, but she's just there, even when I close my eyes. I wanted to save her, Emily, and I couldn't. I failed her.'

'No, you didn't. Sometimes you just can't save them, but you saved Jack—he's in a rehab centre now to carry on his recovery, and without you he would be dead for sure.'

'You would have done what I did.'

'Maybe, maybe not. But it was you who did it. Not me.'

'We all did it.'

'We did, and we do it every day, and we win some, we

lose some, and today, you lost, but tomorrow there'll be someone else you save who would have died.'

He nodded slowly, then moved away from her, and she missed his warmth—not the physical warmth, but the warmth of his compassion, his caring, his empathy, the things that made him Oliver, made him the man she'd loved. Still loved, if only she could trust him...

'So what are you cooking?' he asked gruffly, and she dredged out a smile.

'Chicken and mushroom stroganoff, with tenderstem broccoli and wild rice.'

She turned back to the stove, and she heard the scrape of a stool on the floor as he sat down at the island.

'Anything I can do?' he asked, and she shook her head.

'Not really. I'm almost done. You could get some cutlery out and a couple of glasses of cold water while I dish up.'

She put the plate down in front of him and slid onto another stool, and he picked up his fork.

'Were the kids OK after school?'

'Yes, they were fine. They're lovely together. They spent ages in the garden making a little den behind the Portuguese laurel in the corner, and they took some of Amelie's toy kitchen stuff out there and made a camp-fire and "cooked" on it.'

The smile just about reached his eyes. 'Did you have to eat it?'

'Oh, yes. Frogspawn and toadstool curry, they told me. Apparently they were fairies.'

His mouth twitched, and this time the smile really did reach his eyes. 'I'm glad you didn't cook that for us. I eat pretty much anything, but I might have had to draw the line at that.'

She smiled back. 'You're not alone. Even pretending was hard!'

He laughed, but then his smile faded, and he frowned.

Back in that dark place.

'Talk to me.'

He shook his head slowly. 'Helena's parents. They couldn't understand why she was dead. There was hardly a mark on her, but she started fitting, and her pupils blew, and I couldn't do anything about it. She must have had a massive traumatic brain injury.'

'How long was she with you?'

'Not long. Twenty minutes? And she was OK at first, then—I just keep seeing her parents, the look in their eyes. And I know there was nothing I could do, I'm not stupid, but even so—they were relying on me to save her, and I couldn't.'

He pushed his plate away, and she pushed it back.

'Eat. Now. And then we'll go and sit down and you can talk about it for as long as you need, but just so you know, you didn't fail anyone, and it's not your fault. Eat.'

He knew she was right, and his body was hungry, so he ate, and then they went and curled up on the sofa together, and gradually the warmth of her body against his side began to penetrate the icy wall around his heart.

He felt a tear slide down his cheek, then another, and she wiped them away with gentle fingers.

'How will they cope?' he asked.

'How does anyone cope with loss, Oliver? It's hard. One foot in front of the other, I guess.'

Was that how she'd coped when he'd told her about Sue? Not that it was the same, but it had obviously hurt her very deeply. He could imagine that. It had hurt him, too, even though it had been his fault. And now, despite that hurt, she was here for him.

'Thank you,' he said quietly, and she turned her head and looked up at him.

'What for?'

He shrugged. 'Being here for me? Talking me down off a cliff—'

'A cliff?'

He shook his head and smiled. 'No, not that cliff. I just felt like I was standing on the edge of a deep black hole, and you pulled me back away from it. You and your calm common sense and unquestioning kindness. Your warmth, your generosity…'

He trailed off, because the next step was to tell her he loved her, and he couldn't do that. Not yet, and maybe never. She didn't want to hear it, and he knew he had a long way to go to win back her trust.

He eased his arm out from behind her and stood up.

'I think I'm going to turn in.'

'Are you OK now?' she asked, her eyes worried, and he nodded.

'Yes, I'm fine. It happens to all of us, but yeah, I'm fine. Thank you. Again.'

He pulled her to her feet, wrapped his arms round her and hugged her. 'It's good having you here,' he said into her hair, and then he dropped his arms and stepped away before he did anything stupid like kiss her again, because this time it really wouldn't end there.

To his amazement he slept well, and Friday was fine. No drama, no tragedy for a change, just the usual stuff.

And then Kath came for the weekend, while Steve had Emily's children and she was at work, and while he cut the lawn, Amelie came out into the garden and played in the den she'd made with Billy and Phoebe.

'Why aren't you with Mummy?' he asked as he finished, and she told him Mummy was working. He gritted his teeth, put the mower away and went inside, leaving her playing in the den. Time to deal with this.

Half an hour later, after a fairly blunt conversation with Kath, he ran upstairs, packed a bag and went out into the garden to talk to Amelie in her new den.

'I've got to go somewhere, sweetheart, but Mummy's going to do something lovely with you, OK? I'll see you tomorrow.'

'Are you going to work?' she asked.

'No, but I have to go away and see someone. I'm sorry. I'll be back tomorrow, but you have fun with Mummy, OK?'

'OK.' She hugged him, lifted up her face for a kiss and then ran inside. He could hear her excited voice, asking her mother what they were going to do, and he bit his lips, wondering if tough love would work or if it would bring it all crashing down on their heads.

Only one way to find out. He went back in and found Kath sitting with Amelie, discussing options. Good.

'Bye, guys. See you tomorrow. Have fun,' he said, and kissed his daughter goodbye and left before he changed his mind.

His car was on her drive when she got home, but there was no sign of him and the key was still under the pot, so she rang him.

'Where are you? What's going on?'

He gave a strangled laugh. 'Yeah, Kath and I had a bit of a frank conversation about her priorities, and told her I'd see her tomorrow.'

'Wow. OK. So where are you now?'

'On the clifftop. The café closed so I had to leave, and I didn't like to presume and let myself in.'

'Don't be ridiculous. You can come here whenever you like. I'm all over your house, for heaven's sake. Are you staying the night?'

'If I can? Otherwise, I'll go to a hotel.'

'Don't be ridiculous. Come back now. I'm not doing anything, and you sound as if you need to talk.'

Five minutes later he walked in the door, and she gave him a quick hug and went into the kitchen before she forgot her common sense and stayed in his arms. It was becoming a dangerous habit.

'What do you fancy for supper?' she asked, wondering if there was anything in the freezer that she could throw together, apart from pizzas and the odd bag of frozen peas.

'How about going out again like we did before?' he said, his voice close behind her. 'You've been cooking for us all week, you've been working all day—I reckon you've earned it.'

She hesitated, then turned and nodded. 'OK. Give me ten minutes to shower and change?'

'Sure. I need to ring Amelie and say goodnight anyway, so no rush.'

She didn't rush, because somehow this time it mattered more. She went casual again, but prettier and cooler, in the new floaty floral dress she'd picked up the other day when she'd shopped for the children. She put on sandals and picked up a lightweight cardi in case they sat outside, and ran down.

He was standing at the patio doors staring out at the garden, a jumper knotted casually over his shoulders, and he turned to her with a smile.

'You look nice. Your grass needs cutting, by the way.'

'Feel free. You can earn back some brownie points,' she said, oddly flustered by his compliment. 'How was Amelie?'

'Fine, I think. They seem to have had fun. I think they spent some time on the beach and went to a café for supper, luckily not the one I was in. Which brings me to us. Any suggestions?'

'There's a lovely pub on the river someone was talking about the other day, with fabulous views and lots of outside space. Fancy trying that?'

'Why not? It's a gorgeous evening. We can sit outside.'

It was gorgeous, absolutely gorgeous, and they stayed until the sun was long gone and she was feeling the chill even through her cardi.

'You're cold. Here, have my jumper,' he said, pulling it off, and she slipped it over her head and was engulfed in an intoxicating mixture of laundry soap and Oliver.

She tugged it down and smiled at him. 'Thanks.'

'You're welcome. Another drink?'

'No, I don't think so. How about a stroll to the end of the jetty?'

It was magical by the water, the lights from the boats moored out on the river glinting on the surface, the smell of the riverbank in every breath.

They lingered a little, but all she could think about was how nice it would be if he put his arm around her and hugged her against his side so she could rest her head on his shoulder as she had the other night…

Bad idea.

'The wind's picking up,' she said with a little shiver. 'Let's go back.'

They drove home, and as soon as they walked in the door, she headed for the stairs. 'I'll just change Billy's sheets—'

'You don't need to do that. I can do it later. Come down.'

She turned on the stairs and walked down, and as she reached the bottom step, she met his eyes and something happened, something hot and sweet and irresistible that stopped them both in their tracks.

He closed his eyes and turned away with a sharp sigh. 'I shouldn't be here. This was a bad idea,' he muttered, and she sat down, partly because her legs were shaking and partly because she didn't trust herself not to walk down and wrap her arms around him.

She wrapped them round herself instead, and watched him. His head was bowed, and she could hear the cogs turning, feel the inward battle he was waging with his emotions.

She recognized that battle. It was with her day and night, but the wanting was killing her and the need to hold him was stronger than her resolve.

'Oliver?'

He lifted his head and turned towards her, keeping the bannisters between them.

'I shouldn't be here,' he said again, but she could hear the lack of resolution in his voice this time, the sound of surrender to the inevitable that echoed in her heart.

'Shouldn't you?' she asked softly. 'Are you sure?'

He was silent for so long she was starting to doubt her own judgement, but then he met her eyes again, and she could see tenderness and longing in them. She stood up and took the last step down as he rounded the bannisters and reached for her, and as she went into his arms it felt as if she was coming home.

He held her eyes for another heartbeat, then lowered his

head and kissed her, his lips brushing hers lightly, tentatively, questioningly.

It was nothing like the other night. This kiss was all about them, him rediscovering her as she was rediscovering him?

She took a step back out of his arms, slid her hand into his and led him wordlessly up to her room.

CHAPTER SEVEN

He turned her to face him, and she could feel the tremor in his hands as he cupped her shoulders.

She hadn't put the light on, but there was a full moon and she could make out his features, the set of his lips as he pressed them together, the questioning tilt of his head as he stared down into her eyes, and when he spoke, his voice was gruff.

'If we do this, we can't turn back the clock and undo it.'

'I won't want to undo it,' she told him, and something in her voice must have convinced him, because he gave a tiny nod of recognition and she saw his throat move as he swallowed.

His hands reached down, finding the hem of his borrowed jumper and peeling it slowly over her head. He dropped it on the floor and eased the cardi over her shoulders, before letting it slide to the floor with the jumper, and then he studied the dress.

'How does that come off?' he asked, and she bent and grasped the hem and pulled it over her head.

She heard the intake of his breath, the silence that followed, and she added the dress to the growing pile on the floor and reached for his shirt buttons, undoing them slowly one by one with fingers that trembled.

His breath hissed out but he stood motionless, his hands

warm and firm as they cupped her shoulders, his fingers tightening as she reached for the stud on his jeans. She tugged the shirt out and slid it off his shoulders, and he shrugged it off, then reached for his zip.

She slapped his hands away gently and took over, and as her fingers grazed down over his abdomen, it tensed, and she felt him shudder.

'You're killing me, you know that, don't you?' he murmured, and bending his head he nuzzled into the side of her neck above her collarbone, his breath warm and unsteady against her skin.

She moved her hand, and he caught it and pulled it away.

'No. I'm hanging by a thread as it is. Turn round.'

She turned, and he undid her bra and slid the straps over her shoulders, his warm hands gliding down over her skin, sending goose bumps over it. She crossed her arms, suddenly acutely aware of the changes to her body since he'd last touched her like this.

What if it turns him off? What if he doesn't want me?

She felt the whisper of his breath, the touch of his lips on her shoulder, her neck, her ear, and she arched her neck to give him better access. His breath drifted like fire over her skin, and she could feel the slight graze of stubble, intoxicating as he laid a tiny line of kisses over her shoulder before turning her to face him.

Her arms were still crossed, but he lifted them gently away and cradled her breasts in safe, familiar hands.

'That's better,' he breathed, his thumbs stroking lightly over her nipples, and he feathered a kiss over her lips. 'You have no idea how much I've missed you,' he murmured against them, and she stifled a sob and lifted a hand to cradle his face.

'I've missed you, too. Missed this. The way you always knew how to touch me. Kiss me...'

His mouth found hers again, greedy now, and she slid her hands down his back and under his jeans, her fingers cupping taut, firm buttocks that tensed under her touch. He rocked against her, then pulled away, ditched the jeans and underwear in one hasty swipe and came back to her, the hard jut of his erection nudging hot and needy against the bowl of her pelvis.

And then he swore and stepped out of reach, his chest heaving.

'Stop. I could get you pregnant,' he muttered, and turned his head away. 'Dammit, we weren't doing this. If I'd known...'

She reached out and took his hands. 'I've got an IUCD,' she told him, suddenly glad that she hadn't had it removed.

He stared at her. 'Truly?'

'Yes, truly. I wouldn't lie to you about something like that.'

She felt the hiss of his outbreath as he pulled her back into his arms, toppling her onto the bed in a tangle of arms and legs. His mouth found hers, plundering it, their tongues duelling as her body arched against his. His hands were everywhere, driving her higher and higher until she was sobbing, and then he was there, filling her with one long, slow thrust, his breath shuddering against her shoulder as he dropped his head against hers and held her, motionless, for an endless moment.

And then he started to move, slowly at first and then building, building as her legs locked around him and his mouth found hers again, stifling her scream as he tipped her over the edge into ecstasy.

She felt him shudder, heard the ragged groan dragged

from somewhere deep inside him, then the slackening of his muscles as he lay against her, his breath hot against her skin.

Her heart slowed as their breathing levelled, and he shifted so he could see her face.

'You're crying,' he said softly, and wiped the tears away with a gentle finger.

'I'd forgotten,' she said simply, and she closed her eyes and bent her head down, and he gathered her closer and cradled her as she cried for all they'd lost.

It was still lost, it always would be, and doing this was so foolish. It was only going to make it hurt more, because this was all they could ever have. A few stolen moments in the midst of their fractured lives.

If only Amelie were hers, if Billy and Phoebe were his— but they weren't, and never would be, and no amount of wishful thinking was going to change that.

Could they blend their families? Her two children, his two children? And then what about his mother? And then Kath and Steve on the fringes, adding to the complexity of their lives?

Would Elizabeth move out and go back to her flat and leave Emily in sole charge of both families? Where would Kath stay when she came? And Charlie?

And more importantly, what if, after all of that juggling and compromise, it still didn't work? What could they say to the children, those poor children who'd already lost so much to divorce? How could it possibly be fair to ask them to do it all over again?

It couldn't, and it was too great a risk.

She shifted, swiping the fresh tears from her cheeks with a determined hand.

'Are you OK?' he murmured, his voice soft and filled with concern.

She nodded. 'I'm being stupid. I was just wishing we could turn back the clock, or even just start again from here, but we can't. I know we can't. There's too much at stake for all of us, and we just can't risk it. If it goes wrong—'

'Why should it?'

'Why shouldn't it? It did before. You went and slept with Sue for no very good reason that I can see, and then Steve left me when I thought we were all good and making it work, but I wasn't enough for him, just like I wasn't enough for you. And it doesn't matter what you say,' she added, cutting him off when he tried to speak, 'because it's true. If I'd been enough for you, you wouldn't have slept with her, and we'd be in a completely different place, but as it is I can't trust you not to hurt me again, like you did before, like Steve did—I'm not going there again, Oliver. I can't do it.'

He gave a ragged sigh and wiped away her tears with a gentle hand. 'It wasn't that,' he said, his voice heavy and sincere. 'It wasn't that you weren't enough. You just weren't there, and I was lonely. Lonely, and maybe a bit angry with you for not coming with me, and it was a stupid, stupid mistake and I've regretted it ever since.'

'But you knew I couldn't go. You could have stayed. I know you said you couldn't, but you could, if I'd mattered enough to you. You didn't have to go, but your career path came first, just like it did with Kath. You say she won't compromise, but then neither will you. You just want it all your own way, and you probably would have been the same with me.'

'That isn't true. And anyway, we weren't at that point. It might not have lasted.'

'Well, we'll never know, will we, because you never gave us that chance.'

'I was going to. I was coming back to you, and I instantly regretted sleeping with her. It was a huge mistake and I hated myself, and when I found out she was pregnant, I was devastated. I only stayed with her for the baby, and I never loved her the way I loved you.'

She searched his eyes, looking for the truth but not sure she'd recognize it if she saw it. 'I didn't know you loved me. Why didn't you tell me? I thought you didn't care or you would have stayed.'

He shrugged. 'I don't know. Protecting myself? Maybe also not letting it get too serious, because we were going to be apart for a year and I didn't know what might happen between us in that time, but I always cared and I've never stopped regretting that I hurt you. I thought maybe when I came back—but then it was too late. And you didn't tell me, either. You left it nineteen years to tell me that. And if it helps, I've never loved anyone since the way I—' He broke off, then added, 'The way I loved you.'

His eyes were steady, and she wondered what he'd been going to say. Love, not loved? Maybe.

'I never have, either. I think it broke me. I loved Steve, I was happy enough with him, but it wasn't like it was with you. I've never found that again.'

Until now…

His eyes searched hers, and he reached out a tentative hand and cradled her cheek tenderly. 'Can we try again?' he asked. 'Not involving the kids, but just—maybe we could have this. Just sometimes, like an oasis, a precious retreat where we can be together. Maybe even get away for the weekend from time to time, if the others could have the children.'

She hesitated. Could they? Did she dare? Although what did she have to lose? She loved him anyway, and it was going nowhere, but maybe…

'That would be nice. That would be really nice—but you have to know it can't go anywhere. It's just this, you and me.'

He nodded slowly, his eyes steady, but the silence was broken by a quiet buzzing and he gave a frustrated sigh.

'I bet that's Kath.'

He rolled away from her and sat up, fishing in his jeans pocket for his phone, and then he swore softly and answered it.

He took the phone out onto the landing, and she lay in bed and listened to one side of what sounded like a rather fraught conversation about Amelie. His voice changed and she guessed he was speaking to his daughter, then it changed back again and she heard her name mentioned, and he came back into the bedroom and sat down on the edge of the bed and sighed.

She laid a hand on his arm. 'Trouble?' she murmured, and he turned to face her, his eyes too dark to read.

'Yeah. She won't go to sleep, she says her mother hates her, which she doesn't—she just doesn't have a clue how to be a mother. She also told Kath you were nicer.'

'Ouch. That's why you were talking about me. Is she jealous?'

'No, just protective, I think, although I don't know how she can justify that as she left me. Anyway, it's none of her business.'

'It is if I'm influencing her daughter. I can understand that. Do you want to go home?'

* * *

Did he?

'Honestly? Yes, but I'm not going to. I can't. They have to resolve this, and they have to find a way to be friends. But it is a nightmare, especially her unreliability. You don't know how lucky you are with Steve.'

She smiled wryly. 'I wouldn't say I was lucky, but he's a good father. It hasn't always been easy, though, and it's only because his wife is so accepting that it works at all.'

'Yeah. I haven't even met Kath's partner, and Amelie has no idea what their life is like or where they live or anything.'

'Maybe you should take her over there to meet him?'

He shrugged. 'Maybe one day.' He put his phone on her bedside table and lay down facing her, before reaching out a hand and stroking her hair back off her face.

'You OK?' she asked, and he nodded.

'I guess so,' he said, but he wasn't, not really, because Kath's call had been a brutal reminder that the status quo was finely balanced and could all come crashing down at any time and their little oasis could be wiped out at a stroke.

And again, he was swamped as Emily had been by all the if-onlys.

If only they'd stayed together. If only she was Charlie and Amelie's mother—but they hadn't, and she wasn't, and nothing he could do would ever change that.

Her hand reached out and cradled his face, the tenderness in her touch nearly undoing him.

'Don't worry about her,' she murmured. 'She's not going to come to any harm, and you can talk to Kath tomorrow. For now, you need to sleep, and so do I. I have to be at work at seven.'

'You do. I'm sorry. Come here,' he murmured, opening his arms, and she moved into them with a quiet sigh.

'It'll be all right, Oliver. Don't worry.'

Easier said than done.

Emily drifted off to sleep, and he lay there, staring up at the ceiling and wondering how his daughter was coping with a mother who didn't know how to love her, and whether he could ever win Emily's trust again. What a mess...

He woke her with a kiss, which ended up with her running for a hasty shower and getting to work in the nick of time with a smile on her face, and by the time she got home he was gone.

She made her bed, lingering over the pillows, burying her nose in the scent of him. Could they do this? Make it work?

Maybe.

She heard Steve's car and ran down, and he kissed the children goodbye, and then after they'd run upstairs she had an interesting conversation with him about Oliver.

The children had clearly been talking about him, but she put him straight—or almost—about their relationship, although she wasn't sure he believed her.

He got in the car and drove away, leaving her thoughtful. He wanted to see her settled with someone else? So did she, if only there weren't so many potential pitfalls in their way.

Too much at stake, and wishful thinking wouldn't change that, but she was glad he was open to the idea of her having a relationship. She wondered how Oliver had got on with Kath. She didn't envy him.

And he was right. She was lucky with Steve. At least

for all his failings he loved his children deeply, and they loved him.

She went back inside, rounded up the children and they headed back to Oliver's house, the children predictably talking non-stop about Steve's puppy.

'Will Berry be here?' Phoebe asked as they turned onto Oliver's drive, and she shook her head.

'No, darling. She's with Amelie's grandma. She's her dog, not theirs. You know that.'

'Why can't *we* have a dog?' Billy said, and she sighed.

'You know why. It's not fair. I'm working.'

'You could stop working,' Phoebe said, and she laughed.

'What would we eat? Where would we live?'

'We could live with Amelie,' her little daughter said innocently, and Emily felt her heart squeeze in her chest.

If only life were that easy...

She followed them in, and within seconds they were out in the garden with Amelie, playing in the den. Oliver was sitting on the bench, and he smiled and patted the seat beside him as she approached.

'You OK?' he asked, and she plonked herself down beside him with a tiny laugh.

'Oh, I'm fine. The kids want a puppy.'

'Seriously?'

'Very seriously. Steve's got one, Amelie's got one, why can't we have one?'

He chuckled. 'Yeah, they aren't great with logistics.'

'Oh, they are. They suggested I gave up work and we came and lived with you.'

His eyes met hers searchingly. 'And?'

She laughed again. 'Nice little fantasy. Just a few things in the way.'

He looked over to the children, running in and out of the

den, gathering scattered toys, their excited chatter filling the air, and then back at her.

'We wouldn't have to pretend any more,' he said softly, and she looked away and swallowed.

'Oliver, we can't. You know we can't. Compartments, remember?'

'I remember. I also remember how good it felt to hold you last night.'

She felt his hand brush hers, his fingers tightening around her own, and she gave his a gentle squeeze and eased her hand away. 'We can't do this. They're getting in deep enough as it is. They don't need any added complications.'

'Is that what we are? A complication?'

She met his eyes. 'Well, aren't we? And talking of complications, how did it go with Kath?'

He sighed and looked away. 'OK, I suppose. I think they had fun. Amelie was just trying it on, but she does that.' He got to his feet. 'You stay here and keep an eye on them. I'll go and finish off in the kitchen.'

Keeping their new relationship in a separate compartment proved even harder than Oliver had expected, especially after that conversation, because playing in the back of his mind was always the image of the children in the garden with a new puppy, and him and Emily together.

Married?

No. That was never to happen, for a whole bunch of sound reasons, but it didn't stop him fantasizing about it and wishing it could be.

And every day that passed made it more and more difficult to maintain his perspective, not because of anything Emily or the children said or did, but because every day at work she was just *there*, right under his nose, and every morning and evening she was in his house, in his space, in his sight, and those memories, those longings, were now well and truly refreshed.

Even if he couldn't see her, he could hear her voice, imagine what she was doing, and he wanted more. He wanted all of it, but it was a minefield because their lives were too complicated, and anyway, she'd made it clear as day that that was never going to happen.

Kath didn't help. They'd made some progress over the weekend, but not enough, and then two days before she was due back, she had to cancel because her Japanese client was flying in again and she couldn't reschedule him.

Amelie was gutted, and so was he, not only for Amelie but also because that was his time with Emily, a time they'd both been looking forward to, and it was snatched away from them.

He was at work, of course, just finishing off some notes in Resus when her message landed like a lead balloon, and he could have screamed. He didn't, he just punched the wall and hurt his hand, and Emily found him rubbing his knuckles ruefully.

'What have you done?'

'I might have accidentally hit the wall.'

She studied his face, and he could see her mind working. She cocked her head on one side.

'She's bailed again, hasn't she?' she said, and he nodded. 'Yup.'

Her shoulders dropped. 'Oh, Oliver. What are you going to do?'

'I have no idea. She needs a mother, and Kath just doesn't seem able to step up to the plate. It's not that she doesn't want to. It's just that unless she makes some pretty drastic changes to her work–life balance, she can't do any more. She's basically incapable of saying no to a client.'

'But she can say no to her daughter.'

'Apparently so. I think it's pressure from her boss, but whatever, it's not helping. Anyway, what's going on? Anything in particular need my attention out there?'

'No, it's quiet, so we could go and get a coffee—or not,' she added, picking up the red phone. 'Yoxburgh Park ED.'

She scribbled down the information, hung up and put a call over the Tannoy.

'Code Red, adult trauma call, ten minutes. Code Red, adult trauma call, fifteen minutes.'

His eyebrows creased together. 'Two?'

'Yup. A car's gone through the barrier at the top of a slip road and fallen twenty feet into the field beyond. They've got the driver out, he's on the way, and they're just releasing the passenger.'

'Young men?'

'No. Looks like a married couple, apparently. The man's in the air ambulance, leg and chest injuries, query aorta, GCS twelve at scene, and the woman's coming by road. She has head injuries and query spinal injuries and GCS is seven, so it's not looking great. She wasn't wearing a seat belt, apparently.'

She put out a call to the most relevant departments, ordered extra units of O neg, and as the room started to fill they could hear the air ambulance coming in to land.

'Here we go again,' she murmured, and went out to meet them, leaving Oliver to prep the team.

By the time he'd been wheeled into Resus, the man had deteriorated significantly. An ultrasound showed damage to his aorta, so he was taken straight to Joe Baker and Matt

Hunter in the Interventional Radiology Surgical suite, leaving them free to focus on the woman.

She was on a spinal board, but she had no reflexes, and by the time she'd arrived her pupils were unequal and she was fitting, and she had cerebro-spinal fluid leaking out of her ear.

'Right, we need an urgent CT to see what's going on in her head,' he said, and as soon as they'd stopped the fitting and were satisfied that she was stable, she was taken down to Imaging.

The results arrived back almost as she did, and they confirmed all his fears.

'OK, she's got a massive subdural haemorrhage and a basal skull fracture. This is very not good.' He flashed the penlight in her eyes, but both pupils had blown and were unreactive, and moments later her heart slowed to a halt.

He gave a heavy sigh and looked around at his colleagues.

'OK, I'm calling it. Are we all agreed?'

They all nodded, as he'd known they would. Her situation was hopeless and any further intervention would be futile and an insult to her dignity.

He looked up at the clock. 'Time of death—eleven fifty-six. Sorry, guys. Are you all OK?'

They nodded, but the mood was definitely sombre, and he let out a slow, heavy sigh. 'Are the relatives here?'

'I think their son might be in the family room, talking to the police,' a nurse told him, and he nodded.

'OK, I'll go and talk to him. Thank you, everyone.'

He turned and met Emily's eyes, and she smiled sadly at him. 'You OK to do this, or shall I?'

'No, I'll do it,' he murmured. 'I shouldn't be too long, and then we'll go and get that coffee if it's quiet.'

* * *

She was waiting for him when he emerged looking grim-faced, and by a miracle the department was all ticking over nicely, so they went out into the park and he turned his face up to the sun and heaved a sigh of relief.

'Oh, that's better.'

'How did you get on with the son?'

'Oh, he's in bits. His mother had just phoned him to say his father wanted a divorce, and he was still talking to her when they crashed. His father was yelling abuse at his mother, and he thinks he might have crashed deliberately because she screamed, "What are you doing?" an instant before the crash.'

'Oh, no! That's awful.'

'Yeah. He thinks his father was probably trying to kill them both. Was there any word on him?'

She shook her head. 'No, nothing so far, but he's a mess, too. I wouldn't be surprised if he loses his right leg, and that's if he survives the injury to his aorta.'

'Well, if he does, he could be facing a murder charge. The son's told the police everything he knows. It makes me grateful that Kath's just a pain and not a psychopath.'

They grabbed sandwiches and coffees and headed out, but the café was busy so they sat on the grass under a tree and ate and drank in silence, their thoughts still on the couple.

'Are you all right?' he asked her after a moment, and she nodded.

'I guess. It's just so horrible for the family. How's your mother, talking of families?'

'Oh, she's making progress. Her left wrist is OK, so she can do much more for herself. She's talking about coming home at the weekend, so I've said I'll pick her up on Saturday morning.'

'Well, that's good, isn't it?'

He looked across at her, and she could see concern in his eyes. 'I don't know. She'll try and do stuff to help out. I know she will. I'll have to read her the riot act and she'll give me that look and do it anyway.'

She laughed. 'Don't worry, Oliver, I can be firm with her.'

'Only when you're there, and you're working this weekend and Kath's not there, so I'll have to dress and undress her.'

'Unless I stay over?'

He sighed. 'Could you? That would be really kind of you.'

'Well, I'm not going to be doing anything else on Friday and Saturday night, am I?' she said wryly, and he groaned and shook his head.

'Don't. It was our time, this weekend.'

'I know, but there'll be others.'

'I hope so. I'm so mad with Kath for bailing.'

'Maybe there's something else going on. Why is she so driven? Has she ever been poor?'

He snorted and turned his attention back to his coffee, taking a moment before he spoke. 'No. Her family are wealthy, they're all high achievers, her father was a hedge fund manager and her brother is someone high up in one of the big investment banks. They have money running through their veins.'

'So maybe she feels pressured to equal their success?'

He looked at her thoughtfully. 'Maybe—but if her own daughter isn't enough to make her change, then I don't know what is.'

'Maybe you've made it too easy.'

He laughed. 'You wouldn't say that if you'd seen me two weeks ago. I didn't make it easy, believe me.'

He pulled out his phone, glanced at it and got to his feet, pulling her up. 'Time to go back.'

They walked in just as his phone pinged, and he pulled it out and read the message, then looked at her and she knew it was bad news.

'The driver?'

He nodded and gave a heavy sigh. 'And we think we've got problems? That poor family. I'd better go and tell the team.'

To her surprise, when she and the children got back after the school run on Friday, they were greeted by Berry.

The poor dog was nearly beside herself with excitement, tearing round in circles from one child to another, so Emily opened the door and sent them all out into the garden, then tapped on the dividing door and went in to see Elizabeth.

She was sitting in her chair by the window, watching the children, and she turned towards her with a big smile.

'Hello, Emily!'

'Hello, you!' she said, giving her a hug and a kiss. 'I wasn't expecting you to be here. I thought Oliver was picking you up tomorrow morning?'

'He was, but a friend offered to drop me home.'

'Oh, that's kind. So how are you doing? Are you OK?'

'I'm fine, thank you. So much better. Very bored with it all, and the sling's really annoying, but I'll do and at least it doesn't hurt now, and it's lovely to be home.' She reached out and took Emily's hand with her left one, and gave it a squeeze. 'Oliver says you've been an absolute star. I'm so grateful to you for looking after them for me.'

'You don't need to be. It's been a pleasure and the least I could do,' she said, returning the squeeze, 'and I think the children have quite enjoyed it.'

Elizabeth looked out of the window, a fond smile on her face. 'They do seem to get on very well,' she said, and Emily wasn't sure but she had a sneaky feeling it was a loaded comment. Was Elizabeth matchmaking?

No, surely not...

'Yes, they do, most of the time, which is lucky,' she said, and changed the subject. 'So, Oliver thinks you're going to be really silly and try and do too much before you've had time to heal properly, but I've told him I know you're not that foolish and there's nothing very much you'll need to do during the day, so I'm sure you'll be fine while I'm not here, won't you?'

Elizabeth turned and looked up at her from her chair, a little smile tugging at her mouth.

'What *are* you suggesting, Emily?'

'Nothing at all, because I know you won't do anything rash,' she said innocently.

They exchanged smiles, and Elizabeth shook her head and chuckled. 'You're a dear girl. Such a pity about you and Oliver.' Her smile faded as she looked out of the window at the children, and she sighed. 'I gather Kath's not coming this weekend, letting the child down yet again. She couldn't be less like you. It's such a shame. I don't understand her at all.'

Definitely matchmaking...

'I'm sure she has her reasons,' she said calmly, refusing to be drawn into that minefield. 'I have to take the children over to Steve soon. He normally picks them up but he can't today, so I said I'd do it, but is there anything I can do for you before I go?'

'What are you going to do with Amelie?'

'I was going to take her with me. Why?'

'Because I'm here, and I'm not doing anything. You won't be long, will you?'

'Half an hour, maybe a bit more?'

'Well, leave her here with me. I'm sure we can manage. I'm not that incapacitated.'

She smiled. 'No, you're not, and I'm sure she'll love that. She's missed you. If you don't mind, that would be lovely. I'll get you some tea before I go.'

CHAPTER EIGHT

SHE WAS BACK from Steve's not long after five, and she found Amelie sitting with her grandmother reading, the dog curled up against her side.

'You three look cosy,' she said with a smile. 'Is it nice having Grandma and Berry back?'

'Really, *really* nice,' she said, and she bounced up and ran over to hug Emily. 'What's for supper? Can I help you in the kitchen?' she asked, and Emily looked down at her and wondered how anything could possibly be more important to her mother than this little girl and her happiness.

Not your business...

She smiled at her. 'Yes, of course you can help me, sweetheart. What would you like for supper? There's some of that pasta bake left from yesterday, or we can make something else. What did you have for lunch?'

'Jacket potato and cheese and beans,' she said, tugging the fridge door open. 'So what can I have?'

Something healthy, but what? She peered over Amelie's shoulder into the fridge. 'How about a Thai fish and vegetable curry, like I did before? You liked that, and Grandma will be able to eat it with one hand, so Daddy and Grandma and I can have it later.'

'Can I stay up and eat with you?'

Could she? Oliver was pretty strict about bedtimes, but

the child's mother had bailed on her, and anyway, it was the weekend. She smiled. 'You know what? I think that would be lovely. You don't have to get up early tomorrow, and it's a bit of a celebration because Grandma's back, so why not? Just this once.'

By the time he got home just after seven, he was utterly ravenous and completely exhausted. He hadn't stopped all day, and James had sent him home after his last patient in Resus.

'We can finish off. You go,' he'd said, and Oliver had opened his mouth to argue, shut it and left before he got involved in another case.

And now he was home, to find his mother in the sitting room and Berry overjoyed to see him again.

He cuddled the dog first, because she was the most demanding, then hugged his mother.

'So how come you're here?' he asked, puzzled. 'I was picking you up tomorrow.'

'Douglas gave me a lift.'

He stared at her, puzzled. 'Douglas? Douglas *Buchanon*?'

His father's old friend? Surely not...

She met his eyes briefly and then looked away. 'I told him about my hand, so he popped over to see me.'

Popped? 'I didn't realize he lived anywhere near here.'

'Oh, yes, he moved to Aldeburgh about seven or eight years ago, just before Joanna died, and we've always kept in touch. He took me out to lunch a few times after I bought my flat, but obviously I've hardly seen him for the last eighteen months. Anyway, I think he just wanted to make sure my hand had been done properly, but it turns out he knows the surgeon who did my op and he rates him, so he was happy. Anyway, when I said I was coming back here this weekend, he offered me a lift and I thought it would save you a journey, so I said yes.'

'That was kind of him. I'm glad you're still in touch.'

'Yes, so am I,' she said, and he thought she coloured slightly.

Surely not? His mum and Douglas? And how much had they been seeing of each other before she'd come to his rescue in London? Maybe more than she was saying.

'Where's Amelie?' he asked to change the subject, even though he could hear them in the kitchen.

'Cooking supper with Emily.'

'Good, I'm starving. I'll go and chivvy them.' He headed to the kitchen, and Amelie ran over and threw herself at him, brimming with excitement.

'Daddy, Daddy, I'm making curry with Emily, and guess what? I'm staying up and eating with you and Grandma!'

'Are you, indeed?' he asked, scooping her up, and met Emily's slightly guilty eyes. 'And whose idea was that?'

'Mine,' Amelie said, 'but Emily said it would be OK just this once because it's the weekend and I don't have to get up in the morning. Plus Grandma's come home, so it's a celebration.'

His lips twitched, and so did Emily's, and he had to look away before he laughed.

'Well, that's all right then,' he said, and kissed Amelie and put her down, then looked at Emily again. 'How long will it take? Do I have time to shower?'

'Ten minutes? I just need to put the fish in and cook the rice.'

'Brilliant. Make plenty. I haven't eaten all day and I'm absolutely starving. Amelie, why don't you lay the table while she does that?'

* * *

While he put his daughter to bed after supper, Emily unpacked Elizabeth's bag and helped her get ready for bed, and by the time she'd done that and put the kettle on, Oliver was down again.

'Where's Mum?' he asked.

'In bed reading. She needed the sling off. Want a drink?'

'Yeah, but not coffee. I've been mainlining it all day. A nice cold beer would slip down a treat.'

She smiled at him. 'Yes, I thought it might. You were up to your eyes every time I walked past Resus. Long day?'

He laughed a little hysterically and walked out. 'Give me two minutes. I'm just going to say goodnight to my mother,' he threw over his shoulder, still grinning, and she smiled and made herself a cup of fruit tea. By the time he came back, she was on the sofa with her tea, his beer on the table beaded with moisture, and he dropped onto the sofa beside her, picked up the glass and downed half of it.

'Oh, my word, that's better,' he said, putting his feet up and rolling his head towards her, a smile teasing his lips. 'Thanks for sorting Mum out. She says you laid the law down about overdoing it.'

Her lips twitched. 'Good. I'm glad she realized.'

'Oh, she realized. I think a few people have been pretty firm with her, too, so hopefully she'll behave.'

'Do you know why she came home today? I thought you were picking her up tomorrow, but she said a friend brought her home.'

His brow creased a little. 'Yeah, and that's quite interesting. He's an old colleague of my father's, a family friend. He was widowed a year or two before my father died, and they've kept in touch. He was a hand surgeon, oddly, so she told him about her hand, and apparently he doesn't live far away, so he's been to visit her, and he offered her a lift, but...'

'But what? That all sounds perfectly reasonable.'

He laughed. 'I don't know. I just got a funny feeling there was more to it than that, and she was avoiding my eye a bit.'

'Really? Do you think it's significant?'

'I don't know what to think. She said that after she bought her flat up here he took her out for lunch a few times, so maybe. I mean, for goodness' sake, she's entitled to a life, and to her privacy, but—I don't know. It's probably all totally innocent. I'm just a bit surprised.'

She searched his eyes. 'Would you mind if they were more than just friends?' she asked carefully, and he shrugged.

'It's not really up to me, is it? I know Dad wouldn't want her to be unhappy and lonely, and she's been pretty sad for quite a while, but... I don't know... It would just be really weird. Would I mind? No, I don't think so, and if she wants to be with someone, she couldn't have chosen a nicer, more decent person. To be honest, I don't know what to think. I just hope one of them isn't reading more into it than is meant.'

'Is that likely?'

'No idea. No doubt time will tell, but she seems happier than she's been in a while. Anyway, enough about her, how was your day?'

'Not as busy as yours, thank goodness. Want to debrief?'

His laugh morphed into a groan, and he shook his head. 'No, I'm fine. It was just relentless. Every time I thought I might get a second to grab something to eat or drink, there was another one, then another—James took over and sent me home in the end.'

'Did you argue with him?'

He gave a rueful chuckle. 'No, I was beyond arguing

and I was so hungry I was about to eat my own arm. That curry was delicious, by the way. Thank you. And thank you for letting Amelie stay up. She loved it.'

She pulled a face. 'I wasn't sure you'd approve, but—her weekend's gone AWOL, and—you know.'

'Yeah, I know.' He turned his head and met her eyes. 'So's ours,' he said softly.

His hand found hers, and he tugged her closer, wrapping his arm around her and resting his head against hers with a quiet sigh. 'I thought by now we'd be tucked up in bed together, but it's not going to happen this weekend.'

'No,' she said, feeling a twinge of sadness. 'Still, we get this time together every night after the children are in bed.'

'Yup. I'm not sure if that's a good thing,' he said with a wry smile. 'The frustration's killing me.'

She reached up and cradled his jaw in her hand, and he turned his head and touched his lips to hers.

Not for long, because it just made the longing worse, and then he pulled away a fraction, resting his forehead against hers with a sigh.

'I wish Kath had come this weekend,' he mumbled.

'I know, but there'll be other times. It's just disappointing.'

He moved away, slumping back against the sofa with a frustrated sigh. 'Tell me about it. And if we're feeling like this, how is Amelie feeling?'

'She'll be fine. It's half-term in a week, and she'll be busy with holiday club for some of it, and then Kath's coming over on Thursday for the weekend.'

'But I'm working then, and so are you.'

'Not at night, and this won't last for ever,' she murmured. 'Your mother will be able to do more soon, so I can move home, and we'll get those weekends back.'

'Will we? Suddenly that doesn't feel like enough, and anyway, Charlie will be here, so I'll have to explain to him that I want to spend the nights with you, and that is *not* a conversation I want to have with my seventeen-year-old son.'

She winced. 'No, I can see why. We could spend the evenings together—couldn't we?' she suggested.

He rolled his head towards her, his eyes filled with frustration and a longing that made her heart tug.

'We could, but I want more than that, Em—so much more. An evening doesn't feel like nearly enough,' he said.

It didn't, but deep inside her was still that fear that it could all go wrong. It had before. Could she trust him now? Could she trust herself?

'It has to be enough, and anyway, it's not for long. Charlie won't be here for ever and then maybe...' she said, and kissed his cheek before moving away, because being so close to him was nothing short of torture. So near and yet so far...

'I think I might go to bed. I've got work in the morning and I'm tired,' she said, and he nodded.

'You do that. I'm going to ring Charlie, tell him Grandma's home. I'll see you tomorrow. Sleep well.'

He sat for a while without moving, staring at nothing, wondering where this could possibly lead them.

If anywhere. Could they make a go of it? The children seemed to get on well enough, and she'd slotted seamlessly back into his life and made him feel whole again for the first time in decades.

Yet still in the back of his mind there was that lingering doubt, the risk to the children's happiness if it all went wrong—it had before, for both of them, with two of their three marriages failing due to work pressure.

And being a consultant hadn't really changed that for him. He still had to work some weekends, some nights, and without his mother's help he would have been sunk.

So what if his mother and Douglas got married and she moved out? Where on earth would that leave him?

If it was what they wanted, he wouldn't—couldn't—contemplate standing in their way, but what if he already was? What if they'd been much more in touch than she'd let on, and they wanted to be together, but because of his situation his mother felt duty bound to stay with him and Amelie?

Of course, if he and Emily were together it wouldn't be a problem, but they weren't, and it certainly wasn't a good enough reason to escalate their relationship when neither of them were ready for it.

But if he wasn't with Em and things did get serious between his mother and Douglas, then the impact on his life would be huge.

Back to the au pair idea? A live-in housekeeper? Or go part-time and sacrifice his career?

He dropped his head back and growled with frustration. How could it *get* any more complicated?

Emily left work late on Sunday afternoon, and she found a message on her phone that made her chuckle.

Gone to the beach. Back when we've built the biggest sandcastle in the world—will take photos!

It was followed by a few photos of Amelie looking immensely proud in front of her sandcastle, and a lovely selfie of Oliver with his arm round his daughter. Lucky them. She felt a pang of envy, but it was pointless. She had to work to pay her mortgage, she knew that, but the weekends were always her least favourite shifts. Not that she had anything else to do while the children were with Steve.

Oliver's car still wasn't there when she turned onto the drive, and as she went into the hall, she could hear Elizabeth's phone ringing through the slightly open door to her annexe. She heard her say, 'Hello,' followed by a startled exclamation. 'Oh, no! Hang on—oh, I can't reach…'

Emily dumped her bag on the floor and tapped on the door. 'Elizabeth, are you all right? Anything I can do?'

'Oh, Emily, bless you,' she said, looking a bit flustered. 'I've dropped my phone under the chair and I can't get to it with this stupid, stupid arm and Oliver's not here.'

'Of course—don't move. I can reach it.'

She pulled it out, and she could hear a man's voice asking if she was still there.

'Here you go,' she said, handing it back with a smile.

'Thank you. Douglas, I'm so sorry. It's this stupid arm,' she was saying as Emily went out. She closed the annexe door behind her, but not before she heard a light-hearted laugh.

Was Oliver right? She had a feeling he might be.

And if he was, and if they got together, then where would that leave him and Amelie? She was almost certain Douglas wouldn't be happy living here in the little annexe that was Elizabeth's home, and if she wasn't here, how would Oliver cope?

What if he couldn't find a suitable replacement, someone to live in and look after them both as his mother had been doing until her accident? She was so lucky to have Steve nearby, but Oliver didn't have that luxury, with Kath in another country.

Being a single parent was a nightmare of juggling and compromise, but no matter how accommodating the other ED staff were, they had to have appropriate levels of staffing and James was struggling to provide twenty-four-seven consultant cover as it was. He often ended up doing more than his fair share, so how could Oliver cut his hours?

Unless she stayed?

No. That wasn't an option, not unless they were properly together, and there was no way she was ready for that yet, and probably not ever. She still wasn't sure she could trust him with her heart, and anyway, she was still scarred from her divorce, and so were the children, and she didn't think Oliver was ready, either—and even if he was, it certainly wasn't a good enough reason for them to take that step.

Unless she helped him on an ad hoc basis, having Amelie when he worked nights—and she was totally jumping the gun.

There was no suggestion whatsoever that Elizabeth was going to marry Douglas! Sheer speculation, and probably utterly unfounded.

And then she heard another laugh through the door, and thought maybe it wasn't unfounded. And that could have serious implications for them all.

They were almost home from the beach when a strange car pulled up on the drive. He saw Emily's children waving through the windows, and the driver got out and opened the back doors.

He walked towards him. 'You must be Steve,' he said, brushing the sand off his hand and extending his arm with a smile, and as they shook hands he met a pair of searching eyes and got the distinct feeling he was being interviewed. 'I'm—'

'Oliver!' Phoebe shrieked, getting out of the car, and she flung her arms around his legs and hugged him, and he looked down and smiled at her.

'Hi, Phoebe,' he said, ruffling her hair gently. 'Had a good time?'

'Yup. Daddy wants to meet Berry. Come on, Amelie, let's go and get her,' she said, the two girls running for the door.

He felt his mouth twitch, and met Steve's eyes again, not at all convinced it was the dog he wanted to meet. 'I think you'd better come in.'

Billy had already run inside, and he came tumbling out with Berry, who was so pleased to see the children that she hardly paid Steve any attention at all.

'Come on, you lot, inside,' he said, chivvying them all back in, then he turned back to Steve as they went through the door. 'Can I get you a drink?'

It was after nine before they got a chance to sit down, and she flopped onto her end of the sofa and put her feet on his lap.

'Oh, that's better. Steve likes you, by the way,' she added, and he turned and looked at her.

'A man of excellent taste,' he said with a lazy grin. 'I liked him, too. He's a nice guy.'

'He is. It's just a pity he didn't realize what his priorities were before he met me.'

Oliver rolled his eyes. 'Yeah, we've both got one of those. Come here, you need a cuddle.'

'I do, or you do?' she asked, trying not to smile, and he leaned over and reached for her.

'I do,' he said, his smile gentle and teasing and oh-so sexy...

She went into his arms without argument, settling down

with her head on his shoulder and wishing life wasn't so ridiculously complicated. 'So how's your weekend been?'

He laughed softly. 'Better than yours, I imagine.'

'Oh, don't. It was a madhouse and I'm only grateful I'm not doing nights. Still, just this week to go and I get five days off, and then the following weekend we can be together again.' Unless… 'What will you do if Kath doesn't come?'

He shook his head. 'She has to come, and if she doesn't Amelie's already booked in for holiday club, so she could just spend the whole week there.'

'Or she can come to me midweek and you can keep holiday club in reserve for the weekend?'

He shook his head. 'No. She has to be here, and anyway, you do too much for us already. You need time with your kids on your own, Emily. They can't get too used to this. I know it's short-term, but they're all getting closer, and…'

They were. She nodded slowly. 'I know. I agree,' she told him. 'And actually, I think your mother can manage to dress and undress herself just about now, and she even managed a shower this morning with her arm in a bag, so if you're OK with it, I was thinking I could take the children to my parents for the weekend, because we haven't seen them for ages.'

He turned his face towards her and dropped a kiss on her hair. 'Good idea,' he murmured, but she could tell that, like her, none of this was what he really wanted.

But what they wanted wasn't necessarily what they could have, and at least they both realized that. Not that it made it any easier…

'That was a bit close to home.'

Emily looked up and searched his eyes as they walked out of Resus on Friday. He'd come in to join her in a futile attempt to save the life of a patient who'd suffered a massive heart attack, and his widow was in there now, saying a heartbroken goodbye to the man she'd loved for very many years, stricken with grief and shocked to the core because he had no history of any previous heart problems. Just like Oliver's father…

'I'm sure it was. Are you OK?'

'Yeah, I'm fine. It is what it is and we can't save them all. I've spoken to Kath, by the way. She's coming with Hans and they want to stay in a hotel.'

She stared at him in astonishment. 'Well, how does that work?'

'It doesn't, for us. They'll have to get up early so they're at mine by six, and stay with her till I'm home, but that'll only cover my working hours. I'll talk to her, see if I can change her mind, but she said she had something important to tell me, and she sounded—I don't know. Different. Happier, maybe, so I don't know what that's about.'

'Do you think they're getting married?'

'I have no idea, but if she won't bend that means yet again we lose our weekend nights together, and then Charlie comes. It's going to be ages before we get another chance and the frustration is killing me.'

He looked up at the board to see who was waiting, but it was looking reasonable. 'Coffee while the going's good?' he suggested, and then they heard the red phone ring and he rolled his eyes.

'Oh, now, why did you say that?' she murmured, and as the person who'd answered the phone put a call out on the Tannoy, she went back into Resus with Oliver.

A nurse was leading the sobbing woman out to the family room to make her a drink while her husband's body was moved, and Oliver watched them go, his face drawn.

'Can you handle this next case? I might go and talk to her.'

'Do you need to?'

'Yes, because I understand,' he said quietly. 'Unless you need me?'

She shook her head. 'No, I'll be fine. You do that. I can always call someone else. Just—be kind to yourself.'

His smile wrenched at her heart, but she let him go and made herself focus on the next patient, but at the back of her mind was the perennial threat to their time alone together.

How on earth could they make this work? Because from where she was standing, it didn't look like they could.

By the time he got home, Emily was ready to leave. Their stuff was packed in the car, and she'd remade the beds in case Kath had a change of heart.

'Everything OK?' she asked, and he nodded.

'Ish. Can we have a word while the children are outside?'

'Sure. What's up? Has she backed out again?'

'No, she won't back down about Hans coming and they won't stay here, even though I've offered. They'll be here every morning at six and they won't leave until I'm home, but—well, you know what it means. I'm so sorry.'

She closed her eyes and turned away, swallowing her disappointment.

'So that's that, then. You'll be here, not at mine.'

'You could be here, too.'

'No. Not with your mother here, not with Amelie here. We can't. You know that. It has to be at mine or not at all, and it's looking like not at all.'

She turned to face him, and his eyes were filled with an emotion she didn't want to analyse.

'I'm so sorry.'

'Don't be. I was half expecting it.'

'There'll be other times.'

'Maybe,' she said, not sure she could see how, and went out into the garden to call the children in.

'Do we have to go to Grandma and Grandad?' Billy asked. 'It's such a long way.'

'I know, but they're expecting us and it'll be lovely to see them. Come on. Say goodbye to Amelie and let's go.'

She met Oliver's eyes, and after a moment he looked away.

'Have a good time,' he said to the children, and then looked back at her and mouthed, 'I'm sorry.'

So was she, but there wasn't a thing either of them could do about it.

Kath and Hans arrived promptly at six on Thursday morning, just as he'd put some coffee on, and while it brewed they talked for a few minutes, which gave Kath just enough time to drop a couple of bombshells on him before they heard the sound of running feet.

'Daddy? Daddy, what time's Mummy coming...? Mummy!'

She threw herself at her mother, and Kath stooped down and hugged her hard, tears in her eyes.

'Hello, darling. Oh, I've missed you. Goodness, you've grown!'

Oliver turned away, glad they'd got to this point, sad that it had taken so long to reach it, but at least they were there now, and that, and Amelie, were all that mattered.

So he couldn't stay with Emily this weekend. Tough— and it was tough, but it was the least of his worries and this was hugely important news.

'So, who wants breakfast?' he asked.

'Me, me, me!' Amelie squealed, and he laughed and hugged her.

'Apart from you,' he said, and reached for the coffee.

Maybe it wouldn't be so bad after all...

CHAPTER NINE

IT WAS LATE on Thursday morning before she saw him again after her days off.

She'd arrived to find the department in uproar, and it was gone eleven before she'd dealt with the backlog in the cubicles.

She went to look for Oliver, and found him hunched over a computer in Resus.

She walked over to him with a smile. 'Hello, stranger. How's it going?'

He looked up from the computer and gave her a rueful smile. 'Hi. Sorry, really busy morning. I haven't had a second to call you. You OK?'

'Yes, fine. I've been really busy, too, but it's all suspiciously under control now, though, so I'm sort of waiting for the other shoe to drop.'

'Half-term. They're all on the beach having fun by now.'

'So they'll all be in with sunburn later. Fabulous.'

'Indeed. Look, I'm just finishing up these notes, and then I'm heading for a coffee. Got time to join me? I've got lots to tell you.'

'Absolutely! We might as well make the best of it while the going's good.'

'Tell me about it. Right, I'm done. Let's get out of here.' He pressed Save and they headed briskly for the café.

'So, spill the beans. Did Kath and Hans turn up on time? What's he like?' she asked him as they walked, and he laughed softly.

'I don't know. First impressions are good, but it's early days. He doesn't have children and he said he's always wanted them.'

She frowned. 'I hope that isn't the attraction.'

Oliver shook his head. 'I don't think it is. He told me he and his wife were never blessed with them—his words— and she died, and he's been alone ever since. He seems a very gentle person. He was lovely with Amelie, not at all pushy, and he didn't talk down to her, which I liked. Which is just as well, as he's going to be her stepfather. They're getting married.'

'Wow. OK. Did you know that?'

'Nope. And—wait for this—she's resigned.'

'To what?'

'Not to—from. Her job.'

She felt her eyes widen. 'Really? That's the last thing I expected!'

'Me, too. I was stunned. I don't know if it was because of what I said last time, or if it's been brewing a while, but she just lost it with them, by the sound of it. Anyway, she wants to see more of her daughter, and Amelie is over the moon.'

Emily felt her eyes fill with tears. 'Oh, that's lovely for her. For all of them, really. You must be so relieved.'

'I am. I can't tell you how much,' he said, and stopped at the counter. 'Right, what are you having?'

They picked up a sandwich to share, ordered their coffees and headed out into the park again. The benches were all full, but they found a free bistro table and sat down, his knees nudging hers, and he met her eyes, a sad smile playing round his lips.

'I'm sorry about our plans being trashed again,' he said softly. 'I'm really glad Kath's here and she's happy at last, but I just wish…'

She tried to smile back, but it was pointless. 'Me, too, but it is what it is and it's not for ever.'

'Thankfully not. So how are you doing?'

'Oh, OK, I suppose. It's always a bit flat without the children, but at least they're only ten miles away having fun with their stepbrothers, unlike Charlie. I know he's coming over now, but most of the time he's in America, and I don't know how either of you cope with that.'

That sad smile again. 'Not well, to be honest, and I can't wait to hug him again. It's been so long, literally a year since we spent any appreciable length of time together, and I miss him so much.'

'So what will you do with him while he's here?'

'As much as I can. I've taken a lot of time off, but I need holiday time for Amelie and I can't afford to use it all and he's here three weeks. I can't do that.'

She laughed softly. 'Yes, I know how that goes. It's a constant juggling act when you're a single parent.'

'Well, hopefully it'll be better now with Kath doing a bit more of the heavy lifting, but we'll see how that goes, too. And for some of the time he's going to have to amuse himself, but that's fine. He says he wants to take a look at Cambridge, and he's thinking of applying for medicine there.'

She felt her eyes widen. 'He's going into medicine? Is he a masochist?'

He laughed. 'I know, I know. I've tried to talk him out of it, but I'm a doctor, my father was a doctor, so was his father—as my grandmother would have said, it runs in the blood.'

That made her laugh, but it was a laugh tinged with

sadness, because it was another three weeks where she'd hardly see him, and it was beginning to dawn on her just how deeply she was getting into this.

Not that she begrudged him that time with his son, it must be so precious, but it was becoming clearer by the day that their relationship as it was was unsustainable, and she couldn't see a way round it to save her life.

Two days in, and this was killing him.

Seeing Emily every day at work just ramped up the frustration, and if Kath had been at his, they could have been together every night. Just one evening would have been good, but they couldn't even do that, because his mother had decided to keep out of their way and had gone back to Catherine's until Sunday, so she couldn't babysit.

He drove home, went in and found Kath and Hans in the sitting room, with Amelie snuggled up between them in pyjamas and reading them a story.

She broke off, looked up and said, 'Daddy, sit down. I'm reading a story to you all.'

So he sat, and he listened as she stumbled through it with a tiny bit of prompting from Hans, and then she said, 'The end!' and shut the book, ran over to him and climbed onto his lap. 'Did you have a good day?' she asked, giving him a toothpasty kiss, and he smiled and hugged her.

'Yes, thank you. I had a very good day,' he lied. 'How was your day?'

'Brilliant! We went to a museum and saw all sorts of things, like dinosaur teeth and some bones, and when I grow up, I want to be a arkelol…'

'Archaeologist?' he offered, trying to keep a straight face, and she beamed.

'Yes! An arkelologist, and then I can dig up dinosaur bones and all sorts of stuff from gazillions of years ago!'

His face cracked into a smile, and he hugged her again, happy that she was happy, and that for now was enough. 'That sounds like a great thing to do. Right, I think it's probably bedtime now. Who do you want to put you to bed?'

'Mummy,' she said promptly, and wriggled off his lap and ran back to her, pulling her to her feet. 'Come on. You can read me another story.'

It was half an hour before Kath came down, and he spent it in the kitchen propped up against the worktop, getting to know—and like—the man who was going to be a key part of Amelie's life.

Then Kath walked in, and Oliver saw the warmth light their eyes as they smiled at each other, and he felt a pang of envy that they had that freedom. Unless...

'Amelie would like you to say goodnight,' she told him, and he nodded.

'OK.' He hesitated, then said, 'I don't suppose you'd be able to babysit tomorrow night, would you? Just for a few hours after I finish work?'

Kath's face fell. 'Oh, Oliver, I'm sorry, we can't. We've booked tickets for a late show at the theatre. We aren't busy tonight, though, but I don't suppose that's any good, is it?'

Would Emily be doing anything? He didn't think so. She'd probably be in the bath, if he knew her, or curled up on the sofa reading a book.

'It could be. Have you eaten? There's stuff in the fridge if not, or you could order a takeaway? I'll happily pay for it—'

'Don't be ridiculous.'

'Right, give me five minutes to check and to say good-night to Amelie, and I'll let you know.'

He went upstairs, messaging Emily as he went, and by the time he reached Amelie's door his phone had pinged.

In the bath. Come on over, I'll get out now. Have you eaten?

No.

OK. I'll get you something.

Yes! He punched the air, his face split by a smile of joy and relief, and went to say goodnight to his daughter.

By the time he arrived, the door was on the latch and she was in the kitchen in a silky robe, stirring something on the hob. He toed off his shoes and walked up behind her, slid his arms round her waist and buried his face in the side of her neck with a contented sigh.

'Hello, you,' he mumbled, and she turned in his arms, looked up at him and smiled.

'Hello, you.'

He lowered his head and kissed her smile. 'You smell amazing,' he murmured, and then looked over her shoulder. 'What are you cooking?'

'Beans on toast. I don't really have anything else. Sorry.'

'Don't worry, that'll be fine. Anything I can do?'

'Pour us a glass of wine and talk to me,' she instructed, and he opened the bottle and told her about Amelie wanting to be an archaeologist.

'Well, this week, anyway. Last week she wanted to be a vet, and before that she was going to be an astronaut.'

'Coming down to earth, then, bit by bit,' she said with

a grin, and he laughed. She slathered butter on his toast, poured the beans over and picked up the plate. 'Bring my wine,' she said, and headed for the dining table, and he followed her, still smiling.

'So, how long have we got?' she asked as he ate, and he shrugged.

'I said I'd be back by eleven. It's not long enough, but it's better than nothing and I just wanted to see you.' He scraped up the last mouthful, pushed his plate away and met her smiling eyes.

'We'd better not waste it, then,' she said softly, pulling him to his feet, and he followed her up to her room, his heart pounding.

She turned to face him, and he bent his head and kissed her while his hands found the tie on her robe and tugged it free. She was naked underneath, and he slid his hands inside, her skin warm under his fingers, nipples pebbling against his palms as he cradled her breasts, and he sighed into her mouth.

'Oh, you feel so good,' he mumbled, and moved on, laying kisses down over her throat, pausing over the beating pulse, then on down, over her collarbone, the slope of her right breast, the tautness of the nipple firm against his lips as he closed them round it and suckled deeply.

She moaned and arched against him, and he straightened, sliding the gown over her shoulders and staring down at her body, tracing it with a quivering fingertip.

She sucked in a shaky breath, and his control splintered.

Taking a step back he ripped off his T-shirt, shucking his jeans and underwear, kicking off his shoes as they fell into bed.

There was no need for foreplay, no time for finesse, no time for anything until he was buried inside her, her warmth around him, her body soft and yet firm against his, and then he slowed.

His mouth found hers again, tenderly now, sipping, searching, their bodies in tune as he slowly upped the pace, taking her with him every step of the way.

And when it was over, when their hearts had slowed and their bodies cooled, he lay and held her in his arms and treasured every fleeting moment until he had to leave her...

They both worked on Saturday, but he wasn't there on Sunday because Kath and Hans were leaving, and it felt odd without him. She worked until four, went home and packed up their stuff, ready to go back to Oliver's for the coming week, but her heart was heavy.

Just five more nights, then Charlie would arrive, and she and the children would be back here at home for three weeks, and because Oliver would be off for much of it, she'd hardly see him.

And that mattered more than it should have done. More than she should have let it. He was getting under her skin, filling her thoughts, her mind, her heart—and her body ached for him. So much for compartments.

She put it out of her mind, loaded the car and drove to Oliver's house. Steve was taking the children straight there, and of course after they'd arrived and rushed in to see Amelie and Berry, Billy wanted something from their house.

'I need the chess set. Daddy's been teaching me to play chess, and I want to practise.'

'Oh, darling, you should have told me. I would have brought it. I'll get it tomorrow.'

'I've got a chess set,' Oliver volunteered, and Billy's eyes lit up.

'Really? Do you know how to play?'

'Yes. Well, I used to. I haven't played for ages.'

'Cool. I might beat you.'

To his credit Oliver kept a straight face, and nodded. 'You might,' he said, and met her eyes. 'Do you need a hand unloading the car?'

'That would be great. Why don't you all go in the garden with Berry while we do that?' she suggested, and the children ran out, leaving them alone.

They went out, and she looked across at him as he picked up their bags from the boot. 'How was Amelie when they left?'

He shrugged. 'A bit tearful, but she's been a lot happier this week, which is great. And next time, because Charlie's going to be here, they're just coming for the weekend and they'll take her out for days and bring her back.'

'And your mother?'

'She's home. Douglas brought her back.'

She studied his face. 'And?'

'Well, they were very circumspect, but there was a definite something going on. A sort of unspoken affection—but, you know, they've been friends for decades, and I'm probably just finding things that aren't there. So is that everything?'

'Yes, I think so,' she said, but his words were echoing in her head.

An unspoken affection.

Did people see that in them when she and Oliver looked at each other?

Did the children see it? This love between them that neither of them seemed able to acknowledge?

How long could they keep it up before it broke them? Because it felt like living in a house of cards, and the slightest breath of wind would bring it all crashing down around them.

* * *

They spent every evening together as a family, him, her, his mother and all the children, and every day was just bitter-sweet.

He came home every evening just after seven, and sometimes the children were still playing in the garden, busying themselves in the den or just running about giggling and letting off steam, and he'd grab them and scoop them up and hug them, sometimes ending up with all three at once, and the shrieks and giggles broke her heart.

He loved them all, and they loved him, but they were going nowhere, and it was tearing her in two.

They ended up together on the sofa every night after the children were in bed, and although she tried to keep her distance, it was difficult. Easier if Berry was lying in between them, but mostly she wasn't, and he'd hold out his arm and beckon her, and she'd end up snuggled against his side.

By the end of Thursday, she'd reached breaking-point. Oliver was heading to the airport in the morning, leaving at eight, so she did the Friday morning school run for them all as normal and went to work, then picked the children up and took them back to his to round up all their possessions.

The children ran in, and she found them all in the garden—Oliver, his mother and a young man almost the spitting image of his father when she'd met him.

Amelie was in her big brother's arms, her legs wrapped tightly round his waist, and he was laughing down at his little sister. And then he looked up and saw her crossing the lawn towards them, and he smiled his father's smile and her heart cracked in two.

'Hi. You must be Charlie,' she said, digging out a smile from somewhere, and he freed a hand and held it out to her.

'And you must be Emily,' he said, his eyes searching hers

as her hand was engulfed in a warm, confident grip. 'It's good to meet you. I've heard a lot about you.'

'All good, I hope,' she said lightly, and turned away, swamped with all sorts of might-have-beens. 'Billy, Phoebe, I'm just going to pack your stuff and then we're going home, OK?'

'Oh, Mummy, do we have to?' Phoebe asked, and Amelie said, 'Don't go! Why do you have to go? Charlie won't mind if you stay for the weekend.'

'But Charlie needs his room,' she pointed out, 'and anyway, we don't live here, sweetheart.'

'But we sort of do,' Billy said, pleading, and she looked helplessly at Oliver.

'I'm going to pack. Maybe Oliver will get you all a drink while I do that.'

She headed back inside, blinking away tears, and ran upstairs to the room she'd been sleeping in. She'd packed her own things that morning before the children were up, and changed the sheets ready for Charlie, but the children's room was in chaos because Billy had unpacked his bag to find a different T-shirt before school, and half of Phoebe's things were missing. Hiding under the bed?

She had no idea, but she rounded up what she could, suddenly desperate to get away. Elizabeth didn't need her help with washing and dressing any more, and she really didn't know why she was still there. Maybe it was time to leave for good?

She was on her hands and knees on the bedroom floor when she heard his footsteps approaching.

'Lost something?'

My common sense? My heart...?

She got to her feet and stuffed the few things she'd found into Phoebe's bag. 'All sorts of somethings, but I dare say they'll turn up. I've stripped their beds, Charlie's room is ready for him, so I'm just going to head—'

'You don't have to, Emily. You could stay and eat with us, at least.'

She shook her head. 'No. Charlie's had a long day, and he'll need to rest, and I need to get the children settled back in.'

'Sunday, then. Come in time for supper. We can eat at five, if you like?'

She looked at him, then away again, her mind made up.

'No. I don't think so,' she said quietly, and then made herself look back at him. 'You've got Charlie here now. You don't need me. Your mother's much better, she doesn't need my help with personal care now, and really, Amelie can get herself up and dressed quite easily, and your mother can walk her to school and back, and you can cook when you get home. If you batch cook while Charlie's here, you can freeze stuff so all you have to do is reheat it, and your mother can manage something simple for Amelie. You don't need me here any longer, Oliver. Not in any way.'

His face was confused, his eyes puzzled and hurt. 'That's not true. You know that's not true.' He reached out a hand and touched her cheek, and she flinched.

'Don't,' she said, and her voice cracked, and his face swam in front of her eyes.

'Em, what's going on? I don't understand.'

'Yes, you do. Us staying here was never supposed to be a long-term arrangement, and I don't think we should be seeing each other when Kath's here, either. It just makes it harder for us both and I can't do it any more.'

'No. No, Emily, don't do this to us, please.' His voice was raw with emotion, but she shook her head.

'I have to. The children are getting too deeply into this.

You heard them! And this situation with us, it's too fragile, too uncertain. I can't do it. I'm not ready, and neither are you, and in the meantime they're just getting in deeper and deeper, and so are we.'

She turned and met his eyes again, and they were filled with pain.

'We can do this, if we want it enough,' he said, but she shook her head, trying hard to stay strong, so near to weakening.

'No. No, we can't. We can't keep this in a compartment while I'm living with you, it's just not possible, and what we have outside of that isn't enough. It needs to be all or nothing, and it can't be all. There's too much at stake, and not just for us. We can't put the children through that again if it goes wrong.'

He reached out and wiped away her tears, his fingers infinitely gentle. 'We're older now, we know ourselves better, we know what matters. Why should it go wrong?'

'Because we're both rubbish at marriage, and the children don't deserve to be hurt again.' She stepped back, out of reach of that tender hand that she so wanted to lean into. 'Please, don't argue with me, Oliver. It's better this way.'

'Is it? It doesn't feel better. Not in any way,' he said gruffly, and he turned and walked away.

He watched them go, taking a huge chunk of his heart with them, and as he walked past the sitting room, he saw the chess set sitting on the side table, waiting for Billy's next move.

He walked over to it and stared down at the pieces. Billy was one move away from checkmate, but the boy hadn't realized.

He hadn't got the heart to put it away. He blinked hard

and straightened up, and saw himself in the mirror above, his face raw with emotion.

Pull yourself together.

He sucked in a huge breath, let it out slowly and went back out into the garden to his family, but even though Charlie was there, he still felt that half his family was missing.

She held it together until she got into bed that night, but she hadn't changed the sheets since Oliver had been the week before, and she could still smell the faint, lingering scent of his cologne on the pillow.

Oh, Oliver...

She rolled her face into it and shed a river of silent tears for all they'd lost and all that might have been.

The next day was glorious, and the children wanted to go to the beach.

'I need to do a food order for tomorrow,' she said, but they begged and pleaded, so she scrabbled together a list for delivery the next morning, packed up the buckets and spades, the sun cream, the windbreak, the towels and spare clothes, and they set off for the short walk to the beach.

'Can we have an ice cream?' Billy asked, ever hungry, so she put everything down, dug out her card, paid for them, and they headed off again, with Billy in charge of hers as well as his.

They found a space on the beach, and she rescued what was left of her ice cream from her mischievous son and they sat down on the sand and ate them while she stared out over the sea and wondered how long it would take for the pain to go away.

For ever, she realized. It hadn't ever really gone from losing him the first time, and this time, somehow, felt even worse. Why had she let him back into her heart? Such a stupid thing to do—

'Are you all right, Mummy?'

She blinked hastily and smiled at Phoebe. 'Yes, darling, I'm fine. I've just got sun cream in my eye. Here, have a wet wipe. You've got ice cream all down your chin. Now, what about this sandcastle?'

'There's Billy and Phoebe!'

Damn. He might have known they'd be here today.

'Amelie, come back,' he called, but she was gone, running over the sand to join them.

'They're pretty tight, those kids,' Charlie said, giving him a look, and he let out a short, slightly broken sigh.

'Yes, they are. They've spent a lot of time together at ours because of Grandma, and they're at the same school, so they're bound to be close.'

'Hmm. Pity about you and Emily.'

'What about me and Emily?' he asked, trying to sound casual and wondering where on earth that had come from, but Charlie just raised an eyebrow.

'Uh—I do know about these things, Dad? I'm not a kid any more. And anyway, that's not what Grandma says. She agrees with me. She thinks it's a real shame she's gone.'

Damn. He looked away. 'You're all imagining it. There's nothing going on.' Not any more…

'So why do you look like someone's stolen your puppy?'

He ignored that and looked across at his daughter. 'I suppose we ought to go over there and retrieve her.'

'Well, good luck with that,' Charlie said with a wry laugh, because they were all down by the water's edge now, paddling ankle-deep as they scooped up water in buckets to bring back to the sandcastle moat that Emily was digging out a little farther up the beach.

As they headed towards her, she turned and glanced at them before looking away.

'Gorgeous day,' she said lightly, and carried on digging.

So they were down to talking about the weather. He would have laughed if he hadn't wanted to scream and cry.

'Need a hand?' he asked, and she started to say something when suddenly Charlie grabbed him.

'Billy's gone over in the water,' he said, and without thinking Oliver started to run.

'Where is he?'

'To your right—there.'

He saw a hand, way out, farther out than he'd imagined, and he kicked off his shoes and ran headlong into the surf, his heart in his mouth. He looked frantically around, but the hand was gone and there was no sign of him.

Please, no...

'Billy?' he yelled, ploughing through the waves, and as another one lifted and fell, he saw him briefly, but the beach was shelving sharply and he was suddenly out of his depth.

'Billy, I'm coming,' he yelled, powering through the surf, and then he was there, grabbing Billy by the arm and hauling him up out of the water against his chest.

'It's OK, Billy, I've got you,' he said, and as his feet found the bottom again and he stood up, the boy wrapped his arms and legs tightly round him and clung on.

He could feel the boy's chest heaving under his hand, but he had a horrible feeling he wasn't taking in any air.

Laryngospasm? It wasn't uncommon in drowning accidents, and if that was it, it would be short-lived. Please, God...

'Hey, Billy, it's OK. Just relax. You're safe now. It's all over,' he said, his voice soothing.

He waded out of the water, and as he reached Emily, he

felt Billy suck in a huge lungful of air, and then he started to sob.

She plucked him out of Oliver's arms and sank down onto the wet sand with him, clinging to him and sobbing with relief, and Charlie came up to his father and put his arms round him and hugged him.

'Well done, Dad. That was pretty cool. I thought he was gone.'

He nodded. 'Yes, me, too, but it was your quick reaction that saved him. If you hadn't seen him...'

He hugged Charlie hard, then dropped down onto his knees by Emily, stroking a hand over Billy's sodden hair.

'Hey, little guy. How are you doing? You OK now?'

He nodded, his chest still heaving a bit but with sobs now, he thought.

Emily looked up at him, her eyes flooded with tears. 'I don't know how to thank you. I wasn't watching—'

'That was my fault. Charlie saw him. I wasn't watching, either. He had a bit of laryngospasm as I pulled him out, but I think he's OK now. Might be an idea to check him over.'

She nodded, burying her face in his skinny little shoulder and hugging him with a fierce tenderness that brought tears to Oliver's eyes.

If he hadn't found him under the water...

CHAPTER TEN

OLIVER HELPED HER to her feet, and they retreated to the prom and sat down on the edge of it, and he laid his ear against Billy's back and listened.

'It sounds OK. I think he might have got away with it. I need a stethoscope, really.'

She nodded. 'I've got one at home. I'll check him. Where's Phoebe?' she asked, her heart still racing, but she was just there, standing a few feet away with Amelie, and Charlie was squatting down, his arms around their shoulders, talking to them quietly. Reassuring them?

'Oh, Charlie,' she said, her eyes filling with tears again. 'Thank you so much. If you hadn't seen him...'

He shook his head, dismissing her thanks with a wave of his hand. 'Is he OK?'

'I think so, thanks to you and your father.' She looked up at Oliver. 'I need to take him home.'

'Yes, you probably do. Give me ten minutes. I'll go home and change and bring the car for you. Charlie, are you OK to stay with them all?'

He nodded. 'Sure. Here, I brought your shoes.'

He wasn't gone long, and by the time he got back the children were building the sandcastle again with Charlie's help, and Billy seemed fine.

She wasn't, far from it, but she wasn't surprised. She'd come so close to losing him…

Oliver had brought a stethoscope back with him, and he listened to Billy's chest all over, front and back.

'Is it OK?' she asked, and he nodded and handed the stethoscope to her as if he understood, and she checked him, too, just to reassure herself, knowing he would have done the same.

'Do you still want to go home?' he asked as Billy went back to his sandcastle, but she shook her head, the fear receding now Oliver was back and she knew Billy's chest was clear.

'No. I don't think so. He was scared, but he seems fine now and I don't really want to make it more than it was. But—could I hang on to this?' she asked, holding the stethoscope. 'Just in case?'

'Sure. If he's OK for the next hour or so and doesn't deteriorate, he's fine, but feel free to check if it reassures you.'

She smiled, but it was a feeble effort and her lips wobbled a bit. She firmed them and looked away, and he sat down next to her.

'Do you want me to stay?'

Yes, for ever…

'Do you think you need to?'

'Not for Billy, no. I think he's going to be fine, but you've had a heck of a scare.'

'I'm fine,' she lied. 'And actually, do you know what, it's getting really hot now. I might just take them home. Did you bring the car?'

He left Charlie to take Amelie home while he dropped Emily and the children off at her house, but he didn't go in. He hadn't been invited, for a start, and in any case there was an awkwardness between them that hadn't been there before she'd packed up and left him. No, not him, but his house. Subtle distinction that was pretty much lost on him.

He drove home, and by the time he got there Charlie and Amelie were back, telling his mother all about it.

She looked up at him, her eyes concerned.

'Is he all right?'

He nodded. 'Yes, he's fine.'

'And Emily?'

He looked away. 'She'll be OK. It was a bit of a shock.'

'Does she need you there?'

'No. She's got my number, and I'm sure she'll be keeping a very close eye on him.'

'It wasn't him I was worried about,' his mother said pointedly, but he wasn't prepared to get into this discussion again. It was none of their business and there was nothing he could do to change her mind.

'I'm going for a shower,' he said, and left them to it.

He was standing at the kitchen window, watching the last dying moments of the day when Charlie walked in and perched on a stool, his eyes thoughtful.

'You OK, Dad?'

'Yeah, I'm fine.'

'Are you really? You don't look it from where I'm sitting.'

He swallowed. 'I keep thinking about Billy,' he admitted gruffly. 'If you hadn't seen him get swept out—'

Charlie eyed him steadily. 'You love them, don't you? All of them.'

He looked away, and after a moment Charlie broke the stretching silence.

'I'll take that as a yes, then.'

He looked back at his son, wise beyond his years. 'It's…'

'Don't tell me it's complicated, Dad. It's always complicated. That's what we do, we complicate things, but really, it's simple. You love her, she loves you—what's holding you back?'

'We have—history.'

'I know that. Mom told me. She said you'd never stopped loving Emily, that that was part of what was wrong with your and Mom's relationship, and I guess it was part of what was wrong with you and Kath, too. Neither of them were Emily, and it's Emily that you love, that you've always loved. You and she were meant to be together.'

They were. Had Sue known that? Maybe. Not that it would have made any difference to their relationship ultimately, or to his and Kath's, because Charlie was right—it was Emily he wanted, Emily he loved.

'She doesn't trust me,' he said after an age. 'She daren't. I let her down before—which is how come you're here. And she daren't trust me or anyone else not to let her down again. It wasn't just me. Her husband left her, too, and went back to his first wife.'

'The woman he truly loved, I guess. Just like you love Emily. Go and tell her, Dad. Tell her you love her. Tell her you've always loved her.'

He had, but it had taken until now to realize it, even though it was staring him in the face. Was it really that simple? Maybe.

'If it helps, Grandma thinks you two should be together.'

He shot Charlie a keen look. 'How come you and Grandma think it's OK to discuss my private life?'

Charlie laughed, his eyes crinkling with affectionate amusement. 'What private life? You live in a family, Dad. You don't have a private life. Go. Go now, go and see her, tell her you love her, ask her to be with you. Give yourselves a chance.'

Could he? Did he dare lay his heart on the line?

'What if she says no?'

'What if she says yes? What if she *would* have said yes, but you never asked?'

He couldn't argue with that. Didn't want to. He shrugged away from the worktop, and Charlie slid off the stool and hugged him hard.

'Good luck. And don't hurry home. Amelie will be fine with me and Grandma. She loves Emily.'

'How do you know that?'

He smiled. 'Because she told me? She wants Emily to be her stepmother. And frankly, so do I.'

He blinked away sudden tears and gave Charlie a fierce hug. 'You'd better be right.'

'I'm always right. I love you. Now go.'

He walked round to her house, partly because it would give him time to think, and partly because if her lights were out he'd leave her in peace.

They weren't. There was a faint glow through her bedroom curtains, and the landing light was on. Was Billy in with her?

The downstairs was in darkness, and for an endless moment he hesitated, then he sent her a message.

Can I come in and talk to you?

She didn't respond at first, and he stood there on her drive, staring up at her bedroom window and feeling like a fool.

Of course she didn't want to talk to him. She'd made that quite clear—

Where are you?

Outside.

He saw the hall light come on, and the front door opened. She was wearing that silky robe again, her hair like a messy halo with the light behind her, and she sat on the step and waited as he walked towards her.

'How's Billy?'

'He's fine. You were right, it was just a temporary spasm, but he's been OK all day. He's asleep now.'

'And you?'

She stared at him, then looked away. 'I'm OK,' she said, but her voice was choked and he could tell she wasn't.

He went over to her and sat down, nudging her gently out of the way. 'He's OK, Em. It's all right.'

'I thought he was gone,' she said, her voice cracking, and he slid an arm around her shoulders and hugged her against his side.

'So did I.' He lifted a hand and wiped the tears off her cheeks, but she turned her head into his shoulder with a little sob, and he wrapped his arms around her and held her as she cried the tears that had been pending for hours.

'I don't know how to thank you. I owe you so much. You saved his life,' she said brokenly, and he shook his head.

'You don't owe me anything. And anyway, it wasn't just me. Charlie saw him first, and there were dozens of people on the beach. Other people ran into the water.'

'But it was you who found him, you who saved him, you who knew how to calm him when he was terrified.' She looked up at him. 'And you're here now, just when I needed you. Maybe we should get married.'

'What, just because I rescued Billy? That's not a good enough reason, Emily, not when you still don't trust me.'

She shuffled away a fraction, and swiped the tears off her cheeks before she looked up at him searchingly.

'Why are you here, Oliver?'

Why, indeed. He took a slow breath, and let it out again. 'Because I knew you needed me, and I love you. I've always loved you, and I've never stopped loving you, and I never will.'

Her face contorted and she looked away, her chest heaving as she sucked in a breath. 'You don't know that.'

'I know I'll love you till the day I die,' he said honestly. 'Look me in the eye and tell me you don't love me.'

She slowly turned her head to look at him, and in the light from the hall he could see tears glistening in her eyes.

'I can't.'

'Can't what? Can't love me? Or can't tell me that you love me?'

She gave a shaky sigh. 'I've always loved you, Oliver, and I've never dared to let myself love anyone again, not really, but you're right, I daren't trust you. It didn't work last time, and what if it goes wrong again? What if I move in with you properly and it all falls apart?'

'Why would it? Unless we neglect it. All marriages, all relationships take work. My parents used to argue all the time, but they always worked through it, and they loved each other to the end.'

He took her hand and pressed a kiss to her cold, lifeless fingers. 'I love you, Emily, and I want to be with you for the rest of my life. Don't do this to us. Give us a chance, please.'

'And what if it goes wrong? What if the children fall out?'

'Children always fall out, but they get over it. You know that. It's all part of growing up. And you saw them yesterday. They didn't want to go, and Amelie didn't want you to go. And today, Amelie was so excited to see them on the beach, and so worried about Billy. I was, too. That's why I came here tonight, because he's all I've been able to think about all day. I love him. Emily. I love you all, and we need to be together, for all our sakes.'

He did love them all.

She knew that, deep down in her heart. He'd been wonderful with the children, and they'd loved being a part of his family. Was she just being a coward?

'I'm scared,' she said, her voice a little unsteady. 'I'm scared to love you. It means too much, and if I let it in, and it goes away again—'

'It won't. I won't. I'll never leave you. I know you don't feel you can trust me, but I'd rather cut my own heart out than leave you ever again. Marry me, Emily. Come back to me. I need you. We all need you. Please, give me another chance. Give us a chance.'

She searched his eyes, raw with emotion, filled with sincerity, gleaming with unshed tears.

One slipped down his cheek, and she reached out a finger and wiped it gently away.

I'd rather cut my own heart out than leave you ever again...

'Are you sure?'

He laughed, but it cracked in the middle. 'Yes, I'm sure. I've never been more sure of anything in my life. And yes, it's complicated, yes, it might be tricky from time to time, yes, it'll be a juggling act, but there'll be two of us to catch it if we drop the ball, and we can do this. We can do it together, if you can find the courage to believe in us.'

She held her breath for an age, then let it out and smiled at him as the tears started to spill down her cheeks. 'Yes,' she said, and then just to be sure, she said it again.

'Yes, yes, I love you. Yes, I'll marry you. And please don't cut your heart out. That would be so messy.'

He gave a choked laugh and pulled her into his arms, and they clung to each other for the longest time. And then he let her go and reached into the pocket of his jeans, pulling out something small.

'I don't know if this'll still fit you. I bought it before I went to America, but I never got a chance to give it to you.'

He held it out to her on the palm of his hand, a simple gold ring with a little row of diamonds, and she picked it up and stared down at it, her eyes welling with tears. The diamonds sparkled as they caught the light, and she handed it to him and held out her ring finger.

'Only one way to find out,' she said with a smile, and he slid it onto her finger. She stared at it through the mist of tears. 'I can't believe you've had it all this time.'

He smiled ruefully. 'I couldn't bring myself to get rid of it. Maybe I just never gave up hope. I'll get you a better one.'

'No. I don't want a better one, I want this one, because it has far more meaning than a new one could ever have.'

She swallowed the sudden lump in her throat and, lifting her head, she leaned across and kissed him fleetingly, then stood up and pulled him to his feet.

'Come to bed, my love,' she murmured, and he followed her in through the door.

He sent Charlie a text at six the next morning, and a moment later he got a rude but heartfelt reply that made him laugh.

Emily looked at him sleepily. 'What is it?'

'Charlie. I think he's happy for us,' he said, his arm round her and her head resting on his shoulder. 'We need to go and see them.'

'We do,' she said. 'How will Amelie be? Do you need to talk to her before we tell mine?'

He laughed. 'I don't think so. She told Charlie she wants you to be her stepmother.'

Her eyes widened, and a slow smile bloomed on her face. 'Really?'

'Really. Did you sleep?'

'Off and on. I checked on Billy a few times.'

'I thought you did—ah, I can hear the children. Do you want me to get dressed?'

Too late. The door opened, and Billy and Phoebe came in, stopped dead and then threw themselves at him.

'You're here!' Billy said, and snuggled up against his chest, and as he wrapped his arms around the boy he was swamped with emotion.

If he hadn't been there, if he hadn't found him… Not now.

'Yeah. Mummy's got something to ask you.'

He sat up and they looked at Emily, and she smiled. 'You know you wanted to live with Amelie and Oliver and Grandma? Did you mean that?'

They nodded. 'Are we going to? For ever?' Phoebe asked, eyes widening.

'If that's what you want?'

They leaped up and started bouncing on the bed, and Oliver laughed.

'We'll take that as a yes. Maybe we should go and tell the others?'

They found them in the kitchen—Charlie, Amelie, his mother and of course Berry, who leaped up to greet them.

Amelie's eyes lit up. 'Have you come for breakfast?' she asked Emily, and Oliver gave a strangled laugh.

'Well, yes, but—you know you said you wanted Billy and Phoebe to stay here? Well, how would you feel if Emily and I got married and they all came back to live with us for ever?'

Her eyes widened. 'For ever?' she shrieked, and threw herself at him, hugging him hard. 'That would be the best thing *ever*!' she said, and they all ran out into the garden, taking Berry with them.

He turned and met his mother's eyes, and there was something in them he couldn't quite read.

'Congratulations,' she said softly. 'I'm so glad you've both finally come to your senses.'

'We've both made too many mistakes to do anything rash, Mum. We needed to take our time, and we've done that. This is permanent. This is for ever.'

'Good,' she said, and then went on carefully, 'does that mean you no longer need me?'

'Mum, you'll always have a home here—'

'But what if I don't want it? What if there's somewhere else I'd rather be?'

He searched her eyes, and he felt the smile start from way down inside him. 'Douglas,' he said gently, and she nodded.

'I wouldn't abandon you, I'll always be here to help out, and we'll take it slowly, but we want to be together.'

'You're not rushing this?'

She laughed. 'Darling, I'm nearly seventy, Douglas is seventy-one. Unlike you two, we don't have the luxury of procrastination. And anyway, I've known him since before you were born. It's hardly hasty.'

She was right, and he was just so happy for her.

'Come here,' he said, and hugged her hard. When he turned round, Charlie was hugging Emily, and there were tears in her eyes.

'Come here, you two,' he said, holding out his arm to them, and she and Charlie moved into the hug.

Three generations, two families, one great big happy ending.

Finally…

EPILOGUE

THEY HAD A simple family wedding.

Not a quiet wedding, not with all the children there, but simple and heartfelt, followed by a garden party back at Oliver's house.

No. Their house, the house where they were living now and would continue to live.

Charlie was his best man, of course, and he insisted on making a speech which had everyone in stitches. And then in tears.

'You've waited too long for this moment,' he said, suddenly serious, his voice cracking. 'I don't think I've ever met anyone who deserved their happy ending more than you two, and I couldn't be happier for you—for all of you. For all of us. For the children, for the whole family, but most of all for you two. I love you. Everyone, please raise your glasses for the bride and groom!'

'The bride and groom!' they chorused, and Emily turned to look at Oliver, his eyes filled with tears as he wrapped his arms around her and kissed her tenderly.

Then he turned to his extended family with a slightly crooked smile, his arm still around her shoulders, holding her firmly against his side.

'Relax, guys. I'm not going to make a speech, mostly because I don't think I'd get through it, but I do just need to thank Mum for all the support she's given me, the children for all we've put them through, and most of all I need to thank Emily for giving me another chance, and making me the happiest man alive. I love you, Em. Always have, always will, and that's a promise.'

'I love you, too,' she said, her own voice breaking, and as she went back into his arms, their whole family crowded round them for a massive group hug.

'What a wonderful day.'

'It is. The best day.'

Oliver put his arm round her, and she rested her head on his shoulder with a quiet sigh. He glanced down at her. 'You OK?'

'Very OK. You?'

'Never better. It's just so great to see everyone we love together. I can't believe how well they all get on.'

They did. Their mothers were sitting together on the bench smiling and laughing and getting to know each other, Berry at their feet, and Douglas and her father were standing watching the children play doctors and nurses while Charlie lay on the grass being a very patient patient and hamming it up.

'We feel like a proper family,' she said softly, and she felt his lips press against her hair.

'We are. At last. It's the end of a long, long road.'

'And look where it's brought us. Four wonderful children that would never have existed if we hadn't travelled it.' She turned to face him. 'Did I ever tell you how much I love you?'

His lips twitched. 'I'm not sure. Maybe you'd better do it again.'

'I love you. I love you I love you I love you. Better?'

'Much better.' His eyes were suddenly serious, the smile gone, and he cupped her face in his hands, his fingers oh-so gentle, and as he lowered his head, he murmured, 'I love you, too, so much. And I'm so, so sorry that I hurt you, but I'm here now, and I'm staying, and I love you. I'll always love you—now and for ever...'

His lips met hers, and in the background they could hear a chorus of cheers and catcalls. She felt him smile before he lifted his head and winked at her, then he turned, his arm still round her, and led her back to the others.

Back to their forever family...

* * * * *

REDEEMING HER
HOT-SHOT VET

JULIETTE HYLAND

MILLS & BOON

For all my furry co-authors, past and present.

CHAPTER ONE

"I HEARD THE new vet is stopping by this morning."

Sage Pool didn't roll her eyes at Blaire's comment. Well, at least she tried not to. "You heard right." Nothing ever stayed quiet in small towns. Though Dr. Jacobs had told no one who the new vet was.

Sage doubted it was personal. Dr. Jacobs probably hadn't even thought it mattered. She'd never really fit in. Spring River was insular, but in the eight months Dr. Jacobs was the town vet she had kept herself apart. Whether intentionally or not… she'd cemented her role as an outsider in the community's eyes.

"They're supposed to be here before we open."

"Not even going to feign excitement? Maybe this is the vet that stays." Blaire raised her eyebrows, the playful speech a routine between Sage and the graphic designer that helped her run her small dog rescue.

Usually she laughed at this point in the script they repeated far too often. Maybe if this wasn't their last chance, she could manage it. But too much weighed on the unknown vet showing up this morning.

If this vet didn't stay at least a year, the clinic was done. At least according to the email she wasn't supposed to have seen. The corporate office had recalled it, but not before Sage read the curt note.

Spring River Vet Clinic was on the list for downsizing. It was supposed to happen when Dr. Jacobs left. The new vet stepping in had delayed it…but what were the odds they actually stayed? Based on history?

Zero.

Blaire could work anywhere—the joys of graphic design and remote work. But most people didn't settle in Spring River, California. The tiny upstate town had one doctor, a grocery store, a bus stop to take the kids to the next town over for school and a vet clinic whose veterinarian rotated so much the office should have a revolving door.

The rest of the town catered to rock climbers and hikers spring through fall and skiers in the winter. All passing through on their way to Mt. Shasta. A city with hundreds of people roaming Main Street on any day, but few full-time residents.

Lately investors were buying vacation cabins and apartment complexes. Turning them into short-term rentals. All that did was make it more difficult for the full-time residents to find affordable housing.

"Sage?"

"There's no reason to get excited." She lifted one of the tiny brown puppies from the box Blaire had set down. "A new vet will come in. I will get them spun up on our clients, a few locals, the ones who always get their hopes up, who will actually believe this one will stay. Join the community potlucks and raise a family. Ever the optimists."

"It might happen."

Sage knew her friend didn't really believe that. "Might. But more likely, they'll give a few months' notice, if we're lucky."

"And the process starts over again." Blaire repeated the oft said line…not aware that Sage had intentionally left it off.

Sage couldn't utter the falsehood. She tried to put on a cheery voice as she completed their well-worn script. "Same routine, new vet. It's the role I've played since I became a veterinarian technician."

Except the stakes are so much higher this time around.

Blaire lifted the other puppy from the box and ran her hand over its silky fur. "I keep thinking the corporate shop that set this place up will close it down one of these days."

Ice slipped down her spine as her friend guessed the truth. The email was technically internal communications, but, oh, how she wished she could tell someone! Vet Med Corp had looked at the number of clients, the rotating staff, and decided this place was more trouble than it was worth. There was a small vet in Spring Farm, thirty miles up the road, but Sage knew that their vet techs had worked there for years. She had no hope of a job there, or at the clinic in Jasper, which was an hour commute away.

"Let's keep that idea out of the universe. You can work anywhere…telework isn't much of an option for me."

Anytime she wasn't at the clinic, she spent working with the rescue. It was a tiny network of foster homes right now, though Sage had plans for a standalone facility.

Assuming she ever saved enough money.

"You can always move," Blaire whispered against the puppy she was holding, careful not to meet Sage's eyes.

"Why don't we get these little guys to the back and get them checked out before the paying customers show up?" Sage kissed the brown puppy's nose.

Dogs never judged. Never insinuated that her choices were wrong. They hadn't watched her grow up. Watched her become the parent of her family when her mother lost herself after her dad abandoned them. Or watched her life implode when her brother, Forest, chose the wrong life path.

No. Dogs just gave unconditional love without asking for anything more than a place in your heart and a bowl of food.

"Your mother would understand. Eventually." Blaire didn't meet Sage's eyes as she set her puppy on the scale. "Six pounds. These guys can't be much more than six weeks old. Barely finished nursing."

She appreciated her friend shifting the discussion. Though not before getting one final thought out on her position.

She was wrong, though. Rose Pool would never understand. She'd cry and stay in her room for weeks. Lose the job she'd finally settled into following Forest's sentencing. Her mother wasn't strong. That was Sage's job. It wasn't fair. But life wasn't fair. Complaining about it didn't change it.

Once Sage had dreamed of getting out of Spring River. Dreamed of earning a degree in marine biology and saving the oceans! Big dreams she'd set aside when the small college fund her mother set up went to her brother's defense lawyer.

Not that the man had accomplished much with the funds they'd given him. A pittance compared to his other retainers, but all the money the Pool family had. And her mother had sunk back into the depression that had enclosed her for over a year when Sage was not quite fourteen.

Sage took care of everything…otherwise it didn't get done. And she'd learned never to get her hopes up. Easier to deal with disappointment if you just expected it.

"These look like golden Lab mixes. I bet someone dumped them because they have brown wavy hair and most people want the golden short hair version." Sage knew most dog breeders were responsible, but those that weren't filled already bursting rescues with the dogs they didn't think would fetch a high enough price.

Assuming someone found the puppies.

"Goldendors!"

"Technically, they are called Goldadors. Or even more technically…mutts!"

"All breeds were mutts once," Blaire laughed. "Do you think the new vet will let the rescue use the clinic before it opens?"

Her friend looked at the clock and back at the door. Dr. Jacobs was a creature of habit. She'd walk through the door with the new vet in exactly ten minutes. She hadn't pushed back on

Sage checking the dogs for the tiny rescue. However, if they needed actual treatment, she charged the rescue full price, unlike Dr. Andrews, who'd cut them a deal.

Vet bills were the biggest expenses for a rescue. Even one that couldn't take more than about twenty dogs at any one time. That was going to change when she finally purchased the Rainbow Ranch. She had plans to turn it into the perfect pet rescue location.

Luckily, these puppies were in good condition. Rambunctious, but that was what one got when you crossed a golden and a Lab.

"I'm glad you were on time. The vet before me did not have good time management skills." Dr. Jacobs's sharp tone carried through the small clinic.

And so the clock was ticking.

Somehow, Sage had to convince this vet to stay at least a year.

"New guy is here." Blaire reached for the puppy Sage was holding and put her in the box with his brother. "That is my cue to head out."

Sage kissed the top of each of the puppies' heads. "These little ones are in excellent condition. Call Myka. She should be able to place them with a foster, though once you have their picture on the website, I suspect they will have forever homes soon."

Puppies always went fast.

Blaire held the box in one hand as she dug her keys out of her back pocket. She offered a short wave before darting out the back door.

Sage didn't blame her friend. Dr. Jacobs was efficient…but she lacked the warm fuzzy feeling most veterinarians seemed to naturally exude. She was short with staff and patients. It wasn't personal, but it felt like it.

"Our vet tech is already here. That was her truck out front. Not sure how the thing still runs."

Sometimes it doesn't.

Sage crossed her arms, then uncrossed them. She didn't want to meet the new vet in a defensive posture.

Sure, her truck had seen better days. But she'd used the savings for her home down payment to help her mom get a car three months ago. It was that or deal with her mother losing her job and sinking into despair. Rose was slowly paying her back, but there was no money for a new car. So she kept the truck running on her own.

One could learn most things through internet videos. She'd taught herself mechanics, dry walling, basic plumbing…all things to help her prepare to run the rescue out of the ranch. This was one dream she was going to get. Something of her own.

As soon as Mom pays me back.

"I know you're used to something grander, but we make do." The door to the back opened and Dr. Jacobs stepped through. "Sage, good you're here—"

Sage knew Dr. Jacobs was speaking. Knew words were leaving her mouth, but her ears didn't capture a single one. Her eyes locked with the new vet. He was still so tall she had to look up to meet his gaze.

Of course he is, Sage!

One didn't lose inches, at least not until old age. Holt Cove's lean face had filled out and the last bits of youth had vanished into a well-formed man who probably made many stare.

Including me.

How? What? I… Words raced across her mind in no meaningful order as she tried to process Holt Cove standing less than five feet from her.

Heat rippled across her skin, just like it had the last time she'd seen him. Two days before his high school graduation. They'd shared a kiss after their final school play.

It was everything she'd dreamed a first kiss would be. Fun,

exciting…charged. He'd promised to call the day after gradu-ation. Then Forest was arrested.

And all she'd gotten was his voicemail and unanswered texts.

Pain should wrap around her right now. That was the nor-mal emotional reaction to holding the gaze of someone who'd ghosted you at such an important time. And the pain was there. But it wasn't the only feeling coating her body.

"Sage?" Dr. Jacobs's tone was sharp. She was used to walk-ing in and having Sage immediately discuss the upcoming cli-ents. Not the schedule, that was Lucy, their receptionist's job, but the little things that were expected in a tiny community.

The things that made it seem like Dr. Jacobs knew more about the community than she did. Sage always rattled off the day's internal notes first thing. Before they exchanged any pleasantries. She knew what she was supposed to say.

Mrs. Lowed's daughter was having a baby, a little girl, and she was going to spend the appointment discussing it. Mr. Kipe's wife left him last week—do not ask him how things are—he will break down. And Leonard Owen's dog ate an-other sock…

That one wasn't on the schedule yet, but Leonard had texted her this morning.

Toe ate more socks than any dog she'd ever met. Leonard had taken to keeping them on the top shelf of his closet. He wasn't sure where Toe found the sock, but he'd refused his breakfast. Something the dog never did.

Dr. Jacobs was waiting, but none of the words escaped as she held Holt's deep gaze.

Had he missed her, even a little?

Nope. Not traveling that thought path.

"Sage!"

She blinked, finally breaking the connection. The only sav-ing grace was that he'd seemed as stunned to see her as she was to see him.

"Sorry." She reached for the tablet chart she'd loaded up when she'd arrived. "I—I…" She cleared her throat. Maybe that would jolt her brain into action.

It didn't matter that she'd never expected to see Holt Cove again. Most people who left Spring River didn't return. She needed to focus, but her brain's synapses refused to fire.

What was he doing here?

He could be anywhere. She'd known they worked for the same corporate vet. Holt had appeared in a few of the company's print ads. He was on the fast track, and she hated that she'd looked for him. He was in the big clinics. Boston, Dallas, LA and even the flagship clinic in New York. He shouldn't be here.

And her mind should *not* be even partially happy to see her brother's onetime best friend.

"I…" She looked at the tablet chart, the words still not coming. She could see the frustration in Dr. Jacobs's eyes. If only she could get the words out.

Then she could flee and take a few minutes to gather herself before again being in the presence of the man who'd spent hours learning lines with her in theater class. The connection they'd formed as kids had morphed until she wasn't the tagalong little sister. She was a friend and almost something more.

Yet in the days after Forest's arrest for armed robbery, Holt had vanished from her life. He'd reached out to Forest while he was out on bail. Her brother was angry at the world and the blowup had been epic. But for Sage…all she'd gotten was silence. It had hurt.

Still did, if she was honest. And she was terribly aware that jealousy was mixing in with all the feelings racing through her.

Holt got out of this town, followed his dream. He hadn't had to parent his parent. He'd gone to college and then veterinarian school.

And she was still here. The walls felt like they were closing in around her, and she wanted to be anywhere else. But she had a job to do and, based on Dr. Jacobs's tapping foot, she was about to lose her temper.

Get it together, Sage.

"Mrs. Lowed's daughter is having a baby, a little girl." Her voice shook, and she forced herself to slow down. She was not making a scene. Well…not more of one.

"The baby is all she's going to talk about when you are doing her cat's checkup…" She finished her recitation of the morning appointments without looking up; her mind on auto mode as her emotions locked down.

"Sage is always ready with the local news. The patients' parents like to talk…small-town things."

"Yes. I grew up in Spring River. My dad used to run one of the mountain climbing shops. He retired to Dallas a few years before he passed. Are you referring to April Lowed?"

His voice still made her feel warm. It was calming and resonated easily in the room. The deep baritone was the main reason he'd gotten the part of Prince Charming his senior year. Her insides turning gooey was not helpful.

Holt Cove was hot. Attractive in high school, the lanky boyishness was now a rugged handsomeness. Her body's reaction was surprising, but it was probably just the shock.

More than a decade of quiet, and her body was focusing on such an inconsequential thing. A glutton for punishment. The perfect description for Sage Pool—unfortunately.

"Yes, but she took her husband's name, something with a *B*… Brantley or Breams. Left town not long after graduation." Sage waved a hand, the words inconsequential.

"Of course you know each other. Anyone from Spring River knows the other permanent residents." Dr. Jacobs took the tablet Sage was offering. "So you were in school together?"

The question was directed at Holt, and her chest tightened as she waited for his answer. Waited to see if he would acknowledge a childhood spent jumping into ponds, riding bikes, and then delinquency. He'd righted his path; Forest had barreled forward with poor decisions and paid a big price for it.

And Sage… Sage got left behind.

His blue eyes met hers, then he looked away, but not before she saw a look she feared was pity on his features.

"As you said, all the permanent residents knew each other."

Her fists clenched. Dr. Jacobs didn't need to know their history, but such a cold statement. *No.* She was not having it.

"Sure. But no other permanent resident spent nearly every waking hour at my house. Being my brother's best friend and all. And my friend too…once. Guess time zapped those memories. All the big-city clinics and…"

She slammed her mouth shut. It didn't matter what Holt thought. But the way he'd thrown away their relationship made her see red. Worse, it meant that while he'd forgotten her, she'd acknowledged that she kept track of him.

Barking echoed in the front room.

Thank goodness.

"Toe ate a sock again. And he and Duchess don't get on well." She turned to Holt, hoping her face was blank. "Duchess is Mrs. Lowed's beagle mix."

The dog let out a howl; Holt chuckled. "Beagle…you don't say?"

"Toe wants to play, and Duchess doesn't, so let me go help get them into separate rooms." She hurried away before Dr. Jacobs could point out that Lucy would make sure the animals were where they needed to be.

She needed to be somewhere else. Needed a moment to gather herself. Dr. Holt Cove was home. And would probably stay at least a year. After all, he knew what Spring River was like. That was good for the clinic. Good for the patients and their pet parents who'd come so close to losing their clinic, even if they didn't know it.

This was the best possible scenario, and she hated how much she wished that anyone else had walked through the door.

* * *

"I wasn't sure it was possible to have a worse introduction to our vet tech than mine." Dr. Andrea Jacobs scrolled through the tablet chart, making notes.

Holt was glad the outgoing doctor wasn't looking at his face. Heat coated his cheeks, and he wished, not for the first time in his life, that there was a way to step back in time. To redo a moment.

If genies were real, he wouldn't ask for riches or power. Yes, those were nice, but with enough hard work and time, those accomplishments were within your grasp. The power to fix the awkward moments…or to fix the choices that led to catastrophe. He'd give nearly anything for that fantastical gift.

"Why was your introduction to Sage so poor?" There was no way to ease his guilt at failing to acknowledge their connection.

Did it matter that he'd done it so she didn't feel inclined to claim him? So she could dismiss him? After all, he deserved that.

He still had the messages she'd sent after Forest's arrest. All unanswered. His reminder that inaction was just as much a choice.

He and Forest were best friends, but Sage was only ten months younger than her brother. She'd been a grade behind them in school, but always by their side.

Until the boys started getting into trouble. No, until Holt had dragged Forest with him into delinquency.

"When Dr. Andrews introduced us, he told me that Sage used the clinic to help her animal rescue. I asked if that was within corporate regs. Before even saying hello." Dr. Jacobs handed him the tablet chart. "Research is my skill. I love animals, and finding new treatments is my passion, but the people part…" She shrugged, "At least I know my weakness."

A rescue. That didn't surprise him; Sage had always had an enormous heart.

She was the smart one. The one with big dreams. He knew that Spring River would have changed in his absence. When he picked this assignment, he accepted that. Holt was coming home. Stepping off the career ladder he'd focused on for so long. Proving he could focus on something besides work… besides himself.

The town was supposed to be different. One thing was certain, though. Sage Pool shouldn't be here. She'd wanted out. Even more than he had. His stomach twisted as he looked toward the door she'd used. What if part of the reason she was here was because of his inaction? His choice the night that changed everything for Forest.

That was what he should consider, not the heat layering his heart.

Sage was as lovely as ever. Her dark curls escaping the messy bun, her chocolate eyes full of intelligence as she looked at him. And her lips, the ones he could still remember kissing all those years ago.

Puppy love. High school infatuation. At least that was what he'd convinced himself of when he'd mourned the loss of her friendship and whatever was growing between them. Besides, how could she care for the person who hadn't stopped her brother from making the choice that had doomed him to over twenty years behind bars?

"She's the glue holding this place together. Corporate opened this location five years ago and you're the sixth vet."

Six in five years! He knew it was bad. Hell, if he hadn't agreed to this location, it was slated for closure. Corporate was offering a few vets franchise opportunities…they'd offered him one. Nearly accepted it before his mother passed.

He wasn't sure why that weighed on him so much. He'd understood the grief when his father passed two years ago. His dad was there for him, his cheerleader…even when he hadn't seen it.

His mother? Well, she'd walked out of his life at eight, abandoned him and his father to chase her dreams. She'd reached them too, while missing his birthdays, all the holidays and repeatedly "forgetting" the custody dates she'd sworn to the judge she wanted.

And suddenly the opportunity to work even more, as a franchise owner, wasn't as appealing as it had been. That was as good a non-reason as any for why he'd turned down the opportunity to be his own boss and come to the tiny clinic.

He'd seen the list of closures and suddenly Spring River was the perfect way to show that he wasn't just about the corporate life. Prove that he put people before himself...even if he hadn't always done so.

Perfect way to give back to his hometown and maybe right a few wrongs on his universal spreadsheet.

"Toe just released the sock."

Holt spun to see Sage walk to the sink. "I've gotten the room cleaned, and Leonard is thrilled to only spend for the office visit instead of surgery."

"I'll check on him." Dr. Jacobs turned on her heel. He wasn't sure if she was fleeing this interaction or doing her job. Though it could be both!

"Sage."

She looked over her shoulder, a few wisps of dark hair hovering over her right eye. "Did you need something?" She pulled her bottom lip between her teeth.

Was that still her tell for nervousness?

He opened his mouth, then closed it as he tried to figure out the right words...or even just some words. "I am glad that Toe doesn't need surgery."

She dropped the paper towel in the trash can, then looked at him. He could see the confusion in her eyes. Of course, he was glad that a dog didn't require surgery. Bowel obstructions were dangerous, and the surgery to fix them was major. And expensive.

But that wasn't what he'd wanted to say.

"I need to see to a patient." Sage started for the door, then stopped. "Welcome home, Dr. Cove."

Then she was gone, and he was very cognizant that she hadn't called him Holt. He doubted that was a sign of respect, and if it was, it wasn't one he wanted.

CHAPTER TWO

HOLT ENTERED THE ROOM, his gaze sliding to Sage for a microsecond before forcing his attention to the empty cat carrier on the exam table. "Umm? Where is Starflake?"

"In her regular post." Sage pointed to the top of the cabinets.

He followed the motion and crossed his arms as the calico's bright green eyes met his. Cats were lovely pets, their purr scientifically proven to lower human blood pressure. However, no one did judgmental quite like felines.

"Regular post?"

"My girls weren't the best with her when she was a kitten. Tried dressing her up in doll clothes more than once. They're seventeen and fifteen now, but Starflake doesn't forgive easily." Mr. Stevens held up the bag of treats, but the cat didn't budge. "Skittish is a good description for her."

And mean…if Sage's notes were accurate, and he had no reason to doubt them. Starflake loved Mr. Stevens; she tolerated Mrs. Stevens and liked no one else.

"Before we get her down from her perch, why don't you tell me why you're here?" Holt focused on Mr. Stevens, mostly careful to make it seem like he was showing the cat zero attention. It might not work, but he'd met more than one cat that acted this way but thrived on attention. When they didn't get it, sometimes they hopped down to demand it.

"She is due for her shots. Starflake isn't a huge fan of the vet. Or anyone really."

"Not true." Sage followed Holt's tactic of paying the cat no mind. "She loves you."

Mr. Steven let out a chuckle. "She does. But to stay healthy, she needs shots."

Holt pulled up a hand and pointed to his face, hoping Mr. Stevens got the idea. They were ignoring the temperamental being judging them from on high.

"Her appetite healthy?"

"Yes."

"Any concerns?"

"Outside of attitude?" Mr. Stevens's eyes tracked to the cat before refocusing on Holt. "She's twelve years old and slowing down. Also, there is a lump on her back. Dr. Jacobs thought it was a fatty tumor."

"Fatty tumor?" Lipomas were more common in dogs than cats, and benign. Occasionally they caused mobility issues in cats, depending on the location. "We'll take a look. Have you noticed it growing?"

"Maybe a little. But not much." Mr. Stevens looked at his cat again. "She doesn't really like me playing with it."

"Oka—" The cat landed on Holt's shoulder, and he barely kept the yelp buried in his throat as her claws released. "She's got attitude… You don't say?" Holt gently lifted the animal and saw Sage cover her mouth. Didn't stop the sound of her giggle, though.

Starflake might be a handful, but she'd broken Sage's careful professionalism. He'd seen her interact with the staff and their clients and knew the quiet disinterest she'd showed him today wasn't standard.

Hell, she was warmer with Dr. Jacobs and the two of them weren't close.

Hearing the small laugh gave him a bit of hope that there might be a way to smooth over the morning's misadventure.

The cat started purring, and Holt rubbed her ears as Sage got the shots ready.

"Might want to be careful, Dr. Cove." Sage set the syringes on the counter.

"Why?" He felt the cat's side with one hand while he moved the other, rubbing under Starflake's chin. "Yikes!"

He yanked his hand back and gave Starflake a stern look. The cat hadn't broken the skin, and nips from animals were the main hazard in this field. Still, the nip dashed any hopes he and the calico were bonding.

"We've noted that she likes her chin rubbed for around thirty seconds, then she bites." Sage stepped to the exam table and took a firm hold of the cat.

"Good to know." Holt ran his hand along the cat's back. The tumor was harder than he liked and didn't move as smoothly as he'd hoped. It was probably a lipoma stuck to the muscle around her back, but there was a chance it was cancer and he wanted to be sure. "I want to biopsy this."

Mr. Stevens's head dropped, but he nodded. "I'd rather know than not."

"Understandable. If you have a few minutes, we can give her a local numbing agent and I can take a small tissue sample to send to the pathologist? Should take around two days to know for sure. Or you can come back?" Holt had a few minutes and once you mentioned biopsy, most pet parents wanted results as fast as possible. There were benefits to being in a small clinic.

"She's already here and mad."

Starflake glared at him, confirming what her father had said.

Sage left and returned with the numbing agent, razor and biopsy punch tool. Then she gripped the cat's sides while Holt gave her the numbing agent. The few minutes it took for the medication to work seemed to take forever as Starflake let out a low growl. And her dad rubbed her head.

When he was sure she wouldn't feel it, Holt quickly shaved the area, then punched the small hole in her back and dropped the sample in a tube Sage held out. Then he gave her the shots she'd come for and stepped back as Mr. Stevens opened the door to the cat carrier.

Starflake darted inside, and Holt saw Sage's shoulders relax as Mr. Stevens closed the carrier door. The cat hissed once, then curled into the back of the carrier, her eyes flashing. Yep, he and Starflake had not bonded.

"I'll let you know as soon as the results are back. However, that looks like a fatty tumor, so I wouldn't worry too much."

Mr. Stevens let out a breath and grinned at Starflake through the carrier. "Best to be sure. And the wound?"

"That wound will heal on its own in about a week. If it doesn't, call and make another appointment."

"Will do." Mr. Stevens picked up the carrier, made a few more cooing noises that Starflake rewarded with a hiss. "Sassy, girl. Oh, before I forget, congratulations, Sage."

Congratulations? Was something big happening in her life? There was no need for him to know what, and he wasn't sure Dr. Jacobs paid enough attention to know the day-to-day of her colleagues' lives. There was no ring on her left hand, a thing he wished he hadn't noticed the moment he saw her. Though many vet techs and veterinarians wore rings on necklaces or just left them at home.

It wasn't Sage's birthday. She was born at the end of October. October twenty-first, to be exact. He'd cut ties with this town, with her, after failing his friend, *and her.* But on every birthday, he sent up a silent wish that she got everything she wanted. That she was happy. Fulfilled.

Holt looked at her, but she looked as confused as he felt.

"Congratulations? Is someone starting rumors, Gregg?" She laughed, but he could hear the uncomfortable tone beneath it. Small towns and rumors were synonymous. Stopping one, even a false one, was nearly impossible.

"The Rainbow Ranch." Mr. Stevens, Gregg, as Sage called him, tilted his head. "The for sale sign has a giant 'Sold' attached to the top."

"Oh." She blinked and opened her mouth a few times, but no words came out.

This was a confusion he could clear up. "I bought the ranch." He couldn't hide the hint of pride in his tone. He knew the other vets who'd come to Spring River had left quickly. Most had stayed in a furnished apartment.

He'd wanted to demonstrate that he was staying. He'd seen the ranch for sale and jumped at the offer. His father had mentioned Sage and her mother had moved out before Forest's trial.

He couldn't blame them, but the ranch, the Rainbow Ranch, as Sage's mom had called it, was the site of his favorite memories. His father spent all his time focused on his store. To keep it from failing—a truth Holt had not understood until he'd been left in charge for three months while his father recovered from a heart attack.

When he'd wanted attention, he'd visit the Rainbow Ranch. Sage's mom had taken him in. She'd treated him just like Forest.

They'd had few rules, no bedtimes, unlimited snacks. It was a paradise compared to his lonely home. The fact that it had sat empty for years saddened him. He'd bought it sight unseen, a whim that he'd second-guessed after the ink was dry, but he didn't regret it.

"You bought it?" Mr. Stevens looked from him to Sage, and the undercurrent of the room shifted. There was suddenly an unspoken dialogue going on.

He'd been part of the unspoken looks, the language that the locals used to differentiate themselves from the tourists, once. Now he felt, as he was, an outsider.

"I'm sorry, Sage." Mr. Stevens lifted the crate muttering a hush to the angry cat noises echoing from it. "Thanks for looking after Starflake. I know she is cranky, but she's my girl."

Sage went to the cabinet and pulled out the cleaning wipes. The color had left her face; no brightness escaping her eyes.

He watched her bite her bottom lip and worried she might taste blood.

It had been a long day. Starflake was their last patient. There was usually some excitement regarding the end of the day. Something to look forward to. Particularly with the weekend only a few minutes away.

"Why did he say 'sorry'?" Holt suspected the answer was going to devastate him. Her body language spoke of defeat, but he needed to know. Needed to know why purchasing the Rainbow Ranch, showing that he was staying, was a reason to tell Sage sorry.

"It's nothing." Sage shook her head as she dropped the cleaning wipes into the bin, then tied up the trash bag.

Nothing. A word that rarely meant its dictionary definition.

"I know…" He rocked back on his heels; this wasn't the best place for apologies or discussions about how their lives had shifted all those years ago. "I know a lot of time has passed, but can we agree not to lie to each other?"

Sage let out a chuckle; this one had none of the warmth of the giggle she'd failed to hide before. "Sure, we can agree not to lie to each other. Assuming we talk, right? Return texts or messages, right?"

"Sage…"

She held up a hand. "I shouldn't have said that. Water under the bridge."

Except it wasn't. He'd messed up. He hadn't meant to, but intent didn't overshadow the wrong.

"Sage—"

Before he could apologize, she rushed on… "Gregg, Mr. Stevens, apologized because the whole town has been watching me saving up for the down payment on the Rainbow Ranch for three years. I nearly had it, then Mom's car…well, it doesn't matter now. I hope you enjoy it."

"Why have you been saving for years?" He hated the question as soon as it was out. The property was run-down. The housing market was soaring, but the price wasn't close to market value.

"Because vet techs in the middle of nowhere don't make a ton."

He wanted her words to be angry. Or sad, or something! Instead, there was such a lack of emotion he wanted to scream on her behalf.

"Dreams don't always come true." Sage shrugged. "A lesson I've learned over and over again. There's another property. It's outside of town but…" She looked away, clearly looking for a way out of this conversation.

"Sage…" he started again, not sure what to say but feeling the need to offer something.

"I'm going to take the trash out, then head to my apartment. Unless you need something else, Dr. Cove?"

Holt. Call me Holt.

He'd worked so long to be Dr. Cove. He was proud of that accomplishment. But all he wanted in this moment was for her to call him Holt. Even if she was yelling at him for yanking away her dream.

"I should have called you an old friend this morning."

Her dark eyes held his, but she didn't say anything.

"Should have done so many things, like calling or texting or just showing up. I didn't and I can't change that." He should let her go, but he didn't want to, not without her understanding.

"You don't have to explain—"

"I do." He didn't mean to interrupt, but he needed her to know. "I didn't want you to feel you had to claim me as a friend when I didn't earn that title when it counted."

"I see." Sage's eyes drifted from his to her feet. "We were young."

And good friends…on the path to something more.

Words she left unsaid, but he heard in his soul. "Are you coming to Dr. Jacobs's going away party tomorrow?"

"Of course." Sage held up the bag. "I should get going. See you tomorrow, Holt."

Holt.

He hung on to the hope resonating in his chest. Their lives were completely different now. But his soul felt lighter than it had in a year.

"Sage. I'm sorry. I just heard the Rainbow Ranch is gone. It's my fault."

"It's not." Sage kept her voice level as her mother rocked back on her heels. She'd intentionally not told her mother. Now it was obvious that was a mistake, but she hadn't wanted to deal with the fallout. The tears and upset. Hadn't had the reserves to offer her mom comfort when she was so drained herself.

So she pointed out the obvious. "You needed the car to get to work, and you're paying me back. I'd make the same decision again." Her savings had been nearly enough for the down payment when her mom's car gave out. But that didn't matter now. There was still the property outside of town. It was more expensive, but it was her focus now.

The price tag meant she needed to look for a new apartment, too, because her landlady would not be extending her lease. Her to-do list was ever growing.

She'd make do. Somehow.

"And I don't want to discuss it. Particularly not here." Somehow, Sage kept the smile on her face, wishing for the thousandth time that Dr. Jacobs had hired entertainment for the evening. Instead, people were milling around making small talk, and far too many wanted to talk about Holt Cove and the Rainbow Ranch.

With a DJ this event would still have been awkward…but not a raging disaster.

The hall Dr. Jacobs had insisted on renting out for the goodbye was barely filled. The buffet selection was gourmet, but there weren't enough people to eat it. And it wasn't to many people's liking. Her mother already asked if Sage could give her a granola bar.

Not whether she had a granola bar. Rather than point out that Rose was old enough to hide her own snacks, she'd handed over the granola bar she carried…just in case her mother asked.

This was what their relationship became for the year after her father took off. Her mother was nearly herself again; then Forest was arrested, and she'd stopped taking care of everything. Now she bragged Sage could handle anything. Failing to mention it was because her daughter had no other options.

"I really am sorry, Sage." Her mother's lip wobbled.

If she cried, Sage would too. And that was not happening here. "I'll make do, Mom. Promise."

"You always do." She patted her hand and then waved to a friend and wandered away.

She shifted her shoulders as a bit of the tension in her stomach evaporated. Sage loved her mother. Her mother loved her too, but the dynamic between them was uncomfortable—on both ends.

"This is going fine." Dr. Jacobs grinned as she stepped beside her, her smile doing little to hide the anxiety behind her eyes. She'd been in town less than a year and not made friends. Sage wasn't sure how she'd expected the evening to go, or why the woman had even done this. This event would have been over-the-top for a well-loved veterinarian moving on. For one in town less than a year…

And unfortunately, it was traveling down the exact path she'd feared when the departing veterinarian told her the plan.

Sage had done her best to suggest other alternatives; a small dinner with the staff of the clinic…who'd all feel honor bound to attend. They could have called it a night after dessert was served.

Instead…well, instead it was a pity party with the staff standing around while no music played and the few clients who'd attended wandered around and eventually found Sage. All congratulating and then giving condolences when she said she hadn't purchased the Rainbow Ranch. Before making exclamations about Holt's return.

She understood their excitement. That didn't mean it wasn't exhausting.

She just needed a few minutes to compose herself. To make sure the smile she was faking stayed in place.

To make sure that if Holt looked her way *she* wouldn't break.

He'd arrived twenty minutes late, and all heads had turned his way. Taking in his tall frame, broad shoulders, dusty blond hair and brilliant blue eyes. His tailored outfit hugging him in all the right places.

Or maybe it's just me taking those things in?

Sage had really noticed Holt when he was cast opposite her in *Cinderella*. Prince Charming…and to her sixteen-year-old self. It had felt like he was the character brought to life. Their stage kisses hadn't been awkward. Instead…

Butterflies mixed with horror in her stomach. That was a long time ago. Another lifetime for both of them. But his apology ran in her mind. She even understood.

She'd reacted to Forest's arrest by taking care of her mother and her brother—when he let her. Because no one else was coming to the rescue. But, if she hadn't had to play the role, moving on to the next stage of life would have been her priority too.

He'd been eighteen. An adult by legal definition, but not really. And he's here now.

Ugh! Why was her brain so focused on Holt Cove? She needed a break.

There was a small hidey hole behind the DJ booth. Not big enough to act as more than a one-broom closet. Originally intended to house some piece of equipment long since ruled obsolete. She'd found it at the ripe age of seven when

Holt and Forest had dared her to hide at Ursula Brown's wedding reception. She'd fallen asleep and missed the drama of the bride's sister declaring her love for the groom and the ensuing fistfight.

Holt found her, hours later when everyone in town was searching. She could still remember the feel of his hand in hers as he led her out of the room. Soothing her worries that she'd be in trouble.

He'd felt safe. And he'd told no one where she was hiding.

She just needed a few minutes to collect herself. Then she could step back into…could you call this a party? That was a worry for five minutes from now.

Reaching for the closet light, she frowned when flicking the switch didn't result in the ancient bulb lighting up. She blew the hair out of her eyes, not that she could see it, and leaned against the wall. At least, no one was asking her about the Rainbow Ranch in the dark.

Or about Holt.

She'd gone home yesterday, thrown her plans for the ranch in the trash and crossed out the lists she'd made. Throughout childhood, she'd made lists. Goals she'd accomplish—one day.

She'd stopped after Forest was sentenced to twenty-five years. What was the good of dreams that never came true? She'd only just started putting the list together again. Finally started believing.

And that was why she was so mad at herself. She'd let herself believe. Let herself dream. And now she was dealing with the inevitable fallout.

Sure, there were other properties. And she'd find a place for her rescue. But wherever it was wouldn't be the Rainbow Ranch. She closed her eyes and pushed away the tear at the corner of her eye. It was just a place. Just a place.

Maybe if she whispered the words enough, it would be true.

The door to her sanctuary opened, and she barely caught the sigh. Could she not have five minutes?

Holt slid into the tiny room, his back to her. "No, I know. I just need to grab something. I'll be back in a moment."

She waited for the door to close before offering, "Lying to Mrs. Parsons?"

Holt let out a small yelp, and his hands wrapped around her waist in the dark. "Sage?"

His hands squeezed her waist, and heat tossed through her system.

Do not lean into him, Sage Pool!

Could her body not recognize the difference between teenage puppy love and her adult heart? Her body recognized him as a man…but her brain should put the controls on. Yes, he was hot. Sure, he'd been the only one she'd gotten close to who hadn't told her she was too independent. He'd also been eighteen. What did eighteen-year-olds know about life and love? Not much.

His fingers tightened on her waist; then he broke the connection. Sage kept her body still—barely.

"What are you doing in here?" He was standing right in front of her. Inches separating them in the dark. How she'd dreamed of this moment alone with him, once upon a time.

"I could ask you the same." She raised her chin, aware that he couldn't see her, but needing the armor a life of disappointment had crafted.

He let out a chuckle and tingles traveled from the top of her head to the tips of her toes.

Seriously, get a grip.

Many girls in school had crushed on him. The reformed bad boy who'd turned theater geek. But to Sage, he'd been one of the few people who didn't laugh when she talked of saving the oceans. Who leaned close and shared one special kiss after their last performance. The promise of something more.

A lot of good it did her.

"I'm hiding." He shrugged, or at least she thought he did.

He was so close. If she lifted a hand, it would skim his chest. She swallowed the thought.

"Why?" She leaned her head against the wall, putting a little distance between them. "The town loves a returning resident. You're hot, so finding a partner to talk to…" Dear God, she'd actually said that.

"Hot…" Holt's voice was low, sultry and Sage's body cried out, urging her to step toward him. But they were not teens anymore, and this was not some stolen moment of time.

"You know what I mean. You're the boy who made it. Successful vet coming home to save the day."

"Saving the day?" Holt let out a sigh, and there was a bitterness in the sound. "That sounds a lot grander than the real reason."

"What does that mean?" Without thinking, she lifted her hand, meaning to grip his shoulder, but her palm landed on his chest. She froze. Just for a moment. She was aiming for comfort…but in the dark room…after so many years.

He blew out a breath, his hand lying over hers for a second. The passage of time seemed to disappear. They were once again sharing secrets they didn't want to voice with anyone else.

"Holt?"

"I came home for me, Sage. Not because I was saving the clinic. It's a delightful bonus, but not some grand gesture."

"Oh." There were words he wasn't saying. But why should he? She yanked her hand back. "I—" Dryness coated her mouth as her tongue struggled to connect the dots.

"And any grand gesture they might have thought I was making evaporates when people realize I bought the Rainbow Ranch—" He paused and shifted, his hip brushing hers.

They were too close, but neither seemed able to step out of the room.

"Well, they'll get over it. Another piece of gossip will overtake it soon. You just need to wait to be the old news story."

"I'm not overly concerned about them."

"Then why are you hiding?" She chuckled, though it was nerves, not humor, driving the interaction.

"Touché."

Silence hung between them for a few minutes. Why wasn't this more uncomfortable? Everything about this should be unsettling. She should have taken herself out of this situation as soon as he snuck in.

Yet, she was still standing in the dark with Holt Cove. She and the boy had been close, but she didn't know the man. Still, her feet refused to move.

Finally, she pushed off the wall. Her chest bumped into his, and he steadied her. Again, the world seemed to pause for an instant.

Nope. No, it did not, Sage.

It was just her imagination running wild.

"This room is smaller than I remember." His breath was hot on her cheek.

Her heart raced, and heat bloomed where it hadn't for so long. It was ridiculous. Sure, she didn't date much. She was intimidating...independent...too busy. All fancy words for saying she wasn't what they wanted.

It didn't bother her. Usually. She did everything for herself. She didn't rely on someone to take care of her. That kept her from settling in romance. From getting hurt.

Like Mom.

She hated that errant thought. Though it was true. Her mother had relied on her father for everything, and, when he left, Sage had to step in. She'd never put herself in that position.

Yes, Holt was attractive. Yes, her teenage brain had wanted to kiss him. Those feelings were simply blending together. Sage was not some sex-starved person desperate for a few minutes of fun with a hot man.

"You've been gone a long time." Her tone was soft, almost sultry, and she felt him pull away. As much as the room would allow, anyway. So even if her body was betraying her, his was not.

That shouldn't hurt. She bit her lip, tamping down on the overwhelming bucket of emotions.

She scooted around him, her hips pressing against his, and she barely caught the moan in her throat. Okay…maybe she was a little too lonely.

Dear God, why didn't I leave when he stepped into the closet? "Sage?"

The cool of the metal door handle begged her to open the door, walk out and finish this night with some dignity. But she couldn't force herself to obey. "Yes?"

"I am sorry about the ranch. I assumed…well, it was for sale and I have so many wonderful memories there. Forest and I. And you…" His breath hitched before he finally continued, "I'm not concerned about other's opinions, but I am concerned about yours."

And you. Two little words that hovered in the room as goose pimples raced across her skin.

She flexed the fingers in her free hand, laid her head against the door. It wasn't his fault that she didn't have the money for the down payment. It was a miracle that the ranch had stayed empty this long.

"I'm not mad at you, Holt."

It hurt that so many choices had been stripped from her because of her brother's folly. It infuriated her that the lawyer they'd hired had stolen their funds and provided basically no defense. Furious that her brother had thrown away his future. But none of that was Holt's fault. She'd find another way.

"I'll see you at work." A reminder of what they were now. Colleagues. *Colleagues.*

Such a blasé word, but one she needed to remember. And by Monday morning, she'd have the emotions she was normally so good at controlling back where they belonged.

Then she opened the door and forced herself to step out of the room without looking back.

CHAPTER THREE

SHIFTING THE DRINK CARRIER, Holt hoped he had the right drink order for Sage and their receptionist, Lucy. He was banking on the local coffee shop owner, knowing their regular order. There were benefits to living in a town with only one coffee shop!

He was determined to make a good impression on his first full day as the clinic's only veterinarian. Caffeine was the way to many people's good graces. Anything to make some amends to Sage.

"Good morning, Dr. Cove." Lucy smiled as he walked through the door. "We've a full day." The phone rang, and she gestured to it before lifting it.

He set the coffee in front of her, and she mouthed, *thank you*. One colleague down. Simple and hopefully a premonition of how his interaction with the other would go.

His body had burned since he'd stumbled on Sage during the fiasco that was Dr. Jacobs's going away party. She'd been so close.

None of his feelings were platonic now. No. Holt was drawn to Sage. He shouldn't be, but it had taken all his control in that small room not to hold her for a moment longer. Holt enjoyed the feel of her hand against his chest; her scent seemed to wrap around him all night.

This morning he'd woken up just as his dream self was dipping his head to kiss her. Both furious that his subconscious had delivered that gem and taken it away before it got to the part he wanted.

They'd grown close while playing Prince Charming and Cinderella in the Rodgers and Hammerstein production. Practicing lines together, laughing, as he tried to prove to his dad he'd changed.

All it had taken to drive him from delinquency was his father's heart attack. That still saddened him. It wasn't his father's fault his mother left him when Holt was eight. His dad had done everything to make sure he was secure. And Holt hadn't been able to see it until the crisis happened.

Even two years after his father lost his life to his second heart attack, part of Holt wondered if he'd been a better kid, if his father hadn't been so stressed, would his dad's first heart attack have happened?

Rationally he knew it wasn't his fault. But rational thoughts weren't the ones that dogged him when he lay alone in bed.

It wasn't his father that he'd thought of this weekend. It was Sage.

As teens, Sage had lightened his heart. Made him believe in himself. Helping him aim for success and achievement. When they'd kissed, he'd expected it to be uncomfortable. Instead, it had felt like coming home.

He'd sworn he'd call her after the busyness of graduation was over. He'd meant too. Then Forest was arrested, and he hadn't known the right words.

He hadn't deserved the brilliant girl she'd been, and that was even more true after failing her brother, and now stealing her ranch. His universal balance sheet was bright red where Sage was concerned.

That didn't stop the fire traipsing through his body when he thought of her.

"Good morning, Holt." She didn't turn her head or look up from the cage where Charcoal, a gray cat with bright yellow eyes, was recuperating from surgery to repair a broken leg and lacerations. The gray sweetheart purred for everyone, even when heavily medicated.

"Charcoal all right this morning?"

"Still the sweetest." She patted his head, then stood. "His bandages are holding well. And he's tolerated the pain meds well. I know Steph will be happy to take him home. He's a bona fide hero after all!"

Charcoal had chased off a pair of black bears the day before Holt's arrival. The bears wandered into his backyard investigating the trash Steph had set out. When her two-year-old had seen them, she'd slipped out the back door to "pet the baby."

According to the camera footage, Charcoal had raced to the toddler's aid. The mother bear had swiped at him, knocking the cat down and breaking his leg and putting two slashes in his side. But Charcoal had still chased off the pair before hobbling back to the back porch and sitting with his toddler.

Adrenaline didn't just impact people.

"He's an impressive cat." The video of the incident had gone viral after the local news posted it on their social media account. Holt held out the mocha latte with three shots of espresso and grinned. "Coffee delivery. Your favorite according to Paisley at Up for Caffeine."

Her fingers brushed his. The simplest touch. One most people wouldn't notice. But at the tiny connection, his heart thudded. She was part of his past. A good part.

Holt chased accomplishments after his brush with delinquency. First in theater, then university and finally in his career. After his father passed, he'd dived even further into work. Climbing the corporate ladder, staying as focused as possible. None of the achievements filled the not so tiny hole in his soul.

Standing here felt different, though.

It's coffee with an old friend. Focus!

"Thank you." She took a sip and nodded. "It's good."

There was a look in her eyes that he couldn't quite place.

Not unhappiness or anger but something was bothering her. "You okay?"

Sage raised an eyebrow as she took another sip of her drink. "Of course."

It was a lie. At least he was pretty sure it was.

Once he'd known each inflection of her voice; theater class taught him how to pay attention to the unspoken cues people gave off. It was a skill he used often. There was a time when they'd each joked about how well they'd read each other.

He'd known when she was tired but forcing a point. She'd recognized when he was upset but hiding it. He hadn't realized how much he'd missed that connection until he'd walked into the clinic three days ago.

Still, it wasn't his place to call out her small lie. Not anymore.

She's protecting herself from me.

And why shouldn't she? Just because it touched a sensitive nerve in his soul, didn't mean Sage had to open up to him. Though if she did…

No. He would not wish for something that wasn't his.

"So, is there anything I should know about the day's schedule?"

Sage looked at him, her dark eyes searching his. There were words trapped in her throat, but he wouldn't push.

"We've got a dog coming in, little guy, got loose in a trail parking lot! Hit by a car!" Lucy's voice broke the tension between them.

Sage set her coffee down as they both switched into rescue mode.

"Scalpel?" Before Holt could even hold his hand out, Sage was handing it to him.

She was very good at her job; they'd moved nearly as one during this emergency. Anticipating each other's moves and needs. He'd worked with enough colleagues to know this wasn't the way brand-new colleagues typically worked together.

"He's tolerating the anesthesia well."

Holt nodded as he finished closing the laceration in Boxer's spleen. Shock was a huge factor when animals were struck by cars. With broken ribs, a lacerated spleen and two broken back legs, it was amazing he was tolerating surgery as well as he was.

Little guy was a fighter.

"I am about ready to close." Boxer might tolerate surgery, now, but for every minute he remained under, things had the chance to go south.

"I've got the sutures ready."

"Of course, you do." Holt winked since he knew she couldn't see the smile on his face under the mask. "You are the most competent tech I've worked with."

"Just doing my job." Sage looked at the heart monitor.

Was she avoiding the compliment? Or did she really not know how exceptional her skills were?

"It helps that we know each other too. No awkward get to know you issues." Her words were soft, but he heard the subtle wave in her tone.

They knew each other. Or knew their past selves. He wasn't the same boy he'd been at eighteen, thank goodness. But their subconscious selves seemed to recognize each other. That wasn't the only reason this surgery was going well, though.

"Maybe." Knowing each other was helpful, but that didn't diminish her work. "But having a tech that knows as much as you do is a tremendous benefit."

"No other choice."

"That's true. But I am glad you're the one here, Sage." The words slipped out as he finished closing Boxer.

Maybe he shouldn't be. This wasn't her dream. She'd gotten stuck here and made the best of it. But he could not pretend that he was upset that Sage Pool was his vet tech.

* * *

"Come with me to talk to Boxer's mom?" Holt offered as he wiped the sweat from his brow. "In my experience, it's good to have two people there. Two sets of ears and eyes to make sure we agree the client is hearing all the news."

Sage agreed, but for the first time in forever she wished the clinic was large enough to employ multiple techs. On the weekends they had part-time help if an animal needed emergency care, like with Charcoal's incident. But during the week, it fell to her and the vet.

Holt.

After leaving Dr. Jacobs's going away party, she'd sworn to herself that she'd keep as much distance between her and Holt as possible. Her body responded to him and at least part of her mind wanted to revert to the open-book girl she'd been with him before.

Sage didn't open up to people. She solved the problems. Handled the family issues and kept quiet about her own wants and desires.

But she'd opened up to Holt all those years ago, in between learning lines. Told him all her dreams. How she was going to escape this town, how worried she was about Forest, her hopes for the future, the drama at school, how in a town built on rock climbing, hiking and skiing she wasn't fond of the outdoors.

She'd known his secrets too. How mad he was at his mom for leaving. How hurt he was each time she made a date to see him and then "forgot," or rescheduled. They'd spent a year as friends and barely stepped into something more when her life erupted.

Part of her wanted to go back to that. To step back into that security.

He was right. She'd known what he needed in the surgery. Sure, she was good at her job, though hearing him say it made her heart swell. They'd worked seamlessly to treat Boxer.

If her heart rate didn't pick up just a little each time he

looked at her, she'd be happy to just work easily with some-one after failing to mesh with Dr. Jacobs. If it was anyone other than Holt…

What a selfish thought.

It wasn't his fault she reacted to him. She needed to control her wandering mind because today had proven there was no way to avoid the handsome vet, whose body language she still recognized.

"Lead the way." She wished her scrubs had pockets, some way to make her seem like she was more relaxed.

"Is Boxer going to be okay?" Natalie Grams stood as Holt and Sage stepped into the exam room where'd they had the young woman wait while Holt operated on the little guy.

"Yes."

Sage appreciated Holt started with that one simple word.

Natalie sank to the floor and started crying. "Sorry. Sorry. I know this is good. I just…"

Sage moved to her side and slid to the floor too. Natalie was a tourist. She'd met her long enough only to get the basics for Boxer's care, but she understood the emotions racing through the young woman. "It's okay." She murmured the phrase over and over as Natalie hugged her knees.

Holt didn't rush. She wouldn't have heard whatever he had to say anyway. Dr. Jacobs would have delivered all the basics, then stepped out to catch up on the backlog of patients.

And there was a backlog, though Lucy had done her best to reschedule as much as she could. Rushing away from a client this upset just meant they wouldn't hear what you said, and Sage would have to repeat it.

Natalie hiccupped, then took a deep breath and brushed the tears off her cheeks. "All right." She pushed herself off the floor and Sage followed. "What do I need to know?"

"Boxer is going to be fine, but he'll need to stay with us tonight and tomorrow and maybe one more day too. There was internal bleeding from a broken rib that lacerated his spleen.

I repaired it, but his back legs are broken. The good news is that we could use regular casts. Over the next few weeks, he will need loving care."

"He's already a spoiled little boy; he will love even more tender loving care." Natalie wrapped her hands around her waist. "The other dog just wanted to play, but Boxer is a rescue, and his first home wasn't very pleasant. He fears other dogs and panicked. If I'd been holding his leash tighter..."

"This isn't your fault. And it's not the driver's fault either." Holt's voice was firm, and Sage smiled at him without thinking.

They were the perfect words. Words Natalie deserved to hear. And the bandages on her fingers showed how tight she'd held the leash. But a panicked dog, even a little one, had a lot of strength. And the driver was going the speed limit and had stopped to aid Natalie. This was an accident.

"Can I see him?" Natalie wiped away another tear.

"Of course. Sage can you take her back while I see to another patient?"

She nodded and led Natalie back.

"Boxer is a mutt. I know he is unique looking." Natalie mused as they walked to the cage where Boxer was resting. "He was my elderly neighbor's rescue baby, after his first home. When she got sick, she asked me to take him. I am not sure how the ball of fur weighing less than thirteen pounds got the name Boxer, but he is my little guy now."

Sage couldn't hide the surprise on her face. As a rescue operator, she knew many people feared what would happen if they got ill or passed unexpectedly. Most pets ended up at shelters or stuffed into already-overcrowded rescues. For a rescue who'd come from a rough start, going back into a shelter after losing their person would have been cruel.

"That was kind of you."

More than kind.

"She didn't have any family. Said she was always too busy

taking care of others to see to her own dreams. But she loved Boxer." Natalie let out a soft cry as she leaned against the cage where her little boy was resting.

Always taking care of others. That was a line that Blaire had thrown at Sage more than once. *Need to make sure you're chasing your own dreams. Your own wants.*

She swallowed the uncomfortable feelings as they rushed forward. Natalie had done a good deed, ensured Boxer was well cared for after his owner's passing. It had nothing to do with her.

"Pet his head and talk to him. Even more than half asleep, he will hear your voice and be comforted." She stepped away, "I need to see to a few patients too."

She wanted to race away from the uncomfortable thoughts pressing against her head. Sage was chasing her own dreams.

She was.

It was just taking more time than she'd anticipated. *Because I keep helping Mom.*

Because if I don't who will?

There was no use getting upset about that. It just was what it was.

"You don't have to stay." *And I don't want you to.*

Was that the unspoken phrase following Sage's statement? Looking over Boxer was technically her duty. If there was a problem, which he doubted, he was on call.

But it seemed gravely unfair. In a larger clinic, they'd have a night staff. The clinic could use another vet tech, something he'd bring up with the corporate office. Though he suspected they'd say something along the lines of *we haven't needed one before.*

The reward for good work was more work. And Sage Pool was excellent at her job. That didn't mean he couldn't try to alleviate some of the burden she carried.

"I know I don't have to stay." Holt pulled his phone out of

his back pocket. He'd changed into his jeans and T-shirt when the clinic officially closed. Sage wore a pair of white shorts that accentuated her long legs and a T-shirt with the logo of the rescue she somehow found time to run.

Seriously, the woman seemed to do it all. Did she have an extra six hours in her day that no one else did? "Besides, someone needs to get you dinner."

"Oh, I ordered a pizza."

"With bell peppers and pineapple?" He hoped his voice sounded fine and not let down that one of the few things he could offer, she didn't need. Independence was a good thing, but sometimes letting others help was a sign of strength too.

He'd only been back three days, but his gut told him Sage never asked for help. And probably needed it—something she'd never admit.

The corners of her lips tipped up as she texted someone on her phone. "Surprised you remember that."

He remembered everything about her. Remembered her smile lighting up the room, her passion for animals, and how telling her about his mother had felt so good. Remembered how she'd confided in him too.

And then I just left.

His body shook with desire and pain at odds with the discussion about pizza.

Rather than leaning into those feelings, Holt shifted his position. "To this day, I do not understand how you can stand having the spicy and sweet together. Not my thing."

Sage laughed. The sound a bell his soul craved. Once she'd smiled and laughed often. He'd missed it when he moved away.

More than he'd even realized.

"Some of us like more than just a ton of meat on our pizzas." Her hip bumped his and her eyes widened. She cleared her throat; her cheeks coated a pretty rose color as she grabbed the tablet chart. "Boxer needs his meds. I am going to grab those. Can you make sure the front door is open for Gavin?"

"Gavin?" He knew she hadn't meant to hip check him, but he'd liked the connection. The ease they'd once had slipping through, despite time's passage. Fire coated the back of his throat as he watched her stand on tiptoe to reach the top shelf of the cabinet. She was stunning. His mouth nearly watered as he forced his eyes away.

"Gavin is the delivery kid for Joe's Pizzeria."

"Ahh." He slipped out of the room as relief spread through him. Gavin wasn't a boyfriend. Just the delivery person. Relief… What kind of person did that make him? It shouldn't matter if Sage had a partner. If he were a good person, he'd want her to find someone. To be happy.

That was what someone who cared about others would want.

The front door was unlocked, but he stepped into the evening, taking a few minutes to clear his brain.

Before too long, a tall lanky kid drove into the parking lot. Joe's Pizzeria was quick. Their motto, *From our oven to your table in thirty*, was plastered on the billboard driving into town. A billboard that had been painted in his absence but not updated.

Joe Senior's curly hair was long gone, and his son ran the business now, but the image of the man holding the pizza was a staple.

He opened the door as Gavin, a teen he didn't know, got close. "Good evening."

"Evening. I got two medium pizzas here."

"Two?" Holt took both from the kid, the smell of hot dough and sauce making his mouth water. Maybe Sage was starving. His stomach rumbled, and he wanted to laugh. They'd been so busy today that he'd forgotten lunch, Sage had likely done the same.

"Sage already paid. And included a tip. Have a nice night." Then he was off.

She'd taken care of everything.

Of course she had.

"Your two pizzas are here!" Holt held up the bounty as he stepped into the back. "Any chance I can steal a slice?"

Sage was holding a giant box, but she smiled as he laid the pizzas down. "The second pizza is yours. It's the double meat. Your favorite. Or at least it was." Color seeped into her cheeks, again. "I sent a text to Joe Junior when you said you were staying, and he added it." She looked at the box in his hands, "Anyways, there are plates in the cabinet by the coffee pot."

She'd ordered him a pizza. Taking care of him, adding him to her circle of responsibilities. It was nice.

But will she let me do the same?

"So how do you feel about decorations?"

Sage's question hit him as he wandered back with the plates. "Decorations?" Seriously, her mind must move from topic to topic with incalculable speed. Unfortunately, he couldn't keep up.

She opened the box and held up a banner filled with eggs and bunnies. *Easter/Spring* was written in big letters on the side. He grabbed a slice of her pizza and put it on her plate. She needed dinner as much as he did. And he was going to make sure she took at least a few minutes' break.

Sage took the plate from him and took a bite. She closed her eyes, and he saw the stress of the day fade from her.

"It's good?"

"Delicious! Something about pizza after a long day." Then she tapped the side of the box. "Now decorations."

"Do you ever slow down?" He took a bite of his pizza and sighed. She was right, there was something about pizza after a long day.

"No." She grinned, but there was the hint of something behind her eyes.

"Why?"

Sage just shrugged and opened the box. "I used to decorate the clinic all the time. I've got Valentine's Day, St. Patrick's Day, Easter, Spring, Summer, back to school. Halloween, Thanksgiving, Christmas and Winter decorations."

She'd ignored his question. Once she'd have told him. His chest was tight with the need to push. To demand an answer so he could help. But he didn't deserve one. So he focused on what she wanted to discuss.

"That is quite the list of office decorations. Holt looked at the Hoppy Spring banner. It was handmade, with paper bunnies and carrots. "I like decorations, but I'm not sure why you're asking."

"Dr. Jacobs hated them. Said that corporate sent the decorations we were supposed to use. Which amounts to a few posters with animals and vets dressed for Christmas which are designed to sell product. You looked adorable in the Santa hat."

The smile on her face made his heart skip a beat. He'd done two print campaigns for the company. They'd asked, and he'd said yes. Good for his corporate image, and it kept him busy after his father's death. She was right, though; the posters were not much fun.

"If you want to decorate, Sage, I will not report it to corporate." He grabbed another slice of pizza. "Not even sure if they would care."

He looked over the top of the box. Pastel decorations, all homemade, many from what looked like recycled goods. They were beautiful. "Where did you get these?"

"Made them. I learned from an online video."

"When do you sleep, Sage?"

"Sometimes, I don't." She refused to meet his gaze and grabbed another piece of pizza. "I like to stay busy."

She took a bite of pizza, but he got the impression it was so she didn't have to keep talking. That hurt, but he understood. Once they'd shared so many parts of their lives. But those days were gone.

Shattered by his own choices.

"How about we finish our pizzas, then I'll help you decorate? Deal?"

"You'll help?"

The surprise in her tone didn't shock him. But he was going to ensure Sage knew he'd help whenever she asked. And even when she didn't. "Of course. But we have to finish dinner. It was a long day—it's going to be a long night and we need sustenance. Deal?"

"Deal!" The excitement in her voice was infectious.

"Thank you for helping with the decorations." Sage slid down the wall across from Boxer's cage and yawned. She'd stay for his next round of medicine, then head home to get a few hours of sleep.

Dr. Jacobs hadn't permitted her to hang up her decorations; the other vets hadn't forbidden them, but they'd never helped. It was a small thing, but Holt laying everything out, and getting excited with each new piece was a boost to her ego. A boost she hadn't had in so long.

She'd gotten into a crafting cycle a few years ago. After watching an online video while going through one of her not irregular bouts of insomnia. Better to watch a useful video and focus on something she had some control over than spend the night lying awake running through unpleasant thoughts of issues outside her power.

The insomnia started after Forest's arrest when she could hear her mother cry at all hours. She'd get up to comfort her and eventually it resulted in her not falling asleep, period.

Once she moved out of her mother's place, she gotten some relief. But whenever she was super stressed…which was still too often…she'd spend a few days operating on caffeine and adrenaline.

"It was the least I could do after you got dinner." Holt slid next to her and pulled his knees up to his chest.

Once, so long ago, she'd have laid her head against his

shoulder to talk some theater gossip or discuss upcoming auditions. Now though, she just stared straight ahead, and tried to ignore the not so subtle voice in her mind telling her to do it.

That he was still her Holt. Her safe space.

It was such a nice thought. No one had been safe for Sage in such a long time. The few men she dated bristled at her schedule and independence. Blaire helped with the rescue, but she had her own burdens and Sage didn't want to add to them. And her mom…well, her mom was stronger now, but not strong enough to handle all the anxiety Sage kept trapped in her mind.

"Speaking of dinner…" Holt's voice caught as he leaned his head against the wall.

His blond hair was ruffled, his T-shirt clung to well-toned arms and her fingers ached to run over the stubble on his chin. There were still hints of the boy she'd known as a teen, but the man sitting here now was all chiseled hotness. And the desires pulsing through her now had none of the childish puppy love attributes.

"What if I take you to dinner this weekend? To pay you back."

Her heart leaped as her brain focused on the second line. He wasn't asking her out. Paying one back was not a date. Not that she wanted to date Holt Cove.

You really believe that lie?

Fine. Maybe she wanted a date with Holt. Or part of her did anyway. Wanted to see if the tension that pulled between them so long ago reignited. But that inner girl was easy enough to tame.

"You don't need to pay me back, Holt." She closed her eyes and leaned her head against the wall too. She'd slept as well as she ever did last night, but her body existed in a state of perpetual tiredness. "The next time we have to stay you order the pizza."

"Sure." His voice was tight, but she didn't open her eyes. "How long are you staying?"

"Until his next medication round. If I leave at midnight, I can get a few hours of sleep before I am back here at six for his next round of medication."

"And if you fall asleep on the floor?" There was a touch of worry in his voice, and her heart softened.

Not that it wasn't already soft where Holt was concerned. People didn't worry about Sage. She was the strong one. The one that picked up the pieces of her family's life when it all fell apart. The one who got things done. The one you could always count on.

It was something she prided herself on. But sometimes she wished others asked how she was too.

"You're exhausted, Sage."

He wasn't wrong, but that didn't matter. She held up her phone without opening her eyes. She feared if she saw the worry, she might ask him to stay with her. Might beg. Just to have company. To not be alone on a task. Finally.

She didn't need him, but it might be nice…

"I've set my alarm. But I've got insomnia. On the off chance I doze off, the alarm will make sure Boxer gets his meds. Don't worry about him."

"I wasn't worried about the dog, Sage." Holt's voice was gentle, as he leaned close to her. His arm was warm as he wrapped it over her shoulder.

She sighed as she leaned her head against his shoulder. She'd enjoy the moment, for a few minutes. Then she'd scoot away.

I missed you.

Maybe she couldn't verbalize that thought, but that didn't mean it wasn't true.

The shrill buzz of her phone jolted Sage awake. It took her a few seconds to realize she was sitting on the floor of the clinic. And another second to recognize Holt's arm was still around her shoulder.

He stayed.

No one ever helped Sage with the night shift needs. Not that she'd asked, but it was just the expectation that she'd handle everything. But Holt. Holt was still here.

His fingers tightened on her shoulder as she shifted. Her face turned, meeting his. A loose smile on his lips. The comfort she'd initially felt was slipping into something very different now.

Fire lit through her body. The inferno increasing as she held his gaze. The only thought running through her mind… how did he kiss?

Get yourself together, Sage!

"Time for medicine?" He blinked and stretched, seemingly unconcerned by the fact that she'd used him as a pillow for the better part of three hours.

The question jolted her back to reality. Her phone was still blaring, but it wasn't her alarm.

"No." She slid her finger across the phone. "Hi, Maggie. Is everything all right?"

She knew the answer. No one called this close to midnight if everything was fine, but Sage wanted to give Maggie, one of their most dedicated foster moms, a chance to tell her what was going on. She took in medical cases, puppies that needed training, anything. She was a godsend in the rescue business; if she was calling at this hour, there was trouble.

"I am so sorry about the time, Sage."

"It's fine. What's going on?" She felt Holt's eyes on her, turned and saw the concern on his face. It was like they still had the connection she'd felt all those years ago. What did that even mean?

Most likely she was just lonely. And maybe a little horny.

"My mother fell down the steps and broke her hip. Or she

broke her hip and fell down the stairs. I am not sure, but I booked the red-eye to Boston. I need to head to the airport now."

"Of course." She looked at the clinic kennels. Could she house the animals here? It wasn't ideal but...

"I only need you to take Domino. He's a lovable giant, but a bit of a handful. And the only foster I currently have. Susan is looking after my three girls. Given her age and Domino's tendency to jump—"

"Understood. And taking just him will make it easier on me." It was a lie. Her landlady would love for her to bring Domino home. It would give her the grounds she was constantly searching for to boot her. Even if she was willing to risk hiding a rescue, there was no way to hide the Great Dane mix, who believed he was a lap dog.

She'd started looking at apartments this past weekend, but most were out of town, only offered rentals to tourists on a week-long basis or required a full year's lease. She was hoping to be in her own place before then.

Please.

"I'm still at the clinic. Another pup required monitoring. So if you bring him here, that makes it easier." She mentally started calculating who might foster Domino for a few weeks. Someone who understood giant babies and was solid with training schedules.

"Fantastic. Can I give you the notes on him while I am driving? Save me time."

Sage flipped the conversation to speaker, stood and grabbed a notebook. Fully focused on the task at hand. "Ready when you are."

"He gets two cups of food in the morning and two at six thirty. If you are late, he will whine and toss his bowl. He's better at leash walking, still not great. He pulls—if I didn't regularly lift, he could carry me away."

"Right." Sage ticked off a few things on the list she was making. That ruled out the Kole family and Mrs. Parks. What was she going to do? There was no way her landlady would bend, even with the understanding it was only for a few weeks. Could she board the dog here? *That* would eat through her resources…

"He is a big sweet baby that whines if left alone too long."

And that ruled out boarding. Where was she going to place a gentle giant that needed people? He was already going to be stressed going to a new foster placement; that meant the anxiety would be worse than normal.

"No known allergies or food sensitivities, correct?"

"No allergies. The big goober inhales his food but seems fine with whatever I give him."

"All right." Sage would figure it out, somehow. She always did.

"Can I ask a question?"

"Absolutely." Maggie was one of her best foster parents, and she was dealing with a stressful situation. Sage would do whatever it took to make sure she felt comfortable.

"Is Dr. Cove as hot as they say he is?"

Her face heated as she looked from the phone on the counter to Holt. The smile on his lips combined with the messed hair and five o'clock shadow made her mouth water.

Yes. He definitely is.

"Sage?"

She cleared her throat. She didn't want Maggie feeling embarrassed by the question. It wasn't her fault that Holt was listening.

"He'll be here when you stop by. You can judge for yourself."

Holt knew he was attractive. He hated the stereotype of the lead in the movie or television show, not knowing they were conventionally attractive. He knew it, but it was also the thing he found least interesting about himself. At least until Sage had mentioned he was hot while they were standing in the dark closet. Being attractive to her...

Well, that inflated his ego more than he liked to admit. He'd not fallen asleep. Holding her...he'd liked it. So much.

When she turned her head to look at him when her phone went off, there was a blip in time where he'd thought of dropping his head. Kissing her, asking her out for an actual date instead of pay her back for the pizza. But she deserved more than to be asked out at midnight on the floor of the clinic where she worked, when yet another emergency was brewing.

Was there ever a time when an emergency wasn't brewing for Sage?

Maybe that was something they should discuss, but not here and not tonight.

"So Domino." He saw her shoulders relax. Discussing animals calmed her; that was good knowledge to keep in his back pocket.

"He's a big baby."

"I gathered." Holt stepped beside her. He ached to wrap an arm around her, give her a little support. She needed it. That was a certainty deep in his belly.

And he was going to find a way to make sure she knew she could count on him. This time there'd be no ghosting. Anything she needed...he was her guy!

"Where is he going?" He'd worked with a few fosters before. Unfortunately there were always more animals than there were foster families.

This was why she'd wanted the Rainbow Ranch. So she had a place for late-night placements. And he'd stripped that dream away.

Unknowingly...but still.

Sage rolled her shoulders, her hips sliding toward him before she yanked herself upright.

Did she feel the pull between them too?

"Not sure. It is so late and I can't take him to my place.

My landlady is…" Sage paused, rubbed the back of her neck and sighed. "She's looking for any excuse to yank my lease. Some investor offered her a nice price for the building but refuses to take on any of the leases. I guess he plans to make it short-term rentals for tourists…like nearly every other rental place in town. Not great for those of us that want to stay in the area permanently."

She looked to the ceiling and shook her head. "That was a lot of words to just repeat that I'm not sure." Sage took a deep breath and offered a smile that didn't reach her eyes as she added, "Yet."

She was tired, frustrated, but so determined. Sage Pool would make it work. That didn't mean she had to do it alone.

Without thinking he wrapped his arms around her. "It's going to be okay."

She sighed as she leaned against him. Her body molding to his as her breath slowed. "I just don't know where to put him." The words were soft…so soft he wasn't sure she meant to speak them into existence.

"Why don't I take him?" The offer flew from his mouth, and she turned in his arms. Her chest pressed against his; her mouth hanging open. Sage was just as surprised as him, but it felt like the right choice. He loved animals, and big dogs were his favorite.

His sweet girl Lark, an elderly Lab rescue he'd gotten just after finishing vet school, had been gone about a year. He might not be ready for a forever pet, but he could foster.

Something shifted in her dark eyes, and she stepped out of his arms.

He felt her absence in his soul, but he wasn't going to reach for her again. If she wanted him, all she had to do was ask.

"Have you ever fostered?" Sage rocked back on her heels; her eyes holding his. This was the foster champion, not the vet tech or his friend. This was a warrior for the animals in her care.

"No."

Her nose twitched as she looked at the list she'd made while talking to Maggie, "Pet ownership?"

"I am a veterinarian, Sage." He winked, but she didn't change her stance. "Yes. I had dogs growing up, you know that and then I owned the sweetest Lab mix for the last four years of her life. The family got rid of her when she started going gray. Most ridiculous excuse ever." It infuriated him when people didn't realize pet ownership was a lifetime responsibility.

"She was my sweet girl, crossed the rainbow bridge a little over a year ago."

"An older Lab. Domino has a lot of energy, and you will be here most of the day."

"True." He shrugged. No reason to deny the facts. "I go for a run every morning. Danes aren't great running partners, but he can come for the first mile. That should tire him out." Danes had bursts of energy, but mostly they liked to lie on couches or dog beds and snooze.

They were huge, but generally lazy.

"I can at least take him for a few days until you find a solution you're more comfortable with. I'll take a few bags of food from here, and I still have the water and food bowls I used for Lark."

She pursed her lips as the alarm on her phone went off. There were no better options. Sage had to know that. She needed rest and spending the night in the kennel was not a great option for a dog already going through changes.

Grabbing the medicine for Boxer, she gave it to the drowsy dog before turning her attention to Holt. "I can run the foster supplies over tomorrow after work. Our rescue keeps a welcome packet for new fosters. If you're sure?"

"Absolutely." And it gave him another chance to pay her back for tonight. "What if you come over around seven, I'll have dinner ready?"

"You don't have to—"

"I know, Sage. I want to. Let me help."

She looked at him, but loud barking cut any thoughts off.

"I suspect that is my new best bud." Holt let out a yawn and started toward the door. "Boxer will be fine for the night, let's close this up and get at least a few hours of rest.

"I already got a few hours." Sage covered her mouth and shook her head. "Sorry for falling asleep."

"It didn't bother me at all. You can sleep with me anytime. I…" Heat flooded his body. There was no good way to walk back that unintentional double entendre.

And it was true.

Her eyes darted to his, and he wondered at the unsaid thoughts he saw there. He opened his mouth, then closed it. There was no great way to cover for that lapse of control.

Sage cleared her throat, "We should go let you meet Domino."

"Yes." Holt nodded, in what he hoped was a normal not over-the-top way. "That is what we should do."

CHAPTER FOUR

SAGE YAWNED AND stretched as she stepped out of her truck. Her shoulders were tight; but she loved this time of day. The sun had set but the glint of orange in the horizon made her smile. The days were getting longer. Spring was on its way.

The ranch looked…it looked like home. It always had. Even when it was sitting empty. No other property felt this way. But it wasn't home.

Why was that such a hard thought to get through her mind? Holt owned this. She'd find some other place for her rescue. It just wouldn't be here.

He had done nothing to the front. The weeds were still choking out the native flower beds her mother had planted. The gutter on the left side of the front door was still hanging on…by a few nails.

He's been here a week, Sage!

Not everyone innately needed to stay busy all the time. The need to drive out thoughts with action. To prove to themselves over and over again that they didn't need anyone else. And the ability to stay up all night when rest eluded them.

She liked to think of those things as her superpowers.

"Sage."

Her name…from his lips. Her heart rate increased, and her soul seemed to sigh. *Jeez!*

She needed to find something besides Holt Cove to occupy her thoughts. Since he'd tumbled back into her life, he'd occupied most of the free space in her brain. Last night, standing in his arms. Being held…

Desire had nearly overwhelmed her. Even now she could remember the feel of him against her. The heat, the comfort, the *want* flowing through every inch of her being.

The crush she'd had on him as a teen was nothing compared to the desires racing through her grown-up brain. Stepping to the side of her truck she grabbed the rescue supplies… and the box.

She wasn't sure how she was going to explain its contents. "Domino!"

As if the heavens were answering her silent pleas for some other thought, the dog raced across the yard and bounded to her. She turned her back before he could jump. It was one of the first lessons she taught foster families.

Dogs jumped for attention. Turning your back deprived them of that. Domino let out a whine and sat down. She turned and rubbed his ears—rewarding the behavior she wanted to see.

"That is a good boy." Holt smiled as he walked toward her. A clicker in his hand.

"Working on training?" She was impressed. Yes, Holt was a veterinarian. Yes, he'd recommended training today at the clinic when Mrs. Opiol's rescue, Bailey, had refused to listen. But recommending and following through were two different things.

Holt rubbed Domino's head. "He's a gentle giant. Big dogs don't get the same grace that little ones do. So, he has to listen to commands."

She couldn't agree more.

"Let me help."

Before she could argue, he lifted the box out of her arms; it's beaten edges a testament to the number of times she'd moved with it. Had she subconsciously hoped he'd return?

"This is heavy! You give every new foster a giant box of goodies?"

Her tongue was stuck to the top of her mouth as she listened to the familiar creek of the front porch.

Nope. Only he was getting a box of memories.

The stuff she'd found in Forest's room when she'd packed it up.

And a few things he'd left in hers.

Old playbills. Pictures. Notes. No big deal.

Sure!

She hadn't believed that when she'd packed the box, foolishly hoping that Holt might text back. Hadn't believed it when she moved from one small apartment to another. Hadn't believed it when she'd heard his dad was moving and kept the box…just in case.

She followed him inside and the host of longing she always felt when she returned ached in her chest.

Home.

Clearing her throat, she forced her mind to focus. "Actually, the bag is all you get from the rescue. It has a clicker, which you already have, a list of valuable websites, a few chew toys, a bag of healthy treats. That box—"

Unspoken words pressed against her chest as she looked at the handwriting on the side: *For Holt.* She couldn't seem to force anything out, and Holt just stood there. Heat crept up her chest, her neck and her cheeks. Did she look like a tomato yet?

"That is a box of memories. Things left when mom and I had to leave." She held up her hands. "I—I guess maybe I thought you'd come back." She laughed, nerves sending the pitch close to something only Domino would hear.

"Sage." Holt set the box down and reached for her hands.

His touch was delicate, but she wished he'd opened his arms. She'd have stepped into them. Wanted to step into them…to be held—by him.

"Thank you."

She squeezed his hands, "You don't even know what is there. I mean, thanking me is a little premature. Anyways..." She should leave. That is what she should do. Yet her feet refused to budge.

Once upon a time she'd believed she was meant to be in his life. Then life happened. All the years and distance.

Yet here she was. Feeling like she was meant to be right here. With him. Again.

It made little sense. She wanted to lean into him, to kiss him. To chase long put away dreams. If she was stronger, she could banish the feelings.

"Do you want me to wait until you leave to look in it?"

"Absolutely." She'd kept a box of memories, but there was no telling if he'd actually want it. "That makes the most sense. See you tomorrow?"

"Wait!" Holt squeezed her hand, and she looked down. They were holding hands—again—and she couldn't make herself pull back.

"I promised you dinner." He grinned, the dimple in his cheek making her knees weak.

She'd forgotten that. Or more accurately, she hadn't thought it was a serious offer. Her mother did things like that. Offer something only to conveniently forget. Her father had been a pro at it too. Sage couldn't remember the last time she'd had someone cook her a meal.

"I didn't think you meant that." She regretted the words as soon as she saw his frown. "I mean, it was just pizza and I don't want you to feel like you have to..." Her voice died away. She wasn't sure what she was trying to say.

He stepped very close, the scent of sandalwood and mint trapping her in place. Her hands begged her brain to let them reach up, skim his chest, then beg him to kiss her.

"I want to, Sage. Stay." The words were low, sensual. His eyes flashing with what she wanted to believe was desire. Was that foolish? *Yes*. Didn't change the need flaring through her.

She tipped her head, an ancient part of her begging to let this happen. Just once. Then maybe she could box up whatever feelings his presence had awoken.

Without warning, Domino barked and pushed between them as he bolted toward the door. A large truck on the road raced passed, and Domino scratched at the door, able to hear the loud vehicle even after it had disappeared from human hearing range.

"Domino!" Holt petted the dog's ears, speaking to him in a low, controlled tone. Reassuring the dog that it was okay.

Sage wrapped her arms around herself trying to calm the fire his presence ignited. Unfortunately watching Holt with the dog only intensified it.

There was no yelling. Just reassurance. Dogs got agitated out of fear, and Domino had been through two fosters and one abandonment, when the family claimed they'd expected him to be around forty pounds. He was in a new home. Anxiety was normal.

But if that car had passed a few minutes later she might know how Holt kissed.

"So, dinner." Holt pointed to the kitchen. The moment was gone. "I've got spaghetti and meatballs. Not very fancy but the new stove won't be here until next week. There is a lot to do here. The back room needs all new drywall, a new floor and paint."

He started toward the kitchen, and she followed. She was hungry, and her plans to put distance between them had failed. Maybe if she gave in for a few hours…a few more hours…it would fill the Holt-sized hole in her heart.

"I've tried getting a contractor out here for estimates, but…" He shrugged and grabbed two plates from a cabinet that desperately needed to be refinished.

She understood. The closest general contractor was three towns over and made more money updating and building weekend homes for the ultrawealthy wanting houses with gorgeous views. The tradeoff was the homes were one mud-slide away from sliding all the way down the mountain. But that didn't matter apparently if you had it for a while? She'd never understand.

"They won't come. Not unless you're willing to tear the back half of the house off and replace it. They have better-paying jobs."

The minutes passed as Holt busied himself heating up their dinner. Eventually, Holt passed her a plate, his fingers brushing hers. Did he mean for his touch to linger?

"It looks delicious." She took a bite and closed her eyes as the oregano, basil, garlic and tomato all blended together. He'd said the spaghetti was easy, and she'd figured it was sauce from a can. "This is superb."

"Glad you like it. It's not hard. Dad took cooking classes after he retired. He was always trying to convince me to come." Holt's voice stumbled as he picked up his drink. "At least I learned his spaghetti recipe. If I'd worked less, I might know a few more."

The coat of grief hung on him as she reached for his hand. "I'm sure he understood—he had to work a lot when you were younger."

"Maybe." Holt took a deep breath. He shifted, "So how were you going to fix this place up?"

That was one way to change the topic. From one uncomfortable discussion point to another. Her stomach churned as the question settled around them. The reminder, as if she needed it, that this was another dream that had floated away.

"I learned to drywall, and tile. I've done a few jobs, nothing major, but I had planned to handle it myself." She took a big bite of spaghetti, but the food seemed to have lost some of its taste.

Silence settled around them. Holt ran a hand across his forehead. He looked like he wanted to say something, but instead he finished his dinner.

Domino laid his head on the table, and Holt immediately removed the large head. "Just because we can put our head on the table doesn't mean we do!"

Domino looked at her, his big dark eyes sorrowful, but she shook her head. "Sorry, I agree with your dad."

Dad.

She hadn't meant that. Holt was fostering the dog, but he didn't correct her. If this was a foster fail, well, Domino could do worse.

"I should get going." Sage stood.

Holt pushed to his feet and opened his arms.

Her body moved without thinking, like she was the girl she'd been and she hugged him. Time slowed and for a moment it was just them, again.

Holt didn't hesitate, he wrapped his arms around her. "I'm glad you came."

Lifting her face, she dropped a kiss on his cheek. A light peck, one that could be platonic. Could be... For whatever reason, the heat that burned between them as teens was even hotter now.

Pulling back, part of her sighed as Holt let her go. It was the right move, no one should try to hold on to someone, but if he had...

Her brain romped around the idea of what if? She needed to leave before she gave into the longing being near Holt brought out. "Thank you for dinner. If you need anything, let me know." Then she turned and forced herself to walk out.

Holt watched Domino bound across the backyard, grateful the fence he and Forest put in years ago was still in good shape. It was funny how many things had changed, but the wooden fence, painted all different colors, was still there. Faded, but still a testament to the good work they'd actually managed.

His father had suggested the idea to Rose. A way to keep the boys focused on something besides borderline criminal antics. And Rose was so lost after her husband left, she'd agree to anything.

Looking back, Holt understood they hadn't been bad kids. They'd been lost and angry at the world. Forest pissed at his dad. Completely understandable after the man said he was tired of the obligations family life laid on him.

Obligations.

A crappy excuse. One Holt's mother no doubt would have agreed with. Rather than wallow in joint despair, Holt had helped his friend nurse his anger.

Anger was so easy in those days. His mother had stopped coming to visit him when he was twelve. But the year they'd painted the fence, she'd forgotten his birthday, and his dad had been so busy with the shop he hadn't made it home to celebrate.

Even now, Holt could see the sorrow beneath the anger in the memory. His young eyes hadn't seen how hard his dad was working—for him. All he'd known was that trouble forced his dad to pay attention to him. Complaints about hitting mailboxes off their posts and painting graffiti on billboards advertising shops long closed resulted in lectures. Then shouting matches and finally hugs.

That had been the last summer of friendship for Holt and Forest. His father's heart attack happened just before school started, and Holt had righted his path. To make his dad proud. Joined theater and then noticed…really noticed Sage.

She was the reason the fence was so colorful. The reason this place would forever be the Rainbow Ranch.

She'd saved her money and bought leftover paint from the hardware store. Each bucket enough to paint a handful of fence posts. A happy show to cheer up her mother.

Sage…always taking care of others.

His fingers trailed to his cheek. The ghost of her caress hovering like a beacon.

Sage.

He'd thought of kissing her tonight. Thought of holding on

to her when she was leaving, asking if there was a way to pick up where they'd left off so long ago. They were still so drawn to each other. He wanted her...desperately.

Just thinking of her was enough to drive him mad. Kissing her...running his hands... Nope. He couldn't let that thought flourish.

Strolling back inside, he opened the box and his heart clenched. The picture of the two of them dressed as Cinderella and Prince Charming was on top.

That closing night was forever ingrained in his memory. A core memory of joy before everything changed forever! She'd jumped into his arms just after the curtain closed following their bows.

He'd spun her. Then the world stopped, and, just like tonight, it seemed like only they existed in the universe. Their kiss was brief, so brief. They'd pulled apart, staring at each other, then Sage had smiled at him. All doubts floating away on her grin. He'd asked her out; she'd said yes.

Then their teacher and parents had invaded the moment. With flowers for her and congrats for him.

She'd stepped away, the hint of pink in her cheeks. The promise that maybe there was more to the friendship they'd cultivated on the stage.

He set the picture down surprised by the amount of memory...and need...it restored.

Unfortunately, the next image had the exact opposite effect. Him and Forest in green caps and gowns. His chest tightened as he looked at the snapshot, unable to even lift it from the box. A moment of hope—hours before Forest, and Sage's, world was upended.

The boys were doing an awkward side hug. Rose and his dad had forced the picture. And awkward was a kind description. He and Forest hadn't shared a class in three years. They'd grown apart, as he and Sage grew close.

No. I separated myself.

After instigating the initial trouble, Holt pulled away when his father needed him. And rather than drag his friend with him this time, he'd told Forest he didn't want to be a party to any more antics. Then used worse language, rather than trying to help him. A consequence that eventually impacted more lives than just Forest's, though Holt hadn't been able to see it then.

His phone rang.

Thank goodness for the distraction.

"Hello?"

"Dr. Cove?"

"Yes. Do you have an animal in distress?" The clinic had an answering service that patched emergency calls through.

I probably shouldn't have been so happy about the distraction!

"No. Umm." The woman on the other end of the phone paused.

He waited a minute, and was about to hang up when she whispered, "Sage is going to kill me."

"Sage?" He blew out a breath, "Who is this?"

"Blaire. I help Sage with her rescue. Her truck broke down at the edge of your driveway. Her mom is out of town and I am at the base of Mt. Shasta. It will take me an hour or more. Any chance…"

"Of course." He'd started walking as soon as Blaire mentioned Sage was at the end of his driveway.

"Thanks."

The line went dead as he wandered down the path.

Why hadn't Sage called him? Or walked back down to the ranch?

She had to know he would help.

Didn't she?

Her truck came into view at the edge of the long drive. At least it had died before she got to the highway.

"I don't need this right now!" Her sob echoed down the drive, and his feet shifted into a run.

"Sage?" The hood was up, and he could hear bangs that probably weren't actually bangs, but he'd never really understood anything about mechanics.

"Let me guess—Blaire!" Her head didn't even pop around the hood as more bangs and noises echoed from underneath it. "How does she even have your number? Probably the internet. The woman can find anything."

He didn't respond. Sage was arguing with herself, and the last thing he wanted was to add more stress to her life.

"Anything I can do to help?"

"No! I need a new truck. This one has finally put its wheels up and pleaded no more." She let out a noise that sounded like half sob, half laughter as she walked around the truck and dropped a toolbox in the truck's bed.

"You certain it can't be fixed?" The vehicle was at least twenty years old, but she clearly knew enough to keep it running. Enough to have a toolbox in the bed that looked well used.

"Oh, I can fix it—with a new engine." She leaned against the side of the vehicle and put her head on her crossed arms. "I just loaned Mom part of my down payment money for a car. The ranch is gone, but other properties—"

She lifted her head and kicked the wheel of the tire. "Just once I want something to work out the way I plan. Just once. Is that too much to ask?"

He leaned against the back of her truck as she kicked the wheel over and over again. Anger was a normal emotion. It had taken him years, and unintentionally hurting others, to realize that. If she needed to kick a wheel, he'd wait.

Putting her hands on her hips, she looked at the night sky. "Sorry."

He pulled her into his arms then. "Don't need to be sorry." The hug was meant to offer her comfort. Give her the knowledge that she wasn't alone. But when Sage Pool was in his arms, the world righted. Time stopped, and he felt at peace.

Now wasn't the time for those thoughts. Sage was frustrated and tired. And he'd had the chance to stop her life from up-ending and not taken it. Then he'd stayed away, focusing on his own career and nothing else.

The woman in his arms always thought of others first. Cared for animals; creatures who didn't have a voice for themselves. She'd kept a box of memories for him…just in case.

She was nearly perfect, and he was pretty far from it.

None of that mattered to his heart. All the reasons rampaging through his brain couldn't stop its rapid beat.

His fingers traced down her back. He was offering consolation, but he wanted her. He couldn't deny that. Something about Sage touched a part of his soul that was silent otherwise.

Her arms tightened around his waist, then she stepped back.

"I need to move this hunk of junk."

"If you sit in the driver's seat, put the truck in Neutral, I'll push it to the side. Then I can drive you home."

Unless you want to stay?

He barely caught those words. She'd had a long day. The last thing she needed now was him coming on to her.

"I'll call a ride share. You don't need to be put out."

"Sage, this isn't putting someone out." She opened her mouth, but he put his hand over it. "Damn it, Sage. Let me help. I want to. I owe you."

Her dark eyes widened.

What would it take for her to ask for help?

She was always busy. Always doing something—when did she relax and let others step in?

She doesn't.

That was the answer, but tonight he was helping Sage. Whether she liked it or not!

"If you're sure you don't mind." She wrapped her arms around herself. Rocking back on her heels, there was a look in her face, like there was something more she wanted, but didn't dare ask.

Or maybe he was just imagining that.

"Not at all." He tilted his head. "You steer—I'll push."

She didn't say anything else, just shut the hood and climbed in.

CHAPTER FIVE

SHE WAS GOING to have to get a new truck. Going to drain her precious savings. It would set back her plans—again. Spring River Paws needed a permanent place. Somewhere she could bring animals without having to worry about immediate placement.

Those were the things she should be thinking about. Those were the pressing issues that needed to be solved. Instead, it was Holt Cove running through her mind. Like she was the lovesick teen, still crushing on her brother's onetime best friend.

They weren't teens now...

Her back was still on fire from his touch. He'd been comforting her. Comfort...which no one offered. No, that wasn't true.

Holt had comforted her on three occasions now.

And she craved so much more. She'd wanted to lift her face and kiss him. Complete what it felt like they were starting in his kitchen.

What they'd started so long ago.

Right after kicking the wheel of her ancient, dead vehicle.

And he'd just stood there and let her rage. Hadn't told her to calm down or asked her to control herself. Nope. He'd just let her have all her emotions with no judgment.

"Sage?" He opened her door and offered his hand. "You okay?"

No. Yes. Of course.

The words raced through her mind but none of them came forward. Today had been a lot.

Why was she trying to kid herself? Every day since Holt walked into the clinic had been a lot. A lot…and not enough.

She put her hand in his and slid into the moonlit night. The door of her truck slammed, and the lightning bugs scattered. He squeezed her hand, and she felt the pressure shift. He was getting ready to drop it; she didn't want that.

So she squeezed his hand and then laid her head on his shoulder. Enjoying the connection. The moment of just being with someone who wasn't asking anything of her.

Holt let out a sigh and leaned his head against hers as they started back to the ranch. This would be a perfect moment… if her dead truck wasn't sitting at the edge of his drive.

They reached the front of the ranch in what felt like record time. Even though her feet had been dragging.

"Just need to grab my keys."

"Holt." His name slipped from her lips. She hadn't meant to say anything, but she looked at their combined hands then lifted on her toes.

She was attracted to Holt Cove. And she wanted to know how he kissed. She never got what she wanted, but she wanted this.

The dam around them broke as her lips met his. Holt's hand wrapped around her waist, pulling her closer. No distance between their bodies as she molded to him.

When his mouth opened, she took the opportunity. If this was the only time she ever kissed him, she wanted the full experience. Slipping her arms around his neck, she wasn't surprised when the world slowed. He kissed her softly, their tongues dancing in rhythm as though they'd done this thousands of times.

The smolder in her belly erupted into a desperate need. He wrapped his hand around her head while she pressed her hips against him.

Her fingers ached to reach under his shirt. Her body screamed for his touch. Emotions, desires, wants tumbled together in a potion she'd never experienced. For once she didn't want to be the one making the rational decisions. She'd lived a life cleaning up others' impulsive moves and tonight…tonight she wanted Holt.

"Sage?" His lips were swollen as he finally broke the connection. His fingers ran along her cheek as he seemed to catch his breath.

Her hand ran along his chest. "Holt," she said, enjoying the sigh dropping from his lips.

"Do you still want me to drive you home?" His thumb drew a line along her jaw. Such a simple touch, one that boyfriends had done before. A simple caress, but none before had created flames.

He wanted her…and she craved him. Still, he was giving her the choice. Go home, pretend this never happened.

It might be hard, but he'd do it. Or she could reach for something just for herself. Tonight, she was going to be impulsive. She'd figure out the consequences later.

"Take me to bed, Holt."

"Sage." This time when her name slipped from his lips it sounded like a prayer. The hint of question all gone.

He picked her up.

"Ah!" She wrapped her arms around his neck as he carried her across the threshold. This was the stuff of movies and fairy tales.

The stuff that doesn't last.

She forced that unwelcome thought away. She was not overthinking this. Not tonight.

Sage dropped kisses along his jaw, enjoying the shift in his breathing when she kissed just below his ear. Touching him, knowing how much he wanted her too, was such a turn-on.

When they reached the main bedroom, her breath caught. He'd painted the bright yellow room a dark green. The bed was a light blue; it was relaxing and so Holt. The smell of his cedar and mahogany cologne made her smile. This was his space. Holt's.

And she didn't want to be anywhere else!

He set her on the bed, and she immediately sat up on her knees, pulling his shirt from his head. He had a tattoo of a mountain just above his heart.

Man, he was a masterpiece.

Her fingers ran along the edge of the tattoo, then dipped lower.

His fist wrapped around her wrist as she reached for the button of his jeans. "Not yet." The husky tone grabbed her. "Look at me."

Sage pursed her lips as she followed the command, even though her mind was screaming for her to drink in the mastery that was Holt Cove.

"I want you." He laid his head against hers as his hand stroked the edge of her breast.

The touch took her breath away, even through the light tank top she wore.

"But?"

Why are there always buts in my life?

He ran a hand along her backside, groaning as he cupped her butt. "But." His lips trailed along her jaw, his breath sending lightning across her skin. "I want to take my time with you, Sage. Don't make me rush this…please."

She swallowed, her mouth unable to form any words as she gripped his face with both her hands, kissing him deeply as his hands explored her. Breaking the connection, she leaned back just a little, hooked her hands under her shirt and lifted it over her head.

Holt grinned. If this was what impulsive felt like, Sage understood why so many gave in! Heat flooded every sense as his fingers danced along the edges of her breasts before unhooking her bra.

"You are a work of art." He dipped his head and suckled first one breast then the other, as his fingers skimmed her thighs.

His lips traced her body, his hands never leaving her. Slipping to the floor, he knelt and unbuttoned her shorts, sliding them over her hips. His mouth followed the path of her shorts down her thighs, then back up.

Her knees trembled as he made quick work of her panties. God, she was naked…with Holt.

She purred as his tongue trailed ever closer to her center before dancing away. His fingers were feathers on her thighs as she ran her hands through his hair.

"Please…" The sob escaped, and she felt him smile against her thigh.

His tongue danced around her opening as his hands held her thighs in place—opening her fully to him. She bit her lip as sensation after sensation rocked through her.

Her movements were hypnotic as Holt's mouth devoured her. Just when Sage thought she couldn't take any more, Holt pulled his head back.

His blue eyes met hers as he slipped a finger inside her, his other hand still cupping her butt. Her flesh tightened around him, and her lips parted before he dipped his head to her center again.

"Holt!" She couldn't form any other words. Ecstasy tore through her; she wanted him, all of him.

Now!

His mouth teased her, his fingers working in tandem to take her to new heights.

"Holt." He was tormenting her…in the most sensuous way. But it wasn't enough. "Now." There was a second word she could manage!

She nearly sobbed with relief when he used the hand cupping her bottom to open the nightstand drawer. She grabbed the gold package from the top, her fingers deftly tearing it open. He stood, the last of his clothes dropping to the ground.

Yep, a naked Holt was perfection to behold.

She reached for him, enjoying the length of him while she kissed him. His breath caught, and she smiled against his lips. Two could play the torment game.

"Sweetheart." He reached for the hand holding the condom, pulling it to his manhood. "I need you."

Holding his gaze, she slid the condom down his length, then captured his mouth, pulling him onto the bed with her.

The world exploded as their bodies became one. "Holt…"

"I enjoy hearing my name on your lips."

She wrapped her legs around his waist, arched her back and matched his rhythm. She never wanted this feeling to end!

Holt Cove always made sure his lovers enjoyed their time in his bed. But he'd never had a partner respond to every touch like Sage. It was impossible to overstate what a turn-on that was.

He stepped from the bathroom and saw her curled in his bed. Exhaustion overtaking her. But he didn't mind. Her dark hair was sprayed across his pillow, her lips swollen from kisses. *His kisses.* His chest swelled as he looked at her.

She was beautiful. Tonight she'd rushed in. A rarity for Sage, no doubt. How would she feel in the morning?

He swallowed, pulling her into his arms. That was an issue for tomorrow. Tonight she'd wanted him. That was a gift he'd treasure forever.

Her body molded to his, and he kissed the top of her head. If he was a believer in fates, he'd think they'd crafted her for him.

He grinned at the silly thought. Sage Pool wasn't his, but it was a lovely thought.

Holt woke from a dream…of Sage. The woman was in his arms and his body ached to claim her again. His hands stroked her back. The light touch barely there, just enough to remind his mind that she was here.

With him.

This was the best possible way to wake up.

"Holt." Her lips brushed his chin.

He smiled against her cheek. "I didn't mean to wake you." It was true. He'd just meant to touch her. Reassure his mind that the memory they'd created last night was real.

"Not sure I believe that." She slipped her hand between his legs cupping him before running her fingers along his length. "But I don't care."

Tiredness might plague him tomorrow…and none of it would matter because Sage was here now.

She hooked her foot over his hip, granting him easy access to her as she gripped him. Sage's lips trailed along his jaw, her mouth sliding down his throat. "Sage."

"I like hearing my name on your lips too." She uncurled, pushed him on his back and started working her way down his body. Her dark locks draped over him.

He wrapped his hands in her hair as her lips traveled the length of his shaft. As her mouth took him, he surrendered completely.

Holt gripped the sheets as she drove him closer to the edge. "Sage!" As good as this felt, he wanted her…all of her.

He lifted her head from him and reached for another condom.

"So demanding." She grinned as she slid the condom down his length.

"With you…absolutely." He touched her as she rocked them ever closer to explosion.

His body lighting with every touch. When her body clenched around him, and she laid her head back, he gripped her hips, driving into her, claiming her.

"Holt." Her voice was soft as she lay on his chest. "This was perfect. Thanks."

He kissed the top of her head, but couldn't find any words. It felt like she was leaving this in the past, now. One night with Sage would never be enough.

Not for him.

Still, he'd be whatever she needed.

CHAPTER SIX

THE SUN WAS drifting under the edge of the curtain, and Holt reached for Sage, frowning as his hands came up empty. He sat up in bed...alone.

Looking over at the clock he frowned. Just past five. Too early to be awake—unless he was doing something delightful to Sage.

A sound on the other side of the ranch caught his ear, and he slipped on boxers and his flip-flops to search it out. Domino had been very good his first night, but rescues often took weeks, and sometimes months, to settle into surroundings. He needed to check on Domino and wanted to find Sage.

Her truck wasn't functional; surely she wouldn't have left without waking him. His stomach clenched. As much as he wanted that to be true, if he was honest, it wouldn't surprise him if she called a friend or a rideshare.

The phrase *not wanting to be a bother* might as well be tattooed on her forehead.

Domino barked, followed by quick shushing.

"Domino. Be quiet or you'll wake Holt."

So she was still here. His body relaxed. She'd left his bed, but not run too far.

"Holt is already awake. And a bit grumpy about waking up alone." He felt his mouth fall open as she waved and pointed to the phone at her ear. It was just past five. Who on earth was she talking to at this ungodly hour?

"I understand, Mom. I do. But there are bad days at every job. You've worked for Dr. Jameson for eight years." Sage drained her coffee and mouthed sorry to him.

She was talking to her mom? At this hour?

As much as he'd give to talk to his dad again, the man hadn't recognized an hour before seven. He'd timed his schedule perfectly to roll out of bed at seven fifteen, into the clothes he'd laid out the night before, make a pot of coffee and be at the shop by seven forty-five to ensure he opened at eight. After he retired, Oliver Cove hadn't gotten up before ten.

"I'm not saying don't look for a new job. But do it smartly, while you still have the receptionist job." Sage pulled the phone away from her face and glared at it. "Goodbye to you too!"

"Everything okay?" He shook his head, trying to clear the early morning cobwebs. Clearly everything wasn't okay. "What's wrong with Rose?" He rubbed his eyes and yawned. Seriously, this was too early.

"Nothing. At least not really. She had a bad day at work. One of her friends said she should just retire. Which she can't afford to do. Mom's just in a complaining mood." She clenched her fists and cleared her throat. "Well, those were a lot of words."

"Not really. Parents can be frustrating." His mind was clouded. Lack of sleep, from one of the best nights of his life, and a bloodstream lacking any caffeine were fogging his thoughts.

"Sure…if they act like parents." She pursed her lips, "I—I." She blew out a breath. "We should probably make another pot of coffee. I made that hours ago."

"Sage…"

"It's nothing. Just our relationship. Parenting the parent. I know your mom works constantly." Sage turned, leaning against the counter, the weight of the world easily seen on her shoulders.

"Worked." Holt corrected, surprised by the word. "Mom passed about six months ago."

"I'm so sorry, Holt."

He nodded, accepting the words, hating that people thought he missed her. Maybe he should. That was what a dutiful son would do. A good son would have answered the emails and texts when she reached out.

He'd done neither.

"Dad passed two years ago, another heart attack." He'd sent a notice to the local paper, but wasn't sure they'd actually run it. "I never reached the parenting your parent stage."

"And I've been in it forever." Sage scrunched her nose. "God, I sound awful. Complaining when she is still here. I love her. I do. I just wish…" She bit away the final words.

He reached for her then, leaning his head on hers. Her arms tightened on him. "You sound human. And given that you're the least selfish person I know… I think you're owed a little." He kissed the top of her head and the coffee machine dinged.

Reaching for a mug, he looked at her phone. "I must have been dead asleep to have not heard it ring."

"Oh." Sage laughed and shrugged. "I've been up for a while. Insomnia reared its ugly head after…" Her cheeks darkened as she filled her own coffee mug. "No big deal. Besides it was good, because Mom likes to call early."

Insomnia.

Sage mentioned not sleeping at the clinic. And now she was trying to spare his feelings, given that he'd woken her.

Seriously, Holt!

The woman fell asleep, in his bed, in his arms and that hadn't been enough for him. No, he'd let his baser needs take root. Determined to enjoy as much time with her as possible.

So he'd made the selfish choice…and impacted the beauty before him.

He couldn't fix that, but he could make her breakfast. "How about some pancakes? Or would you prefer waffles?"

"You don't—"

"Sage, I am not letting you leave without breakfast. And since I am your ride, you might as well tell me which one. I owe you."

"Waffles." She tapped her fingers on the table.

Did she realize she was doing it? He tried to think of a time when she was still. Not a single instance came into his mind.

"And you don't owe me anything." Sage crossed her legs then uncrossed them.

The woman never stopped moving. And he was not going to argue about owing her. He knew he did…and that was enough.

"Do you have any plans after work today?" He'd like to pretend that the question was an easy one, one meant as simple morning conversation after spending a fun night with a woman. But it was deeper. He wanted to know if she had plans…and if she might want to include him in them.

"Besides finding a new car or truck?" She laughed but the sound wasn't joyful.

Before he could offer to help, she changed topics, "I need to figure out the spring fundraiser for the rescue. We have done all the regular things in the last two years. A 5K run, a bake sale and three car washes. I need something that makes the rescue stand out, and I'd love it if we could bring the rescue dogs. Let people meet them. Best way to get them into a new home." Her fingers started tapping again…this time faster. "Maybe a spring theme…or something."

"How about an egg hunt for the dogs?" He chuckled as he dropped the dough into the waffle iron. Images of dogs racing after pastel-colored eggs dancing through his head. It was hilarious.

"I don't think dogs would hunt for Easter eggs. And chocolate…"

He opened his mouth to point out that he'd meant it as a joke but held the words back as Sage tilted her head. He could almost see the thoughts pulsing through her brain.

"But we could hold a dual event." She pulled out her cell and started typing into a notes app. "What if we had a small hunt for kids and a bone hunt for the dogs? We could even 'rent out' our rescues."

He leaned against the counter watching her work. His mind was barely awake, but Sage was planning an epic event, after sleeping less than four hours and dealing with her emotional mother far too early. She closed her eyes and her mouth moved but no words escaped.

And it shifted him back in time. They'd had to debate in their theater class to work on emotions. The topic their teacher chose was whether women faced more pressure than men. The boys had all argued that everyone was equal, while quietly believing men faced more pressure.

Sage had done this exact thing. Closed her eyes and started talking to herself before she'd eviscerated the boys using logic, drawing on what she'd heard from boys in the halls. All about how women were inferior, how they were lesser. Repeating misogynistic jokes spoken in her sweet tone. It was humbling.

The lesson was meant to work as a segue for the powerful speeches in *To Kill a Mockingbird*, but all he remembered now was Sage.

She was amazing. In that moment, he'd known that she'd get a degree in marine biology and convince the world that action was needed—and then make it happen.

Now she used that same intellect, that same strength, to plan an egg hunt for dogs. What if he'd forced his friend to listen to his arguments? Gone with Forest that night? Would Sage still be in Spring River?

Probably not.

He'd gone to veterinarian school, worked all over the country, chased every professional accolade he could…and Sage? Sage took care of her mother and didn't believe that dreams came true anymore.

How was that fair?

She opened her eyes and grinned. "Waffle ready yet?"

He shook his head, time's spell breaking around them. "I got lost watching you work through the puzzle."

Sage took a sip of her coffee and wandered over to where he was standing. She didn't touch him though or lean into him. Was she already moving past their night?

He wouldn't push. Though if she leaned her head against his shoulder, if she bumped his hip, or kissed his cheek…

He forced his mind away from his baser desires.

Focus on caring for her this morning, Holt.

He lifted the iron, then dropped the waffle on the plate. It didn't look great. The first one never did. Sage moved to scoop it up, but he grabbed her wrist. Heat bloomed, and he'd never wanted to drop a kiss on someone's lips so badly.

"The first one is always a mess. I'll take this one—you take the next."

Sage's dark eyes looked at him, and he felt as though she was staring deep into him. He swallowed as the urge to shift under her gaze settled on him. "This waffle is fine, Holt. Perfection…well, it's not for me."

She lifted the waffle and took a deep bite of it. "Now it really is mine. Got my germs on it and everything."

He took the plate from her, setting it aside. "I think we are past sharing germs. And you deserve the good waffle!"

Her eyes flashed as she pulled her hand away, though she didn't take the waffle. A tiny step, but an important one.

"About last night…" She grabbed her coffee mug, "I've never been impulsive… I just…"

"You do not have to explain yourself to me." Holt shrugged, trying to make it seem like it didn't bother him that she was putting distance between them. "We are adults. And I enjoyed every minute."

"Right. Adults. Having fun." Sage opened the fridge and then looked back at Holt. "Where is the maple syrup?"

He opened his mouth, but no words tripped from his tongue. "I…"

"Offered me waffles without having maple syrup?" Sage laughed, the bell tones ringing off the ceiling of the ranch's kitchen. It was both lovely and heartbreaking… After all when would he get to share breakfast with her again?

Maybe never.

"I didn't think. I am sorry." He'd offered the suggestion to get her to stay. Not that she could leave until he took her home, but he'd wanted to stretch the encounter. Now he lacked the main thing people ate waffles with.

"I can just use butter. But you owe me waffles with syrup, Holt. I am putting it on your tab." She hit her hip against his. The connection lasting the briefest moment.

It wasn't much, but he was holding on to the tiny bloom of hope erupting in his heart.

Sage covered her yawn as she rubbed Jack's ears. She'd slept well for the few hours she'd managed in Holt's bed. Better than she'd slept anywhere in years.

But she couldn't regret him waking her either. Kissing him; spending the night in his arms was the most impulsive move she'd ever made. But she refused to regret it.

The time they'd spent together—it was almost enough to make her want to daydream. And that was why Sage needed to stop herself.

She'd daydreamed often as a girl. After her father left, she'd fantasized that he'd return. Fix everything; lift the world off her plate. Then she'd imagined one of the host of men her mom dated might stay, play the role Sage had taken over.

None of the daydreams ever paid off. And leaning on others wasn't who she was. Though it had been nice for a night.

It wasn't like her life was terrible. It was fine. Maybe it wasn't the daydream of her past, but few people's lives were.

Blaire called her pessimistic. Sage preferred to think of herself as realistic.

Even if she wasn't working by the ocean, she still got to spend her day helping animals. And right now, there was a light gray cat with barely there white stripes rubbing his head against her hands. It was nice, though she knew Jack was angling for treats. Treats she couldn't give the friendly guy until Holt saw him for his tail injury.

A decade plus of working with animals told her that the tail didn't require surgery. The X-ray looked like a clean break. But Holt was the final diagnosis authority. The arbiter of Jack's treats.

A fact that Jack did not appreciate as he rubbed against her hand, turning it over, hoping something might fall out of it.

"Sorry, Jack. I just keep moving my hand to cover yawns, not to grab treats!"

"Late night?" Amber Plodi winked. The woman loved gossip and was always hoping to be the first with juicy news. Amber always started conversations with a question, hoping she might elicit some new information from the unsuspecting.

In a small town the news was recycled over and over and Sage had no intention of letting anything about her night with Holt drop into the rumor mill. The gossipmongers would have them walking down the aisle and breaking up all within a matter of days.

"My truck broke down. Nothing too exciting, and unfortunately an expensive fix. So, you know…lying awake thinking about that." That was close enough to the truth.

Her truck had broken down, and she had lain awake thinking after he woke her. But not about the truck.

No. It was Holt Cove occupying all her thoughts. Her body still heated from his fingers exploring every inch of her.

It was everything she'd imagined since the night they stood in the dark closet. Kissing Holt…and everything that came after.

"Car repairs stink. Miles used to fix mine; then the divorce—" Amber blew out a breath.

And Sage nodded. Clients often talked when their pets were injured. Inane things to keep as much worry at bay. Though divorce wasn't inane.

"Now if I ask for anything, even with the girls, he'll say sure, then mention I owe him." Amber ran her fingers down Jack's back, careful to stop before his tail. "I swear the man keeps a universal spreadsheet. Everything has to be even—though what's the cost of cheating on your wife?"

"It should be priceless!" Sage crossed her arms as she made sure Amber knew she agreed with her.

Amber let out an uncomfortable laugh. "Sorry. I don't know what came over me there."

"It's okay." What else could she say?

"Beware a man who says they owe you or you owe them! Love doesn't keep track."

"Good advice." The words felt hollow, but she forced them out.

Holt had said he'd owed her several times since returning. Even last night after her truck broke down.

For what?

She hadn't asked. And didn't want to know.

Besides, they weren't in love either.

Sage pushed away the thought. Seriously—they'd had one good night. She did not need to overthink this.

"Sorry, I'm running a bit behind today." Holt yawned as he stepped into the room.

"Sage is yawning too. Veterinarian work must be exhausting." Amber looked between the two of them.

They'd just had a personal conversation about her ex, her cat had a broken tail, but could smell gossip a mile away.

"It's often rated one of the most demanding career fields." Holt's voice was calm, but there was a hint of color at the collar of his scrubs. "Tell me what happened to Jack."

"Right." Amber nodded and looked at the cat. "The girls were playing in the back room. I didn't get the full story, but I heard Jack squeal and a door slam. I think Matilda slammed her door and caught him." She gave Jack a sympathetic look.

"Matilda and Kaitlynn were in tears and Jack looked uncomfortable and there's the kink in his tail. I swear you wouldn't know it by his behavior here. He just keeps asking for treats."

Jack rubbed his head against Holt's hand and started purring. Holt was a great vet, but the cat's reaction surprised Sage.

"He clearly likes you." Amber leaned toward Holt, smiling…

Sage's belly twisted, and she bit the inside of her cheek. Amber had an injured animal; she wasn't flirting with Holt.

Knock it off, Sage.

And even if she was, Sage had no right to be jealous. They'd spent one night together.

One glorious night. And it wasn't enough. Just like all dreams…a taste only led to wanting more.

Holt pulled back a little then started toward the wall where the X-ray Sage had captured was waiting for him.

"This is the break." Holt pointed to a portion of Jack's tail, about an inch from the end. "The good news is that it is far enough down, it shouldn't impact his ability to walk or use his litter box. Is he still jumping?"

"Not really." Amber batted her eyes at Holt. "If we need to make any accommodations for him, I'm afraid I'm not very handy. Are you?"

Sage hated dissing other women, hated it that society often pitched them against each other in everything. But… Amber was flirting with Holt. While her cat had a broken tail.

White-hot jealousy flooded her system. Whether she had that right or not be damned!

"Not handy myself." Holt turned his attention back to the cat.

She went to grab the X-ray off the wall, taking a little too much pleasure in the fact that Holt didn't take the bait from the blonde beauty. Dr. Andrews had dated a few of the clients... and when he'd left with nearly no warning, it was a headache for the entire staff.

That was a good reason for Sage to appreciate his inattention to Amber. But it wasn't the reason for the flutter dance in her belly. This...this was one of the million reasons she did not give in to impulsivity.

"That's too bad." Amber's pouty tone made Sage's skin crawl.

"Well, the good news is that he shouldn't need any accommodations. This kind of break heals on its own usually. Though the kink in his tail might remain, only time will tell."

She could hear the hint of frustration in Holt's voice. The subtle tightness in his words, the clipped question. When they'd been in theater class, she could read each of his tells, but she hadn't expected the ability to return so quickly.

Or at all.

"That's good." Amber ran her hands down Jack's fur.

Sage saw all sorts of reactions in this room. Amber cared for Jack, but she wasn't as attached to the cat as Sage would have preferred. Still, the cat was well taken care of, and she'd made an emergency appointment after the injury. However, this must be one of the top ten worst places to flirt!

"He should be himself in a few weeks. If not call back and make another appointment. Anything else?"

"Umm." Her gaze darted to Sage. "Well, yes, but..."

Sage could read the body language. Amber wanted her to step out of the room, but unless Holt asked her too, her feet were planted.

Plus, Holt was uncomfortable. He kept shifting on his feet and his eyes had captured hers more than once. Even if the protocol wasn't to have a vet tech in the room during the visit, his body language was enough to keep Sage right where she was.

"I just wondered if you might like to grab dinner." Amber's cheek's bloomed as she ran her fingers along Jack's back. "Or coffee?"

Holt's left eye twitched, but he kept the smile on his face as he rubbed Jack's belly, then looked at the cat's eyes and in his ears. Jack purred, rubbing against Holt's wrists. Gray cats really were the friendliest, even in the worst circumstances.

"We could catch up on the town gossip—I mean goings on." Amber shook her head. "Wow I am botching this."

Points for self-reflection.

Most people would stop, but Amber just barreled on. "I mean, I'm just so glad you came back. Found your way home. It's so nice for someone to choose us for once."

A look passed across Holt's face, and Sage's blood chilled. He didn't like Amber discussing his return. *Why?*

He'd mentioned that his choice for coming home wasn't altruistic, but hadn't said more.

"Keeping Jack healthy should be our focus." Holt looked at the electronic tablet in his hand.

"Of course." Amber's eyebrows scrunched together; her cheeks colored, and she cleared her throat.

Sage felt a twinge of secondhand embarrassment. She was a single mom, with two great kids, and not a lot of free time. Holt was attractive...no, he was a stunning specimen of a man. Why not shoot her shot? She might be a gossip and hitting on a man not interested. But Jack was well taken care of.

And that was what mattered.

Amber looked at Holt then at Jack, resignation hovering in her eyes. "Well. I should get going. If you change your mind, I'm easy to find." She winked but the flirty undertone had died away. "I'd love to hear why you came home."

Holt didn't say anything. No platitudes about coming home or being excited about it. No statement that moving here would help his career...though she knew that would be a lie.

Silence was a statement.

She ached to reach across the exam table and squeeze his hand.

But now that she thought of it, he had not brought up his reasons for returning at all. He'd deflected each query. Expertly adjusted the conversation back to the patient or to something else.

Maybe she should drop it; it was a topic he clearly wanted to avoid. Spring River wasn't most people's first choice. She knew that better than most. But he'd bought the ranch, come to the clinic when it was in need. All things one could brag about. Instead, he avoided the topic.

Something was bothering him. And Sage hated that. There had to be a way for her to help.

No ideas immediately came forth, but with enough time, she'd figure it out.

CHAPTER SEVEN

"So Tina was the fifth client who asked why you came back. *And hit on you.*"

Was that a hint of jealousy?

And wrong of him was it to hope it was? He followed Sage and locked the clinic's door. She grabbed her bike but didn't swing her leg over it. It was the routine they'd developed. Close up shop and chat for a few minutes; he craved this precious time.

She hadn't been in his bed in a week and with each passing hour it became more difficult for him to keep from begging her to come home with him. If she even hinted she was open to the idea he'd jump at it.

"Who was hitting on me?" Holt grinned, hoping the expression looked realistic. The only person he wanted hitting on him was standing in front of him...not hitting on him.

Sage cocked her head, her dark eyebrows raising. "You are in your late thirties. You can tell when people hit on you. It's the question about Spring River you avoid."

She wasn't wrong. "I'm here—do the reasons matter?" It was the line he'd used so often he felt he should wear a sign around his neck. Maybe that would stop people from asking.

Holt Cove came home. The reason doesn't matter.

He'd wanted to prove to himself that his life wasn't all work. That he could focus on other things.

That he cared about people more than achievements...more than corporate prizes...unlike his mother.

The mother who'd reached out to him just before she'd passed. And he'd ignored the summons.

Would I if I'd known she was so close to death?

He wasn't sure. That was the piece that niggled at him. He'd made a choice, stuck to it, not caring about the consequences… until the consequences arrived.

The letter from his mother was brutal. He'd memorized each word before lighting it on fire. Then he'd felt bad about torching her final words.

It was exactly what she'd have done.

Holt prided himself on not being like her. Except that was exactly what he'd done after leaving Spring River. Gone to school, focused on his career.

He'd wanted to show his dad he'd changed. That he wasn't the rebellious kid who'd caused him so much stress. Unfortunately, he'd been so wrapped up in that he hadn't had much time for his father.

What he wouldn't give to have a do-over there.

He'd earned so many promotions, awards, bonuses…praise for putting work above everything else. But what did he really have to show for it?

"Earth to Holt!" Sage playfully snapped her fingers. She'd put the kickstand down on her bike and stepped in front of him.

She was closer now than she'd been since they'd left the ranch after their night of passion. His body cried out. She was inches from him and it was too close and not enough all at the same time. The urge to ask to kiss her, to lose himself for the night in her arms.

Drive away the uncomfortable thoughts…

"Sorry. Lost in my own thoughts, I guess."

"I get it." Her fingers grabbed his. Grounding him.

It was likely meant as comforting, but there was no way to pretend the energy blazing through him was anything less than desire for her. Need…passion. All for her.

"When I have an idea for the rescue, whether it's an online

video to draw attention to the egg hunt—brilliant suggestion, Holt. Or a new idea for recruiting foster families…or what I will do when I finally have a place of my own—my mind wanders." Sage winked and hit her hip against his.

He playfully rolled his eyes and slid an arm around her shoulder. He squeezed her; dipping to drop a kiss on her head—pulling back just in time. A simple motion that was so much more difficult than he could have imagined.

"Always thinking of others."

Of course she was.

The woman was part saint. Holt gestured to his car. Needing just a few more minutes with her. "Why don't I give you a ride? Your bike will fit in my SUV's trunk."

She looked at her bike, then at him. He could see the mental hoops racing through her mind. But he didn't know if it was because she wasn't sure she wanted a ride…or to be with him? Was she craving him as much as he craved her and trying to keep a lid on what felt like a boiling pot, destined to bubble over?

"I'd like that, assuming you don't think Domino will mind you delaying getting home?"

"I was actually hoping you wouldn't mind if we picked him up from doggie daycare on the way to your place."

"Doggy daycare?" Sage raised a brow. "What?"

"I worked a deal out with Peter Olikee. He has kids now. Which… I mean, it's like I blink and suddenly…" He'd known Spring River would change. He'd changed after all, but in some ways, the town was untouched. In others, it was almost unrecognizable.

He pushed a hand through his hair then took Sage's bike and lifted it into the back of his SUV. "I just didn't want him lonely and with the kids, I figure we can make sure he is compatible in a house with a family. Which he completely is—such a big baby."

The gentle giant was quickly becoming his pet. He rationally knew he was just a foster parent, but the ranch felt more like home with Domino lolloping around.

"I don't mind. And if you decide you want to adopt him…" Sage let her voice die away as he shot her a look before they climbed into the SUV.

He would not be a foster fail. Domino was great, and maybe when Holt was a little more settled, he could get a dog for the ranch. Though the idea of letting Domino go made him sick. But that was a worry for another day.

"So, why don't you talk about why you came home?" Sage leaned her head back against the seat and closed her eyes.

Today had been a long day, but that didn't mean he was going to chat about his mother.

"It isn't some grand reason. In fact, it's kind of crappy."

He didn't elaborate, and she didn't push. That should make him happy. He never wanted to discuss his mom. He'd spent his adult life making sure he made up for his antics with his father, but promotions and accolades didn't give you time… or memories.

After vet school, when his father wanted to retire, he found a great place near where he worked. If Dad was tight on money, Holt made up for it. It was the least he could do.

But his mom. He hadn't even called her.

It was a decision he couldn't change. And one he did not discuss.

He was in Spring River to help the clinic. Right a little of the wrong he'd put into the universe. That didn't mean he wanted to discuss it. So why was he fighting the urge to open up as he drove? Hoping she'd ask one, just one follow-up question?

Peter's house came into view. He was grateful to have a reason to shift away from the uncomfortable feelings trampling through him.

"Think Domino had fun?"

"How could he not!" The door opened before he could knock, and Domino barreled out. Wearing a T-shirt!

"Aren't you stylish!" Sage bent and rubbed the dog's head as he happily panted and turned in circles.

"I hope it's okay. The girls wanted him to wear it. I put it over his head for a second and he stepped into it. He hasn't wanted to take it off." Peter shook his head as he looked to the dog, whose tail was hitting the side of the door so hard Holt was a little worried it might dent the wood.

"Do you like clothes?" Sage's voice was sugary sweet as she rubbed his neck. "We have a pittie mix right now, that is always dressed! People think of little dogs as the stylish ones, but big guys can rock an outfit too. If they like it."

"I have plenty of old shirts at the house, Domino, but we should leave this one with Peter." He pulled the shirt off and attached the leash. "So he did okay?"

"He did great. If we didn't have baby number three on the way, I'd adopt him tomorrow. Great with the girls, and with our cat. He jumped up a few times, but we corrected it just like you showed us. He's a quick learner." Peter ran his hand along Domino's back. "See you tomorrow!"

They started back toward the car, and a weight lifted off his chest. Peter didn't want Domino. That should upset him. He should want Domino adopted. But dropping him off this morning had made him sick to his stomach. He didn't want to think of the day when he'd drop him off somewhere for forever.

"So you have a foster that loves clothes." Sage giggled the mood lightening.

He reached for her hand without thinking. He saw her head dip out of the corner of his eye as they walked to his car. But she didn't pull her hand back, so he didn't question it.

"I guess so." Holt loaded Domino into the back seat and buckled the dog into his special harness.

The ride to Sage's apartment took no time. Why did the town have to be so small? Traffic was something he'd hated when he'd lived in Boston and Dallas but spending extra time with Sage would have been completely worth it!

"Do you want to come up? I have taco meat in the slow cooker, and I was planning to make a salad to go with it."

He wanted to say yes. So badly! But Domino...

"Domino needs to be fed."

"Of course. But you know I run an animal rescue, right? A network of foster families. I can't have a dog full-time, per my landlady's requirements, but I have dog food. Lots of it!"

Color spread across her cheeks. "I mean. It's just tacos. Anyways. No big deal." She looked at his hand holding hers, then broke the connection. A hint of pink climbing her neck. "So, umm. Thanks for the ride."

"Sage."

He waited until she looked at him. He took a deep breath. "I want to come upstairs. I want to eat tacos with you..." This was a pivotal moment, he knew that.

His choices had changed the course of her life forever. How did one ever make up for that?

He also didn't want to miss out on anything with her. So this was what the bards meant by being torn in two?

"But..." Her eyes held his and the urge to lean forward and kiss her sucked nearly all the air from his lungs.

"I want to kiss you." Those weren't the words he meant to say. They were true, though.

Her mouth opened, a delicate O that made his heart race. He wanted her to say something. Anything, so his body would know how to react to this moment. If she turned him away, he'd accept it, but the world seemed to stop spinning as he waited for her answer.

Anything!

"I think you should come have tacos." She kissed his cheek, then slid out of the car and moved to get her bike.

And Holt followed with Domino. His soul singing. The dog padding after Sage, having dinner together, kissing. This felt so right.

The smell of tacos hit him as soon as Sage opened the door to her apartment. Domino didn't miss the scent, either!

"No tacos for you!" Sage wagged a finger and Domino licked it. "Thanks for the reminder that I need to wash my hands before making the salad."

Stepping into her apartment, Holt wasn't surprised by the cozy and overstuffed feeling it had. There was dog food, leashes, bowls and other rescue paraphernalia stacked in the corner next to the television. A well-worn blue couch and a small table.

Pictures of animals and their families covered her walls. And an oceanography magazine sat on the table by the couch. A nod to the life she'd planned and lost.

"Grab a bowl and some food for Domino. I am going to get out of my cycling outfit, then I'll get started on the salad." Sage darted into her room and took a deep breath.

Holt wanted to kiss her, and she'd invited him up. Because she wanted to kiss him too.

Who was she trying to kid?

Sage wanted so much more than kisses. Wanted more than one precious memory. One impulsive night.

Everyone Sage saw eventually told her she was too independent. Didn't have enough time for them. That she didn't need them. But did they ever need her?

Nope. So she made sure she didn't need them either.

She stripped out of the cycling outfit she'd worn to the office. Holt had changed before leaving the clinic. She looked at her closet, trying to convince herself it didn't matter what she wore.

"Come on, Sage! It's tacos and salad."

And kisses.

So much for the pep talk.

After grabbing a pair of shorts and a pink tank top, she

threw the outfit on and refused to look in the mirror. It was dinner in her apartment, not some major event.

She walked into the living room and stopped.

Holt stood in the kitchen rinsing vegetables. "Hope you don't mind. I just grabbed the veggies I saw."

He'd helped…without being asked. A foreign concept for her, and it was a little unsettling.

When her mother fell into her depression, Sage handled almost everything. Chores, shopping, doctors' appointments… Even now, her mother relied on her for little and not so little things. Blaire helped with the rescue, and they had some volunteers, though volunteers sometimes didn't come through. At the clinic, she just did what needed to be done without being asked.

This was nice…at least it should be. So why was her body itching to take over? To do it herself?

"I don't mind." It felt weird to utter those words—odd not to be as comforting as she expected. Sage was proud that no one ever wondered if she needed anything.

But it was lonely too.

She reached over him and grabbed a paring knife and began chopping the tomatoes he'd already washed.

The silence surrounding them as they prepped should feel uncomfortable. That was what people said. Long silences on dates were uncomfortable. But this wasn't. It was like he'd walked back into her life after almost two decades away and just picked right back up where he was meant to be.

By her side.

"So tell me about your favorite place?" Sage tapped his hip with hers as she pulled a few taco shells from the cupboard. It was easy to touch Holt, so very easy.

"My favorite place?" Holt raised a brow as he tossed the salad. "I like the ranch. It's fine for now."

For now. Two little words she heard so often where the vets were concerned. So he'd purchased the ranch but wasn't sure it was forever. That should make her happy. That meant it might come on the market again. Except she wanted to be in a new place soon.

And the thought of Holt leaving left a hollowness in her stomach. Part of her wanted to scream at him, to make him listen to the reasons he should stay. Choose Spring River... choose her.

It was a foolish thought. He deserved better than the small clinic in a resort area. He'd had it too. The big clinics, the promotions. She was stuck in Spring River...at least until her mother wanted to leave. Assuming she ever did.

"Oh, please." Sage rolled her eyes. "I've never even been on a plane, so let me live a little vicariously."

A look crossed his face that she couldn't quite comprehend. "Holt?" What about that bothered him? Lots of people didn't get to travel.

"I liked Boston." The words dropped out, like he was rushing one thought to stay away from another. "Except for the winter. Bitterly cold and windy. At least here the cold comes with views of snowcapped mountains."

"Interesting way to describe your favorite place." Sage laughed and dropped meat on the tacos, then layered lettuce, tomatoes and cheese on top.

"I liked Dallas until Dad passed. Then I wanted to be somewhere else." The words were soft as he followed her to the table.

That was understandable. The local paper had run the obituary for Holt's dad, but they printed it a few weeks after his funeral, and she hadn't had Holt's address to send along her condolences.

Sage sat opposite him, but she didn't say anything. His brows pulled together, and he was working through something. She wanted to know what it was, but she figured if she asked, he'd shut it down completely.

"Do you ever think about life paths not taken?"

"No." It was true. She'd didn't think about other paths. At least not for long. That was a recipe for bitterness, and disappointment. And Sage refused to let bitterness hold sway over her.

"Life isn't fair. That is a lesson I learned when Dad walked out. Learned again when Forest was arrested, again when the college scholarship I was banking on to attend university fell so short of what I'd needed to graduate that it didn't make sense to go. I like to give myself twenty-four hours, forty-eight at the most to mope...then move on time!"

"How do you manage that!" Holt's eyes shot open, and his reaction surprised her.

They were supposed to be discussing his favorite places. This had dissolved fast.

"I started when I finally realized Dad wasn't coming home. As an adult, I know that was best for us. That he left, I mean, but as a kid... No one was coming to the rescue but me. Besides, Forest was already taking on the role of rebellious teen, so the only role left was the responsible one."

It was meant to be a joke. But she saw the flash of panic in his eyes. He'd been rebellious once too. And felt awful about it. The teen boy had beaten himself up over his dad's heart attack. Taking all the responsibility, when none of it resided with him. And Forest's rebelliousness wasn't anyone's but his fault.

He knew that, right?

Before she could ask, he started, "I loved the busyness of LA and Boston." He chuckled, but he was looking at her in a way that made shivers run down her back.

Busyness...that was the exact opposite of Spring River. Would he be happy here?

"I think you'd like it." He took a big bite of his taco, "There is so much going on. Particularly for someone who likes to stay busy."

"I stay plenty busy." She winked. Sage appreciated the vote of confidence. Once she'd have preened at someone saying she'd do well outside of Spring River. That had been her primary goal.

But she'd found other ways to occupy her time.

"I know. So how is the rescue Easter egg hunt going?"

She wagged a finger. "Nope. We are talking about LA or Boston or somewhere else besides Spring River. Let me live vicariously! You take me to dinner later this week and I will tell you all about the rescue project."

Sage watched the smile spread across his cheeks.

He reached his hand across the table, capturing hers. His thumb rubbed the inside of her palm and her body lit up.

"Dinner later this week. I am going to hold you to that."

"Absolutely! Now chat, Holt Cove. If you liked big cities so much, why are you back here?"

"Mom died."

The phrase was succinct. The mood at the table shifting immediately on two words with a lifetime of hurt behind them. Priscilla Cove left Spring River when he was eight. Sage had a few foggy memories of the woman, but most of what she knew was from the year they'd spent in theater together.

The missed phone calls, the ignored birthdays and events. The woman abandoned her family. Her father had kept a loose relationship with Sage and Forest until she graduated from high school. After that, he'd basically vanished. Every few years he'd send along a birthday card…never in the right month. She wanted nothing from the man.

Holt's mother hadn't bothered to stay in her son's life at all.

"She reached out when her cancer was deemed terminal, though she didn't tell me that. I didn't contact her. It's one path I wish I'd walked differently."

"Really?" She squeezed his hand. Holt's mother hadn't thought of him. He didn't owe her anything, but grief was a unique emotion. She knew people who weren't bothered when their absent parents passed and others who mourned deeply—

particularly the idea that the relationship they'd hoped for was forever gone. Both responses were valid.

"In her letter she was cruel."

"I'm sorry, Holt. That isn't fair to you."

"I didn't go see her."

"Would you have gone if you'd known her time was short?"

"I don't know." He pulled his hand back and crossed his arms. Closing himself off.

She'd opened the wound, so she would stand by while he dealt with the cascade of feelings tramping through his soul. After sliding out of her chair, Sage went around the table and grabbed his hand, pulling it from his crossed-arm position. She led him to the couch, grateful when he let her.

Holt sat down and she snuggled up next to him, running her hand along his leg. A reminder that he wasn't by himself. Not now.

"There wasn't a right or wrong answer. Your mom left you and your dad. You didn't owe her something. Even final peace." She kept her voice even, careful not to put any inflection in it. She didn't know what she'd do if her father reached out. There was so much anger and pain in that relationship.

"Maybe." He wrapped an arm around her shoulder, and she leaned her head against him. "But in her last letter, the one her estate sent, she called me ungrateful. Said I couldn't even leave work for a few days to complete her dying wish."

"She didn't tell you it was her dying wish." The words were more forceful than she intended. Manipulation was not okay. Period. And manipulation from the grave, when her son could do nothing about it. That toxic behavior bordered on evil.

"She didn't." Holt kissed the top of her head, his voice so soft, she wasn't sure if he was talking to her or to himself.

"So you came here because she died?" Sage didn't understand. His mother left this place when he was young. But Spring River was also the only place he had memories with her.

"It was the last line. That she knew work was important. It was why she left me…that at least she could pass knowing I was like her." He scoffed, "Left me a sizable inheritance— her proof that work was more important.

"It was enough to finish paying off my student loans and buy the franchise corporate started offering…but the idea of working more…of being like her." He blew out a breath. "I saw the closing notice for Spring River and volunteered. Give something back instead of bettering myself. *For once.*"

She was glad he was back. Glad he'd chosen here, and she didn't think the reason was a bad one. Though telling people why meant touching a raw part of his soul. No one was owed that. However, he wasn't like his mother. He had to know that, didn't he?

"I am so sorry she put that on you, Holt. But you are nothing like her."

"If she hadn't passed, and I'd seen the Spring River notice of closure, I wouldn't be here. At least, I don't think I would be. I'd have taken the franchise opportunity. Sure, I'd have needed a loan to do so, but I could have gotten it. I am not some returning hero, Sage. Not some knight riding in to save the day."

"You're not." Dropping a kiss on his cheek, she slid into his lap. "Hero is a term that should be reserved for the few. And knight…a bit over-the-top in description for coming when the call went out. But you said, *'At least I don't think I would be.'* You're not certain."

"No one can be certain." His eyes were soft, lost in the pain his mother had delivered to his doorstep. Unsolicited trauma to pile on the trauma her abandonment delivered.

"Not true." She leaned her forehead against his. "Your mother could have answered the question. She left here and never looked back. My father too. That you aren't certain means you aren't them."

His jaw started to move and Sage covered his mouth with

a finger. "Bad things happen. Choices are made, but we are only responsible for how we respond."

It was something Forest had told her on one of her visits, when she'd railed that their father had started the downfall of their family. He'd told her that their father had made bad choices, but he'd chosen how he responded to the ripples his father had tossed into the pond.

"You'd really never walk another path?" Holt's face was so open, so trusting. "Change a seemingly small decision that had drastic consequences you never expected? Look for a redo?"

"If I'd walked another path we wouldn't be here right now, would we?"

"No."

She dropped her lips to his. "This is a pretty good place to be Holt, for now." She hated that she'd added the small caveat. It wasn't intentional. Not really. Just a mental reminder to herself that this dream might not be for forever. Most things weren't…and nothing in her life had been.

The rumble from his chest sent tidal waves of desire through her. There were so many ways her life could have gone… should have gone, if people had made different choices. Would any of them have led to Holt here and now—with her?

Probably not. And that was why she refused to think of other lives. Because he was here…now. That was what mattered.

"Sage…"

"If you are about to say something other than I want you, take me to bed, keep it to yourself, Holt Cove."

Life didn't promise you anything. So you took what you wanted when you could. And Holt was who Sage wanted. There might be a point where he decided she was too independent, or he wanted to focus on growing his life outside of Spring River. But for now, she'd cling to the feelings he'd awoken.

His lips parted beneath hers, and he pulled her into his lap. "I want you."

* * *

"I want you too." Sage moved against his groin.

Dear God, she was going to be his undoing.

But what a way to come undone.

His fingers edged to the bottom of her shirt, desperate to touch her. To kiss her. He wanted to claim her and drive the words *for now* from her vocabulary. It was a new sensation for him.

Holt had had a few semiserious girlfriends. Nothing felt like the need he had around Sage. The burning ache to protect her, to right all the wrongs life had dealt her.

Sage's fingers ran across his belly, and she lifted the shirt over his head. "You are so beautiful." Her lips spread as she ran her nails over his chest.

If he wasn't so turned-on, he could sit there for forever letting her admire him.

Lifting her shirt, he unhooked her bra, then dropped the clothes to the floor. "You're the beauty." The words were hoarse as she shifted her hips against him. Had he ever needed someone so bad?

Her skin was like silk under his hands, their bodies remembering the touches they'd liked. And discovering new ones.

Her hands wrapped around his neck, pulling him closer as her breasts brushed against his chin. Holt gripped her hips as she molded herself to him. "Sage."

Her head fell back, and he trailed kisses down her throat. Reckless abandon chased at his heels. He looked at the kitchen table, the idea of pushing their plates from the table and taking her there materializing and then evaporating.

Mostly because he knew Domino would investigate the crumbs. And he planned to savor every moment with Sage.

"Sage."

"Mmm-hmm." Her voice was soft as she slipped her hands between their bodies, unbuttoning his pants and sliding the zipper down. Her hand grazed him. The flimsy hold he had on his self-control cracking but not breaking.

Not yet.

"I want you." He captured one ripe nipple in his mouth, drinking in her taste and the need flowing through her. "Let me take you to bed," he breathed as he kissed his way to her other nipple.

"I was supposed to seduce you tonight." Her bottom lip slipped out as she pulled his face to hers and trailed kisses down his chin. "I wanted to drive you mad."

Her hips rocked against his groin, and he grabbed her hand, kissing her fingers. "Mission accomplished, honey! I need you, Sage. Just you."

"Then take me to bed, Holt."

Holding her tightly, he stood, and she wrapped her legs around him. Her hands danced through his hair as her mouth captured his, claiming him. If it were possible for steam to rise from his body, the room would be filled.

The walk to Sage's room was less than twenty feet, but it felt like forever before he dropped her on the bed. Before she could reach for him, he stripped her shorts and panties. She lay before him, naked and glorious.

"Holt." Sage grinned as she ran her hand along her nipple, circling the bud with her finger.

He let out a soft breath, enjoying the show. But it wasn't enough; he needed to taste her.

Ignoring the storm of his own desires, he worked his mouth down her thighs. Edging ever closer to where she wanted him…then pulling back.

Her hips bucked. "You're teasing me."

He couldn't stop the smile as he nipped at her sensitive inner thigh, stroking her core. When his tongue finally flicked her pleasure bud, Sage let out the greediest groan.

The world's most perfect sound.

He brought her to completion with his mouth, enjoying

each plea, each movement. She was like putty beneath him. All Holt wanted was to find every single touch, every kiss, every movement that made her scream his name.

"Holt. Now." She reached a hand over her head, fumbled in a drawer, her movements uncoordinated as he continued pleasuring her.

He heard the package rip and felt her shift. Before she could touch him, he gripped her wrist. If he let her roll the condom down his length, he feared he'd come just from her touch.

"I've never wanted anyone so badly." He sheathed himself, then pushed himself into her—but not all the way. He wanted this to last. Wanted more time with her pliant and panting.

Pushing another inch in, he dipped his head, trailing kisses up her breasts and finally capturing her mouth. She tasted sweet and fiery.

She tasted like home.

Sage broke their kiss, her mouth swollen from pleasure, her eyes dilated and breath heavy. "Holt."

He joined them fully then, his eyes holding hers as she clung to him. Time stopped; the world disappeared. For a few minutes it was only Sage and Holt in the universe.

CHAPTER EIGHT

SAGE SIGHED AND rolled over. She'd slept through the night. It was a feeling only an insomniac really understood. The moment your eyes opened, and you felt rested. Such a delicious feeling.

Holt's arm lay over hers. He'd stayed. That brought more joy.

The only times in her life she'd given in to impulsivity were with Holt. So far they'd worked out. And he'd agreed to dinner later this week too. He felt like hers.

Was that dangerous?

No. As long as she didn't rely on him. And that was easy enough. She was going to embrace whatever connection was between them, for as long as it lasted.

"You stayed in bed all night." Holt grinned as he opened one eye and looked at his watch. "Though it is still painfully early!" He dropped a kiss on her cheek, his hand running across her body. It was sensual, but not sexual.

That was a nice experience. They'd had an amazing night. Her body still sang with memories of his touch. But this was one of the few things she longed for when listening to others describe their relationships. The satisfaction of being next to another person, of hearing their breaths, and feeling settled.

No need to preform or expectation for intimacy. It was a special feeling no one had stayed in her life long enough to achieve.

His arm tightened against her waist, and he pulled her close.

"Don't get up. We have several hours before the clinic opens. That is a nice benefit of a small practice."

"Once I am up, I am up." She dropped a kiss on his nose. "But you can lie about as long as you like."

Holt rolled over. "I just might take you up on the offer!"

He yawned, and she kissed his cheek. "You should!" Was there too much excitement in her voice? She liked him being in her bed.

After quietly dressing, Sage slipped out of the room. Domino blinked as she walked into the living room. He was curled on one of the dog beds, one meant for a smaller animal, but he seemed comfortable enough.

Grabbing his leash, she held it up and wasn't surprised when he bounded toward her. She could count on one hand the number of dogs she'd helped who saw a leash and didn't go into ultraexcitement mode.

Ruff!

"Shh!" She glanced over her shoulder, hoping Mrs. Clark hadn't heard the barking. Her landlady was a sourpuss on the best days, and she hated dogs. Well, dogs, cats, birds and most humans.

Sage had a few months left on her lease…and she needed them.

The tourist industry had gobbled up so much of the available rental units. Now they were limited leases, meant for hikers and skiers staying a few days instead of long-term renters.

Time was ticking on her lease, but she'd hoped to have enough of a down payment ready for the property outside of town. But now she needed a new vehicle too.

Pressure coated her chest. Pushing her hand against it and taking a few deep breaths didn't release any of it. She needed to figure something out. *Soon.*

"Let's go. And please be quiet." No need to alert Mrs. Clark to his presence.

Domino wagged his tail, and she wanted to pretend that he understood.

He did his business quickly and she cleaned up, enjoying the hint of sun rising over the mountains. Holt might enjoy staying in bed, but she loved this time of day. When there was still so much promise...

"Now what shall we fix for breakfast, big boy? She opened the door to let Domino in, turned to close it and her stomach dropped to the floor.

"Good morning, Mrs. Clark."

Her landlady was still in her bathrobe and didn't crack even the hint of a smile as she glared at Domino. "I've warned you, Sage."

So they weren't even going to try for a collegial discussion. "Domino is my overnight guest's dog." She had no intention of discussing Holt with her judgment-filled neighbor.

Mrs. Clark let out a grunt as she crossed her arms. "I want you out by the weekend."

"What!" The call echoed down the hall. She was the only resident right now...because Mrs. Clark had found a way to push the others out.

"Mrs. Clark..." The desire to rail at the woman, to scream that this was unfair raged in her. All of that was true, but it wouldn't help her case.

For this she needed rational arguments. Because the lawyer she'd had look at her rental agreement had made sure she understood that Mrs. Clark had far more rights in the contract than a regular landlord. Sage had signed when she'd been desperate to get out of the place she shared with her mom. Needing her own space for once, and not paid close attention.

"I don't want to hear it. The lease says no animals."

"I don't have any animals." Her heartbeat echoed in her ears. She needed this apartment. For at least a few more months. By then her mother would have repaid her. If she biked... There were options. There were always options, even if they weren't ones you liked.

Her skin prickled as she tried to think of something, anything. "Domino is just a guest. One that is leaving in a few hours."

Mrs. Clark shrugged. "I don't care."

"Sage? Oh!" Holt's voice was coated in confusion, and she didn't have to turn around to know that he'd walked out of her bedroom without putting on his shirt based on the appreciative look crossing Mrs. Clark's face.

"Domino belongs to Holt."

"I mean not technically."

"Holt!"

"I…" A look crossed his face, as he stepped to her side. It wasn't his fault he hadn't known the script.

And it probably wouldn't have mattered.

"As I said, I want you out by the end of the week. And put that dog somewhere that isn't my condo by the end of the day, or I will have the sheriff put your stuff on the curb."

Sage wasn't sure Sheriff Thompson would comply, at least not right away, but if Mrs. Clark went to Justice Barrett—that woman was a friend to no one. She'd happily put Sage and anyone else out of their home with the barest legal justification.

"Wait."

But Mrs. Clark didn't turn as Holt called after her.

Her mind usually racing with ideas, with plans or thoughts, next steps was blank. Silence…at any other time she might squeal with joy, but right now she needed a plan. Needed to think through her options.

There were options…options that kept her plans alive. There had to be. Her brain just couldn't think right now.

"Sage."

Holt's fingers were warm, but they didn't calm her racing heart. Her throat tightened. She needed to react, needed to do something, but for the first time she couldn't make herself do anything.

"Sage."

Why wasn't she responding? Was this emotional shock? He'd never wanted to practice human medicine, but right now he'd kill for better knowledge on treating non-life-threatening shock.

"Let's go inside. You can sit on the couch." He took her hand and didn't know if he should be happy or terrified that she let him lead her to the couch.

Sage sat down and Domino climbed up on her couch. He started to tell the dog to get down, but Domino laid his big head in her lap and Sage started petting his ears. "I am going to make us coffee and then we can figure out what to do."

He took the lack of comment as approval for the actions. Somehow he'd turned a fun night into a nightmare for Sage. When she'd fallen asleep in his arms, he'd held her and tried to figure out if he should stay or head out. She'd rolled over and he'd gotten up, taken Domino out…then crawled back into bed with her.

They hadn't discussed any next steps, except for a vague agreement for dinner this week. He wanted to date her, and he'd wanted to be here when she woke.

She'd mentioned a nightmare landlady. And her no pet policy. But he hadn't remembered that when he'd answered the question about Domino. And now his flippant response had resulted in Sage's landlady kicking her out.

The coffee started brewing, and he slid in front of her. "I know everything is stressful right now." Understatement of the year, but what else was he supposed to say?

He put his hands on her knees, hoping she knew that he was there for her. No matter what she needed. "I need to know how you like your coffee, sweetheart."

"Almond milk and a spoon of sugar."

The words had no inflection, which worried him. But they were spoken. Small steps.

Pressing the mug into her hands, Holt waited a moment wondering if he was going to have to lift it to her lips. This was a woman who took care of everything. Who bounced from pizza to decorating to taking care of rescues. She was always on the go.

"Sage, this can't be legal." He took a sip of his drink, hoping she'd follow suit. "A lawyer—"

"Will cost money. Fighting to stay when she won't renew my lease is pointless. I…" She took a deep breath, "I'm all right. I'm all right. It's going to be fine." She shook her head and downed the coffee.

"Okay, um that had to burn your throat."

"Yep." Sage's head bobbed and her eyes widened. Then she clapped her hands on her knees. "All right, I need a new place to live." Her bottom lip trembled. "That is all. A new place."

"I am so sorry." He had no idea what to do.

"Not your fault." She ran a hand over her forehead. Like she was trying to activate her mind.

"Domino staying is my fault." This wasn't about him, but he wanted her to know that he was sorry.

"Mrs. Clark has looked for reasons to kick me out. Many landlords shifted to temporary lodging for tourists. Those apps have really messed with the already-tiny rental market here. Figured I could last a few more months, get a down payment ready…" She cleared her throat.

The Rainbow Ranch no doubt popping in both their minds.

"Then Mom's car, and mine…" She didn't fully manage to catch the sob.

"Come stay with me." The offer flew from his mouth.

Sage's wide eyes and her open mouth told him the words were as unexpected to her as they were to him. This made sense and was the least he could do considering his foster created the problem. "Not for forever of course."

"Of course."

It shouldn't bother him that she agreed with him quickly. But he hated putting even some fantasy end date on this.

"Not sure it's a good idea, Holt."

He wasn't, either, but he also didn't care. He wanted her there. "It's not any worse than no place to go." He grabbed her hand, "This is the best answer in this moment. Come stay, for a week or two, at least."

"That would give me time to find a new place instead of running into another bad lease." She stood, confidence filtering back into her body. "I swear I won't be a burden… I'll carry my own weight."

"Sage…"

Burden was the last word he'd use to describe her.

She didn't turn around, instead she opened the kitchen cabinets and started taking notes.

Where had the notepad come from? Was she taking inventory?

She knew she was allowed to worry about being evicted right? Allowed to worry in general? It was a normal human reaction.

"Do you mind if I have Blaire drop the flyers for the rescue egg hunt at the Rainbow Ranch? She was supposed to drop them by after work today." She rubbed the back of her right leg with her left and opened a drawer. "We do most of our promotion online, but there are still a few places around town that put up flyers. And some people really like looking at them."

His dad's shop had had a board full of notifications. But that was twenty plus years ago in a completely different technological landscape. "Of course that is fine. After work today we can get some boxes and…"

"This isn't fair!" She slammed the drawer then drew a deep breath. "Sorry." Her shoulders shook. "It's just a lot."

Her body trembled as she repeated the words. "I can do this. I *have* to."

How many times in her life had she muttered, or screamed that mantra?

Holt pulled her to him. She was stiff in his arms, so he just held her as she mourned for today. Maybe this wasn't the place she'd dreamed of, but to be so unceremoniously kicked out was a nightmare.

She hiccupped and shuddered. "I always have a plan—a next step. But everything in the air and...and now I'm burdening—"

"Nope! You are not using that word to describe yourself... period." He kissed the top of her head. This was not an ideal situation; he would not pretend it was.

However, Sage Pool should banish that word from her vocabulary!

"Thank you." She stepped out of his arms. "While I am staying at your place, I can help you with some of the projects for the ranch. You know—earn my keep." She winked, but he could see the wheels already moving in her mind.

She was shifting, moving to the next thing. How did she do that?

"I'd love some help with those things, but you don't have to pay me back. I owe you—after all, this big guy is the reason today happened.

Her back stiffened for just a moment. Or maybe he was imagining it. He looked at his watch. "I need to head back to the ranch. Anything you want me to take?"

"The dog food in the corner." She crossed her arms. "This isn't a huge place. It won't take long to clear out. I'm petty enough to not turn over the keys until the last day!"

"I support that." Holt kissed her cheek. "See you in a few hours."

"Thank you." Sage ran her hands over his cheeks. "Promise it won't be for too long."

He couldn't say anything. They'd gone from an impulsive night, to last night and the promise of dating to living together.

By society's standards this should terrify him. They were not ready to move in together.

Once again though this felt right. Like everything with Sage, it just fit.

"I just don't understand why Mrs. Teacups keeps getting sick." Amalie Berkins rubbed the overweight cat as it purred.

She reached into her pocket, and Sage held up a hand. "Why don't we wait for Dr. Cove to take a look at her before we give her any treats?" She knew it was a losing quest, but Sage felt duty bound to suggest it.

There was nothing wrong with Mrs. Teacups that couldn't be fixed with weight control and exercise for the tabby. Something every vet had recommended for the four-year-old cat. Amalie just didn't like that answer.

"She's earned a little treat. Unlike my children." She held out the treat making a little noise as the cat greedily snapped it from her fingers.

She'd driven her children away. That wasn't a kind statement, but it was true. Her daughters had gone no contact years ago. Her son following suit a few months ago.

"They take and they take. But they never give anything back. Just expect to live off my generosity. Or they did."

Sage looked to the door. If she had an ounce of magic in her body, she'd pull Holt through the door right now and out of this ongoing drama. She had no part in the circus of Amalie's life and she didn't want one!

Melody, Amalie's youngest daughter, had graduated with her. They'd been friendly enough, though they'd each had so much going on that a deep friendship never developed. Still, when she was leaving town, she'd adopted a small white Lab mix with black and brown spots, named Cleo.

She sent pictures of Cleo to the rescue every once in a while, with the request that it not be shared with her mother. A request Sage honored.

"I gave them eighteen years of living expenses, a roof over their head. And what do I get in return?"

Some might call that the bare minimum a parent should provide.

Sage kept that statement to herself. Only Mrs. Teacups got love…and the over-the-top application of the emotion here was killing the cat.

"Good afternoon, Mrs. Teacups." The cat blinked as Holt walked in. It sat up, but its belly was nearly dragging on the exam table.

"You are a big girl."

Sage could see the same thoughts run through Holt's mind that she'd watched the other vets think. Could a homegrown vet make Amalie finally listen?

Holt graduated with Lance, Amalie's son, who had tried so hard to make his mother happy. She wasn't sure if Holt and Forest had known Lance, but they'd have to have least known of him and the rough situation at home.

"She has big bones."

"Cats do not have big bones, Ms. Berkins." Holt's voice was stern as he looked at the cat and then it's owner. "What brings Mrs. Teacups in? The chart says not eating."

I find that hard to believe.

He didn't add those words, but Sage knew he wanted to.

"I mean she *is* eating." Amalie took out another treat, and Mrs. Teacups moved as quickly as possible to get it. How many treats did the woman have in her pocket?

"So what did you want me to look at?"

"She gets sick." Amalie held up her hands, her cheeks darkening as she glared at Holt. Like he was supposed to divine the issue.

Holt didn't react—right choice. Dr. McKay had reacted to everything Amalie did, all the attention-seeking behavior. It never worked well.

"Okay. Is there a specific time where she is ill?"

"After dinner. She eats her bowl of food in just a minute or so, then gets a handful of treats, then gets sick! And then I have to give her a little more food, cause I can't let the baby be hungry, and sometimes that makes her sick too."

"Handful of treats?" Holt leaned against the counter. "Are you trying to kill your cat?"

Sage knew her mouth was hanging open, but she couldn't quite believe what she'd just heard.

"How dare you! Mrs. Teacups is my life. She never talks back, never takes me for granted, never…"

"I knew your son. I know what you think of your children. What I am concerned about in this moment is Mrs. Teacups."

Shutting down the expected rant about her kids. Wow, Holt really was on a roll.

"We rate cat weight on a scale of one to nine. One is severely underweight. Nine is morbidly obese. Mrs. Teacups is a nine, and on the high side of nines I have seen."

"She is not that overweight." Amalie huffed and reached for the cat carrier. One Sage knew Mrs. Teacups hated as it was too small for her.

"She is. An average lifespan for a cat is eleven to eighteen years. I have treated many cats close to twenty. At the weight Mrs. Teacups is at, she will, and it is not an if, *will*, develop many health-related issues. Diabetes, joint problems, heart disease, even some cancers are tied to weight in cats. She is four. I doubt she makes it to six if she stays this weight. You are killing her by letting her be this heavy."

"Well, I never!" Amalie shook her head; if it were possible for steam to pour from her ears it would. "I love my cat."

"Then work with me to get Mrs. Teacups healthy. For each week she loses weight, even a small amount, we will celebrate you."

"Celebrate how?"

Yeah, how?

Amalie had played the same game with the other vets. Got

mad at the suggestion, then stormed off. She was furious with Holt, but still here. No small accomplishment.

"How about for each week of lost weight, you get a gift card to the local coffee shop?"

"With six dollars. I like the big fancy drink."

"With enough to cover one big fancy drink. And if she puts on weight, you will give me the money for a big drink." Before Amalie could say anything, Holt held up his hand. "What's fair is fair. We want a clean slate."

Amalie looked at Mrs. Teacups and crossed her arms. "Fine. I will try it for a few weeks."

"Excellent." Holt nodded. "Ideally, Mrs. Teacups needs to lose at least ten pounds. Twelve would be best. It will take time—probably close to a year."

Amalie looked at the cat then at Holt. Sage could see the wheels turning as she calculated how many coffees Holt would pay for. Could this actually work?

"Amanda will be in with your discharge papers shortly. Sage, can you come with me?"

She moved a little to quickly, but she didn't think Amalie noticed. She was too busy murmuring to the cat that there were going to be some changes.

"You got her to listen." She still couldn't quite believe it. No one got Amalie to listen. No one!

"I went to university with Lance's new wife. She's a bio-technology engineer now. One of the smartest people I've ever met."

"Wow. Small world."

"Right! I met up with them in LA, accidentally at a bar and we reconnected some." Holt laughed. "Anyways, Amalie is a classic narcissist, unfortunately. Nothing is her fault, but she likes rewards, even small ones for things she should be doing. Play into that, and she'll at least consider it."

"I guess if it works."

"Kinda my feeling. Though I never want to talk to a client

that way. I'll have to let Peyton know I owe her. Without her insights on her mother-in-law not sure we'd have gotten Mrs. Teacups the help she needed."

An uncomfortable feeling slid down Sage's spine. The wording was off. Like he owed them a debt. Helping Peyton and Lance if they needed it would be the right move. Period.

It's nothing.

They'd had a long day. It was a turn of phrase. Nothing more.

"Now—" Holt pulled her into his arms "—what should we make for dinner? Whatever it is, we have to stop by the store… my pantry is bare." He dropped a kiss on her nose.

"Still need maple syrup?"

"Nope. Picked that up the day after…" He cleared his throat and kissed her cheek. "I wasn't taking any chances that you might spend the night again. Tomorrow, I'll make waffles… with syrup."

CHAPTER NINE

"THIS IS THE last bit." Sage wrapped her arms around her waist and rocked as she looked at the few boxes of clothes and her bed.

Holt stepped behind her; she leaned into his chest as she processed the moment. "You have two more days. We can leave the bed here, until Friday night."

Working together they'd packed and cleaned the small unit faster than he'd expected. A motivated Sage was a sight to behold.

"Waiting isn't changing the outcome. I just wish I wasn't imposing."

"There's that word again. You aren't imposing. We should strip that from your brain." He kissed the top of her head. It was selfish to be happy that she'd be at his place. Selfish to relish the consequences of his decisions.

"What… What are we doing…" She blew out a breath. Whatever she wanted to say caught in her throat. "Bravery isn't my best skill."

"I won't agree to that statement." Holt squeezed her tightly. Bravery flowed through Sage's blood. It was such a part of her that she didn't see it. But he had a guess at what she wanted to ask. "What are we doing with your bed?"

"Yes."

She'd spent the last few nights at his place. They'd come

here, box up part of a room, then head to the Rainbow Ranch. It had become a near perfect routine in just four days.

But this was still very uncharted territory. They'd slipped from one night of fun to something different to living together without any discussions.

They needed to have those conversations. Needed to make sure they were on the same page. Hell, how often had he told a friend to just ask what the relationship status was? *Have a conversation* was such an easy phrase to utter.

When you weren't the one risking getting hurt.

"I thought we would put it in your old room, but—"

Blood rushed in his ears; his chest was tight. Finishing a sentence had never made his insides crawl. Wow, he owed a dozen or so friends apologies. This really wasn't as easy as he'd always assumed.

"But I want you in my bed, Sage."

"That was direct." A small giggle erupted from her lips. "I like direct."

"Good." He spun her in his arms.

"But I think we should agree to something." Her nose twitched and she looked at the floor before looking at him.

If she was worried about earning her keep, he wanted to lay that thought to rest. "You don't have to earn your stay at—" He stopped as a look crossed her face. She needed to help. Not letting her would hurt her.

"Okay. I could certainly use the help." But he'd be beside her the whole time, whether she liked it or not. She was used to being the one offering help and she planned for letdowns, because unfortunately too many people had let her down.

He swore he would never be one of those people.

"But I actually meant…" She gestured between them, her body tensing.

He wanted to pull the words from her lips. Wanted to know what she wanted…and also wanted to pause life right here. Right now, things weren't perfect, but they were good.

"When this ends, we agree that it doesn't impact work." She coughed and ran a hand on her chest. "If we decide to step away from this, life reverts back to what we were. Right?"

What if it doesn't end?

He understood her need to plan, but his heart seized on that *when*. He couldn't force that question out. Instead he heard the word "agreed" slip from his lips.

But what were we?

They'd been childhood friends—almost more, colleagues, lovers and strangers. The only one they could truly go back to was strangers. An association he hated even thinking of ascribing to Sage.

"Okay." She raised on tiptoe, her lips brushing his. Looking around the apartment, she pursed her lips then straightened her shoulders. "Let's get out of here."

Her bottom lip trembled, but she didn't break. Her strength was so impressive. He'd turned her life upside down. And hated how he didn't want to change anything.

"Great plan. We can get the bed tomorrow? How about we grab takeout on the way back to the ranch? Spend the night watching a movie?"

Other words hung in the air. The desire to tell her he didn't want to consider what happened when. That he wanted to ponder the idea of never. But the moment was fading, and he wasn't strong enough for it.

"Perfect recipe for tonight!" Sage grinned, but the look didn't quite reach her eyes.

"Why are there so many eggs?" Holt laughed as he slid a piece of tape across the egg's seam. It was a trick her friend had recommended after carting a box of eggs to the local hunt and having half of them burst open, spilling their contents before they could even be hidden a few years ago.

"Donations!" They were filling their third box. She'd gotten almost six hundred eggs for the hunt, and several foster families had donated eggs and candy too. The children were going to have a field day. Full baskets of candy.

"You don't have to help. I know this isn't exciting."

"Sage. I offered to help—and I am helping." Holt's tone was soft as he leaned over and kissed her.

His mouth opened and she deepened the kiss. There was work to do, but she'd be up for a distraction. And Holt was a great distraction!

He pulled back and grabbed another one. "Besides, without me, this will take forever. And I have fun plans."

"Motivation to finish." Sage grinned as she looked at the box before them. Stuffing them was taking longer than she'd expected. It was a blessing Holt was so willing to help.

None of the men she'd dated ever helped with the rescue. She'd gotten so used to doing things alone, it made her feel weird to have a partner sitting here with her joking. Treating this like it was just a normal relationship moment.

It was a sad statement, but so many people promised to help, and then other things took priority. If you ran a volunteer network, you got used to assuming people wouldn't turn up and excited when everything worked out.

Holt didn't complain about helping either. Even his question about the eggs was in good spirits. It was lovely and unsettling. Part of her kept waiting for the other shoe to drop.

For him to get frustrated and tell her she was on her own. It wasn't fair, but that didn't stop her mind from watching for the warning signals.

"Do we have enough kiddos in town for all this candy?"

"Are you worried that we might have to bring bags of chocolate home?"

Home. Such a loaded word. One that Holt didn't seem to notice. This was home. Her home. She'd lived in several places since her mom lost this place. None had just felt like hers.

But here did…particularly with Holt beside her.

But it's not, Sage.

"Is it an option to keep some of the chocolate?" He held up a bag of chocolate peanut butter candies. "I mean…"

She shook her head and pointed to the unstuffed eggs. He dutifully ripped open the bag and started putting the candy in. Though he did pop a few in his mouth. She couldn't blame him for that.

"I promise, if there are any eggs left, you can stuff yourself silly with candy."

"Hmmm." Holt held up another piece of candy. "I might hold you to that. Feel like I'm a little owed with all the work." He winked, again.

It was a joke. She could see the humor dancing in his eyes. But her mother always said her father joked about responsibilities being too much before leaving. Said she'd missed the signs.

Holt was not her father. He was helping. Though he did seem to keep track of debts…

"I've stuffed myself enough tonight." Holt chucked another egg in the box. Then leaned across the couch and kissed her.

He tasted of chocolate, and fun and home. *Home.* Was that a silly, or worse dangerous, thought? He loved the big city. Had chosen here to prove he wasn't like his mother, something that should be so painfully obvious.

Would he leave when he was content with the truth she saw so easily?

"Funny isn't it, candy as an adult."

"Funny?" Sage tilted her head as the thoughts floating around her mind meshed with the silly conversation. "Candy is candy, no matter your age."

"I disagree." He held up a piece of chocolate. It was a circle, wrapped in bright colors. But she knew the candy was cheap chocolate, with rice crisps inside. "As an adult I can buy whatever candy I want."

"The good kind, too!" Sage grabbed the candy from his hand and put it in an egg with another piece of chocolate. Kids didn't mind the chocolates.

It was a fun memory. "Forest always managed to get the most eggs. I swear his basket was always overflowing. But not with good chocolate."

He looked at the next circle. "His egg hunting skills were top-notch. I used to love exchanging candy after the hunts."

"Forest always wanted the peanut butter chocolates." Sage looked at the bag her brother would love. A hint of wistfulness making its way through her. Such a little thing they'd taken for granted. "I add a little money to his canteen each month so he can get some candy. Little treats are different as adults."

Particularly when you can't go to the store to pick your own.

Her eyes blurred for just a minute, but she blinked back the tears. He'd made a poor choice…and was paying a steep price for it. But that didn't mean she forgot about him; that she didn't miss him.

When she looked back at Holt, he didn't quite meet her gaze. His eyes hovered on the peanut butter candies, then drifted away, somewhere lost in the past.

Sage waited a minute, but Holt didn't say anything else. Setting her eggs and chocolate to the side, she climbed across the couch and sat in his lap. She kissed his cheek and pressed her forehead to his. She didn't know what was rumbling around his mind, but she wanted him to know he wasn't alone.

Holt pressed his lips to Sage's head as she snuggled in his lap. He'd seen the tears she'd blinked away. He let out a sigh as they sat in silence.

Easter candy wasn't a trigger he'd anticipated.

As kids everything seemed possible. The whole world just waiting for you. As a kid, adults liked to say *you can be anything you want*.

It was a nice lie.

But most people couldn't. Sage was the perfect example. She'd had good grades. Was an accomplished high school student. And her dreams of leaving for university had crashed around her the night of his graduation.

It wasn't her fault. But that didn't mean it hadn't impacted her...catastrophically.

It was easy to forget. Particularly when Sage was warm in his arms. Her head leaning against his shoulder. This wasn't the past, but she was tied to it so closely. Tied to a decision he'd regret for the rest of his days.

Children didn't realize how the lives around them were impacted by what they did. Heck, even as adults it was so easy to miss the ripples your choice made on others.

"I think we could use a break." Sage grabbed his hands as she stood and pulled him off the couch. "So, let's talk about the back room."

"The eggs aren't done."

"We still have two days to stuff all of them!" She held his hand as she walked them to the back room. They'd spent two days ripping out the drywall with Sage's tools. She swore demo was the easy and fun part, but he couldn't believe how motivated she always was.

How was her body not constantly on the brink of exhaustion?

"Okay, what do you want to talk about?" The room was dusty, the studs and empty spaces behind the walls highlighting just how much a place could change with a little work.

"What do you want to do with it?" She rocked on her heels. "What is the plan? Demo is fun. But now the real work comes."

"The drywalling?" He knew she'd trained herself for this. Figured out how to drywall and do handy projects for when this place was hers. A fact that gnawed in his belly.

"Yes. The drywalling is the next step. After you get the electrician out here to make sure the wiring is still fine. I know a lot of things, but electricity and major plumbing issues—those are jobs we hire out!"

We.

He liked that word. We...he and Sage. No timeline in that

statement. No indication of *when it ends*. Words bubbled in the back of his throat, but he couldn't pull them forward.

Instead he went for what he knew she wanted to hear. "I already called. Rick is supposed to stop by tomorrow afternoon. I told him where the spare key is, since we will still be at the clinic. He said checking the wires will be quick. If anything needs to be replaced, he'll call me."

"Good. So what is this room, Holt?"

"A room?" He shook his head. "I am sorry, Sage, but I am not sure what you mean. This is a room. Though it needs real walls, of course."

"Right. But is it a guest room or a study, or a library, a home office? A room that can be turned into a playroom with warm colors and built-in storage for when you have a child?"

Color coated her cheeks. And his mouth fell open. He'd never discussed kids. Never really thought of them. Always to busy with work…like his mother.

"I just mean, what was your plan for this? I guess if you don't have a plan that is okay. But, I mean…you know…it's your house."

"What did you plan this room to be?"

Sage's mouth opened. Maybe it wasn't the question she expected, but he really wanted to know.

"Come on, I know you had a plan. Was it the playroom?" The last suggestion was too detailed.

"Yes."

So Sage wanted a family. She'd be an excellent mother. His body turned cold as he imagined a fictitious partner standing beside her.

So this was jealousy. This feeling so close to bordering on anger and hatred for a person he'd never met, for a person Sage hadn't met. But one she'd hoped for.

"But not for kids." She sighed as she looked around the room. "It was going to be my puppy room. Puppies are the hardest to foster."

"They're so cute though!" Holt laughed, knowing exactly what she meant. Puppies were adorable, and just like newborns, a *ton* of work. Many people got puppies because of the cute factor without realizing how difficult it was to train them.

"Sure. Cute. For twenty minutes then disaster!" She stepped into the middle of the room and pointed to the back wall. "I planned to cut a doggie door there. One I could lock but would let the dog mom exit and eventually her puppies for potty training."

She spun as she outlined the plan. "Over there was going to be a little play area, dog toys, chewy bones, steps for climbing. And of course I wanted to take the door off and build a permanent dog gate."

She looked at her feet then back at the walls, "Painted teal... a nice relaxing color."

"Not sure puppies care about the color of the wall."

She batted a hand at him. "They are not really colorblind. You're a vet. You know they see shades of blue and yellow."

"Yes." Holt pulled her into him. Enjoying the feel of her against his body. This was perfection, even in an unfinished room. Her in his arms, talking about the future.

Could he give that to her? Would she want it from him?

"I don't think teal will calm puppies."

"But it will calm me!" She leaned her head back and kissed his cheek. "Sometimes it's about me...well, at least it's nice to think about me once in a while."

It should be about her more often.

"A puppy room." He saw it clearly. Puppies tumbling over the toys. A tired mom dog hurrying out of the room for a few minutes of peace when the puppies were occupied. Sage passing out treats and diligently training the dogs. Giving them their best shots at a forever family.

"Let's do it."

"Do what?" Sage looked at him, her eyebrows knitted together.

"Make a puppy room." He tried not to let the surprise dropping over her features bother him. They'd just talked about this. She'd eloquently outlined the plan. It was a good plan, a better one than another guest room.

He already had one of those. With his dad gone, he hardly needed a second empty visitor suite.

He had a living room, no need for a gaming studio and he refused to bring paperwork home with him. His dad had turned the kitchen table into an office. He'd never seen his mother's place, but he'd bet money she had a home office. If he needed to stay late at the clinic he would. The ranch was not becoming a second office.

"How often are you planning to foster puppies, Dr. Cove?"

He didn't like that she'd used his title. There was a hint of distance in the question. A pinch of reality. The ranch wasn't hers and even with everything building between them, she didn't seem to see that as a possibility. They were having a blast together, but the idea that this might be theirs…she wasn't letting herself dream that.

He swallowed as white-hot pain cascaded through his soul. He didn't want reality intruding on this moment. He'd figure out later what the twists of emotion really meant.

"I'm a vet, Sage. I'm fostering Domino. He's a puppy."

"A housebroken six-month-old is not a puppy. That is an adolescent, and you know it."

He did. Dogs were technically said to be puppies up to two years, depending on the breed. But by six months they were really adolescents. Still learning socialization techniques and good manners, but not nearly as needy as a true puppy.

"You don't have to know what you want the room to be tonight. But start thinking of it. And remember, teal is a very calming color."

He made a mental pledge. Whatever this room was, it would be teal.

CHAPTER TEN

"MOM, YOU PROMISED to help today." Sage looked at the gathering crowd. Holt's idea was a success…maybe too much. Most of the town had to be here!

"I know, Sage." Her mother covered the phone, saying a few words to someone before coming back. "But I…well, something came up. Besides you always have everything under control. I'll talk to you later. Love you."

"Sage?" Holt pulled her to him, Domino pushing against their legs. "What's wrong?"

"Mom has something else going on, so down a volunteer. I'll make it work. Always do!" Her voice was bright, even as she watched more people arrive. But her mother was right, she had this…because there wasn't another option.

"Are you ready for today?" Sage rubbed Domino's head, focusing on something besides the pain that once more her mother had thought Sage could just figure it out. The dog panted and rubbed its ears against her hands. The card table rocked as his tail batted the leg. "You're going to knock over the table, Domino."

"Are you asking me or the dog if we're ready?" Holt's grip on Domino's leash was best described as a death grip. He'd helped her set up the Easter egg hunt, then gone back to the ranch to grab Domino.

She needed to be laying out adoption applications and checking in with foster families, figuring out who would help Blaire with registration, but Holt looked miserable.

"Sweetheart." The endearment slipped out and Sage almost covered her mouth with her hand.

Like it was responsible for her calling Holt sweetheart.

Nicknames were things for couples.

Which we are, right?

She wasn't seeing anyone else. He wasn't either, but they'd never really discussed it. Never labeled it. Normally that didn't bother her. So why was her heart racing?

Because she wanted to label this. Maybe after she found a place for herself, when they were on more equal footing. Though given that she'd put in four applications for rental units and been turned down for all four, that might take more time than she planned.

And she liked living with him. Liked waking up next to him. A lot!

"If someone fills out an adoption form for him—"

"If!" Holt opened his mouth, his cheeks coloring as he looked at Domino then back at her. "How could someone not put in an application for this guy? He is a giant baby. An adorable goober. The bestest best boy! If? Please. Everyone should want him."

Crossing her arms, she tilted her head.

Mixed signals much, Holt?

"So you are happy with him being adopted?"

"I didn't say that." Holt kicked the dirt; his hand automatically reaching for Domino's head.

Fostering was difficult, she understood that. It was easy to get attached.

"This isn't a foster fail."

"I didn't say it was." *Yet.* Sage knew a foster fail when it happened. Domino couldn't do better than Holt Cove as his owner. Maybe Holt hadn't realized that, but he would.

Clearing her throat, she pointed to the adoption application. It was a formality. Spring River Paws's foster families were preapproved to adopt, but it was still a requirement. "But if you wanted to keep him…"

"The ranch does feel more like home with him there. And you—"

"Sage!" Blaire's voice echoed across the field. It was a skill her friend reserved for when she really needed help. "I need help!"

Timing was everything. Sage desperately wanted to know if he was about to say the ranch felt like home with her there too. If, despite liking the big cities, he might really choose to stay here. *Forever.*

"Mom was supposed to help with the children's section. I have to get the fosters checked in here." She needed to be in two places at once. "I need—" She looked over to where children were starting to swamp Blaire.

The registration booth for the egg hunt was giant. Their foster dogs were already registered for the bone hunt and just needed to be checked in. But they'd not thought to do preregistration for the children.

Oversight central. But one easily made when the rescue's focus was dogs.

"What can I do?" Holt looked to Domino then kissed her cheek.

"You sure you don't mind?"

"When are you going to stop asking that? Domino and I are at your service. Just tell me what needs to be done. I am happy to help."

"Think you can handle registering the few extra dogs we're expecting? I'm betting most of the dogs hunting today will be our fosters, but I know a few people are planning to bring their pets too."

"Of course." Holt pulled Domino to stand with him beside the dog registration table and waved his hand. "You do what you need to do and I will be here."

"Thank you." She ran a hand on Domino's head. "Categories are pretty easy. Under ten pounds, ten to twenty pounds, twenty to fifty and then our over fifty-pound category."

"Sage!"

"Blaire needs you. I got this. Promise. You can count on me."

Count on me.

The words rested on Sage's heart. She handled everything and everyone just let her. Everyone but Holt. It was a gift she couldn't calculate the price on.

"Thank you!" She waved a hand overhead as she took off.

"Took you long enough." Blaire handed pens to a few parents. "Just put names and ages. Please."

"Sorry. I had Gina and my mom scheduled, but…"

"Enough said." Blaire nodded. Gina would probably be here. At some point. It was the nature of volunteer work; you always planned as though at least a portion of volunteers wouldn't show. And her mother was a complete no-show.

"Holt is running the dog registration."

"Of course he is. You're here. The man would do anything for you."

Sage's cheeks were hot, and it was too early in spring to blame a summer heat. "We are enjoying each other."

"Clearly, but he's here for you." She handed a reusable bag to a child who'd forgotten their Easter basket.

"We haven't even put a label on it." Sage took the pen and registration form from a mom with four kiddos clinging to her legs, pointing them to the area for the kids' age group. This wasn't the best place for a conversation, but Blaire had never let the optics of a time and space interrupt her when she had something to say.

"Love doesn't need a label."

"Uh-huh." Sage nodded, hoping her friend would take a hint for the first time in her life.

"Enjoy the egg hunt!" Sage waved back at the small girl who'd started waving at her the moment she'd gotten to the front of the line. "Do you think we have enough eggs?"

"Yes. And I think you're trying to change the topic." Blaire chuckled as she pointed a family in the right direction.

"This isn't exactly the time or place. We're a little busy, after all." Sage gestured to the gathered crowd. Not that it mattered because she wasn't in love with Holt. He was loveable, and great and they were having fun, but love... Love was what crushed her mother.

And Holt was here to prove a point to himself. When he did...what then?

No falling in love. No relying on others. No getting hurt.

She had the rescue she loved. A job she enjoyed. A full life. Sure she was lonely sometimes.

Not since Holt got home, though.

The thought pounded in her head as she passed out a bag. The fact that her heart raced, her chest heaved and her soul cried out at the thought of Holt leaving meant...

Well, she wasn't sure, but it didn't equal love. She'd kept her heart secure from that emotion her entire adult life.

"There is no time and place where you are not busy. I gotta take my opportunities when they present themselves."

Sage didn't respond. She didn't need to. Yes, she was busy. Yes, always.

Holt would be easy to fall in love with. She could do it so easily.

But she hadn't. *Not yet.*

"Domino." Holt shook his head as Domino jumped with the rescue pittie being "rented" for the bone hunt by Chad Dye. All the rescue dogs had found a person to take them on the hunt. If even one dog was adopted out of today's event it would be a success. But Holt had a good feeling that several were going home.

"Bucky. Aren't we supposed to be hunting for bones!"

The pittie barked, Domino barked and Holt just looked at Chad. "I guess we know they're dog friendly."

"I guess we do. Honestly that was my main concern." Chad laughed and rubbed the tan pittie's giant head. "Though I guess they think this guy is closer to three so not so much a puppy."

"In my experience pitties have two speeds for most of their lives. GO! And nap. They're active dogs that get an undeserved bad rap."

"I'm moving in a month." Chad looked at the mountains in the distance before redirecting his attention to the dogs. "Never thought I'd leave Spring River. It's been home for so long."

Home.

The word kept circling in his brain. What was his fixation with it? The ranch was nice. It felt nice being there, with Domino…and Sage.

He'd lived all over and never considered the place he laid his head anything more than a house. Moving was easy each time. Another step in the career ladder. A new adventure to try.

He didn't have roots to break…at least he hadn't felt like he had until he returned to Spring River.

His gaze found Sage. She was across the field, laughing and helping a kid carry what looked like an overflowing basket. His heart exploded.

He'd run from Spring River once. Now he understood Chad's wistful look as he stared at the mountains. "You going far?"

"New York." Chad sighed and rubbed Bucky's head. "Upstate. I have a great little place rented. But I don't know anyone. So, thought bringing along a buddy might make that easier."

"And he is such a good boy!"

"Abby!" The golden retriever bounded up, her tail wagging as she joined the boys in play. "That chocolate German short-haired pointer is going to get all the bones!"

Abby didn't seem to notice her companion's frustrations. Goldens really were the happiest things on the earth.

"I think Ginny, the pointer you mentioned, *is* going to get most of the bones. Between her and Pepper, the Lab mix, who

Sage told me is one of the most food driven dogs she's ever met, all the bones will be found." Holt laughed as he looked over at the dogs running in the open field searching out bones.

Sage had set it up as a run. So each dog ran down a line and found four bones. That way none of the dogs were hunting for the same bones. The rescue tested the dogs for food aggression, and the one dog known to be food aggressive had had a spa day at home instead of coming to the event.

But now that three were out of the hunt, Ginny and Pepper explored the unused lanes, scavenging for extra bones.

"Living their best lives." Holt laughed as Bucky and Abby both rolled over on their backs exposing their bellies. "I guess you're the dominant one here, Domino."

His black and white ears bounced as he playfully pounced on his new friends.

"Anyone thinking about putting in an application?" Sage beamed as she moved to stand next to Holt, a few clipboards and pens in her arms.

"Yes." Chad and the woman holding Abby's leash said in such an echo the dogs looked up, tilting their heads at their soon-to-be parents.

"I am going to need one of those too!" The man running beside Ginny let out a pant. "She is driven, but so sweet."

"Just be warned. If you throw the ball for her, she will keep bringing it back for you. Forever!" Happiness danced in Sage's eyes as she looked at Holt. This was what she'd hoped for, and he was glad it worked out.

"I believe it."

"Those the applications?" Pepper and her partner walked up, the Lab panting and looking at the pocket of the person holding their leash. "I let you have the four you found on your run. The other eight...we don't want you getting a stomach-ache, honey."

Already talking like a responsible owner.

"Wow." Sage shook her head. "I didn't bring enough clip-boards."

"Here you can use my back." Holt turned and winked at Sage as Pepper's soon-to-be owner used his back to fill out her application. He'd actually been joking, after all it wouldn't take too long for a clipboard to become available, but once the offer was made!

Thank you. Sage mouthed the words.

Turning to her small audience, she clapped her hands. "Your puppies still need to have their final vet check. And we need to do a home inspection. Pictures of your new place will do, Chad. I will have them ready for pickup by the end of the week."

"If the foster family okays it, can we stop by to check in on them?" Chad handed Bucky a treat. "Not sure you really earned this, since you didn't hunt at all!"

Bucky politely took the treat and grinned at Chad.

"Today was a good day. Busy, overwhelming but good." Holt wrapped an arm around Sage, as they, and Domino, walked the field to find any leftovers. Though the results so far had been dismal. One lonely egg, and no bones.

"Today was a great day!" Sage leaned her head against his shoulder. "Only one foster puppy in attendance didn't have adoption paperwork placed."

"About that…" Holt kissed the top of her head.

"Mmm-hmm." Sage raised her head and dropped a kiss on his lips. This perfection, this night. Another he'd cherish in his memories forever, no matter what happened between them.

"Do I have to do the home check?"

"Nope." She beamed and he could see the *told you so* echo-ing in her eyes. "As I said, all our fosters are preapproved for adoption. He's yours as soon as you fill out the paperwork."

"Let's do it when we get home."

"I like the sound of that." A look passed over Sage's eyes. Satisfaction…he thought. Or was he just imagining it?

* * *

"I love this time of year!" Sage was dressed in old overalls, her hair in a bun with a bright red bandana tied around the rest of her hair. She was carrying a box from the garage, with Domino at her heels. "Everything is starting to bloom. The world is reawakening and hope for a new start is everywhere."

Spring cleaning was a chore many hated, but it was her favorite. A freshening of your space. She'd climbed into the attic, seen how much clutter he'd inherited from previous owners and decided to go through it. Some of it might even be her mother's.

Holt's addition to this morning's cleaning was a welcome surprise. Though maybe she shouldn't be surprised anymore. The man was always willing to help.

She was already dressed and ready to move. Anything to keep her brain from drifting to the reality that she was so happy here. Too happy here.

With Holt.

And his dog.

She'd recognized the foster fail the first time she saw the two of them together at her old place. But recognizing one and the person following through were not always the same thing.

"A new start. So poetic." Holt shook his head and he handed her another box from the attic. "So, you think any of this is your mom's stuff?"

"Probably." Sage blew across the top of the box watching the dust lift into a little cloud. "If we find anything I think she misses, I'll let her know."

"You aren't frustrated with her? She promised to help at the egg hunt and ducked out at the last minute. Literally."

The question didn't surprise her. Her mom wasn't as strong as Sage. She'd let life break her. She was never going to take care of Sage. It didn't mean her mother didn't love her, just that she wasn't capable of being the type of mom people thought she should be.

Sometimes it hurt, but dwelling on it didn't change things.

"She is who she is, Holt. I should have asked someone else. That's on me."

"It's not." Holt looked at her, but she couldn't hold his gaze.

She knew better than to expect her mom to follow through. Getting angry about it…well, life was too short.

"Stay!" Holt held up his hand as Domino started to get off the bed he'd placed in the garage. The dog had hit the jackpot. Now that he was officially Domino Cove, goofball dog of the local vet, Holt was training him to come to the clinic.

The bank foreclosed on the ranch not long after Forest's conviction. The little apartment her mother had wasn't big enough for all her furniture, let alone the memories and junk she'd stashed in the attic above the garage. And there was no money for a storage unit, so they'd taken only what mattered most.

"Well, if she doesn't have room, and you don't mind, she is welcome to store any of it here she wants to keep. I don't mind indefinite storage." He held his hand up, made sure Domino saw the sign then climbed back into the attic.

Indefinite storage. The words rooted Sage in place. *Indefinite.*

Such a fancy word for *forever.* Her throat was tight. Her mind fixated on a single item.

"Sage." Holt had another box in his hand as he stepped down. "What are you…"

"Indefinite storage." She interrupted whatever he was about to say. "Did you mean that?"

"Of course. I can't imagine that I will ever need that full attic space. It's huge. Unless the rescue needs me to store stuff."

"The rescue?" So many words. Too many feelings. "Holt, what are we?" That wasn't exactly the question she meant to ask. Or maybe it was.

So much had happened in just a few short weeks. She'd resisted labels, resisted getting close. Resisted needing anyone. But it was so easy between them.

She was looking for another place. And not having any luck. But her heart wasn't in it. Because of the man standing before her...who she'd just asked to define their relationship.

Holt stepped off the last step and put the small box down. "We are whatever *you* want us to be?" He took the box from her hand.

Tiny explosions were echoing in her heart. In her mind. *Whatever I want.*

Except the world never gave Sage exactly what she wanted. People left, dreams evaporated...

"What if I want you to name it?"

What if I say the wrong thing? The thing that makes you walk? The thing that makes me too independent or too much or...?

Her mind wrapped around so many thoughts, unable to put any into real words.

"Sage..."

She hated the soft tone. That was a tone for crushing dreams, not starting relationships.

"I want you."

Physical connection. *Check.*

"I care about you. You're one of my best friends."

Yikes, this was just getting worse.

"But?" Sage crossed her arms. She'd thrown the gauntlet down. She'd demanded an answer; so she had to accept whatever it was.

"There isn't a but, Sage." Holt pulled her arms away from her body. Holding her hands, he squeezed them, but didn't pull her closer. "I'm yours. Pure and simple, for as long as you want me around. So you get to choose the label. Or leave it off all together. I have no plans to see anyone, while we're us."

"For as long as I want you around?" Sage looked at him,

really looked. There was a darkness in his eyes. A sadness of some kind.

For what?

"You think I will get tired of you?"

Holt smiled, the darkness fading, but not quite vanishing. "I know that you make me happier than I've ever been."

There felt like there was an unspoken but there. A piece of the puzzle he was holding back.

Or you're looking for the problem, looking for a way to protect yourself.

"All the other vets leave Spring River." And now the fear was finally voiced.

"So I've heard."

She swung her hands pulling his along with hers. She was falling for him. Hell, who was she kidding. Sage Pool was tumbling headlong into love with Holt Cove.

It wasn't the plan. Love was so dangerous she'd never let herself believe it possible. But her heart seemed not to care that it could get crushed.

The cluttered garage, in overalls was not the place for this conversation but there was no turning back now. "I don't want you to leave." Five little words. Not quite the big three words, but closer than Sage had ever gotten.

"No plans to." Holt kissed the top of her forehead.

"Okay." Sage lifted on tiptoe and grazed his lips. He was staying. He was staying. The fear that had engulfed her since that first return.

He'd left her once. Left town. Dropped out of her life. A person that was once a seamless part of it. The hole it created, no one else had filled.

Or maybe she hadn't let anyone.

Closing the tiny distance between them, Sage wrapped her arms around his neck. "Can you make one promise?"

"I can try."

She wrinkled her nose and tightened her grip on him. She'd

expected a yes. Though maybe his caution was the right move. "We talk through the big things?"

"The big things?" Holt tightened his grip. "Like you moving out…and me not wanting you to?"

She smiled against his chest, "Yes. Like that." He'd really just asked her to stay. Not with a big gesture, just a simple statement. Her heart felt lighter than it had in years.

"Are you sure, Holt?" She wanted to stay. Wanted to be here…with him. But it had all moved so fast.

"It's one of the few things I am absolutely positive of." He captured her mouth then, holding her tightly. Perfection.

But he hadn't actually agreed to what she was asking.

Pulling back, she ran her fingers along his chest. Would she ever tire of touching him? She hoped not.

"Holt, I am serious, though. The big things. Life changes, career, new dogs, we discuss those."

"Sure. Feels like something one should do in relationships."

"Agreed." Sage took a deep breath; he was right. One should do that, but so often people didn't. "I've always wondered if Dad let Mom know how much he was struggling—"

"If he'd have left?"

"No. He was always going to leave." Sage shook her head against his chest. Still not willing to break the connection they had. "But if she'd known, maybe she wouldn't have been so blindsided. Maybe I wouldn't—" Sage cut the unkind thought off.

Holt ran his fingers along her back. "Maybe you wouldn't have had to step in as much?"

She didn't trust her voice, so she just squeezed him tightly.

"We talk about the big things." Holt lifted her chin, his blue eyes sparkling. "Little things too. Deal?"

"Deal." Blowing out a breath, she looked at the garage. Maybe this wasn't the most romantic place for their relationship to officially enter its next stage, but that didn't matter. "Seal the deal with a kiss?"

"You will never have to ask me twice to kiss you." His lips were soft as they met hers; almost begging hers to open. She met his need with her own. He was hers.

Forever wasn't a word Sage used but it was starting to feel like maybe it could be…

CHAPTER ELEVEN

HOLT WHISTLED AS he set up for the day. He hadn't expected to find Sage in Spring River. He knew that Forest's crime trapped her here. And that maybe he could have changed that. But having her in his life, in his bed, by his side…it felt too perfect to let worry seep through.

"Good morning, Dr. Cove." Amalie beamed as she held up a very angry Mrs. Teacups. The cat glared through the mesh of her cat carrier.

It was almost like she knew who was responsible for the diet.

"Here for our weekly weigh-in and gift card."

It was a weird agreement to put into place with a client and a patient. But Mrs. Teacups desperately needed to lose the weight.

"Do you have the gift card?"

Holt held up the gift card he and Sage had gotten on the way in this morning. The same thing they'd done for the last three Fridays.

Sage stepped into the room; her face clear of any emotion. The clinic didn't officially open for another twenty minutes, but they'd scheduled this interaction early. In case Mrs. Teacups hadn't lost any weight and Amalie threw a fit. The first two weeks were successes, but Sage was waiting for Amalie to revert to her old ways.

Holt wasn't.

"Moment of truth." Holt motioned for Amalie to put the cat on the scale. "Down point two pounds. That is nearly a pound." It wasn't much, but for a cat in a few weeks, it was a good start.

"Yep!" Amalie beamed and held out her hand. "Gift card please!" Holt passed it over, and she bundled up the cat and headed out.

"I can't believe this is working." Sage kissed his cheek, surprise coating her eyes. "I have watched every vet try to find a way to get Mrs. Teacups to lose weight and you do it with a six-dollar-a-week gift card."

He didn't like the way the woman treated people, but part of him understood her transactional nature. "At her core, Amalie sees life as a list of transactions. It's why she is so horrid to her children. She raised them, cared for them, provided a roof and food, etcetera."

"So they owe her?"

He understood Sage's open mouth. People wanted to believe all parents loved their children. That there were a few cases of abuse, and when it happened the state could step in.

But the truth was more nuanced. And heartbreaking. A happy and healthy home was far rarer than people wanted to believe.

Shoot! Look at Sage's upbringing. Nothing criminal…but nobody would call it healthy?

"In her mind. Yes. They owe her."

"That's horrid."

He agreed, but that didn't change the reality. "Mrs. Teacups can't give Amalie anything but love and attention. So the cat will always get more than she should."

"How did you figure that out?"

"I think in a similar fashion."

"You do not!"

Daggers danced where shock had hovered in her eyes. "I've lived with you for almost a month now. You help out all the time and…"

She put her hands on her hips and he got the distinct impression she wanted to wag a finger at him. "I refuse to believe that you are as calculating as that."

"That is nice to hear." He leaned forward, dropping a kiss to her nose. They didn't touch much in the clinic, but it wasn't open yet. "I don't think anyone owes me anything. But I do think you reap what you sow. The energy or choices or whatever come back."

"Like karma?"

"Yeah. That's as good a label as any. So no, I don't think anyone owes me something because of what I have done, but I can grasp Amalie's thoughts."

Sage opened her mouth, but whatever argument was hovering on the tip of her tongue was drowned out by someone screeching her name.

"What the?" Holt wasn't sure who was on the other end of the voice, but they sounded desperate.

Sage made it through the door before he did. A teenage boy was cradling his dachshund.

"What's wrong with Roxy, Parker?"

The little boy sobbed as he held his lethargic dog. He looked at Sage and then Holt, his mouth opening but delivering no words.

Holt knelt next to him. "Parker." He didn't know Parker, but he did need to get him to focus on helping them. He waited until the boy looked at him. "I'm going to help Roxy, but I need to know what is going on."

"She hasn't been eating, but Dad lost his job and vet care..."

"I'll cover it."

Holt didn't look up at Sage as she said the words. It was a kind offer, but he would handle it.

"This morning she was so weak. I put her in my backpack, slung it in front of me and rode my bike. Mom is going to be so mad."

Sage looked to Lucy. It took only a moment for Holt to hear the receptionist letting Parker's mom know where he was.

"We are going to take Roxy to the back and take a closer look at her, okay?"

Parker wiped the back of his hand across his nose as tears slid down his face. He didn't say anything as he handed the dog to Holt.

Roxy licked his fingers, that was a decent sign. The dog was lethargic and clearly sick, but not despondent.

"Can you set up a full blood panel? Then we will get some fluids into her." Holt used his pen light, glad to see Roxy's pupils react.

Sage was back quickly with the blood draw material and the fluid. "Any ideas?"

"Too many." Holt looked at the sick dog, hating that there was no way for him to know immediately what was wrong. The symptoms could be liver failure, age, even unintentional poisoning, if Roxy got into something without her owners knowing. There were just too many possibilities in the moment.

"Right now we need to stabilize her." Holt listened to Roxy's heart rate. Elevated but not as bad as he'd figured.

"The last time she was here, she weighed just over twenty-two pounds."

Sage didn't say it, but he knew what she was thinking. The dog had lost at least five pounds. She was far too skinny.

"I've got fluids ready." Sage ran a finger on Roxy's ear and she held the needle out and the bag up.

Holt started the fluids, flinching when the dog didn't react to the stick. "I want to stay with her a few minutes, make sure she is stable before we move her to the back."

"Underst—"

Lucy stepped into the back before Sage could finish, "Peanut is here. Should I tell Mike to take him to the emergency vet?"

"Peanut?" Holt was trying to learn all his patients, but that name did not ring a bell.

"Orange cat with white stripes. Sweetheart…but likes to push things off counters."

"Did he land in glass again?" Sage pushed past Holt. Most cats didn't land in the mess they made.

"Fraid so."

"How about I get the glass out then you can check him?" Sage grabbed one of the tablet charts. "I think it's going to be a long day."

Unfortunately, he agreed.

"Sage here?" Lucy yawned and looked to where Holt was reading Roxy's blood work. Thiamine deficiency.

"No. She ran to grab us dinner. Should be back in about twenty minutes or so. I thought you'd already left?" The day had gone on far too long and he and Sage were staying even longer to make sure Roxy responded well to the thiamine pyrophosphate injection. The dog would need at least a week's worth of injections and then two weeks' of oral medications, followed by a lifetime of supplements.

It was going to be an expensive regimen, but he'd make sure Parker's family got the support they needed.

"I was in the parking lot when Rose stopped by. She's looking for Sage and she's not answering her phone."

"She left it here." Holt nodded to the counter. They were all so tired, but he'd noticed the buzzing a few minutes ago. In fact he'd planned to answer the next time it rang in case it was an emergency. "I'll see to Rose, you head out, Lucy. See you tomorrow."

"Thanks, just a heads-up, Rose is crying."

"Good to know." With any luck this was something he could clear up so Sage didn't have to.

Rose was wringing her hands just inside the doorway. She offered a quick goodbye to Lucy then looked at Holt. "Where is Sage?"

"Getting dinner. It's been a long day, Rose. What's wrong?"

He kept his voice even, though the exhaustion of the day clung to him.

"Forest needs money added to his commissary. I tried three times, but I must have done something wrong because it isn't working. I've tried calling Sage all day, but she hasn't answered."

"We had a couple of emergencies." *And she is working.*

"Forest called today. Collect—that's the requirement—and mentioned that he wanted to get some treats for his dog, but has to wait until next month. He enrolled in the dog program the prison has a few years ago. Trains them to be placed in homes." Rose let out a deep breath. "Sage always puts the money on the first of the month."

"You don't?" He didn't mean to ask the question. Sage took care of things for her mother; he knew that. But still, this seemed like something she should be able to handle.

Rose looked at her feet and wiped away a tear. "It upsets me to think of him there."

"It upsets Sage too, but she manages." Slamming his mouth shut, he stuffed his hands into his pockets.

Rose looked at him but didn't say anything.

"Did Forest say he needed the money right away?"

"He didn't say he needed it at all. Just that he was waiting, but I don't want him to have to wait, we can add a bit."

The day had been too long already. That wasn't Rose's fault, but did she ever think of Sage this way? The immediate need? Holt suspected her daughter's needs never crossed her mind. And they should! "I will tell Sage, but we are going to be here for several more hours—"

"It can be done via an app. That way it's there tomorrow—"

"No." Holt pulled his hand across his face. How could she not see that this wasn't an emergency. It was already late, and Forest could wait another day. Particularly because based on Rose's own statement, he was just making conversation.

"This can wait until tomorrow, Rose. Or you can figure out how to do it."

Her brows crossed and she turned and went back to her car.

She pulled out, just as Sage was pulling into the parking lot.

"Why was Mom here?" Her stomach rumbled as she stepped next to him.

"She's fine, though probably pissed at me. Come on, let's go inside. I'll explain over dinner."

Her phone buzzed, and he saw her look at it and type out a message. Frowning, she turned the phone over, then picked it back up and powered it down. Frustration radiated from her, but she didn't look at him. He didn't think she was as frustrated with him as she was with her mother.

But he was certainly a close second. Very close.

Of course. Her mom showed up and I was too forceful.

He didn't actually feel bad about that. There was no reason for Rose to act like this couldn't wait a day. No reason to put her son above her daughter.

Particularly considering everything Sage did for her.

But it was deeper than just wanting her mother to think of her daughter first…or at all. If Rose couldn't, then Holt would make sure he stood in front when necessary.

He wanted to protect Sage, wanted to help, to be her partner—in everything. If that included messy family stuff, that was fine.

He loved her.

Holt couldn't turn back time. Couldn't give her the dreams she'd lost, but he wanted Sage to have everything. The puppy room. The ranch. All her dreams.

And he wanted those dreams to include him.

"So, if you're not too busy this weekend, want to help me paint the back room?" He kept his tone light. Sage preferred to work, to stay busy. He didn't want this to seem like he was

adding more work to her plate. He'd be just as happy loung-
ing on the couch.

A goal of his own. One day he and Sage were going to spend
all weekend relaxing!

"You haven't picked a color." She leaned against the counter, her eyes locking on his.

"Teal. As someone wise said, it's comforting." He smiled
but the motion was fleeting as she crossed her arms.

"That was my pick. It's your home."

The words stabbed his heart, but he kept the rush of emotions buried. "We are living together. We said that. I—I want
to see this place as ours."

He meant to say I love you. He'd started to, but her stance,
the long day, the issue with Rose. It just didn't seem like the
right time.

"My name's not on the deed, Holt." Her lip wobbled as she
pushed a hand through her hair and looked away. "We seem
off." She gestured to the distance between them.

There were several feet between them like they were duel-
ing. It wasn't intentional…or maybe it was.

"We're not fighting." Sage blew out a breath.

But we could.

Her unsaid words weighting the already tense energy
around them. He'd taken care of Rose for her. And she hadn't
wanted it. She was already exhausted. Her mother was being
irrational—which Sage knew, but still, he could tell she wished
he hadn't stepped in.

That stung.

She never expected help. Sage was independent; it was one
of the things he loved about her. But he didn't want to just accept the help she gave him. He wanted full partnership.

"Do you want to fight?" Holt put his hands in his pockets
and rocked back on his heels. If she wanted to blow off steam,
needed to vent her frustration, he could handle it.

"Are you joking?"

He was a little surprised the octave registered in his ears.

"Sure. Tell me exactly why you're frustrated with me."

"I didn't need your help with Mom."

That hurt to hear, but he didn't interrupt.

"Mom is better than she was. I know it maybe doesn't look that way all the time, but she's working full-time. She has her own place." She blew out a breath as she blinked back tears. "There are still things I wish she could do—"

"She can add money to an account, Sage. She is an adult."

"You didn't see her before."

"Sage…"

Holt opened his arms, but she shook her head.

"You weren't here when Forest was sentenced!" The cry echoed off the walls. "You didn't live in a tiny studio apartment, trying to make her eat, or shower, or just move. I did. I was the one who handled all of that. I watched dependence on my father destroy her and then kept her alive when Forest followed destruction.

"If putting money in an account that she can't stand to look at helps her, keeps her from going back…"

She sucked in air, like her body couldn't decide between releasing tension and taking it in. "You left, you chased all your dreams and you got them. I am happy for that, for you but what happens if you want to chase other dreams? Because I am trapped."

She didn't trust that he was staying.

His chest heaved. He wanted to move toward her, wanted to pull her into his arms but couldn't make his feet move.

Because she was right. He hadn't been here. He'd fled, gone about his life.

And he hadn't returned for her.

"I am not going anywhere." He kept the words even as he repeated them. "Sage. I am not going anywhere."

"I'm sorry. I don't know what's come over me. I…" She

stamped her foot as tears slipped down her cheek. "Nope. No tears, Sage."

Her command didn't stop the flow. Instead the water streamed faster, as she brushed it away.

"You're allowed tears of frustration, Sage. Or sadness. Or anger. Or just because your eyes produce them." He moved then, pulling her into his arms.

"My dad hated when my mom cried. My mother can't handle my tears. Yes, I hear the irony there. I never cry in front of anyone."

"Well, I'm not just anyone." Holt kissed the top of her head, tension leaking from her.

"You're not." She sighed into his shoulder.

He felt her open her mouth, but she didn't say anything else.

"And that makes you uncomfortable?" He kissed the top of her head wanting the connection between them. Just to touch her.

"I don't want it to."

"Sometimes our bodies don't respond the way we want them to." But it all boiled down to trust. He'd broken it once. He'd been a teen. Sure, his brain hadn't been fully developed, but that didn't change it.

She might have accepted his apology and forgiven him for the teenage judgment lapse. It didn't mean she didn't remember it…or fear it.

But he was going to find a way to prove it to her. To show her she didn't have to fear him leaving, and that he would help…always.

"I know you aren't planning to leave, but…" She sighed as she looked up at him. "Even if you aren't planning it, you're free to come and go as you please. And it's selfish of me, but I am a little jealous." Her eyes rolled to the ceiling before she closed them.

"I hate myself for even saying that. But it's why I want you to choose the color of the back room. I know that is a mental twist, but if you choose, then that means you're putting your own stamp on this place."

"I painted my bedroom the moment I got here."

She sniffed and a soft chuckle left her throat. "That is a good point. One I should have considered."

"Maybe." He grabbed her hand. "I still say teal. It's a nice color, calming." He winked. "But we can discuss paint tomorrow or the day after, or in a week. Why don't we get a shower and a few hours' sleep?"

"Okay. Sorry, I overreacted."

"It happens." He wrapped his arm around her, glad she was still here.

She has nowhere else to go.

That thought sent a chill down his body.

A look passed over Sage's face that sent tickles of comfort through him. He wanted her to have a puppy room here, but what she said struck him. Her name wasn't on the deed.

Maybe it was time to change that. After all, she deserved a dream that came true.

CHAPTER TWELVE

SHE'D DRIVEN HERSELF this morning, in her new truck. Well, new to her anyway. The truck had been bright red, once upon a time. It was faded now, but the engine ran well, and it had room for her to cart supplies.

And it was in her price range…the main factor in her purchasing decision.

She'd loved riding with Holt each morning, but he liked to sleep in. And she needed to check out a new rescue found abandoned on the mountain.

She also wanted a few minutes on her own. After her breakdown last night, she'd slipped out of bed, and sat on the couch drinking a tea that was supposed to help her fall asleep. Maybe it helped some people, but it seemed to do nothing for Sage.

Letting it all hang out was the best definition for last night. She'd been frustrated with Holt for interfering with her mom. Which wasn't fair. She knew that.

She was just frustrated with her mother. With the situation. And she'd been exhausted.

None of which was Holt's fault. It was nice to have support, but Sage took care of her mom and herself.

Doesn't mean I always have to.

Last night she'd almost told Holt that she loved him. That the reason she was so frustrated was because she wanted to rely on him. The words had ached for release.

But last night, in anger and frustration, had not been the

best time. Particularly when she was still coming to grips with the idea that loving Holt meant accepting his help. She could rely on him…couldn't she?

Pulling into the clinic's parking lot, it surprised her to see a car that looked like it was due for the junkyard any day. A man leaned against the trunk, holding the smallest dog carrier.

Bright pink carrier.

She couldn't stop the smile that spread across her face. "Paul!" Her brother's former cellmate waved as he stepped away from the car.

"Sage." He clutched the carrier close to his body. "You are a sight for sore eyes." Paul was a giant, almost six feet, seven inches. He was muscular and intimidating looking, but a big softie once you got to know him.

He'd helped Forest transition to life behind bars; helped him recognize that just because he was institutionalized it didn't mean he wasn't still a person. Something Sage would be forever grateful for.

"What's wrong?"

"I hate that the first time I'm seeing you on the outside is to ask a favor. I meant to get up here after they released me, but gas is expensive and work and a million other excuses."

"It's fine, Paul. What's wrong with your baby?"

Paul had participated in the canine incarceration program. He loved the animals and always included notes to her when he wrote. Which was often when he was inside.

He'd trained six dogs by the time Forest was his roommate. It had taken her brother almost a year after they paroled Paul to get into the highly competitive program, but it had saved her brother.

"My baby is not eating very well. She started panting this morning. I found her behind the apartment I rent last month. She was tiny, underfed, but I got some nice weight put on her. I shoulda taken her to the vet, but…"

But vets were expensive.

Healthcare in the US was pricey, even if you were fortunate enough to have good insurance. Pet insurance was a thing, but expensive. So far too many pet parents were forced to wait until it was an emergency.

Which then increased the cost of treatment.

"Let's get her inside. I'll have a look and see if we need to call Dr. Cove. I have another rescue coming in soon too.

"So what is her name?" Sage needed to know, but she also wanted to calm Paul down.

"Princess."

She didn't hide her grin as she led him into an exam room. "You named her Princess?"

"Figure she deserved a name that matched her spirit, not her circumstances." Paul held his chin up as he opened the crate and looked at his Princess.

Princess didn't stand, and it took only a quick look for Sage to see what was going on. "I'll be right back!"

She hurried to the back room where there were boxes and old towels. She brought both back and Paul opened his mouth and shook his head.

"How could I miss that?" He smacked his head, a ridiculous gesture normally, but on the giant, it was more cartoonish.

"Because she is your baby, and your first worry was the worst one." Tapping her own head she shrugged. "Overthinker here, too!"

"Sage?"

"That's Blaire. There is a rescue I need to run a heartworm test on."

"She..."

Sage understood the concern running across his face. The good news was this was a surprise, not an emergency. "Most dogs deliver with no issue. I suspect she still has a few hours to go. If you want her seen by Dr. Cove, to make you feel better, he'll be in soon."

"I'm already here." Holt kissed her cheek then passed her a coffee.

"I'm getting used to this." Sage took a sip of the coffee, happy to see the joy radiating off Holt too.

"You should. You take care of everyone, so you deserve someone taking care of you."

Taking care.

A turn of phrase, Sage. Not a sign she was relying on him. *Dear God, it's coffee! Stop overthinking this.*

"How is Princess?"

Paul stood as soon as Holt closed the door, standing almost like he was at attention. Then he shifted and shook his head. "Been out years and still feel like I have to jump to attention in new places."

Holt didn't have a ready comment. He'd read more than most about incarceration after Forest's sentencing. Knowing the basics and understanding were two different things.

"Princess is panting, and I feel like something is getting ready to happen. Not a great judge of that though 'cause I've been thinking something was about to happen all day."

"Labor takes time." Holt looked over the small dog. "See that? The discharge means we should see a puppy soon."

Paul's shoulders dropped, relief clear in his face. The man loved his little Princess. "I'm ready, and I know Princess is."

"You ready for puppies? Sage mentioned you have a small place." Small places for small dogs worked. Provided he didn't have a nightmare landlord.

"I reached out to the rescue I worked with when I was inside. They can take the puppies in when they are weaned. I can keep them at my place until then. Oh, look!"

Princess was delivering the first puppy. Headfirst, which was best. Dogs could deliver tail first, but it was tougher. It didn't take too long before the puppy was free, and Princess had taken care of the placenta.

"Now she rests." Holt nodded. "We'll have another puppy in the next half hour or so." He'd seen several pet parents worry when the puppies didn't come one right after the other. But real life didn't work like movies.

"Good to know." Paul shifted on his seat, his eyes moving from Holt to the floor and back again.

"You make Sage happy."

Holt had expected a question about the puppies. Silence stretched in the room, before he said, "She makes me happy too."

"That's good. Forest talked about her often." Paul leaned his head back on the wall, his eyes closing. "Worried about her. Not as much about their mother, but some. Mostly he just hated that his screwup cut her chances of college off. He wanted her to be happy and felt terrible his choices changed her life."

"She should be happy." Holt didn't hesitate. It was true. Sage deserved to get everything she wanted.

And it wasn't just Forest's choices...it had been his too.

"Did he ever mention me?" It was a selfish question. One he hadn't meant to ask, but couldn't reel back in. Forest had told him not to return the one time he'd stopped by after his arrest. Holt had considered writing so many times, but what was he supposed to say?

"He was mad at you, if that is what you're asking?"

It was. And it didn't surprise Holt. He didn't even really blame him. He'd been the wayward one. The one that was acting out. He'd encouraged the first pranks, and the small vandalism they'd done at first. If he hadn't, what path might Forest have walked?

No way to know.

"But he was mad at most of the world. At least for a while. I was too. Takes time to adjust, to accept."

"Another puppy." Paul grinned and leaned forward. "You got this, Princess."

The puppy came quickly, and Princess relaxed; her body

language shifting slightly. They hadn't gotten Princess in for X-rays since she was in active labor, but she looked to be a Chihuahua mix.

Litter sizes for the breed usually ranged from two to six puppies.

"There is a good chance that was the last puppy. It's possible she'll deliver another, but if she hasn't in two hours, we'll know for sure." The placenta for the second pup was delivered, and Princess was taking care of her puppies.

All activities you wanted to see after a delivery, and more confirmation that she was likely done.

"Can't say I will complain about two. Puppies are a lot of work. We had a few young ones in the program I was in, always a handful."

"How are we doing?" Sage beamed as she saw the tiny black and white puppies. "Good job, Princess."

"I can't thank you both enough for letting us hang here today."

Sage hugged Paul, "I'm glad that it wasn't anything bad. Though puppies?"

"Yeah." He shrugged. "I forgot to ask. Did you buy the ranch? Forest used to talk about you wanting to, and I'd love to see it."

"Oh." Sage shook her head. "Actually, Holt owns it."

"Oh." A look passed across Paul's face.

"At least it went to someone who cares for it, right?" Sage's tone was bright, but the light in her eyes was a tad dimmer.

The idea that had sprung into his mind last night spun faster. He wasn't exactly sure how he could manage it, but this dream was one she was getting.

CHAPTER THIRTEEN

Saw Holt by the smoothie shop. You should warn him they've been shut down three times for health code violations. Don't know why they keep opening back up.

BLAIRE'S TEXT SENT shivers down Sage's back. There was no way Holt was at the smoothie shop. Even being gone for years, he'd heard the rumor that the shop was terrible. It only stayed open because tourists didn't know the history.

He'd acted weird this morning, telling her he had an appointment but not who it was with.

Actually, he'd been off since Paul's visit to the clinic two days ago. When she asked, he'd kiss her and then change the subject. Saying there was nothing wrong. He just had a lot on his mind.

She always had a lot on her mind. So she didn't want to push. But her emotions seemed clogged in her stomach. It ached with a worry that she couldn't quite force away.

It's nothing.

Intrusive thoughts got her nowhere. She knew this.

The real estate office is there.

There was also a doctor's office, a chiropractor and an attorney. They were supposed to talk about the big things. They'd promised each other that. And this felt big.

"Honey, I'm home."

The smile on Holt's face released a little of the tension held tightly in her gut. Why didn't it release all of it?

"You seem happier."

Holt pulled her into his arms, kissed one cheek, then the other. "I am happy."

"Care to tell me why?" She wrapped her arms around his neck, willing the doubts creeping along the back of her mind to vanish.

"It's a surprise."

Surprise. A word she hated.

"Never been great at surprises, Holt." Her life felt like a series of surprises, and she could count on one hand the number of them that were good.

"Are you making a big decision?" His cheek twitched, and she felt her stomach clench. "We discuss those, remember?"

Holt sighed. "I know, but I am asking you to trust me. Not even sure the surprise is possible."

Then why not tell me?

Instead of pushing, she took a deep breath. There was no reason for her not to trust him. So she switched topics.

"I found the box I brought that first night." Sage lifted on her toes, kissing him. She was pretty sure she'd never tire of kissing this man. "You didn't go through it."

"I got distracted by the pretty woman with car trouble at the end of the driveway." Holt wrapped his arm around her waist, "Want to help me go through it, now?"

Did she? When she'd dropped the box off, she'd rushed away. Embarrassed because she'd kept a box of memories for a man she never expected to return. Now she was living with him. Seemed a little silly to let that embarrassment continue.

"I can't even remember everything in it. I was seventeen when I packed it up. So you have to promise, not to judge the contents."

"I mean, I looked like a beanpole the day I graduated high school, and I found a journal I kept in middle school after Dad passed—I think embarrassing is the best descriptor for child-hood. And teens are children, even if they don't think so."

"I put the box on the kitchen table when I was cleaning, didn't know exactly where you wanted it."

"You ever just relax?" Holt's lips grazed the top of her head as he squeezed her.

"I don't understand the question." Her fist playfully struck his side.

"I know you don't."

The box was worn on the edges and stuffed to capacity. She remembered packing it up along with so many other things. By the time she'd put her life in boxes the tears had mostly dried, but this box had unleashed the waterworks for the final time.

She couldn't even remember why now. Probably stress and the realization that one part of her life was over.

The top of the box contained a weathered image of her brother and Holt. "I remember when that was taken." She ran her fingers on the edge. "Mom wanted you two to smile, but…"

"But it was awkward."

Awkward was an appropriate description. Her mother had never understood why their friendship had suffered. Forest had blamed Holt for his troubles. Blamed everyone.

His mom for not getting a better attorney. Their dad for leaving. Their teachers for not reaching out to him, like he felt they had with Holt. Never mind that Forest had rebuffed every overture.

Only Sage was spared her brother's wrath. He felt guilty about hurting her future too. Then he'd used that guilt to fuel his anger.

A vicious circle Paul had helped him break.

"He wanted me to hang out with him that night." Holt's voice was soft as he ran his hand over the edge of the picture. "Always wondered if I could have changed things."

"Maybe." Sage leaned her head against his shoulder. She felt him shudder, but it was the truth. If Holt had gone out with Forest that night, he wouldn't have robbed the store. Not that night anyway.

That *didn't* mean Forest would have chosen a different path.

"For a time at least, Holt. But, Forest was so mad at the world. He was bent on destruction. Mom refused to see it, and so many people threw him away when he started acting up."

"Including me."

"You were eighteen." She slid into his lap. Straddling his legs and forcing him to look at her. Forest wasn't his burden to carry.

"There were adults who should have stepped in. But even with those fail-safes faltering, my brother was responsible for his choice that night. I will always be thankful no one was harmed. But armed robbery leaves a mental scar on the victim too."

He leaned his head against hers, his fingers traveling up her back. A comforting motion that still made her body heat.

"Holt—" she waited until his eyes met hers "—if you'd hung out with him after graduation, life might be different. It might not. There is no use dwelling on the what-ifs. And my life is fine."

"Fine." Holt raised an eyebrow. "You wanted out of Spring River, if I recall. Wanted to study the ocean…save the whales."

There was a bitterness in his tone she hadn't expected.

"If I'd made different choices, hadn't been so focused on myself. I got out, and you got trapped."

Her angry words thrown back at her in such a quiet tone.

He wasn't responsible. She needed him to know that. "Those were good goals." Sage held his face between her palms, desperate to make him understand. This wasn't a debt on any balance sheet. "But then I wouldn't be here to help the animals that need it."

This felt like some internal tipping point. A place of no return. She was happy. Sure, there were things she would change—that was life.

She shifted her hips, enjoying the catch in his breath. This was better than fine. Couldn't he see that?

"I wouldn't be here. Right now. With you." Sage drew her fingers along his chest, wanting to push away the hard questions. Ignore the uncertainty flowing in this moment.

"You're trying to distract me." Holt kissed the base of her neck, his warm breath adding spikes to the bead of desire she always felt in his presence.

"Is it working?"

"A little too well." Holt's fingers slipped under her shirt as his mouth devoured hers.

"We still need to talk about this." His breath was hot as she rocked her hips against him.

"No." She captured his mouth. "We don't. I'm happy. With you. That is what matters."

"Let me help with that." Holt reached for the box but Sage shook her head.

"I got it." She slid the heavy box into the back of her new truck then turned back to the house. Only a few more trips, then the rescue donations they'd received at the egg hunt would be at the rescue's storage unit.

He'd told her she could keep them here. He had more than enough room. But she'd told him that the rescue rented the unit so the volunteers could get what they needed if she wasn't around. He understood but expected there would be more rescue material at the ranch soon.

Because...*they* would have enough room. At least if all his plans went through.

When her name was on the deed, he could come to her as a full equal, having restored something his actions...or rather inactions, stole. Then he'd tell her he loved her.

Following her into the study where they'd dropped the donations, Holt grabbed one box.

"I promise, I got it, Holt."

"I know you've got it, but you'll get it a lot faster if I help." Why was this the recurrent theme? She never asked, but he'd never wavered in his willingness to be by her side.

And still she never asks.

"You don't have to do everything on your own, honey." He had to bite back harsher words. The anger and bitterness that flared each time she did things on her own when he was there to help.

Her mother looked to Sage for support. That wasn't fair. She should support her daughter. And her brother was gone for at least another few years.

But she didn't have to be on her own. Not when he was right here. He wanted to be her partner. Her full partner.

"I've gotten good at doing things on my own." Sage stacked two boxes and started for the truck again.

Grabbing the final box, Holt followed her. "Sure, but I'm right here and can help. You don't have to!"

"I gave up on the idea of Prince Charming saving the day years ago. The good news is that nowadays princesses save themselves." Her chest was puffed out. She was proud of this feeling.

And he didn't want to take that feeling away, but he wasn't trying to save her. He was glad she could take care of herself. Glad she wanted to.

So what was the crushing weight in his chest?

He loved her. Loved the strong woman she was. But she was protecting herself…from him. He couldn't look away from that truth—and the fear bubbling in his belly.

What if she never fully trusted him?

No. He wouldn't contemplate that.

"I want to help." The words were soft, barely audible to his ears. "Need to help."

"I don't need you to help, though." Sage wiped her hands on her blue jeans. "This isn't a balance sheet, Holt."

It was—at least a little. But that wasn't the reason for this disagreement. Holt climbed into the truck bed, carefully stepped around the supplies she'd loaded up. "It hurts when you don't want my help."

Sage blinked, her head snapping back. "I'm not trying to hurt you."

"I know that too." He kissed her, enjoying the way her body molded to his. Like they were two pieces of the same puzzle. "I love…" His throat closed on the words leaping to escape his throat.

She wasn't sure of him, not completely. That would come when he gave her the surprise…hopefully by the end of the week. Then he could let all the emotions loose.

"I love how strong and independent you are."

"But?" Her dark eyes glittered as she stared at him.

How he wished there wasn't a but this time. Wished this joke just got to lie there.

"But…" He ran his hands along her waist, enjoying the soft sigh that fell from her lips. "I also want you to need me a little too."

"Need." Sage made a face as she seemed to swirl the word around her mouth. No doubt it tasted weird. "That word terrifies me. But—" She looked over the boxes then back at him. "Come with me to drop it all at the storage unit? I could use your help unloading it all."

It was a small step. But one that lifted his heart.

"Of course."

CHAPTER FOURTEEN

"So, you still don't know what he was doing at the real estate office two days ago?" Blaire passed Loki, a mischievous tabby, to Sage.

The rescue usually only took dogs. But Loki had been found with a boxer mix they were calling Thor. The two were inseparable, so they'd made an exception. Luckily, Elise Major was willing to take both. The real estate broker was picking the two up shortly.

"I don't even know that that is where Holt was at. He's got some kind of surprise." Sage rubbed the cat's head as she looked over the tabby one more time. Most orange tabby cats were male, so she'd been named Loki to match her brother. The name had stuck once she'd figured out how to break into the treat cabinet. "And I am doing my best not to worry about it."

"You could always ask Elise. If he was there, she'd love to tell you."

"I'm sure she would." Sage peeked into Loki's ears. Dr. Andrews had checked the pets out when they'd first come into the rescue. The cat had had a nasty ear infection and Sage had worried he'd lose hearing in at least one ear, but he'd recovered well.

"You're really not curious?"

I didn't say that.

She was too curious. Too focused on what it might mean.

They'd promised to discuss the big things and whatever he was hiding was something big.

That wasn't fair to him. Sage understood that. But something in the looks he gave. In the words he uttered. No matter how she tried, worry chased her. There was a tension, like he wanted to say something, but couldn't force the words out.

She'd seen that look before. The week before her father left, like he was trying to tell her mother. He never had. He'd pulled the cliché, gone out for cigarettes and never come home. Except he'd said he was grabbing beers with a friend.

Another thing that wasn't fair to Holt. He wasn't her father but there was also his karmic balance sheet. His need to prove he wasn't like his mother. If he couldn't see clearly how obvious that was, could he ever be happy?

And was whatever he was planning some grand gesture to prove that? If so, was it for her...or for him?

She wanted to be so much more than a ledger item on a universal oopsie sheet.

He'd listened when she'd told him that Forest was responsible for his own choices. Life might have taken a different path if he'd agreed to go out with Forest after graduation.

But maybe not.

Forest was so lost in his anger. At not getting into college, not getting out of Spring River, not having the opportunities he saw so many have. Never mind that he'd thrown those opportunities away. He might have dragged Holt down with him.

"Earth to Sage!" Blaire waved a hand in front of her face.

"Sorry. Too many thoughts, I guess."

Blaire raised a brow but didn't push.

"How is Loki?" Holt stuck his head in the room. "Elise just pulled in."

"Cleared to go to his new home."

"This guy too." Holt let Thor in. The boxer bounded through the room and put his front paws up on the exam table. "I need to finish up paperwork before we head back to the ranch. If you're okay?"

Loki rubbed her cheek against the boxer's. It was a picture-perfect moment.

"I'd say everyone is great."

"Are my babies here!" Elise's voice echoed through the entry. The real estate agent was tiny, just over five feet tall; but she made sure everyone knew when she entered a room.

"Ready for their new home." Sage beamed. This was her favorite part of rescue life. Helping animals find their forever homes, seeing them go from having no one to being loved family members. It never got old.

"This is so exciting." Elise rubbed Thor's ears. "It took me forever to get my own place, no landlord. And less than two weeks after closing to get furry children."

She was nearly bouncing. This was the perfect type of placement.

"I am glad that you and Dr. Cove gave them their check-ups. Now, Sage, you'll always be here."

"Yep." Sage helped Loki into her carrier.

"But do you know who the new vet will be, yet? Or will they close this location when Holt moves on?"

"New vet?" Sage heard Blaire's intake of breath, but she couldn't look at her friend. Couldn't focus on anything other than Elise's question.

"Yeah. Holt was in talking to my partner the other day. I admit I had hoped he'd stay in Spring River, being a home-grown guy, right?"

"Right. I think he is staying. Must have been about something else." The walls of the room weren't closing in on her. They weren't. Air was still reaching her lungs. But her brain was locking her heart down.

Holt wasn't leaving. He'd have told her that. But that still meant he was keeping big news…life-changing news, secret.

"Here is your welcome kit, and if you need anything, or

have questions on pet ownership, you can reach out to the rescue at any time." Blaire's words echoed in the room. Or maybe
it was just that the blood was pounding through Sage's ears.

"I can't wait."

As soon as Elise closed the door to the exam room, Sage
leaned into the exam table. She needed…something. What
was he planning, and why hadn't he told her?

"I just need to talk to him. Get an answer, even if he doesn't
want to give one." The words were soft, but she saw Blaire's
eyes widen.

"You should ask. Directly. Miscommunication in a relationship is a death knell."

Miscommunication.

He'd told her he'd had a surprise. Told her she'd like it. So
he wasn't leaving. But why go to a real estate agent?

And not tell her immediately. He knew how this town
talked. How rumors bloomed from nothing.

She knew he felt bad about buying the ranch, but that wasn't
his fault. And he couldn't undo it.

Undo it.

No. He couldn't. But if he could, he would in an instant.

For her…or to balance his universal balance sheet?

"If I need a place—"

"You might not—"

"If I do," Sage pushed on, "can I crash at your place tonight? I haven't found…" The words died away. Not only had
she not found another place, but she'd stopped looking when
he'd said he wanted her to stay.

She'd given up that piece of independence…and now what
if…?

This was why she'd never relied on others. Or at least she
hadn't before Holt stumbled back into her life.

"Please, Blaire."

"If you need it, my place is always open."

The door to the exam room opened. Her body was numb. A weird feeling, the absence of feeling.

No anger, no sadness, no worry. Nothing.

Like she was already placing her heart behind the independent walls she'd let crumble with him.

"Ready?"

No. Not all.

"Whenever you are." The words tasted like ash, and she saw Holt's eyes flicker to Blaire and then back again.

"Sage…"

"We need to talk but not here, Holt."

He opened his mouth, then closed it. "As soon as we get to the ranch?"

She nodded, not trusting her voice. It was a fifteen-minute drive. She had fifteen minutes to box up her heart and find a way to accept whatever the surprise was.

And if it was really for her.

Holt thumped his fingers against the steering wheel and looked in the rearview mirror. Sage was still following him back to the ranch. Was she brushing away tears?

What had happened?

Blaire's face had no color, and Sage had locked down.

Like the first day I saw her.

Holt shuddered. Domino leaned over the console, licking his ear. "I'm okay, boy." He ran a hand over his boy's ears, wishing it was the truth.

The day had seemed so normal. Yes, he'd been a little distant these last few days…afraid he'd spill the secret before it was ready. Before he knew if it was even technically possible to add an unmarried party to the deed. Without incurring a tax burden on Sage.

Today was supposed to end on a high note. Elise was picking up Thor and Loki.

Elise…

She was the real estate broker he'd met with when purchasing the ranch. *And I spent three hours with her partner, Neil, earlier this week.*

Working on the surprise for Sage. Assuming he could pull it off. He'd sworn Neil to secrecy. But this was Spring River.

How did I not consider that?

The ranch came into view and his body shifted between relief and fear.

Domino bounded out of the back of the seat, racing to the front door. Amazing how fast the giant had gone from seeing this as just a place to his home.

The door to Sage's truck slammed and he saw her cross her arms as she looked at the ranch. Her bottom lip trembled but no tears coated her eyes.

"I'm not leaving Spring River."

"I know." Her voice was wobbly as she rocked backward. Away from him.

"I wanted to surprise you. Wait, you're not worried I'm leaving?" How had this slipped so far from his control?

"No. You'd have told me that."

"Then why are you so upset?"

"We are supposed to talk about the big things, Holt. You promised. So, knowing that I hate surprises, please tell me why you were at the real estate office?"

Pushing his hands into his jeans, he hung his head. This was not how this was supposed to go. She knew he wasn't leaving but was waiting for some other shoe to drop. Expecting something bad.

Because that is where her brain always goes.

"I was talking to Neil about titles."

"Titles." She rubbed a hand over her forehead and closed her eyes. "Titles…deeds? The ranch, right?"

God, she was so smart. If she'd gotten that scholarship, there was no telling where she'd have landed.

"Neil still has his real estate license, but most of what he does is title changes, now. I think he works with the high-worth clients. I was asking about adding you to the title."

The bottom of Sage's lip disappeared; this wasn't a moment to be nervous. He waited a minute but she didn't ask.

"I inquired how to add you to it. It's not a quick process, since we aren't married and I want to make sure that you don't end up with a big tax bill or something."

"Why?" Her face was clear of emotions.

"Why?" He hadn't meant to repeat the question. But it wasn't what he'd expected in this moment. Excitement, joy, surprise, sure. But the suspicion in her eyes—that was unexpected.

"Yes, Holt. Why?" She gestured to the ranch, her eyes hovering on the window that had been their bedroom for weeks now.

"Because you wanted it. This is your dream. One I took, unintentionally."

"So you feel like you owe me the ranch. Owe me my home." Her voice cracked and she stepped back as he moved toward her.

"It's not exactly like that. Sage, baby."

"Not some check mark on whatever universal spreadsheet you are keeping? Proof that you can right a wrong? Proof you aren't your mother?"

"That is not fair."

"You're right. It's not. But is that part of why?"

"I…" He blew out a breath. "Are you saying you don't want it?" Holt didn't understand. This was what she'd worked toward. It wasn't a line item on his balance sheet. Well, it was, but it was the best kind of item. A chance to rectify a wrong. A debt he could pay, for the woman he loved.

And she doesn't want it.

"No. I don't want it. Not like this."

"Yes. Yes, yes you do. I know you do." Holt had never understood why dramas had people stamp their feet when they were frustrated, until just now. How could she not want the thing she'd worked so hard for?

"If I accept this, does it square everything you think you created when you didn't go with Forest?"

"Of course." He shook his head. "That sounded wrong."

"No. It sounded right." Sage laughed but there was no joy in the sound. "I don't need to be saved, Holt. I do not need the ranch. You don't owe me anything. I don't want anything from you." She choked back a sob and pulled the keys from her pocket.

She was diminishing this, and he felt his defenses rise. He wanted her to have it, wanted to give it to her. To help her. To be her full partner. But Sage never wanted his help. Not really.

"Is this because you didn't do it yourself? You don't have to be this independent!" They were the wrong words. Disastrous words. But pain was piercing every part of his soul.

"I told you I don't need saving. I'm not the princess in the castle—this isn't some play."

"Don't go." His hands were shaking. He'd hurt her; crushed her, while trying to give her everything.

Except she didn't want everything from him.

Sage looked at the ranch then back at him, "Goodbye."

One word. One sealed fate.

He stood in front of the ranch watching her taillights disappear down the driveway. Hoping she'd turn around.

Knowing it wasn't going to happen.

CHAPTER FIFTEEN

SAGE LAY ON Blaire's couch, staring at the ceiling and waffling between wishing her phone would ring and hoping Holt wouldn't reach out. He'd offered her the ranch. The thing she'd wanted most since her family lost it.

Because he owed her.

That cut to the core. If he'd told her he loved her. If he'd said it was because he needed her. Hell, if he'd indicated it was anything other than fulfilling some debt, she'd have jumped into his arms and told him how much she loved him.

She knew he felt bad about Forest. She did too, but he'd been a teen. And so what if he worked a lot after his father died, and didn't see the mother who'd abandoned him? Those were appropriate trauma responses.

Everyone had moments in life they wished to redo. Life didn't offer do-overs. And she wasn't keeping track.

"So what are you doing about work?"

Blaire padded into her kitchen and started the coffee pot. Thank goodness, because Sage had managed maybe two hours of sleep. And that was being generous.

But for the first time she hadn't worked through the insomnia. No, rather than be productive, she'd sunk into listlessness. *Another first.*

"Go in I guess." Her body ached at the idea of crossing the clinic's threshold. There weren't enough techs as it was.

"You want to talk about it?" Her best friend passed her a

mug and pointed to the coffee bar she had in the corner. Blaire loved sweet coffee treats and had more syrups than the local coffee shop.

Normally, having coffee here lifted her spirits.

"What's there to talk about?" She put some syrup and almond milk in her coffee, not caring what the flavor was as long as the caffeine got into her system. *Fast*.

"Is he moving?"

"No. I told you he wasn't." Sage hated the bitterness hanging in her throat. She almost wished he was. Wished he'd broken her trust that way.

How selfish am I?

A tear slipped down her cheek, and she didn't even lift her hand to wipe it away. She'd experienced more than her fair share of life letdowns. And she'd pushed past them.

She didn't wallow. She just started a new thing, focused on the next goal. Anything to keep busy.

But she didn't want to be busy. She wanted...she wanted Holt.

"He was looking for a way to put me on the ranch deed." Sage pulled her legs up in the chair; if only there was a way for her to disappear.

"Wow."

"Yep."

"And so you left?" Blaire clicked her tongue. "Seems like a good choice."

Normally she'd rise to the bait. Which her friend was probably hoping for. Instead, she just shrugged. "He feels guilty for what happened to Forest and guilty for buying the ranch since I was saving for it. Balancing his karma."

"Pretty big balance."

The scoff escaped Sage's lips before she could stop it. "I don't need saving. The girl that believed in Prince Charming riding to the rescue died a long time ago."

"Independence is a good thing."

"Exactly!" Finally, Blaire was seeing her side.

"Provided you don't use it as an excuse to avoid getting hurt."

Before Sage could say anything, Blaire continued, "I'm not saying that is what you are doing. But it's good advice.

"Also, I ordered cinnamon rolls from Deb's Bakery. Not saying sugar fixes everything…but it doesn't hurt. They should be here shortly." Her phone went off. "I gotta sign in to my computer for a meeting. Thank goodness no one expects me to be on camera at this ungodly hour."

Blaire turned and headed into her room. Obviously this part of the lecture was over.

Sage took a deep breath and texted Lucy saying she was taking a few days of paid time off. She apologized for the short notice but said she needed at least three days.

What was the use of having saved up so much leave if you weren't going to use it?

Lucy responded that she hoped everything was okay.

It wasn't. And she wasn't sure it would ever be okay again.

A knock at Blaire's front door sent Sage's heart racing. It was the cinnamon rolls, she knew that, but part of her hoped Holt might be behind the door.

Swinging the door open she opened her mouth but found no words as she met her mother's gaze.

"What are you doing here?"

"Sage, honey, why are you here?"

The words echoed in Blaire's small apartment as the women's words blended together, then her mom held up the box. "Blaire ordered these. Already tipped." Her mom bit her lip, looked at her watch then continued, "Are you okay?"

"Of course." Two little words. Words she'd muttered a million times, but her throat closed with the sobs her body ached to release. "Why are you delivering cinnamon rolls?"

Her mom sighed, then shrugged. "It was supposed to be a

surprise, but I started delivering food, and groceries and pretty much anything else one can order through an app."

"Did you lose your job?"

"No." Her mom shook her head. "No. But I've earned enough to finish paying off your loan. I'll drop it off after finishing up at Dr. Jameson's."

"This is a lot." Could she handle this? Without getting lost, despondent?

"Not really. I could stop now, but I'm going to keep at it. Put a little aside for my savings and to put on Forest's commissary card.

She pulled her phone from her pocket, tapped a few buttons then kissed Sage's cheek. "I lost myself when your dad left and then with Forest, but I am the parent and it's time I started acting like it. Better late than never."

"I never would have asked." The smell of cinnamon strolled through her body as tears coated her eyes.

Her mom nodded. "I know. But maybe you should have." Her mom choked up and Sage lost the hold she had on her tears. "Just because you can do it all on your own, doesn't mean you should have to."

"Thanks, Mom."

Holding up her phone, she grinned. "I need to get my final delivery in, but if you decide you aren't okay, and you need me, I am a phone call away." She kissed Sage's cheek again, then headed out.

Holt hated knocking on Rose's door so early, but he needed to see Sage. He wasn't sure what to say, but he didn't want to say it over the phone.

And she hadn't shown up at the clinic for three days now. And the last of her clothes had disappeared while he was at the clinic yesterday.

He'd messed up. But there had to be a way to fix this.

Three days of hoping he'd see her. Find the right words and

convince her to come home. The ranch wasn't right without her. He needed her.

It was as complicated and as simple as that.

"Holt?" Rose's voice was soft as she yawned and looked at her watch.

"I know it's early, and Saturday, but I need to see Sage."

Rose blinked, her head tilting in the exact way that Sage's did. God, he missed her. Nothing was right in her absence.

Rose stepped to the side and Holt rushed in.

"She isn't here."

The words hit his back like a hammer.

"What?" Holt looked around the living room. Rose's place was small, but he'd been so sure she was here.

Images of Forest and him covered the mantle, but the only one she had of Sage was her working on a theater set in high school.

Even though she wasn't required to help with set design as Cinderella; she'd done it. Worked herself to the bone for the theater teacher, for everyone.

"She stopped needing me a long time ago, Holt." Rose looked at the image catching his attention. "My girl—always on the go. Earning her way through life. Helping everyone."

"But who helps her?" The words slipped out, and he hated the flinch he saw on Rose's face.

"She was always so strong. Too strong." Rose crossed her arms and looked at him. "Forest needed me. I didn't help him either. I was so lost, and Sage was so capable. Doing everything for everyone. I didn't see it, until you put it not so delicately."

He couldn't apologize for that. Wouldn't.

"I wonder what she will do when someone finally just needs her." Rose's gaze met his and his heart cracked.

I need her. Desperately.

And instead of telling her that, he'd offered her the ranch. A thing. Instead of making sure she knew life was bleak without her in it, he'd told her the ranch balanced the scales. Trying to prove to himself he wasn't like his mother.

His mother never thought of others. The fact that he was so concerned about her should have showed him, but he'd let worries about Forest, about life and fairness cloud what really mattered.

Of course she walked away.

He hadn't even told her he loved her.

"Any idea where she might be?"

"She was at Blaire's the other morning. I asked if she was okay and she…well, she lied to me." Rose shook her head. "But, when you find her, make sure she knows you need her, just her."

Don't repeat my mistake.

He didn't intend to. Holt was done weighing himself against the past.

He loved Sage and that was enough. Just on its own, assuming she felt the same way.

The bank had come through. With her mother's repayment, she had enough to qualify for a loan. Enough to cover the cost of the place she'd considered her second choice. It was a good location, outside of town, a longer drive…but it could be hers in a few weeks.

So why hadn't she put in a call to Elise, started the process of making an offer?

There was nothing to think about. Yet she'd hesitated.

Pulling up to Blaire's apartment complex she laid her head against the steering wheel. Blaire's couch wasn't a forever place. She should call Elise, let her know how much loan money she'd qualified for. That was the next move.

Pulling out her phone, she pulled up the number. Her thumb hovered over the call button.

Just push it!

She wanted to throw it.

Independence is good, provided you aren't using it to keep others out.

Part of her wanted to hate Blaire for that line. But she was right. She called Blaire, not surprised when her friend picked up on the first ring.

"Holt's looking for you. He was here a few hours ago. I didn't tell him you were talking to a loan officer, but this is a small town."

"Can you do me a favor?"

"Another?"

"Yes." Sage laughed, this was either going to be a great night, or the worst of her life. "I need to do something. If it goes south…well, make sure the freezer is stocked with ice cream? Chocolate."

"I don't think whatever you're planning results in you sleeping here tonight."

"Just in case."

"Just in case." Blaire sighed, "Good luck."

"Thanks." Sage started the engine back up. It was time to stop hiding behind independence. She needed Holt…forever.

He hit Call and listened to Sage's voicemail pop up on the first ring. Either her phone was off, or she'd blocked his number. He didn't want to consider the last option.

She wasn't at Blaire's, though he was pretty sure that was where she was staying. Not that her friend had admitted that. Which Holt respected.

He needed to feed Domino, let him out; then the search started again. Spring River wasn't that big. He'd find her. If necessary, he'd sit outside Blaire's door.

Pulling up his drive, Holt saw her truck parked in her regular spot. "Sage!" Rationally, he knew she couldn't hear him, but he couldn't stop her name falling from his lips. She was here.

Here!

He cut the engine and nearly fell getting out of the car.

"Sage." Blood pounded in his ears; his throat was tight and aching to tell her so many things.

"I'm around back."

Her voice was so sweet; he broke into a run.

She lifted the ball thrower over her head as Domino sat at her feet, his tail wagging. The contraption let you throw a ball at least twenty feet, it would keep Domino going for a minute or so…

The dog took off and Sage turned. "I love you."

There were hundreds of things he'd expected her to say. Expected she'd demand the apology she was owed. Instead it was the words he'd longed to hear. The words that made the world right, that made him whole.

"I love you, so much, Sage Pool."

Domino returned, dropping the ball at their feet. Holt chucked it, and reached for Sage. "Honey…"

"I don't need you." Sage kissed the tip of his nose. "I can do everything on my own. But I need you. Does that make sense?"

"Yes." The word rushed out of him as the world righted.

He'd fallen for an independent woman. And he wouldn't have it any other way. "I can't say I don't need you, because I'd be lying." Holt let the truth out. "I need you, Sage. Not to right any wrong or balance any sheet. To prove anything. I just need you. My life isn't complete without you."

"You aren't the one that needed saving… I did." Holt's lips captured hers. The world stopped as her body melted against his.

The moment could have gone on forever and he'd have happily stood in the moonlight kissing Sage. But Domino had other ideas.

When neither of them acknowledged the tennis ball he'd dropped between their feet, he jumped, joining the hug and licking Holt's cheek!

"Ugh!"

Sage giggled and picked up the ball, then threw it. "I think he is a little jealous."

"He'll have to get used to the feeling, because this is forever for me."

"Me too." She hit his hip. "But I'm not kissing you again until you've cleaned the dog slobber off!"

Fair enough. He grabbed her hand and whistled for Domino to follow them.

This was love.

Not earned, but freely given.

EPILOGUE

"COME BACK!"

Forest's voice echoed into the kitchen, and Sage looked to Holt. "I am not sure what puppy got loose but you will have to help him. I'm too tired. These practice contractions are exhausting."

"My lovely wife admitting to being tired. Look at that growth!"

"Yeah. It's nine months of growth!" Sage gestured to her swollen belly. She was beautiful, and he hoped their daughter looked exactly like her mother.

Though if she didn't arrive soon, Sage might start walking until she induced her own labor. She'd had Braxton-Hicks for the last two weeks. They'd even gone to the hospital once, only for her to be told to go home. Their daughter was stubborn…just like her mama.

And he wouldn't have it any other way.

"You're gorgeous." He kissed her cheek, before starting toward the back of the ranch. They'd taken in a very pregnant golden retriever named Lula about six weeks ago. The puppies were nearly weaned and starting to get into everything.

Stepping into the backyard, Holt was surprised to find no sign of Forest. Sage's brother was released on parole a little over a month ago. He was staying in their spare room until he found more permanent housing, and the rescue employed him as a trainer. A job he excelled so much at; he'd already had a few consulting clients to help with their wayward pets.

"Forest?"

"Ginger escaped!" The call came from the side gate, "I've got her, any chance you can let me in."

Holt raced to the side gate. "How did she get out this time?" The runt of the litter was always into mischief.

"No idea." Forest rubbed the puppy's ears, while she playfully licked his hand and squirmed, completely oblivious to the worry on Forest's face. "I woulda sworn I got all the loose fence posts fixed. But clearly!" He wagged a finger before pushing the cutie through the puppy door.

"I hate to say it, but I think we have to put in a new fence." Holt crossed his arms, knowing it was the truth, and hating letting this piece of the past go. The rainbow fence…the project that had bound the two boys, now, men together.

"I hate to agree, but yeah, it's time. I'll make a run to the hardware store tomorrow. Get it put in before the baby gets here. Least I can do for all you and Sage have done for me."

Holt slapped his friend on the back, happy to have him back in Spring River. "No one is keeping a tally, man. Least of all me. How about we do it together?"

"Whatever you're talking about doing is going to have to wait," Sage called as she stepped onto the back porch. "I think this is the real deal."

Holt smiled but didn't want to get too excited in case it was another false alarm. "You think so?"

"Considering my water just broke…yes." She took a deep breath, placing her hands on her back.

Forest let out a hoot and Holt grinned.

This was his universal slice of perfect, and he'd have it no other way.

* * * * *

COMING SOON!

We really hope you enjoyed reading this book. If you're looking for more romance be sure to head to the shops when new books are available on

Thursday 13th April

To see which titles are coming soon, please visit

millsandboon.co.uk/nextmonth

MILLS & BOON

MILLS & BOON ®

Coming next month

THE NURSE'S ONE-NIGHT BABY
Tina Beckett

Serena waited for him to say something. To respond to what she'd just told him. None of this was happening the way she'd wanted it to.

But now that she'd said it, she couldn't take the words back.

He blinked as if not quite sure what to say. "Sorry?" He shifted her on his legs, easing out of her.

She hated the feeling but understood that he was probably in shock. Maybe she should backtrack and try this again.

"I...I..." She took a deep breath. "I haven't been feeling quite right for the last couple of weeks, and I couldn't figure out why."

"You didn't look like you felt at all well when we were running. And add that to what you said before we parted ways..."

Her teeth scraped against each other a couple of times as she tried to drum up the courage to say again what she needed to say. "I couldn't get up the nerve to tell you what was wrong that day."

"And now you want to."

He looked confused. Maybe Toby hadn't actually heard what she'd said a minute ago. She hadn't exactly shouted out the news. "Yes. As I said, I wasn't feeling well and realized my cycle was later than it had ever been. So… I decided to take a pregnancy test."

"I see."

He was calm. Too calm.

A sense of horror and foreboding rushed over her. "I'm pregnant."

"You're pregnant?"

Continue reading
THE NURSE'S ONE-NIGHT BABY
Tina Beckett

Available next month
www.millsandboon.co.uk

LET'S TALK

Romance

For exclusive extracts, competitions
and special offers, find us online:

- **f** facebook.com/millsandboon
- **𝕏** @MillsandBoon
- **⬛** @MillsandBoonUK
- **♪** @MillsandBoonUK

Get in touch on 01413 063 232

For all the latest titles coming soon, visit
millsandboon.co.uk/nextmonth

OUT NOW!

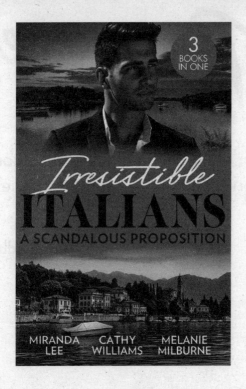

Available at
millsandboon.co.uk

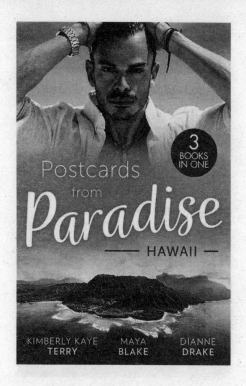

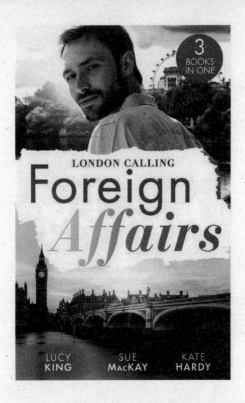

MILLS & BOON

THE HEART OF ROMANCE

A ROMANCE FOR EVERY READER

MODERN

Prepare to be swept off your feet by sophisticated, sexy and seductive heroes, in some of the world's most glamourous and rom locations, where power and passion collide.

HISTORICAL

Escape with historical heroes from time gone by. Whether your pas is for wicked Regency Rakes, muscled Vikings or rugged Highlande awaken the romance of the past.

MEDICAL

Set your pulse racing with dedicated, delectable doctors in the high-pressure world of medicine, where emotions run high and pa comfort and love are the best medicine.

True Love

Celebrate true love with tender stories of heartfelt romance, from rush of falling in love to the joy a new baby can bring, and a focus emotional heart of a relationship.

Desire

Indulge in secrets and scandal, intense drama and plenty of sizzlin action with powerful and passionate heroes who have it all: wealth good looks…everything but the right woman.

HEROES

Experience all the excitement of a gripping thriller, with an intens romance at its heart. Resourceful, true-to-life women and strong, men face danger and desire - a killer combination!

To see which titles are coming soon, please visit

millsandboon.co.uk/nextmonth